MY
HUSBAND'S
LOVER

BOOKS BY JESS RYDER

Lie to Me
The Good Sister
The Ex-Wife
The Dream House
The Girl You Gave Away
The Night Away
The Second Marriage

MY HUSBAND'S LOVER

JESS RYDER

bookouture

Published by Bookouture in 2022

An imprint of Storyfire Ltd.
Carmelite House
50 Victoria Embankment
London EC4Y 0DZ

www.bookouture.com

ISBN: 978-1-80314-520-4
eBook ISBN: 978-1-80314-519-8

For my family

ONE

SOPHIE

Sophie struggles up the bank, legs shaking, swimming shoes baggy with water. Her breath swirls in the cool morning air. Grabbing her dryrobe from the rock, she puts her arms through the loose sleeves and drags up the chunky zipper. The lambswool lining licks the water off her skin.

How different to those childhood holidays on Cornish beaches, she thinks as she gazes across the lake. She always stayed too long in the sea, jumping the waves, emerging with blue lips and shivering limbs. Nan made her a changing tube out of an old beach towel, gathered at the neck. It was thin and rough and became sopping wet within seconds. She remembers Nan rubbing her all over in her no-nonsense way – drying her with love.

Sophie laughs to herself. Nowadays she wouldn't dream of going in without her beloved dryrobe to return to, with its quick-dry technology, ingenious waterproof pockets and a zip that can be fastened from both sides, and all made from recycled materials. It's supposed to be oversized, roomy enough to go over several layers of clothing, even other jackets, but it completely swamps her small frame. *All the gear and no idea,* scoffed Ryan, although he still agreed to buy it for her birthday and didn't complain about the heavy price tag. It's part of the unspoken agreement between them – the sad fact that he will never be out of her debt.

Her fellow swimmers are still in the water. They went in a couple of minutes after her, so their maximum fifteen minutes isn't up yet. Sophie always tries to slip into the lake first, to experience the wonder of being alone, at one with the elements. She loves the silence lapping around her, the sensation of her heartbeat accelerating in response to the cold. The others always break the spell. They gasp and squeal as they wade in, as if it's the first time they've ever swum in open water. Once submerged, they bob about in a loose circle – exclaiming how good they feel before lapsing into mundane chat. Sophie always swims over and joins in, tries to find something relevant to say. She likes these women and would never dream of telling them to shut up.

The group is a lifeline, but what she *really* wants to do is swim completely by herself in some remote and beautiful location: a secluded pool, an old quarry with turquoise water, a rushing mountain river. It would be intensely peaceful, yet also exhilarating. She would have to face her fears, test her limits, put her body at risk, knowing that nobody would rescue her if she got into trouble. But that fantasy is never going to happen. 'Swim with others' is one of the main rules, and Sophie is not a strong swimmer. She's not interested in swimming as a sport; doesn't do it to get fit or lose weight. She does it because it keeps her sane.

'Oh my God, that water is colder than ever,' says Fern, hobbling towards her over the stones. She points to her robe – cerise with navy trim, same brand as Sophie's but the limited edition. 'Chuck it over, will you?' Sophie obliges.

Fern puts on the coat and zips it up, then dives into the interior to peel off her costume. As she wriggles and squirms, she reminds Sophie of a giant pink worm. The costume plops to her feet like a discarded skin. That's what some wild swimmers call swimsuits these days – skins. Sophie thinks it's a bit pretentious.

None of them wear wetsuits, not yet, but if they ever do, Fern will lead the way. She lives in one of those detached executive houses just outside town with her husband and two children. Sophie meets a lot of women like Fern at the chiropractic clinic where she works as a part-time receptionist. Some of them are a bit sneering and entitled, but Fern is warm and generous.

Elise and Grace make land next, gabbling away as if they've just emerged from a shopping mall. They are the youngest members of the group. Probably. Sophie doesn't know their age exactly. Late twenties? Early thirties? Neither is married or has kids and that makes them seem sweet and playful, like a couple of kittens. They are younger than her, for sure. Their flesh is firmer too, stomachs flatter, thighs smoother.

Sophie tries not to stare, not to make comparisons, not to feel inferior. There's nothing wrong with her body – okay, so it's a bit flabby in parts, but what can you expect after giving birth to two babies in twenty months? She never had a chance to get her figure back in between. Now she's glad the boys are so close in age – they always have someone to play with and are no trouble to look after. Ben and Louie are not what drive Sophie mad. They don't keep her awake at night, nor make her wonder whether she's made a terrible mistake. They are not the reason she decided to start a wild swimming club at Elizabeth Lake.

Sophie changes into her T-shirt, sweatshirt and jogging bottoms as the last of their group – Keira and Ariel – leave the water. Keira takes off her orange swimming cap (bright colours are advised for safety reasons), making her cropped black hair stick up like a hedgehog. She has intensely blue eyes and long lashes, smooth skin like pale pink marble. She's pleasant enough, but hard to draw out. According to Fern, she works for an insurance company and lives alone. Sophie thinks Keira must be a few years younger than herself, early to mid thirties. Not married. No mention of any children. Divorced, perhaps?

Ariel is the oldest in the group. She wears baggy patterned trousers and is letting her hair go grey. The purple swimsuit she always wears has lost all its elasticity. She doesn't wear shoes despite the sharp stones underfoot and dries herself with a threadbare towel. Sophie's pleased that Ariel has returned. She missed so many swims recently that they all assumed she'd given up. But it turns out she was looking after her sick mother.

These six are the core. Another four come and go. Open-air swimming all year round, come rain or shine, is not for everyone. Some women turn up once, literally put a toe in the water and run away; some stick it out for a few weeks, then disappear. Sophie never misses. The other day, Elise called her the 'beating heart' of the group, and it almost made her cry. She wears the epithet like an invisible badge. If Nan was still alive, she'd ask her to sew it to her costume.

'Hot chocolate at the Shack, everyone?' asks Fern, gathering her things together. Grace and Elise nod immediately. Keira checks the time on her phone and says she has to go.

'Can't make it either, sorry,' says Ariel. 'I promised Mum I'd help sort out her stuff. There's a whole lifetime of junk to get rid of.'

Sophie frowns sympathetically. 'Is she going into a nursing home?'

'Yes. She's protesting, but there's no choice.' Ariel tugs a brush through her wiry hair. 'I feel terrible about putting her there, but she can't manage alone any more, and I can't put my life on hold...' She tails off, biting her lip.

'You're doing the right thing,' declares Fern. 'You mustn't feel guilty.'

Elise takes Ariel by the arm. 'Come on, have a quick one.'

.   .   .

The Shack is a mobile unit, the only catering facility at the nature discovery park. The area was once a large open-cast coal mine, the land reclaimed and replanted, with the new lake as its centrepiece. Work is under way to build a visitor centre with its own café, but until then, the Shack is allowed to serve tea, coffee, scalding hot chocolate, organic fruit juices, paninis and home-made cake. It's not the most idyllic spot, but as it's a five-minute walk down a rough path to the lakeside, customers tend to hang around. There were just a few folding wooden tables and chairs at first, but they seem to have bred, and now take up several parking spaces.

The five of them queue to place their orders, each paying for their own drink. That's how it works. Nobody is allowed to treat the rest of the group – it could easily become complicated and unfair. Ariel suggested that rule and everyone quickly agreed. Sometimes Sophie would like to buy them all a hot drink and a slice of cake, just to say thank you for sticking it out week after week, through the winter and everything. She'd like to thank them for being unwitting companions on her journey to recovery. But she can't tell them the truth about why she swims. It's too shameful, too embarrassing.

They sit down with their various cups of steaming liquid. Grace is tempted by a piece of flapjack and Fern offers everyone a bite of her panini. There are a few exchanges about the latest Netflix series they're all hooked on. Elise lowers the hood of her sweatshirt and turns her face up towards the sun. Her pale skin burns easily, but she doesn't seem to care. Grace remarks on how surprisingly cold the water was today, despite the good weather. It's late September, but you wouldn't think it.

Sophie nods and sips her hot chocolate, but she's hanging right on the edge of the conversation, slowly losing her grip. It happens all the time: at work, when she's supposed to be liaising with clients; while she's helping the boys with their homework; when she's at the hairdresser's, during Sunday lunch at her parents' house. Her inner voice butts in, demanding her full attention, pulling her deep into her head and away from the present moment.

The only place where it doesn't happen is in the water. She's not sure why. Something to do with the intense cold, perhaps. Or the concentration needed to avoid getting tangled in the weeds. Or the overwhelming feeling of positivity that swimming gives her. Suddenly she wants to put down her hot chocolate and run back to the lake, to throw herself in like a fish that's been given another chance to live. But she stays where she is, the monologue twisting insidiously in her brain.

She tries to snap out of it, to re-engage with the chat. Fern is telling them that she's had this amazing idea. She loves Elizabeth Lake, absolutely adores it, but it's getting a little boring only ever swimming in the same place.

'Why don't we all go away together for a wild swimming holiday?' she says, her gaze lightly falling on each of them in turn.

'What, like a school trip?' Elise laughs.

'Yeah, why not?' says Grace, her brown eyes laughing. 'I'm desperate for a break. Where would we go?'

'I've been browsing online, and I've found some incredible places,' Fern continues, reaching into her sports bag.

Sophie's jaw tightens. There's nothing wrong with Fern suggesting a group activity. Sophie isn't the leader, after all. There *is* no leader. And yet she feels that since she is the 'beating heart' of the group, Fern should perhaps have mentioned the idea to her first before announcing it to the others.

Fern passes around some printouts from a website. She's clearly done a lot of research. 'I've marked the places that look the best. Some of them are extremely remote. A couple don't even have electricity,' she laughs.

'That's going a bit far,' says Grace, no doubt thinking of her hair tongs. She is the vainest of the group, the only one who swims in full make-up and never puts her face in the water.

'A few have generators, but none have Wi-Fi or landlines. It's supposed to be complete digital detox,' Fern explains. 'We could all do with that.' The others nod thoughtfully. Sophie feels a small quiver of excitement in her stomach. Actually, this is what she needs: a chance to spend some time away from Ryan and the boys, some time for herself. To think. God only knows, she deserves it.

'Wow, check this one out,' says Elise, flicking through the pages. 'It's got its own loch!'

Fern grins. 'Yes, that one caught my eye too. Just look at those views.'

'A loch. Does that mean it's in Scotland?' Ariel says.

'Yes – north-west, I think. You leave your car at the road-side, then it's a two-hour walk to the house along a track.'

Grace releases her long brown hair from its scrunchie. 'That's a long way to go for just a weekend. We'd have to stay for at least five days to make it worth the journey, maybe a whole week.'

Elise sighs. 'Looks really cool, but I won't be able to afford it.'

'Don't rule it out. It's surprisingly cheap off season, and we'd be sharing the cost,' says Fern. 'I took the liberty of enquiring about availability. As luck would have it, they'd just had a cancellation for the last week of next month.'

'Half-term,' says Sophie immediately.

'Yes, I know.'

'Mum will be in the nursing home by then,' murmurs Ariel, almost to herself.

Elise turns to Sophie. 'What do *you* think? You're the one that started all this. We couldn't go without you – it wouldn't be right.' She passes the printouts over.

Sophie's eyes wander over the photos of Condie's Retreat, a

traditional Scottish stone house dating back to the 1700s. It sleeps up to eight, and the facilities are basic to say the least. There is no mains electricity or running water. There's a compost toilet in an outside shed, the oven runs on propane gas, oil lamps and a log burner provide light and heat. Outside, it's a walker's paradise, with babbling burns and hidden waterfalls and a strong chance of seeing deer and eagles. No shop, no pub. No neighbours for miles. Just the six of them together. Swimming, walking, cooking, eating, drinking...

She looks around at the group. She hardly knows these women. They are of different ages, from different backgrounds, and they've been together for less than a year. All they have in common is their addiction to immersing themselves in freezing-cold water once a week. She wouldn't call them friends as such, and yet these are the women she wants to spend time with in this remote and beautiful place.

Ryan betrayed her. *These* are the people she trusts.

TWO

SOPHIE

'You must be out of your mind,' says Ryan when she mentions the trip over dinner. 'No running water, no electricity, compost toilets?' He laughs and turns to their sons. 'Mummy wouldn't last five minutes, would she, boys?'

Sophie rests her fork. 'Why are you being so negative?'

'Remember that holiday in Menorca? You had hysterics when you found a cockroach in the shower.'

'That was a four-star hotel. This is *supposed* to be basic, a digital detox.'

'You'll never survive.'

'We're only going for a week,' she retorts.

'I don't object to you going away, it's just that this is not your kind of thing. You should go on a spa break, have yourself a bit of luxury.'

'I don't need luxury.'

'At least go somewhere warm and sunny, not dreary old Scotland. Spain, Portugal, Tunisia...'

'Why don't we all go together?' suggests Ben. At nine, he's the image of his father – blue eyes outlined with dark lashes, a sprinkling of freckles across his little snub nose, sandy-coloured hair that is almost ginger, but not quite.

Sophie feels a pang of guilt. 'Well, I love going away on holiday with you lot, but... sometimes mummies need a bit of time and space to themselves.'

He pouts. 'Everyone in my class is going to Disneyland for half-term.'

'I doubt it.'

'*And* in my class,' lies Louie supportively. 'Everyone's going. Why can't we go too? It's not fair.'

'He's got a point, we never do that kind of stuff,' agrees Ryan. 'Hey, guys, let's go to Disneyland Paris! That would be so cool, eh?'

'Disneyland! Disneyland!' the boys chant.

'Enough!' Sophie tries to keep her temper. 'We're not going to Disneyland, okay? Maybe one day, if we can afford it, but this half-term I'm going to Scotland with my friends.' The boys groan. 'You can stay with Granny and Grandad, how about that? You always have a lovely time with them.' She gathers up their plates.

'That just leaves me,' says Ryan. 'What am I going to do, all by myself?' He pulls a sad face.

'Poor Daddy!' laughs Louie.

'Huh. Thanks for the support,' Sophie mutters sarcastically as she goes off to the kitchen.

She hates it when Ryan gangs up against her with the boys, even when it's in fun. They're too young to understand the subterranean battle that's being waged here. Ryan knows she'll never tell them. She hasn't told anyone – not her parents, or her brother, or any of her close friends. Only their couples counsellor knows the whole sordid story.

Ben and Louie jump down from the table and run off to the lounge. Ryan brings the glassware into the kitchen and puts it by the sink.

'Sorry. I didn't mean to shoot you down in flames,' he says. 'Why not go to Scotland? Sometimes it's good to get out of your comfort zone.'

'That's what I thought.'

'It'll be an adventure.'

'Yes.'

He pauses to look at her directly. 'As long as you don't decide you're not coming back.'

'I'd never leave Ben and Louie.'

'I meant to *me*...' He moves to embrace her. 'Maybe, when you come back, all renewed and refreshed, we could go away for a romantic weekend, just the two of us.'

She shakes her head. 'I can't. Not yet. I'm not ready.'

'It's getting on for a year, Sophie.'

'I don't need reminding of the date.'

He sighs. 'I thought we were over it. That we were mended.'

'Look, all I want is a week away, relaxing, walking, swimming with my friends. I can pay for it myself, out of my work savings.'

'Sure, I've already said it's okay. Go away without me, do whatever you want,' he says. 'You've got me by the balls, I know that.' He leaves the room, immediately shouting at the boys to turn the TV off and come upstairs for their bath.

Sophie puts her hands into the soapy water and leaves them there for a few minutes, remembering their first session with the counsellor, an elegant older woman called Miriam David. She hadn't wanted to go for couples counselling any more than Ryan had – it was something other people did, people who couldn't communicate with each other, who had no friends to confide in, no family to turn to. But when it came down to it, she realised that the only person who could help them was a stranger.

The consulting room was light, decorated in a pale green that was presumably supposed to be calming. Miriam suggested they take their coats off, explaining that it was a small room and tended to get quite hot. She gestured to them to sit in the beige armchairs in front of her, then reached for a folder and asked for their names, contact numbers, email addresses. Had they had couples counselling before? They shook their heads. She explained how it worked. How she was not there to judge, how she would not take sides. Oh, but you will take sides when you hear what happened, thought Sophie. She was a woman, how could she not?

'So...' said Miriam, putting the folder back on her desk and smiling at them like a benign primary school headmistress. 'Who would like to tell me why you're here?'

There was the inevitable pause. Sophie looked down and noticed the woman's very expensive shoes – Italian, she guessed. Ryan stared out of the window and watched the traffic pass in the gaps between the cream vertical blinds. Half a minute ticked by on the small clock placed discreetly behind a pot plant. Miriam seemed unbothered by the length of the silence. But for Sophie it was unbearable. Coming all this way, paying all this money and then not saying anything was just plain stupid.

'Whose idea was it to come here?' Miriam asked after another thirty seconds.

'Mine,' replied Sophie, unable to contain herself a moment longer. 'But I think Ryan should tell you why.'

The counsellor slowly turned her head. 'Ryan?'

There was a longer, more terrifying pause. Sophie felt the emotion rising, a sick, empty sensation, a faint dizziness as the blood drained away from her head.

'Ryan – would you like to tell us what brought you both here?'

'I had... an affair,' he mumbled.

Sophie felt as if she was hearing the news for the first time. The words punched her in the stomach, taking her breath away. Tears immediately began to roll down her cheeks; they were uncontrollable. She rummaged in her bag for a tissue, but Miriam deftly produced one from a box at her side.

'I'm sorry,' Sophie sniffed.

'No need to apologise.'

She didn't know why his words had shocked her again. Maybe she'd hoped that once they were in front of the counsellor, Ryan would say, *Actually, this is all a joke. Of course I haven't had an affair. I would never do anything as bad as that. Does this look like a woman you'd want to be unfaithful to?* But he had not.

'And is this affair still going on?' asked Miriam, evenly. Not *You bastard! How could you?*

'No. It finished ages ago.'

'What do you mean by ages? Weeks? Months? Years?'

'Does it matter?' interjected Sophie, irritated by the purely factual direction the conversation appeared to be taking. 'I want to know *why* he did it, but he won't tell me.'

'I keep telling you, I don't know why,' he muttered. 'There was no reason.'

She appealed to the counsellor. 'I don't understand. We were happy, there was nothing wrong with our marriage.'

There was more silence while Miriam wrote something in her notebook. Then she said, 'How did you find out about Ryan's affair, Sophie?'

'He told me.'

'It was her fault,' Ryan said. 'We'd been to this party, and she'd been flirting like mad with this guy all night.'

'That is so not true – we were doing "Auld Lang Syne", wishing everyone a Happy New Year.'

'She was all over him.'

'I was not!'

'As soon as we got home, a row started. One thing led to

another. She accused me of being an unattractive slob, so I just came out with it.'

'With what exactly?' Miriam asked.

He sighed irritably. 'You know. That I'd slept with someone else.'

'I see. How would you describe your relationship with this woman?'

'There wasn't one. We just had sex a few times.'

His words sent a fresh chill through Sophie as she instantly imagined their two naked bodies writhing together.

'How many times?' Miriam pressed.

'I don't know, two or three. Maybe more. I don't want to go into details.'

'He won't tell me anything about her,' interjected Sophie. 'I don't even know her name.'

Miriam made another note. 'How long did the affair last?'

'Not long. A month or two? I don't remember. It didn't mean anything.'

'It meant something to *me*,' said Sophie sharply.

Miriam turned her gaze. 'Yes. Tell us about that,' she said.

And that's how it started. Weekly sessions of saying 'truths' to each other that seemed perceptive and helpful at the time but that later felt cruel and unnecessary; of making accusations that hit hard and were impossible to take back. After seven months, they were both exhausted from churning their marriage over and over, as if they'd put it in a really long wash cycle. The horrible stains still hadn't come out and Miriam's fees were draining their bank balance.

In the end, they were brought together by a desperation to stop tearing themselves and each other apart. At their last session, six weeks ago, Ryan said that he was incredibly sorry for all the pain he had caused the woman he truly, madly, deeply loved and Sophie declared she'd forgiven him. Miriam David wished them well and sent them on their way, perhaps pleased with herself for a job well done, or perhaps not fooled for a second.

Sophie rinses the last soapy items under the tap and sets them down on the draining board with a long, tired sigh. The counselling sessions have left her feeling oddly responsible for the marriage's survival. Ryan has apologised; what more can he do, other than never betray her again? The onus is on her now to accept his apology and move on. She's been trying to hold the broken pieces of their relationship together, stuck with the glue of forgiveness, but eventually she's going to have to take her hands away. Will everything stay in place, or will it shatter? She can't be sure, can't risk it yet. Maybe this trip to Scotland will help.

She finishes clearing up the kitchen and goes into the sitting room, slumping on to the sofa. Her phone has been pinging with messages on the Sophie's Swimmers WhatsApp group. She reads through the string of enthusiastic comments, punctuated with exclamation marks and emoticons. Fern has offered to pay the rental fee up front as long as everyone confirms that they definitely want to go. *Yes please!* texts Ariel, quickly followed by Elise, Grace and Keira.

How about you, Sophie? Fern asks.

She takes a deep breath and types, *Yes. I'm in!*

THREE

SOPHIE

Sophie pushes her feet into the walking boots and pulls the laces tight across her instep. They feel hard and unforgiving, but maybe they are supposed to be like this. Maybe this is how they protect her, with tough love.

'Comfortable?' asks the sales assistant, a young bearded guy in khaki cargo pants and a black T-shirt.

'Not sure... I think so.' She stands up and paces up and down the floor, trying to imagine trudging through mud, clambering up mountains or skipping over streams. They seem okay, just a bit inflexible. She's thirty-eight and has never bought a pair of proper walking boots before. It makes her feel middle-aged. Until now, the most sensible footwear she's ever possessed is a pair of floral-patterned wellies she wore to Glastonbury. As it turned out, it didn't rain once that year and she spent most of the time wandering around in flip-flops. That was long ago, before the boys were born, before she and Ryan married even.

'I'll take them,' she says, returning to the bench and easing them off.

The assistant puts them back in their box. 'Great. Anything else you need? Hiking socks?'

'Um, yes, probably.'

'Spray protector for the leather?'

'Suppose so.' She glances at the bewildering display of jackets hanging on the walls. 'I also need a waterproof. A decent one that will actually keep the rain off.'

'We've got a great range, going from two- to five-hour protection, depending how much you want to spend.'

'Not too much,' she admits. 'All this outdoor gear is so expensive.'

He nods. 'Yeah, I know, but it's important to be properly equipped. Can I ask where you're going?'

'The Ardnish Peninsula.' He looks blank. 'West coast of Scotland, near the Hebrides. We're staying in a traditional house near a loch. It's very remote. No electricity, no Wi-Fi or mobile signal. Totally off-grid!' She laughs nervously.

'That's hardcore. And Scotland this time of year? Definitely go for the five-hour protection. And buy a decent pair of waterproof trousers.'

Her heart momentarily speeds up as she thinks of what her credit card balance will be this month. She promised Ryan she would pay for the trip out of her savings, but the costs are mounting up. There's no choice. She can't wear her skimpy shower-proof raincoat in the Highlands, and her winter ankle boots have heels and pointy toes. No, she'll have to go the whole hog and be done with it. 'Pay up and look big,' as Nan would joke. It was one of her favourite sayings.

Half an hour later, she emerges from the outdoor adventure shop laden with bulging carrier bags. She's spent nearly four hundred pounds – Ryan would have a fit if he knew. Not that she's going to tell him. She feels much easier about having secrets from him these days. Nothing she might keep from him will ever compare to the deception he played on her. It's a sad thought, but also liberating. She spent all those years trying to be the perfect wife, and look where that got her. What a waste of effort. Now she can relax and do what she wants. What's more, he doesn't dare criticise her, because her sins will never be as great as his.

She stashes the hoard at the back of her wardrobe when she gets home, covering it with a blanket. She feels childishly excited, as if she's bought a load of Christmas presents, all for herself. The trip is less than three weeks away now; it's come around so quickly.

All that shopping has given her an appetite, so she goes downstairs and makes herself some lunch. Normally she works on Tuesday afternoon, but Nigel has gone to a conference on alternative medicine and the practice is closed for a couple of days. Although she likes being a receptionist, the job can be boring at times. During those really dark months, when it seemed like she and Ryan were going to split up, she struggled to maintain her friendly smile as she greeted clients. They had to fit in counselling sessions around their shifts, which often meant Sophie had to go straight to work afterwards – eyes bloodshot with crying, insides all shaken up, her emotions wrung out like a damp cloth. Nigel asked if she was all right a few times, but she always denied there was anything wrong. He never pushed, thankfully. And she made sure she still got her work done, double-checking the appointment schedule, biting her tongue when clients complained unfairly to her. Being professional. She had lost so much, she didn't want to lose her job as well.

Maybe, she thinks as she eats a sandwich in front of the lunchtime news, she might look for a new job when she gets back from Scotland. Something more interesting and challenging. Full-time, perhaps. Or she might enrol on a course. She's often thought about becoming a physiotherapist. Now could be the time to revisit some of her earlier dreams.

This trip is starting to take on a new importance. It feels like she's drawing a line under the past and moving on – almost literally. When she returns, refreshed and renewed, she'll be able to look at her life with new eyes. She might decide to change everything or do nothing at all. It doesn't matter, as long as she's in control. She's had enough of feeling like a piece of litter tossed about in the wind.

The following week, the swimmers meet up after work to discuss arrangements. They've never socialised together before, and when she arrives late at the pizzeria, Sophie barely recognises them huddled at the corner table. With the exception of Grace, she is used to seeing them without make-up, their hair scraped back or stuffed under a swimming cap. When they're wearing their goggles, they all look the same, like alien aquatic creatures. But tonight, everyone has dressed up for the occasion, and it makes her realise how different they are, not just in facial features but in personal taste. Elise is wearing a long pink floral dress that matches her strawberry-blonde hair beautifully; Grace looks sexy in a tight black shift and Keira is stunning in a simple shirt and skinny jeans. Ariel is sporting the fairground fortune-teller look – gathered skirt, coloured scarves and dangly earrings – while Fern is smart in designer labels and a touch of bling. Anyone observing the group would wonder what on earth had brought them together.

'Sorry I'm late,' Sophie says, wishing she'd changed out of her work clothes for the evening. 'I couldn't get out the house.' They shuffle along the bench to let her sit down.

Elise smiles. 'Don't worry, we haven't ordered yet.'

They crowd over the menus, trying to decide whether to have a starter or save room for dessert, whether to mix and match pizzas or order for themselves, and whether two side salads would be enough for six to share. Everyone is trying their best to be generous and easy-going. It's as if they're auditioning for the trip and want to prove that they will be good team members. The atmosphere is jolly. Within minutes they are on their second bottle of Chianti.

'Right, girls,' says Fern, once everyone has eaten what they can of their pizzas and the waiter has cleared away the debris. 'No dessert until we've made some plans.' They groan good-humouredly as she takes a notebook and a shiny pen out of her handbag. 'I only booked the accommodation, remember – Grace, you still owe me for that, by the way – I'm not organising the whole thing.'

'We understand that,' says Sophie.

'I know, but there's a lot to arrange. Everyone has to do their bit, okay?'

'Yes, Mum,' quips Elise, and they all laugh.

'I'm serious,' Fern continues. 'Everything we're going to need for our stay has to be taken on foot – clothes, toiletries, food, booze, bottled water, gas cartridges for the oven... We can't afford to forget anything. There's no popping to the corner shop for a pint of milk.'

'We could take it in turns to cook,' says Ariel, 'and each bring the ingredients for that meal.' They all murmur agreement.

'I like the idea of taking turns, but we need to coordinate, otherwise we'll end up with everybody cooking sausages or whatever,' Sophie points out.

'And we should share basics,' says Grace. 'Cooking oil, butter, sugar, tea, coffee, breakfast cereal. Cheese and ham for lunch. Bread.'

'Any veggies?' asks Keira. They all shake their heads. 'No allergies? Intolerances...? Good. That'll make life easier.'

'I suggest that everyone decides what they'd like to cook, bearing in mind that the facilities are extremely basic, and sends their shopping list to me,' says Ariel, sounding quite excited. 'I'll pull them together to make sure there are no duplicates. How does that sound?'

'Brilliant,' says Fern. 'Now, moving on... We've all got to try to bring the minimum clothes-wise. I know I'm the worst for overpacking, but it really is important to cut down as much as possible. Otherwise we'll never carry it. We have to be sensible and look out for each other – a chain is only as strong as its weakest link.'

'And it's not like there'll be anywhere to go,' says Keira. 'We can be scruffy all week.'

They pause the discussion to order desserts and coffee. Sophie feels a warm glow inside her as she drains her glass of wine and tries to think of what she'll cook when it's her turn. Something simple that can be done in one pot, she decides. Chilli con carne or a ratatouille, perhaps.

'Next item on the agenda is transport,' announces Fern, once they've stuck their spoons into various calorific puddings. 'It makes sense to travel up together in one car. I'm happy to take my seven-seater, which will save on petrol costs. But I've looked up the route, and according to the AA, the journey takes about seven hours. Too much for one person. I can put some-body else on the insurance, but we'll have to share the cost.'

'I don't mind driving,' says Sophie, feeling full of bonhomie and chocolate brownie.

'Thanks. Anyone else? A third person would be good...'

'Sorry, don't drive,' says Elise. Grace and Keira say the same, and Ariel confesses that she gave up her car years ago and has let her licence lapse.

'Oh well, we'll have to manage between the two of us, I guess,' says Fern. 'Anything else we should discuss?'

Keira raises her hand. 'Just that I've got a trolley that I use for my kit at festivals. Shall I bring it? Might be useful for the walk to the house.'

'Absolutely,' says Fern. 'If anyone else has got one, bring it too.'

'This is so exciting,' Elise chimes in. 'I can't wait.'

'Come on, girls, we need a selfie!' says Sophie, taking out her phone. Fern shuffles closer to Elise, while Ariel and Keira put their arms around each other's shoulders. Grace gets up and stands behind the group, and they all beam at the lens.

Sophie checks the shot, then immediately shares it with their WhatsApp group. It's only a photo, but it's about to change the rest of her life.

FOUR

SOPHIE

The boys go to an after-school club on Tuesdays. Normally Sophie picks them up by car on her way home, but today she walks there at a leisurely pace, arriving half an hour earlier than usual. She enters the hall, where the children are involved in a game of something vaguely akin to basketball.

'Ben! Louie!' Her call is lost among the shouting and the teeth-hurting squeak of trainers on the polished floor. 'Come along, time to go home. Now!' They ignore her, forcing her to enter the chaos and extract them physically.

'But we're in the middle of a game,' moans Ben. 'I was about to score, and you stopped me.'

'Sorry.'

'Why are you so early, Mummy?' asks Louie. 'Nobody else is going home.'

'I finished work early. I thought it would be nice to spend some time together.'

'Doing what?' frowns Ben suspiciously.

'I don't know. Anything. We could go to the park. Or make a cake, perhaps?' Both boys look unimpressed by her suggestions.

'Can't we just stay here? You can collect us later.'

'No. Put your coats on, please. And don't forget your backpacks.'

She drags them out of the door. It's only a ten-minute walk home, but they insist on jumping on every available wall and kicking litter down the street, then suddenly being too tired to put one foot in front of the other whenever she asks them to speed up. It's torturous, but also comforting. Because it's normal. And preferring to stay at the after-school club with their friends is normal too.

Things with Ryan, however, are *not* normal. The last few days, he's been behaving like a kicked dog, and she can't work out why. It's connected to this holiday, she's sure of it. At first he was supportive, even though he took the piss out of her for going on a digital detox rather than a luxury spa break. He agreed that she deserved time off from him and the kids. Now he seems to have decided that she's abandoning him. It makes her so angry when she remembers what he put her through – trampling all over the sanctity of their marriage with his appallingly selfish behaviour. Has he forgotten how much he still owes her? Sometimes she wonders whether he is genuinely sorry for hurting her or just sorry that he confessed. Did he only apologise because he wanted the counselling to stop? It was tough for them both, but she learned important stuff about herself – her perfectionism, her absolutism, how hard she finds it to forgive. Ryan, however, has just gone back to being Ryan – charming, funny, a bit lazy when it comes to doing jobs in the house, but good with the kids. He's the same man she fell in love with when she was a teenager.

As the boys linger by some puddles, she thinks back to that time at university. In the first few months of their relationship, she was the only one who actually thought it *was* a relationship. She didn't realise it at the time, but it was something that came out during the counselling. Yes, they really did go back that far...

'Retrace your steps,' said Miriam David, sitting there smugly with her notepad and her shiny Italian shoes. 'Describe those early days.'

Sophie talked about how much she'd wanted Ryan to treat her as his girlfriend. He was very happy to have sex with her, but less keen on making arrangements to see her, or putting her before football, or seeing movies he didn't particularly like, or going on double dates with her friends.

Ryan was clearly feeling uncomfortable. 'I don't want to talk about those times,' he said. 'I'll walk out.'

'Why does that make you feel threatened?' asked Miriam, her curiosity sparked.

He ignored her and turned to Sophie. 'I married you, didn't I? What's your problem?'

'There you go,' huffed Sophie. 'Denial followed by aggression. That just about sums it up.'

'This is all bollocks, a waste of time.'

Miriam allowed a pause, then said, 'It can be very enlightening to investigate the beginnings of a partnership. Often a pattern is set that is repeated over and over again.'

'You're exactly right, it's extremely relevant,' agreed Sophie.

'Do you want to expand on that?'

'Our relationship has always been lopsided. I make all the effort and Ryan just comes along for the ride. I organised our wedding virtually single-handed. All he did was turn up on the day.'

'That's not true,' he interjected.

'I book our holidays, plan our social life – what little there is of it. When we bought our first place, I did all the house-hunting, researched schools, handled the legal work, found the removal company. I do most of the cooking, I've always sorted the childcare—'

'And I suppose you conceived the boys by yourself too, did

you?' he butted in. 'Like I don't go to work and bring home money for you to spend on new furniture and—'

'Yes, yes, you go along with my plans, but you don't *initiate* anything,' she cried, adding bitterly, 'Apart from going online and finding some tart to screw.'

There was a pause, as if someone had let off a bad smell. 'Maybe that's why I did it,' he said finally. 'Because you don't leave room for me to—'

'That's not—'

'I'm afraid our time's up,' cut in Miriam, putting her notepad on the desk. 'Some very interesting issues have arisen today. Let's explore them more fully next week.'

But they never went back to the past again, and in one way, Sophie was glad. There were dark corners she didn't want to investigate any more than Ryan did. Enough damage had been done without making it even worse.

As soon they arrive home, Ben and Louie rush into the sitting room and switch on the television, pleased to be in time for one of their favourite cartoons. Sophie starts to prepare the evening meal. It's home-made meatballs tonight, served with spaghetti and fresh tomato sauce. She takes the minced beef from the fridge and is dividing it into sixteen equal portions when her mobile phone rings. She presumes it's Ryan, telling her he's on his way home, but to her surprise, it's Fern.

'Hi,' Sophie says. 'Everything okay?'

'I'm really sorry to do this to everyone,' Fern replies in a shaky voice, 'but I can't make it.'

'Can't make what?'

'The trip. I've got to pull out. I'm really sorry.'

'Oh.' Sophie's heart sinks. 'Why? What's happened?'

'Personal reasons,' Fern says quickly. 'It's complicated. I don't want to talk about it. *Can't* talk about it. Sorry.'

'That's okay.'

'I was so looking forward to going, but... well, it's out of the question now. Impossible.'

'I'm really sorry to hear that. I'll miss you. If there's anything I can do—'

'Obviously I won't be taking my seven-seater, so you'll need to organise alternative transport.' Fern talks over her.

'What? Oh, of course, yes... I'd forgotten... Well, we won't all fit in my little car. Not with everyone's luggage and the supplies.'

'That's what I thought. You'll just have to hire something. More expense, I know, but... I'll still pay my share of the accommodation. I feel so bad about letting everyone down, but there's no way out of this.'

'Okay. We'll sort it out. Thanks for letting me know. Take care, Fern. If you need anything, just ask.' Sophie puts the phone down and returns to the meatballs.

It's a blow. What on earth could have happened to make Fern withdraw? Some health issue? Marital problems? Perhaps her husband has put his foot down and demanded she stay at home. She's always assumed that Fern is happily married to her successful businessman, living in that posh executive home with him and their high-achieving kids. Could it be that she's been pretending as much as Sophie has? Maybe they are *all* pretending. And maybe the wild swimming club is everyone's lifeline, not just hers.

She mulls this over later that evening, after she's put the boys to bed. How everyone has secrets. How you never know what's going on in other people's lives.

'Fern's not coming,' she tells Ryan, stopping by his man cave (otherwise known as the third bedroom) on her way to bed. They managed to eat together, but he has spent the rest of the evening gaming on his computer. She stands at the threshold, not wanting to enter his lair. He is sitting at the desk, his face illuminated by flashes of coloured light from the screen.

'Who's Fern?' he replies, without looking away.

'One of the women in the swimming group. It's such a nuisance. Means I'm going to have to do all the driving.'

'That's not fair.'

'There's no choice. None of the others has a licence. And there are no trains – not that stop anywhere nearby, anyway.'

'It's not a goer, you should cancel.'

'I'll be fine as long as I take breaks.'

'You're not a very confident driver, Sophie, you hate twisty country roads.'

'Yes, but I can do it. I've been driving for over fifteen years.' She frowns at him. 'What's wrong? You were all in favour when I first suggested going away. This has nothing to do with the driving, has it? You just don't want me to go.'

He shrugs. 'It's boring being left here all by myself.'

'I thought you'd enjoy it. Can't you... go and look up a friend? Or visit your parents?' He throws her a filthy look. 'I know you don't get on, but you haven't seen them for ages, and...' She throws her hands up. 'You're grown-up, you'll find something to do. As long as it's... you know... a wholesome activity.'

He groans. 'Jesus, Sophie, did you have to say that?'

'I'm sorry, I wasn't having a dig.'

'Yes, you were.'

'Look, I trust you. Surely leaving you here for a week by yourself is proof of that.'

'Ooh, thanks, so gracious of you.'

'Stop being so arsey. It's just a week, you can manage, can't you? This isn't about you. It's about me, for once. Just me.'

'I know, I get it.'

'I'm really looking forward to this trip. It's an important step in the healing process.'

He curses as his avatar is killed, then swivels around to face her, giving her one of his puppy-dog looks. 'I'm going to miss you, that's all. So will the boys.'

'You won't miss me, Ryan – you'll hardly notice I've gone. And the boys will have a lovely time with my mum and dad.'

'I still don't get it. Going all that way for a freezing-cold swim...' He shakes his head disbelievingly. 'How many of you crazy women?'

'There were six of us, but it's only five now. And we're not crazy.' She gets her phone and shows him the photo taken at the pizzeria. 'See? We're all perfectly normal.' She points at their tiny faces smiling to camera, one by one. 'That's Grace at the back. That's Elise. I suppose you'd call her ginger, but she insists she's a strawberry blonde. Keira's the tall one who looks a bit like a boy. That's Fern, she's about my age, I think, and the one with the funny turban on is Ariel. You should meet them one day, they're all really nice.'

He takes a sharp breath and stares at the screen, suddenly transfixed by the Image. 'And, er... they're *all* going to Scotland with you?' he asks after a few seconds. His voice sounds a little strangulated.

'Yes, except Fern. It's such a shame, I can't believe she's not coming. It just won't be the same without her.'

He's still looking at the photo. 'How... er... how did you meet them?'

'I formed a Facebook group, sent a message out and they turned up. Not all at once, at different times... but you know all this. Why are you asking?'

'I just, er...' He trails off. 'Doesn't matter.'

'Is something wrong?'

'No. Nothing,' he says abruptly, shutting down his computer. His face is twitching with emotion, although he's trying his hardest to hide it. 'I really don't think you should go on this trip.'

She sighs irritably. 'Not again.'

'It's too far to go with only one driver.'

'We can't cancel now. It's too late. We've already paid in full. I'll be fine, as long as I stop for regular breaks.'

'It's not safe.' He turns to face her. 'Honestly, Sophie, the trip can't go ahead.'

'You can't stop me,' she replies gruffly.

'Please! It's too dangerous.'

'You don't know what you're talking about.'

'Swimming in unknown waters this time of the year, it's stupid... You're miles from anywhere, there's no phone, no internet. If someone got hurt...' His voice sounds brittle, as if it's about to snap.

'Yes, there are risks,' she admits. 'But we're very sensible, we always follow the safety rules. Nobody wants to drown.'

'I'll be worried sick about you all week.'

'Well, you mustn't. I'll be fine.'

'But what if something awful happened? Think of the boys, they'd be devastated.'

'Please don't try to guilt-trip me. That's not fair.'

'But—'

'I'm going to Scotland, and that's final.'

'I'm begging you, Sophie. Pull out. Now.'

'No. I won't. Why are you being so difficult? I really need this.'

'Oh no you don't,' he replies. 'You absolutely one hundred per cent don't.' He stands up, almost pushing past her to leave the room, and runs downstairs.

She goes after him. 'What's wrong?' He takes his jacket off the peg and puts it on. 'Ryan – what are you doing?'

'I need to go out, that's all.' He shoves his feet into his trainers and quickly ties the laces.

'What, now? It's gone ten o'clock.'

'I won't be long.' He picks up his keys and opens the front door. A blast of cold night air invades the hallway.

'Where are you going?'

'Nowhere. Just need to clear my head.'

'Why are you so upset?'

'I'm not upset. Got a headache, that's all, need some air. You go to bed, don't wait up.'

'But, Ryan—' He leaves before she can finish her sentence, shutting the front door behind him with a firm click.

FIVE

THE SWIMMER

I lay everything on the bed – jeans, joggers, tops, jumpers, underwear, pyjamas, two swimsuits, microfibre towel, dryrobe, swim hat, woolly hat, walking boots, wellies, flip-flops... It's too early to pack, of course, but I like to plan carefully in advance.

I'm going to need some toiletries, and I'll probably throw in a dress or two, although we're not likely to go out anywhere fancy. It's a lot to carry on my back for the trek to this Condie's Retreat place. And what about all the food and drink we've got to bring with us? Can't we just order a delivery and make them bring it to our door?

My phone bleeps – it'll be another message on the WhatsApp group, no doubt. It's been buzzing all evening, everyone competing to say the nicest thing about Fern and how much they're going to miss her. Apart from her first message, telling us she was dropping out, she has stayed unusually silent, only offering hearts and sad faces in reply to our outpourings of love and support. Secretly, of course, we're all dying to know what her 'personal reasons' are for withdrawing. She's made a few hints recently about feeling trapped in her marriage, and how it's only since she started wild swimming that she's felt her 'authentic self' – whatever that's supposed to mean. She was the one who suggested the trip in the first place, and I'm sure she's gutted. Something major has gone wrong. I messaged her privately to say how disappointed I was and offered a shoulder to cry on. I was hoping she'd divulge a few details, but she didn't take the bait. She was most worried about Sophie being the only other person who could drive.

I *can* drive, I just don't want to. Not all the way to bloody Scotland and back.

I add a string of thumbs-up emojis in response to Sophie's latest missive, saying how we'll have to leave even earlier on Saturday morning because she's going to need to take more breaks from the wheel. Oh God, I hope this trip is going to be bearable. The booking website is full of warnings not to expect luxury. I don't mind basic accommodation, but the idea of an outside compost toilet is freaking me out a bit. Also, with only four bedrooms, two of us will have to share.

I want to share with Sophie. I wonder if she snores or talks in her sleep. Maybe she dribbles on to her pillow or has night-mares that wake her up in a sweat. I wonder how she might feel about letting it all hang out in front of me. Of course, I've seen her in a swimsuit many times, so I already know about the stretch marks on her thighs and the roll of fat that sits under her ribcage. Apparently she's still trying to get rid of the weight she put on in pregnancy. If she's self-conscious, I'll do my best to put her at her ease. We'll be like schoolgirls sleeping in a dorm; giggling in the darkness, telling secrets, sharing our hopes and fears. We'll get to know each other so much better. No longer just swimming buddies, we'll become proper friends.

I think back to when we first met. I'd been tracking Sophie covertly on social media for months, browsing through her unflattering photos and boring posts – so-called inspiring poems, pics of cakes she'd made with her sons, shares of tedious articles about women's issues. She went quiet for a bit around

New Year and I almost stopped checking. Then a month or so later, I saw that she'd formed this new Facebook group – Sophie's Swimmers – inviting other women to join her at Elizabeth Lake at 8 a.m. every Tuesday for a wild swim.

I was only planning to go once, just to see her in the flesh, hear her voice, observe her mannerisms. I had no intention of actually swimming. Give me a sandy beach and the warm Mediterranean and I'll willingly strip off and dive in, but a freezing cold lake in the UK? In February? I thought it was insane. But everyone was so friendly and encouraging – especially Sophie – that I felt obliged to wade in up to my ankles at least.

It turns out I'm a mermaid in disguise – who would have thought it? Now I'm addicted to open water, can't get enough of the stuff. It's free. *And* legal. There are no side effects and no hangover to deal with the next day. Honestly, since I started wild swimming, my mental health has improved, I've been more productive at work, and I have even more sexual energy. I've given up my expensive gym membership and ditched the yoga class. The water gives me everything.

It's the coldness that's my drug. The colder the better. It anaesthetises my memories, dulls the pain of the past and forces me into the here and now. When I think I can't take one more second of it, I deliberately swim out further. The thought that my heart could suddenly stop beating excites me. Is that what the moment of death is like? A few seconds of feeling at your most alive.

And afterwards, when I'm wrapped in my wonderful dryrobe with my hands around a cup of coffee, I love the way my body fizzes and tingles as it warms up. I go home and have a tepid shower – not hot, because that actually lowers your body temperature – then get dressed and skip into work feeling like I've just had sex with the most attractive man on earth.

The doorbell chimes, waking me from my watery fantasy.

There's only one person who calls this late in the evening. *Shit.* I quickly gather up my neat piles of holiday stuff and shove everything under the bed. The bell sounds again, impatiently, and I run down the stairs.

'You can't keep doing this,' I say, opening the door. 'I'm not on call, you know, always available to service your needs.'

Ryan has a strange expression on his face, kind of angry. 'Can I come in?' he says, stepping over the threshold without waiting for my reply.

'Er, you just have. What's up?'

'I can't believe you would do this to me,' he says, marching into the sitting room.

'Do what?'

'Don't fuck with me. I know what you're up to, I saw you in the photo. At the restaurant.'

Ah... I pull my dressing gown across my chest and sit down on the sofa, cursing myself for making such a simple mistake. I've been so careful not to participate in any of the photos Sophie has taken for her FB page, thinking Ryan might see them, but I forgot all about it when we were at the pizzeria.

'Well?' he says. 'What's going on?'

I shrug. 'Nothing. I just like open-air swimming.'

'That's bullshit. You're stalking my wife.'

'Hmm, maybe I was at first – a teeny-tiny bit. But not any more. We're friends now.' His eyes widen in horror. 'Honestly, babe, it's all okay. She doesn't know.' I pause, studying his expression. 'You haven't told her, have you?'

'Course I bloody haven't. I'm not *that* stupid.'

'Well then, what's the problem?'

'You, you're the problem. This whole thing's the problem,' he wails. 'I can't cope, it's too much. There's no way you're going to Scotland with her, no way!'

'Oh yeah, and how are you going to stop me?'

'I asked you to come away with me this half-term, it was the perfect opportunity to spend some time together. But you said you were going to London to see your best friend.' He pushes out his bottom lip. 'You lied to me.'

'So? My lies are nothing compared to yours. You have to face it, babe, you've got no choice but to let us go off and have a lovely girlie time together.'

'I don't trust you,' he says. 'You're up to something. Please leave her alone, she doesn't deserve it.'

'I'm not up to anything,' I laugh. 'It's just a bit of fun. I wanted to find out what was so great about her, why you were still with her when she blatantly wasn't giving you what you wanted. I did a bit of googling and found out about her little swimming group. Now I'm hooked. Honestly, I love it.'

'If you tell her who you are... if she finds out we're seeing each other...'

'She won't. Not from me.' I fix him with a look. 'And not from you either – if you want us to carry on.'

'I do, you know I do, but this is... scary.'

'It's just a game!'

'You can play games with me, but not with her. She's a good person, a great mother...' His voice breaks.

'And this is how you repay her.'

'You think I don't feel shitty about myself every time we hook up?'

'Oh thanks, that makes me feel really great.'

'I *do* love her,' he says, 'but I love you too.'

'No, Ryan, you have sex with me, that's all. You keep your love for sweet, boring little Sophie.'

'You just said she was your friend.'

'Yeah, well...' I roll my eyes. 'Hadn't you better get back to her? She'll be wondering where you are this time of night. Don't want her to get suspicious.'

He stands up. 'Please don't go on this trip.'

'Sorry. Bags are packed.'

'Okay. Then promise me, from the bottom of your heart, that nothing bad is going to happen to her.'

'Like what? I'm hardly going to push her off a mountain – at least not in front of the whole group.'

'It's not funny.'

'Oh, relax, Ryan. She's safe.'

He puts his hands on my shoulders and looks me straight in the eyes. 'I want you to promise.'

'Okay, I promise, cross my heart, hope to die and all that shit.' I give him a long, lingering kiss. 'Everything's going to be fine.'

I am such a liar.

SIX

SOPHIE

Sophie walks into the boys' bedroom. 'Ben... Louie...' she says softly. 'Time to get up.'

They are fast asleep in the bottom bunk. She often finds them like this, arms around each other, their identically coloured hair mingling on the pillow. Louie suffers from nightmares, which wake his big brother up, and Ben climbs down from the top and gets into bed to comfort him. She loves it that they are so close – playing together, sleeping in each other's arms, hardly ever a cross word between them. They will need each other, she thinks, if she and Ryan go their separate ways, leaving them in no-man's-land, not knowing in whose camp they belong.

She draws the curtains, letting in the pink morning light. The boys don't react, so she has to shake them gently.

'Hey... wake up, please.'

Ben opens a bleary eye. 'Wha-a?'

'Mummy's going to Scotland today, remember? I'm dropping you off at Granny and Grandad's on the way. I need you to get up.'

He makes a groaning noise. 'Do we have to go *now*? Can't Daddy take us later?'

'No. Sorry.' She strokes Louie's back until he starts to stir. 'Morning, sweetie... wake up.'

Ben sits up. 'I don't want to go,' he says. 'I want to stay here for half-term and play with my friends.'

'Don't be silly, you love staying with Granny and Grandad. Come on, be good boys for me. Get dressed and come downstairs straight away.'

She leaves the room and goes down to the kitchen, where the mug of tea she made earlier is getting cold. She swallows the tepid, milky liquid in one gulp. An excited shiver runs through her as she thinks of what lies ahead: living the simple life, hiking through beautiful scenery, creating bonds with the other women, and most of all the swimming. She can already feel the icy water soaking her skin.

Ryan is still asleep in bed. She won't wake him until she's ready to leave. He's been in a strange mood ever since he left the house a couple of nights ago and didn't return until two in the morning. She was still awake when he came in, trying to puzzle out why he'd gone out in such a state.

'Where the hell have you been?' she hissed as he crept into the bedroom.

'Nowhere,' he whispered. 'Just driving around. Thinking.'

'What about?' She switched the bedside lamp on and sat up.

'All sorts of stuff.' He perched on the side of the bed next to her and took her hand. It was as if she was ill, and he was visiting her in hospital.

'Why did you flip when I showed you the selfie?' she asked.

He shrugged. 'I felt jealous, left out. You all looked so happy, so together. I realised you have a whole other life now, with people I've never even met. They're the ones you want to go on holiday with, not me.'

'I see... Well, I guess that's true. To some extent. I'm not saying we'll never go on holiday again, just that right now...' Suddenly she felt cruel, and didn't want to finish the sentence.

'I'm so sorry, Sophie.' He took her hand and stroked it. 'You know, for what happened.'

'For what you *did*,' she corrects. 'It didn't just happen. You went out of your way to find it.'

'Yes, yes, I did. It was the biggest mistake I ever made, and I know you haven't really forgiven me.'

'I'm trying my best. It's a process. You can't just say "I forgive you" and expect it to be over. It doesn't work like that.'

'I know...' He sighed heavily. 'I really wish you weren't going away on this trip. I'm scared that when you come back, you won't want to be with me any more. Or you won't come back at all.'

'I don't think that's very likely,' she said, although she knew he had a point.

He took her in his arms and squeezed her tightly, jamming her face into the crook of his neck. 'I love you. Forget bloody Scotland. Let's go away together, just the two of us.'

She pulled away. 'No. I can't. It's too late to back out now. I'm not going to let everyone else down. Anyway, I *want* to go.'

That conversation took place in the early hours of Wednesday morning, and they haven't really spoken since then. He hasn't mentioned the trip again, and nor has she, although evidence of it is everywhere. Her new waterproof is hanging over the end of the banisters and her walking boots are in the porch. Her rucksack is already packed and waiting by the front door. The grey seven-seater she collected last night is sitting on the driveway.

It was extremely expensive to hire, and she had to pay for it with her credit card. She hopes the others will be willing to chip in. Ryan is right to be anxious about her being the only driver – she's not looking forward to that. It makes her feel like a teacher taking a group of students away on a field trip. She feels responsible.

They are meeting in the car park at Elizabeth Lake at 6.45, with the aim of leaving as soon as possible. There's a long way to go. They have to reach their destination by 4 p.m. at the very latest, otherwise they'll be walking to the house in the dark, which will be difficult, if not dangerous.

She checks the time: 5.20. If she's to get to her parents' house then double back to Elizabeth Lake, she has to get the boys out of the house in ten minutes.

'Ben! Louie! Are you dressed yet?' she shouts from the bottom of the stairs. There's no reply, so she runs back up. Louie emerges from the bedroom with his trousers around his thighs and his jumper on inside-out.

'Oh, look at you!' laughs Sophie, yanking the trousers up. She whips the jumper over his head, and he yawns as she pulls the sleeves through and pops it back on. 'There, that's better. Where are your socks? Go and find them, please.'

Ben is also dressed, but instead of wearing the smart clothes she laid out for him last night, he has put his beloved Spider-Man top on – the one with the fraying sleeves and the indelible stain on the front. The navy chinos she washed and ironed specially yesterday have been cast aside in favour of a pair of tatty old jogging bottoms, only suitable for the garden.

'You can't go to Granny and Grandad's looking like a scare-crow,' she says. 'They might stick you in the garden to frighten the birds.'

He scowls as she hands him a checked brushed-cotton shirt – a present from her mother – and the chinos. 'Put these on. Quickly, please. I don't want to be late.'

She stands over them while they finish getting dressed. Their hair is sticking up in knots and in need of a good brush. No doubt Grandad will make some comment, but there's no time to deal with it now. She picks up the little wheeled suitcases that she packed yesterday and herds the boys downstairs.

'I'm hungry,' says Ben.

'You can have breakfast at Granny and Grandad's.'

'Pancakes?' Louie asks hopefully.

'Sure.' She hands them their jackets. 'Put your shoes on, please. *Now*. I'm in a rush.'

Ben looks upwards. 'Is Daddy going to come down and say goodbye?'

'I don't think so. He's still asleep.' Both boys look crestfallen. 'It doesn't matter, you'll see him again very soon.'

'Bye, Daddy! Love you!' whispers Louie, blowing a kiss up the stairs.

She thinks about going back upstairs to say goodbye herself, but there really isn't time.

Sophie pulls up in the car park at the top of the lake, surprised and relieved to be only two minutes late. The boys were deposited on time, but her mother wouldn't let her go – quizzing her about the trip, asking why she was going away on her own, whether everything was all right. Mum and Dad know that she and Ryan have had some difficulties this past year, but not the root cause. Sophie decided to keep Ryan's adultery from them, reasoning that while *she* might be able to forgive him, her parents never would. She is a favourite daughter, and they've never liked Ryan much anyway. Even if the marriage was patched up, it would create problems in the future. Family get-togethers would be tricky, Christmases excruciating. When her mother has a couple of glasses of Prosecco inside her, she has a habit of making mysterious barbed comments, and Ryan isn't the type to pretend he hasn't heard.

The car park is empty apart from Grace, Elise and Ariel, who are standing next to their luggage: three large rucksacks, two bulging plastic carrier bags and some crates of food and drink.

'Hi,' Sophie says, putting on a cheerful face as she jumps down from the Zafira. 'No Keira?' she asks.

'She messaged to say she's on her way,' says Elise. 'Her taxi didn't turn up, so she's had to order another one.'

Sophie opens the back door of the car. 'Right. Let's get all the stuff in, then we can leave as soon as she arrives.'

'Such a shame about Fern,' says Grace, heaving the biggest, heaviest rucksack into the boot. 'This trip was her idea in the first place. She was so excited about it. Something really bad must have happened to make her pull out.'

'Yeah. Anyone know the reason?' Elise picks up the first crate, which seems to be mainly full of root vegetables, and staggers over. 'Her WhatsApp message was really vague.'

'Some personal problem... Maybe to do with her kids?' suggests Ariel.

They hear the sound of a vehicle approaching, and a few seconds later, a minicab rounds the bend and stops. Keira gets out and takes her rucksack and a folded trolley out of the boot. They stow them in the back of the Zafira and then everyone climbs aboard.

Keira parks herself next to Elise. 'Sorry,' she says. Ariel, who is sitting in the front passenger seat, waves the apology away.

'No worries,' calls Grace from the very back. She has commandeered the empty seat next to her and is sitting at an angle with her legs up. 'Hope you brought your swimsuit!'

'Of course.'

'I've already got mine on,' jokes Elise.

Sophie restarts the engine. 'Everyone okay? Seat belts on?'

'Yes, Mum!' they chorus, breaking into laughter.

She pulls out of the car park and takes a right turn that leads to the M6, heading north. Most of the journey will be spent on major A roads and motorways, with the final leg towards the west coast promising some spectacular scenery. It's easy, monotonous driving. Normally the challenge would be to stay awake, but Sophie is feeling surprisingly alert considering she was up so early. It's a relief to be leaving all her troubles behind her – physically and mentally. The further she gets away from home, the more she realises how much she needs this break.

There's a lot of lively chatter behind her, peppered with outbreaks of laughter. Ariel keeps turning around to join in, leaving Sophie feeling like a taxi driver. Not that she cares too much about being ignored. Putting her foot down, she keeps the car cruising at just below the speed limit and tries to concentrate on the road ahead. She is hungry to eat up the miles.

After a couple of hours, they stop at a service station for a comfort break and breakfast. Sophie turns on her mobile and sees that she has several missed calls from Ryan. She listens to the message he left on her voicemail. His tone is rather plaintive as he complains about her not waking him up to say goodbye.

'I really need to talk to you,' he says. 'Please ring me as soon as you get this. It's extremely important.'

It annoys her that he's not letting her break free, still invading her peace. She hesitates, not wanting to speak to him.

'Everything okay?' asks Grace. She is halfway through an almond croissant and has smudges of white dust around her mouth.

'Yes. Just my husband,' Sophie replies. 'He's a bit miffed because I forgot to say goodbye... I suppose I'd better call him back. He'll only keep trying.'

Grace dabs a paper serviette over her mouth, careful not to remove any of her lipstick. 'At least he cares.'

'Hmm... Excuse me.' Sophie picks up her cup of coffee. 'I'll be outside, waiting by the car.'

'We won't be long,' Ariel assures her.

Sophie rests her coffee cup on a picnic table and calls

Ryan's mobile. It barely has a chance to ring before he answers it.

'Hi, thanks for calling back,' he says. 'I've been going out of my mind.'

'Look, I'm sorry I didn't wake you. You were fast asleep, and—'

'I wanted to talk to you before you left.'

'I'm sorry, I ran out of time. And I couldn't use the phone while I was driving. We've stopped for a break now.'

'This is really difficult.'

'What is?'

He pauses; she can hear his quick, anxious breaths. A strange feeling of dread starts to creep over her.

'What's wrong, Ryan?'

'Did they all turn up? Your friends. Are they all there?'

'Yes...'

He swears under his breath.

The others spill out of the service station, laughing and talking as they wander past her towards the car. She pulls an apologetic face. 'What's wrong? Please, just spit it out. I've got to go. Everyone's ready to press on.'

'Are you alone? Can anyone hear you?'

'No...'

'Good. There's something I need to tell you,' he says.

SEVEN

SOPHIE

'We can't start a heavy conversation now, Ryan. It's not the right time. Or the place.'

'We have to, there's no choice,' he replies. There's an odd tone to his voice she's never heard before. It's as if he's about to tell her that somebody close to her has died. 'You're going to be shocked, but I want you to react calmly. Whatever you do, don't let on to the others.'

'What's happened?'

'The woman I had the fling with...'

Her hackles rise. 'If you're about to make another confession, I don't want to hear it. Ever. You can't keep dumping this stuff on me, it's not fair.'

'Listen to me! This is important.' He inhales sharply. 'She's part of your group.'

She genuinely can't understand what he's saying. 'What group?'

'She's one of your swimmers – she's with you now.'

'What?'

'I had no idea, Sophie, honestly, swear to God. Not until I saw her in that photo. She's been stalking you all this time. God knows why. I tried everything to stop her going, but she refused. I was going to tell you this morning, but...'

She has that sick, empty, dizzy feeling again, like everything is falling away. 'Who is it?' she rasps.

'Better you don't know. Just get back in the car and drive home. Make up some excuse, say that your dad has had a heart attack or one of the boys has been in an accident.'

'Tell me who it is,' she demands, her voice cold and hard.

'No. She mustn't find out that you know.'

'Why not? She needs calling out.'

'I'm scared of her.'

'Scared? What do you mean?'

'I don't know why she's doing this – what it is she wants... I'm sorry, Sophie, so, so sorry. I never meant for this to happen. Just come home, yeah? I'll tell you everything and we can sort it all out.'

'Forget it. It's over. You and I, we're finished.'

'Don't say that... let me explain. Please, come home.'

'Not yet. I need to sort this out first.'

'No, no, you don't understand, she could be dangerous—'

She ends the call before he can finish and immediately turns off the phone. Her knees are shaking violently, and she has to sit down on the bench. It's as if her insides have dissolved to jelly. The taste of her bacon butty rises back into her throat, and she gags.

Looking across the car park, she sees the others standing around the Zafira. The three younger ones, Grace, Elise and Keira, are chatting to each other, oblivious, but Ariel is watching her. Sophie gives her a feeble wave as she tries to compose herself.

What to do? She has a strong urge to go up to the group and demand to know which of them is sleeping with her husband. She would like to have it out with her right now, right here in the car park. Maybe there'll even be a punch-up. She'll get back in the car and drive off, leaving her stranded in the middle of nowhere. That would serve her right.

But something stops her. Why should she sink to her level? And how awful it would be to accuse all of them. They are her friends – at least, three of them are. No, she can't do that. She's bound to deny it and then what would she do. It would be so humiliating.

Ariel walks over. 'Everything okay?' she says. 'You look like you've seen a ghost.'

'I'm fine. Honestly.' Sophie blinks back the tears and forces a smile.

'You don't look fine.'

'Just a bit tired, that's all. It was an early start.'

Ariel studies her. 'Um... everybody's ready to go, but if you need more of a break...'

'No, I'm coming.' She tries to get up, but her legs are still wobbly.

'Are you sure you're okay?' Ariel touches her arm.

'Yes!' she replies, a little too sharply. 'Sorry. Just give me a moment, and I'll be right along.'

Ariel goes back to the car. Sophie watches her as she has a few words with the others. She studies them from a distance, her heart still pounding with anger and shock. So... which of them is the bitch from hell?

She discounts Ariel immediately. She's too old, for a start, and she's not Ryan's type. The idea of him shagging an older woman is completely absurd. It has to be either Elise, Grace or Keira. They are of a similar age – late twenties to early thirties. Each has a different look and style but is attractive in her own way. She tries to picture them in turn with Ryan, but the thought makes her feel physically sick.

Whoever she is, she mustn't know that she's been exposed. In that respect, Ryan is right. She's been playing a nasty game for months and thinks she's got away with it. Well, now it's time to turn the tables on her. Sophie tightens her muscles, summoning up what little remains of her emotional strength as she gets to her feet and totters towards the group.

'Sorry about that,' she says. 'Husbands, eh?'

Elise's face puckers with concern. 'Everything okay?'

'Yeah, fine. He wanted to know which programme to use on the washing machine.' She points the key fob at the car, and it unlocks. 'Right, we'd better get going.'

They get back in and fasten their seat belts. Sophie starts the engine and pulls out of the service station. She grips the steering wheel tightly as she stares at the wide, sweeping road ahead, trying to concentrate on the basics of driving – looking in the mirrors, keeping an eye on her speed. But her heart is still pounding against her ribcage and her mouth is dry with fear. She's not afraid of *her*, only what she herself might be capable of doing once she's worked out who she is.

The car snakes through the barren landscape in a series of long bends. Lorries storm past, impatient with her slowness, but she can't drive any faster. Her mind is continually being dragged away from the task in hand and into the darkest of places. It's as if she's gone right back to the beginning, those awful, traumatic days when she first found out that he'd been unfaithful to her.

Only now it feels worse, because he's been lying to her all this time. She thinks back to those ghastly, torturous sessions with Miriam David. How she wept and raged and begged him to tell her the truth. How he assured her that the fling had meant nothing – it was just sex, that was all, not a proper relationship, over almost as soon as it had begun. No wonder he wouldn't tell her his lover's name – because the affair was still going on.

How stupid she's been. How naïve. Over the past year, she has spent an unhealthy amount of time imagining what her rival looks like, what her name is, what she does for a career, where she lives, whether she's also deceiving a partner. And all this time, the woman has been right under her nose. Mocking her, presumably. Gloating. Pretending to be her friend. And worst of all, *swimming* with her, week in, week out. Polluting the one activity that was keeping Sophie sane.

She drives on, lapsing into automatic mode while observing the others with surreptitious glances through the rear mirror. Grace is listening to music through her earphones, nodding her head and looking out of the side window. Keira and Elise are both absorbed in their phones. Elise is scrolling through her feed, while Keira appears to be texting somebody. All of them look completely at ease.

She can't imagine any of these women plotting against her. What did Ryan mean when he said he was scared? Surely he was exaggerating, trying to make himself sound like the victim when really *he's* the predator.

Even so, befriending your lover's wife is creepy behaviour, especially when the relationship is still going on. The woman needs confronting, and that's what she's going to do. But first she has to work out which one it is. Elise? Keira? Grace? She peers at their reflections in the small rectangle of mirror. *What is my instinct telling me?* She asks herself.

'Sophie!' Ariel cries. 'Look out!'

Her eyes flick back to the front, and she sees a line of traffic, suddenly come out of nowhere as she rounds the bend. She slams on the brakes, but the car's going too fast, and they continue to move forward. Relentlessly. Inevitably. The red car at the back of the queue ahead looms before her. They're heading straight for it and there's nothing she can do. Everyone screams. Sophie heaves the wheel sharply to the left, skimming past the car with only millimetres to spare before screeching to a halt on the hard shoulder.

. . .

There is silence and stillness for a few moments. *My God, I've killed them all*, thinks Sophie, slowly lifting her head. Beside her, Ariel is covering her face with her hands.

'Jesus, Sophie, what happened there?' says a voice. She turns around to see Elise, mouth open in shock, still clutching the sides of her seat.

'Everyone okay?' asks Grace.

'Yeah, think so,' answers Keira. 'That was close.'

Ariel peels off her fingers. 'I thought we were going to die. My whole life flashed before me.'

'Come on, it wasn't that bad,' says Grace. 'Sophie did a good job avoiding that car.'

'I'm so sorry. I didn't see the tailback until it was too late. It's all these bends, they're more dangerous than they look.'

'All the more reason to concentrate,' says Keira stiffly. 'What happened? Did you nod off?'

'No, of course not.'

'You were looking in the rear mirror all the time,' says Ariel. 'I know you're supposed to keep checking the cars behind, but...'

'I know, I'm sorry... Really sorry. I didn't mean to give you a fright. Is anyone hurt?' They all shake their heads. 'Thank God for that.'

'It's not a good idea only having one driver,' says Elise. 'It's too much pressure. I don't drive, but I can imagine how hard it is to concentrate hour after hour, especially when the road is so boring. The important thing is that we are all fine.'

'A bit shaken,' murmurs Ariel.

Keira leans forward. 'What do you want to do, Sophie? Do you need a rest before you drive on?'

'No, I don't think so,' she replies. 'We can't afford to keep stopping or we'll never get there on time. There's obviously a traffic jam ahead – who knows how long it's going to take to get through it.'

'Remind me, what's our deadline?' asks Elise.

'Four o'clock,' Grace replies. 'Any later and we'll be walking the last bit in the dark, which would be a really dumb idea.'

'Well, it's up to you, Sophie. We're in your hands.'

'Thanks, Elise, but I feel okay.' She restarts the engine. 'We'll stop for lunch as planned, but maybe not for too long.'

The car doesn't seem any worse for its close brush with disaster. They join the queue of traffic, which has lengthened, and find themselves behind a large truck. It's impossible to see past it, or around the bend.

'Let's have some music, cheer us all up,' says Elise, ramping up the volume on her phone. Chill-out house music fills the car.

'Yay! We're going on holiday, remember?' Grace wiggles about in her seat, pumping the air with her fists. 'Not exactly Ibiza, but who cares?'

'Not so loud, please,' says Ariel. 'I've got a headache. I think it might be whiplash.'

Sophie doesn't say anything; just drives and tries not to think about why she nearly crashed the car. Everyone except Ariel is being very understanding, which is ironic, given that she's the only one Sophie doesn't consider a candidate for Ryan's lover. Whoever it is is doing a great job of being nice. But then she's been working undercover – so to speak – for months. She's not going to slip up so early on in the trip. But if Sophie lulls her into a false sense of security, there's more chance that she'll reveal herself eventually – in some small, subtle way. She just has to watch all of them closely, every minute.

But first she has to get them to their destination in one piece.

EIGHT

SOPHIE

Sophie draws into the lay-by just after 3.30 p.m. Considering the various delays, she's made excellent time. That last stretch of road demanded all her concentration, with its sharp bends lined with crash barriers. She drove it in a kind of trance, leaning forward, her eyes fixed firmly on the road ahead. Not once did she allow herself to look at the others through the rear mirror. And every time her thoughts strayed into dangerous territory, she pulled herself back to the here and now. But the effort has exhausted her. She puffs out a sigh of relief and turns off the engine. Her passengers break out in spontaneous applause.

'Well done,' says Ariel, who seems to have forgiven her for the earlier scare.

'Yeah, incredible effort,' agrees Elise.

Grace peers out of the passenger window. They seem to be in the middle of nowhere. Barren hills dotted with brown scrub and rocky outcrops loom around them. 'Is this *it*?' she asks. 'I was expecting a car park at least. Maybe even some public toilets.'

'This is definitely where we leave the car,' says Sophie defensively. 'I followed the instructions to the letter. Besides, it's the only big lay-by we've come across.'

'Okay, I believe you. It's just so quiet. What if the police think it's been abandoned and tow it away?'

'I wouldn't worry. They're probably used to vehicles being left here for days,' says Ariel. She opens the door, and a blast of fresh mountain air fills the stuffy interior. 'Come on.'

They get out and stretch their legs, shaking out the cramp from sitting still for so long. Sophie unlocks the boot, and they remove their rucksacks, together with the crates of food and drink. Keira unfolds her trolley, and they load it up, fastening the crates with luggage cords.

Sophie feels incredibly nervous. How can she possibly have normal conversations with these women knowing that one of them – if *only* she knew which one – is screwing her husband? They are about to be trapped together, with no escape, for an entire week. For a moment she contemplates driving off and leaving them to it. It's tempting, but it would be the coward's way out.

Elise walks over to a signpost sticking out between two large trees. 'Hey, this is it!' She reads the sign aloud, stumbling over the Gaelic words. 'It's less than three miles. We'll do that easily in an hour and a half.'

'We won't,' Keira assures her. 'Look at the terrain. There's a steep climb ahead and the ground is really uneven. You know, I'm not sure my trolley's going to make it.'

Ariel joins them. 'See what you mean. You're right, Keira, it won't last five minutes, and we'll never haul it up that hill. We'll have to distribute the stuff amongst us and put it in our ruck-sacks. The rest can go in plastic bags, and we'll have to take it in turns to carry them.'

'Hmm, that won't be easy, but yeah, it's the only solution,'

Elise agrees. She turns to face the group. 'Okay, everyone. Make some room in your rucksacks, please. Leave behind anything you can do without. Extra jumpers, make-up bags, teddies, sex toys...' Everyone except Sophie laughs. 'Seriously, girls. It's that or starve.'

By the time they have unpacked and repacked and put discarded items safely in the boot, it's almost four o'clock. Sophie is feeling impatient. According to the information sent by the booking agent, dusk falls at 6.36 today. The light will start to fade well before that. They really have to get a move on.

Ariel leads the way. It turns out that she has bought an Ordnance Survey map of the area, 'just in case'. The gravel path is narrow, not wide enough for them to walk in pairs, so they go in single file. Sophie brings up the rear, hanging back to create a small distance from the group. The others are still trying to keep up a conversation, but their voices sound like birdsong and she can't understand what they're saying. Not that she wants to join in.

Luckily the temperature is mild and it's not too windy. The big sky is extraordinary – streaks of brilliant sunlight and patches of bright blue amongst swathes of dark grey clouds. It looks as if heaven itself is peeking from behind a curtain. They are walking through heathland, most of it brown, the heather being past its best. But there are still a few pink-and-purple clumps to marvel at.

The easy gravel path soon peters out, giving way to an uneven track made up of stones of various shapes and sizes. It has sunk in the middle like an old mattress, giving them hardly any space to walk. There are large boggy puddles in places, some of them deeper than they look. The going is slow. Sophie is already feeling the weight of her rucksack, the straps digging into her shoulders. She stops, putting her hands behind her back and under the bottom of it, taking the strain and relieving the pressure for a few seconds. The others disappear around a bend, and for a moment she thinks about turning back without telling them. But they would only worry and come after her and then it would get dark... She can't do that to them, it's not fair. It would be dangerous.

She sets off again, catching sight of them as they enter a wood. It seems to be entirely made up of birch trees – not straight and firm as she's seen elsewhere, but thin and spindly, their branches bent into strange angles by the wind. Their silvery bark is worn and scratched. They are losing their autumn leaves, but some still remain, dotted among the branches like gold coins. Through the trees she can just make out a long line of dark grey water below. One of the many lochs they are meant to pass on the way.

Elise is last in line, her bright blue rucksack bobbing awkwardly on her back. She is the shortest of the group. She has removed her woolly bobble hat to reveal her long golden hair, which has been put in an untidy ponytail. It's the same colour as the birch leaves, and complements the rucksack, making her look as if she's on a photo shoot for a magazine.

As Sophie plods at a safe distance behind her, she tries to remember exactly how and when they first met. Elise didn't respond to the Facebook posting, just turned up one morning with her swimming costume on under a tracksuit. She was one of the first to join the group, which was very unstable during those early months. Hardly anybody attended two weeks running, and there were lots of women Sophie never saw again. She remembers how open and friendly Elise was. She knew from the beginning that she wanted her to love it and keep coming.

It must have been February, or perhaps early March. The weather was mild for the time of year, but the water was still insanely cold. Only two other women had turned up that morn-ing. They'd swum their ten minutes and were making their way back to land. Sophie needed to come out too, but she was treading water, waiting for Elise to join her.

She'd stripped off and was standing at the edge of the lake, her arms wrapped around her like a blanket. Shivering.

Sophie waved. 'Come on!' she cried encouragingly. 'You can do it!'

Elise took a cautious step forward. 'Oh my God, it's fucking freezing!'

'Yeah, I know. Sorry!' Sophie shouted back, wondering why she always felt the need to apologise for things that were beyond her control. 'You'll feel better once you get your shoulders under.'

'I can't!' Elise cried.

'Yes, you can. But don't stand around. You have to just go for it!'

Suddenly Elise hurled herself forward, plunging the rest of her body into the water with a gigantic splash. She immediately resurfaced, emitting a loud, guttural cry, like a wild animal. Her face was streaming wet, and spittle was running down her chin. Then she started laughing. After that, she turned up more or less every week. She still complains about the cold water, but more out of habit than anything else. It's part of her ritual.

Sophie stares at the bobbing blue rucksack. She hopes it's not Elise, because she has always liked her.

After a short while, the group ahead comes to a halt. They turn around and wave at Sophie. She quickens her pace, dodging a couple of boggy puddles, and joins them by a small stone bridge. They take their rucksacks off and drink water from their flasks.

'You okay, Sophie?' asks Ariel. 'You seem to be struggling with the pace.'

'Not at all. I just needed a bit of time to myself. To take in the scenery, listen to the birds.'

'Fair enough,' says Keira. 'But don't lag too far behind or you might lose us.'

'Don't worry, I won't.'

'This bridge crosses the train line to Mallaig,' announces Ariel. 'Steam trains run in the summer.'

'I love steam trains,' says Grace wistfully. 'They're so romantic.'

Keira picks up her rucksack and heaves it on to her back. 'Shall we move on?' They all nod.

'Time to swap round the food bags,' says Ariel. 'Sophie, do you mind taking this one?' She passes over a large plastic carrier. 'The handle's not great, I'm afraid. I hope it lasts.'

'Me too.'

They load up and press on. A few hundred yards later, they meet another bridge, which goes over a small stream. It's wooden and far less stable than the stone one, so they cross one by one. After that, the landscape opens out, offering wide views of the grey-green hills and a large glassy loch dotted with small islands. The sun has gone behind the clouds, but Sophie can sense it sinking ever lower. There is a new chill in the air.

She hangs back again, holding on to her separateness. The path starts to ascend steeply, and she feels her heart rate increasing. The plastic handle of the carrier bag is digging into her fingers, but it was right to ditch the trolley with its flimsy wheels. Just imagine trying to haul it up here... impossible.

Grace has taken up the rear position in the group ahead, so it's her turn to be analysed. Sophie can't remember when she first joined the wild swimmers. Soon after Elise, she thinks – the two of them are quite friendly. Maybe they even knew each other before. She never thought Grace would stick it out; she just didn't seem the type. She's a townie, very concerned about her appearance. Her swimsuits are glamorous, she even wore a bikini a couple of times when the weather was hot, and Sophie has never seen her without make-up on. In fact, she probably wouldn't recognise her without those painted eyebrows. Grace always keeps her chin above water and never gets her luscious dark locks wet. She says it's because she has to go straight to work after the swim. Sophie has a vague memory that she's in the beauty business. Perhaps she sells make-up in a department store, or the duty-free lounge at the airport. That last thought stops her in her tracks. Ryan works at the airport – could that be how they met? He's always claimed it was via some hook-up site, but he could easily have lied. She can't believe anything he says any more. She has to start with a blank page.

The others are waiting for her at the top of the hill, standing by a heap of stones. Everyone except Keira is visibly out of breath, and Ariel is actually gasping.

'I didn't realise it was going to be that steep,' she says, clasping her chest.

'Nor did I. I'm really hot.' Elise takes off her waterproof jacket and drapes it over the top of her rucksack.

'It was worth it, though. These views are incredible,' says Grace, slowly spinning around in a circle to take it all in.

It's true. They can see the coastline from here, a distant wavy line of inlets and bays, sea lochs and winding rivers. Snow-capped mountains loom to their right, while the lower hills are a patchwork of heather and bracken, long straggly grasses and grey rocks. Sophie feels tears in her eyes as the contrast between the beauty around her and the ugly feelings she has inside hits home. She turns away, wiping her face with her sleeve, hoping nobody has noticed.

'Which direction do we go now?' asks Elise.

'We just follow the path,' says Ariel. 'It's downhill all the way from now on, heading towards the sea.'

This time Sophie decides to forge ahead, not wanting to be blamed for a late arrival. The skies are definitely darkening. Her backpack feels heavier with each step. She packed so abstemiously, not wanting to overload herself, but now there are tins of vegetables, a bottle of cooking oil and a large packet of rice bumping around among her jumpers and jeans. The plastic carrier bag she's carrying is extremely uncomfortable, the handle slicing into her fingers.

They reach a stream. There's no bridge this time, just a jumble of stepping stones that look as if they've been carelessly thrown in the general direction of the water. The bank is steep and there's nothing to hold on to. With the heavy bag in one hand, it's impossible to stay balanced. Her foot slides on a rock and she stumbles forward, letting go of the handle. Potatoes, carrots and a large head of broccoli spill out. She swears, bending down to retrieve them.

'Honestly! I just knew that was going to happen,' says Keira, who is first to the rescue. She crouches next to Sophie and gathers up the rest of the potatoes. Their eyes lock, and Sophie feels the younger woman looking straight through her, like she's made of glass. Her gaze lasts less than a second, but it's long enough to make Sophie feel uncomfortable.

'Thanks,' she murmurs, holding out the bag so that Keira can drop the potatoes into it. Then she stands up and makes her way across the gurgling stream, careful not to slip and fall in. Jumping on to the other bank, she strides ahead, trying to create some distance between the two of them.

Keira is the most enigmatic of her three suspects. She joined the group a month or two after the others and has turned up virtually every week since. Sophie knows very little about her. She's calm and reserved, but as Nan would say, 'still waters run deep'. The swimming is very important to her; she seems to need it as much as Sophie does. It's created a bond between them, although they've never spoken about it, or even acknowledged its existence. Sophie has sometimes wondered what it is that Keira is trying to deal with – a past tragedy, a broken love affair, a cruel injustice? But maybe she has been misinterpreting this all along. Maybe it's Ryan they share.

She stops and turns around. The others have paused to look at the stunning panorama. They are pointing and taking photos, even though there's barely enough light. Sophie sighs impatiently. There's still about another kilometre to go, all downhill through woods of birch and oak. The house is tucked away somewhere, and they need to find it before it gets dark.

NINE

SOPHIE

They only just make it to the house before pitch black descends. Keira holds her phone screen up to illuminate the key safe, while Elise punches in the code. Taking the key, she unlocks the door, and they tumble into the porch.

'Shoes off, everyone,' says Ariel. 'House rules.'

They unlace their walking boots and heave them off, then open the inner door into a narrow hallway, where they dump the rucksacks and food carriers. There's no mains electricity, and the house, which is laid out on one level, is so dark they can't see a thing. Taking out their torches, they walk excitedly from room to room. Narrow beams of light criss-cross over the dark, heavy furniture set against roughly rendered white walls. But the decor is soft and welcoming. In the large sitting room, there are rugs on the stone floor, two squashy sofas draped with tartan blankets, thick curtains at the windows and a stack of logs and kindling in a large wicker basket. Beautiful pieces of ceramic and small driftwood sculptures adorn the alcoves on either side of the fireplace. A bookcase is stuffed with old paperback novels with worn spines, and a pile of glossy hardbacks about the local flora and fauna sits on the coffee table.

But there's lots to do before they can sit down and relax. There are paraffin lamps to light, the log burner to get going; they need to work out how the camping oven and gas fridge operate, where the compost toilet is... Everyone is desperate for a cup of tea, but unfortunately they arrived too late to fetch water from the nearby stream. Using bottled mineral water instead feels like an extravagance, but they have no choice. It's either that or crack open the wine.

Ariel is the only one of them with experience of log burners, so she gets down on her hands and knees and sets to with kindling and firelighters. Elise and Grace follow the instructions in the visitors' manual and light the paraffin lamps, which soon give the sitting room a warm but slightly eerie glow. Keira busies herself in the kitchen, putting away the food and making a pot of tea.

Sophie goes to inspect the compost toilet, which is in a brick shed just outside the kitchen door. A handwritten sign on the wall explains how to use it. The set-up is far from luxurious but seems okay. She goes back indoors and hovers in the kitchen for a bit before wandering into the sitting room.

Her brain is spinning. She feels discombobulated. Three of these women are her friends, but one of them is her enemy. She is no nearer knowing, and she won't be able to function properly until she has worked it out. This evening she can play at being tired after all the driving, but what about tomorrow and the day after that?

Keira carries a tray of steaming mugs into the sitting room and sets it down on the large, sturdy dining table. 'Tea's up,' she calls. 'Come and get it.'

'Marvellous,' says Ariel, getting to her feet and coming over. The fire has caught, and flames are already licking the glass door of the burner.

Sophie murmurs a thank you as she selects a hand-thrown pottery mug and sits in the armchair by the fire.

'Listen up, everybody,' says Elise. 'Me and Grace would like to unpack, but we don't know where we're all sleeping.'

There are four bedrooms: two doubles and two twins, one with bunk beds. Some are bigger than others, but they are all nicely furnished, equipped with a small candelabra, candles and a box of matches.

'How are we going to decide on rooms?' asks Keira. 'Draw lots?'

'Seems the fairest way,' says Elise.

Grace frowns. 'Not necessarily. Two of us are going to have to share, right? If anyone snores, or sleepwalks, they should have their own room.'

'Any snorers?' asks Elise. They all shake their heads.'

'Not as far as I know,' says Ariel, 'but it's been a while since I shared a bed with anyone. Sadly.' They all chuckle, except Sophie, who cannot force it out no matter how hard she tries. Inside she is thinking, *please, please don't make me share with anyone.* What if she ends up with *her*? How excruciating that would be, how utterly impossible to sleep.

'Actually, there's a sofa bed in the little room next to the kitchen,' Keira says. 'It doesn't look too bad, although it's hard to tell until you try. I know it's not ideal, but it would mean we could each have our own space.' They all seem to think that this is a good idea.

'Personally I think Sophie should have her pick,' says Ariel. 'She deserves it after doing all that driving. Even if she did almost kill us,' she adds with a twinkle in her eye.

'Good point,' says Grace. The others nod in agreement.

'Are you sure? That's incredibly kind of you all,' Sophie replies quickly, her prayers for once having been answered. 'In that case, do you mind if I have the double at the front?'

'Okay, so Sophie's sorted, what about the rest of us?' asks Elise.

'I'll organise the draw if you like.' Sophie unzips an outer pocket of her rucksack and takes out a notebook and pen. Tearing off a sheet of paper, she divides it into four pieces and writes down the name of each room. She pops the folded pieces into the woolly hat, then passes it around.

Keira gets the other double, Elise the twin, Grace the bunks and Ariel the sofa bed in the snug.

'If the sofa bed is too uncomfortable, you can share with me,' says Keira.

'Thanks,' says Ariel, 'but I'm sure I'll be fine.'

They put their empty mugs back on the tray and go into the hallway to collect their rucksacks. Then everyone disappears for a short while to unpack and make their nests.

Sophie puts her bag on the bed and loosens the drawstring. She takes out her clothes and toiletry bag and the food items, then shoves the rucksack down the side of the chest of drawers. At last she's alone and can drop her guard. All the emotion she's been suppressing since the phone call with Ryan suddenly rises to the surface like boiling soup, and she collapses on the bed, pulling the quilt over her. She sobs into the pillow, letting its softness absorb the sound. She has become an expert in this technique after having to hide her crying from Ben and Louie.

Sad thoughts of her gorgeous little boys tug at her, and the tears flow more freely. When she gets home, she'll have to tell them that Mummy and Daddy are splitting up and Daddy won't be living with them any more. She knows how upset they'll be, especially Ben, who is older than Louie and more likely to understand the implications for the future. It's not what she ever wanted for her children. That's why she went through all that counselling, why she tried to forgive Ryan – it was to save the marriage for *them*.

She endured months of torture with Miriam David, attempting to understand what had led Ryan to betray her, believing that it must have somehow been her fault, beating herself up for not being beautiful enough, or sexy enough, or

interesting enough, or funny enough = for just not being
enough, full stop. It was easy for Ryan. He had little soul-
searching to do because he could blame male wiring. Men are
genetically predisposed to scatter their seed as widely as possible, he told her. Whereas she, as a woman, only needed one
partner – a strong man to build the shelter, bring home food and
protect her and the children from attack. It was her responsibility to hold on to her husband while purely natural forces
pulled him in the opposite direction. When he crossed the
middle line in that tug-of-war, it was *her* fault. Nobody ever
articulated it so openly, but that was the underlying argument.
Even Miriam – a woman = seemed to support the theory.
Sophie suffocates a guttural cry. Just thinking back to those
sessions makes her feel violent.

But she needs to control these feelings. She must douse the
flames of fury, silence the sobs of despair = put on her game
face. Pretend just as her enemy is pretending. It's really important that she doesn't give herself away. If this woman is out to
get her, Sophie has to get to her first. This time she has to win.
Right now she's not sure what she's going to do, or what
winning might entail. She fought for Ryan before = a long time
ago = and look how that turned out. Now she has to fight for
herself.

She lies there in the ghostly candlelight, listening to the
sounds of activity beyond her room = the clatter of pans in the
kitchen, the tinkle of conversation, a sudden burst of laughter.
How long has she been 'resting'? Did she fall asleep? It's
suddenly become very cold. Of course, there are no radiators to
come on as soon as the temperature drops. No heating in the
bedrooms at all.

Pulling herself up, she swings her legs over the side of the
bed. The last thing she wants to do is join the party, but she *has*
to. She stands up and takes the candle over to the dressing table,
where there is a swivel mirror on a wooden stand. She tips it

back to illuminate her reflection, sighing as she observes her puffy eyes and a red patch on her cheek from burying her face in the pillow. Ah well, it's so gloomy, maybe they won't notice.

She puts her belongings away, then leaves her room and goes into the kitchen. Ariel is on cooking duty, heating up a stew she made in advance and took out of the freezer this morning. Keira is sitting down, chopping up fruit for a salad. A large oil lamp glows in the centre of the table, illuminating her face from beneath, hollowing out her eyes.

'Have a good rest?' Ariel asks.

'Yes. Sorry if I was too long. I think I must have dropped off. How's it going? Anything I can do to help?'

'No, no, everything's under control, thanks. The potatoes are under way – I'm doing wedges because we don't have water to boil them in. I'm not sure how long it's all going to take. I've never used a camping oven before.'

'I didn't even know they existed,' Sophie admits.

'Maybe you could lay the table,' suggests Keira, slicing into a peeled kiwi fruit.

Ariel shakes her head. 'Elise and Grace have already done that.'

'Oh. Well then, you can just relax.'

As if, thinks Sophie, retreating. She can hear the other two women talking in the sitting room. Raising her candle, she lights her way down the narrow hallway. She feels nervous, but arms herself with a smile as she enters.

'Hi,' she says. Elise and Grace are sitting together on the sofa, their slim legs tucked under their bottoms, glasses of wine in hand. They look up and greet her simultaneously.

'Red or white?' asks Elise. 'We have both. The red is on the table. We put the white in the porch to chill. Who needs a fridge, eh?'

Sophie crosses to the dining table, which has been beautifully laid. She surveys the blue-checked linen tablecloth, its creases still in place. Matching napkins have been folded into miniature crowns, while the table mats and coasters feature illustrations of purple thistles and various species of heather. In the centre, a glowing lamp adds lustre to the heavy silver cutlery. She picks up a long-stemmed glass from the setting at the end of the table, pours in a good slosh of red wine and takes a sip – as she suspected, it's too cold. Choosing the armchair by the log burner, she sits down and warms the glass between her hands. The air smells woody, drying her throat.

'We were just saying, the cottage is really gorgeous,' Grace says. 'Perfect for a romantic getaway.'

Sophie flinches at the word 'romantic'. Is Grace making a dig?

'Hmm, I think hot running water and central heating is more romantic than faffing about with paraffin lamps,' remarks Elise. 'Although I *do* love it here. It's really special.'

'Can't wait for our first swim,' Sophie says, sipping at her wine.

Elise grins. 'It's gonna be effing freezing, that's for sure.'

They continue chatting, though Sophie dips in and out, her thoughts constantly flitting to the overwhelming issue. This trip is already ruined, she can see that now. Even if she doesn't manage to work out who Ryan's lover is, even if she decides not to confront her.

'Grub's up!' Ariel calls out, walking into the room carrying a heavy casserole pot. She plonks it down on a metal trivet in the middle of the table. Keira follows closely behind with a dish of roasted potato wedges.

'Wow! Amazing!' says Elise, leaping up.

Ariel removes her oven mitts. 'You haven't tasted it yet.'

They take their places at the table. Sophie finds herself sitting next to Elise and directly opposite Keira. They raise their glasses to the cooks, the driver and finally to themselves.

Ariel gestures at the food. 'Come on. Dig in before it gets cold!'

They help themselves, but Sophie hangs back, suddenly realising that she has no appetite. She's too churned up inside. She knows that it's not good to drink wine on an empty stomach, though, so forces herself to take a small portion. Everyone makes enthusiastic noises and comments about the food, which is indeed delicious.

Sophie does her best to join in with the banter, but she's struggling. The others start talking about their plans for tomorrow. After some debate, they decide to go for their first swim at 8 a.m., then come back to the house for a cooked breakfast. Later, they'd like to go for a walk, possibly as far as the coast.

Keira serves up the fruit salad. Once they've finished eating, they clear the table and stack the dishes in the kitchen, ready to be washed in the morning, once they've fetched the water. Grace rootles around in the sideboard and finds a stack of board games, but everyone is either too tired or too drunk to start playing now. It's only just after ten, but it seems much later than that.

Nobody has thought to stoke the log burner, and the fire has gone out. The room is starting to feel chilly. Sophie stands up. 'I'm going to turn in now,' she says. 'I'm exhausted.'

'Me too,' agrees Ariel. 'Sleep well, everyone.'

Sophie closes the door of her bedroom behind her. Unfortunately it doesn't have a lock or a bolt. If she had a suitable chair, she'd wedge it under the handle, but there's only a small stool in front of the dressing table. She removes her clothes and quickly puts on her pyjamas. Then she gets into the icy bed and lies there nervously watching the flickering shadows on the wall. This is no good, she thinks. She can't stay on guard all night – she has to get some sleep.

After a few minutes, she blows out the candle, plunging the room into thick darkness.

TEN

THE SWIMMER

So, here we all are then. All girls together, tucked up in our various cosy beds. Lights out, no talking, no whispering in the dark. Night-night, sleep tight, don't let the bed bugs bite... See you in the morning.

I don't think I'm ready for sleep yet, still got a load of brain-work to do, evaluating the events of the day. I pound the pillow into a better shape and snuggle down beneath the duvet. The mattress is surprisingly comfortable. I was expecting a wobbly iron frame and worn-out springs, but you could have quite vigorous sex on this bed and nobody would hear you. Mind, I'd be surprised if the house sees much in the way of bonking – it's too bloody cold and the lack of bathroom facilities are a real turn-off. I just knew that compost toilet was going to be disgusting. There's no way I'm getting up tonight to use it. I'd rather wet the bed.

Condie's Retreat may have five stars on all the organic hipster websites, but I'm not sure it's for me. Of course, I joined in with all the oohs and ahs over the tatty old furniture and the log burner, the smelly oil lamps and the camping gas oven. How quirky not to have mains electricity! How reassuring that there's no landline or a mobile phone signal or that you can only reach the house on foot down a really difficult path. I can't wait to fetch water from the stream at dawn, and if anyone needs any more wood chopping, just give me a shout.

Am I the only sane person here? Or do we all think it's a bit grim but are afraid to admit it?

The scenery I *will* give five stars to. And I'm sure swimming in the loch tomorrow will be an incredible experience. I can't wait to feel the pain the cold water will bring. My nerve endings are fizzing in anticipation. I'm hoping it's going to calm me down a bit, because right now, I'm wired.

I draw myself into a ball, hugging my knees as I consider the Sophie situation. Here's the question: Did Ryan tell her about me? I think, on balance, not, although she is behaving quite strangely. Her driving was really erratic. At first I felt safe, but after we stopped for coffee, she seemed to stop concentrating. When she nearly hit that car, I thought we were going to crash into a tree. It shook her up too, and after that she didn't take her eyes off the road, didn't say a word. She lagged behind on the walk to the house, making it clear that she wanted to be on her own. Maybe she was feeling guilty about nearly killing us, or maybe she had something else – *somebody* else – on her mind.

Then again, I simply don't believe Ryan would have had the guts to tell her. And if he *had*, there's no way she would have still come on this trip. I mean, how humiliating would it be to spend an entire week with your husband's lover? No, it doesn't play, as they say. According to Ryan, Sophie hasn't a clue that he's having an affair, let alone that it's with one of her lovely new swimming friends.

I feel like I'm okay. The group selfie was a blunder, but in a way, it's made things more interesting. I've got Ryan by the balls and Sophie in an invisible armlock. Now I just need to bide my time, wait for the right opportunity.

And I *will* do it. I made a promise to the lads. They don't believe I'll go through with it; they think I'm all mouth and no action, the girlie girl, the useless runt of the litter. But I'm going to prove them wrong. I'm doing this for all of us, but especially for Carly.

I think back to last Sunday. The whole family – or what's left of it: Mum, my brother Drew, Auntie Jill, Uncle Rob, my cousin Billie and me – got together to celebrate her birthday, as we have done without fail for the last God knows how many years. It's always the same. We eat her favourite food – roast chicken dinner followed by apple crumble and ice cream – washed down with as much alcohol as we can get into our systems and still stand up. We seem to need more booze as the years go by, not less. It has become an ordeal that can't be avoided, like a dental appointment only a lot more painful.

As soon as the year turns, I mark the nearest Sunday to her birthday on my calendar, knowing that on that date at 1 p.m., I will definitely be in my home town at the house where I grew up. The same foil *Happy Birthday* banner, now creased and torn at the edges, will be hanging over the mantelpiece, and there will be a place laid for my sister at one end of the dining table. We'll all be there in our usual seats, but hers will remain empty. She'll never turn up, no matter how long we put ourselves through this agonising ritual. When Mum dies, I hope someone has the guts to call time, but for now it's Groundhog Day. Mum is only sixty-four, and there's a lot more life in her yet, a lot more tears still to cry.

After lunch, we look at photo albums and watch a home movie that Uncle Rob filmed at Christmas in 1990. It used to be on a DVD, but now it's on a memory stick that he plugs into Mum's telly. I find it quite boring watching my relatives open the same old presents year after year, and also quite annoying that nobody ever mentions that I'm not in the scene. I didn't exist in 1990, I was just an accident waiting to happen. My father, who left Mum four years later, makes an appearance, however, skulking in the corner behind a glass of beer, but nobody mentions that either. I think their brains must pixelate him out. I'm sure Mum would much rather watch something with a more appropriate cast, but it's the only moving image we have of her – five-year-old Carly in her Christmas pyjamas unwrapping her new Barbie again and again and again.

After the photos and video torture, the people I still think of as the grown-ups go into the kitchen to clear up. We kids run upstairs to play – only these days we take a bottle of wine and Drew rolls us a joint with his dirty fingernails. He's a gardener for the local council. It's a good job for a damaged person, not too much stress.

Last Sunday, everything was panning out as usual. We'd eaten Carly's favourite food, wished her a happy birthday and watched her thank Santa for the hundredth time. Now the three of us were lounging around in the time capsule that was once my sister's bedroom, getting pissed and stoned. Talking about stuff.

We're aware that it's ghoulish pretending that Carly's with us, hiding behind the curtains or under the bed perhaps, listening to our conversation without ever joining in. She would have been thirty-seven this year, but in our heads she's still a teenager who listens to Westlife and used to have a crush on Peter Andre. We should stop doing this, but there's nowhere else to go if we want to have a private chat.

Drew's smelly pit of teenage angst was fumigated as soon as he left home and is now a lovely guest room, which Mum never uses and hates being messed up. My minuscule box room was converted into her sewing den many years ago. As the youngest, I always got the worst deal: the smallest bedroom, the hand-me-down clothes, the garden chair when we had visitors for lunch. By rights I should have moved into Carly's room, but the idea was never even discussed.

Nothing has changed. The wardrobe is still full of her

dresses and jeans, her underwear and crop tops are still crammed into the chest of drawers. Her nightie is tucked under the pillow, a pair of laddered tights nestles in the waste bin. Even the dressing table is exactly as she left it: hairs tangled in her brush, a tube of mascara with the lid not screwed on properly, a palette of eyeshadows, a pile of sparkly bangles, splashes of scarlet nail varnish on the white melamine surface. It could be a Tracey Emin installation, hidden in a former council house, only available for private viewings on one day of the year.

'So, how's it going, sis?' asked Drew, rolling the joint so perfectly and tightly it looked like another work of art.

'I'm good, thanks,' I replied, almost telling the truth.

'Seeing anyone?'

'Yes, but only for sex.' They laughed, slightly nervously, I thought.

'Sounds good to me,' said Billie. He never has any luck with women, can't seem to keep a girlfriend for more than about five months. He'll be forty this year and he's still not ready to settle down. Never been married, let alone divorced, no kids, accidentally or deliberately conceived. Most men of his age have left some mark on the world by now, but not our Billie. His life is a pond that has conveniently iced over so he can skate across the surface. Sometimes I want to break the ice and push him under, see if he'd fight to survive, but I suspect he'd just sink to the bottom. All three of us are fucked up in different ways.

'We've got to stop doing this,' I said after a long marijuana-infused pause.

Drew passed the spliff to Billie. 'You mean getting stoned in our dead sister's bedroom?'

'No – the birthday party, all of it. We're colluding in Mum's depression – normalising it. It'll be twenty years next year. It's really unhealthy.'

'I agree, but what do we do? Refuse to turn up? Tear down the posters, put Carly's belongings in a bin liner?'

'It'd kill her,' said Billie.

'Yeah, but this is death by a thousand cuts,' I argued. 'If she's going to have any chance of a happy old age, we have to confront her, tell her this needs to stop right now.'

'Go on then, you talk to her.'

'She doesn't listen to me. Carly was always way ahead in the favourite daughter stakes. Sometimes I think that if Mum had been given a choice over who to lose, she'd have given me up without a second thought.'

'That's not true. It's hard for her. Every time she looks at you, she sees Carly.'

'Except I look nothing like her.'

'No, but you're a girl, so...' Drew tailed off uncomfortably.

'Anyway, I thought you should know this is my last birthday bash,' I announced. 'I'm breaking free of the Carly Cult and moving on.'

'You won't do it,' said Billie. 'You can't.'

'Well, I can actually, because I have a plan.'

Drew frowned. 'What kind of plan?'

I played a drum roll in my head, then told them how I'd found Sophie.

'What – the Sophie?' asked Billie. 'Sophie Sophie? The one who...' He broke off. Even after all this time, he couldn't bring himself to say the words.

'Yup, the very same. She runs this wild swimming group. I joined up. I've been swimming with her once a week for the last six—'

Drew swore under his breath. 'Jesus... How could you bring yourself to spend even one minute with that...'

'I know, it sounds disgusting, but actually it's been okay. It helps that she has no idea who I am.'

'Is she married?' asked Drew. 'Does she have kids?'

'Oh yeah. And guess who the lucky guy is?'

He gapes. 'Don't tell me she's married to him?'

I nodded. 'We'd always hoped they'd burned in hell, but they all lived happily ever after, I'm afraid.'

There was a long pause while the two of them absorbed the shocking information. I have to say I felt a surge of triumph. At last, I'd impressed them.

Drew inhaled deeply, letting the smoke permeate his lungs before breathing out. 'Jesus... that's a blow. They just carried on, like nothing happened...'

Billie reached for the bottle of wine. 'Have you seen the bastard?'

This was where I had to part company with the truth. My brother and cousin aren't strong enough to cope with the news that I'm in any kind of relationship with the man they hate most in the entire world.

'No, not yet,' I replied. 'I'm trying to steer clear, but I'm sure he wouldn't make the connection. He never took any notice of me back then – I was too young.'

'Okay, so what's this plan, then?' Billie topped up our glasses. 'You going to kill her?' He laughed, like it was a joke, only he was also being serious.

I told him about our all-female swimming trip in the wilds of Scotland. They listened in awe – and a little fear – as I explained how Condie's Retreat was miles from anywhere, how it was the perfect location for an 'accident'.

Drew shifted uncomfortably on the bed. 'You can't do this,' he said.

'Yes, I can. I've got it all worked out. Have you any idea how dangerous swimming in freezing-cold water can be? People drown every year.'

'I mean, you *shouldn't* do it. Get caught and you could end up in prison for the rest of your life.'

'Yeah, as much as it hurts to say it, he's right,' said Billie. 'It's too risky.'

'I know what I'm doing.'

'No, I don't think you do,' said Drew. 'This is serious stuff, kiddo, you can't—'

'Don't call me that. I'm not a kiddo, I'm thirty. I've thought about this a lot.'

'Then think again. This is way out of your league. You'd fail, or you wouldn't be able to go through with it.'

'How dare you say that? What have you achieved in your life? Nothing, big fat zero. At least I hold down a proper job—'

'Hey, let's not go there. Your bro's doing all right,' cut in Billie.

'Just walk away, kiddo, walk away and forget about her. She's not worth it.'

I jumped off the bed and swept everything off the dressing table. A cloud of dust rose as the items scattered themselves across the carpet. 'I've had enough of this morbid shit, enough. You can sit around here for the next twenty years if you like, but I'm going to *do* something. I'm going to get justice for Carly – or revenge, or whatever you want to call it. The nightmare ends now.'

Drew got down on his knees and started picking up the stuff while Billie just stared at me open-mouthed. I stepped over the bangles and the hairbrush and left the room, more determined than ever to carry out my promise.

And now here I am on the battlefield, ready for action, poised for the kill. Just the thought of the possibility of doing it sends a thrill through my body. I lie in the darkness, imagining my hands on Sophie's shoulders, pushing her down and holding her under the water. Getting her alone is going to be the most difficult part, but I'll find a way, I know I will. There's a whole week ahead.

ELEVEN

SOPHIE

In the morning, Sophie wakes to the sound of her name being called through the door.

'Hey – are you awake?' It's Grace's voice, she thinks.

'Er, yes... sort of.' Leaning on her elbow, she reaches out and picks up her phone. With no signal for miles around, it's only good for telling the time. She's surprised to see that it's so late. Kicking off the covers, she gets out of bed and opens the door, pushing her nose through the gap. Grace is wearing her huge dryrobe and a pair of black leggings, reminding Sophie of a giant insect. As usual, she is wearing full make-up.

Sophie pulls an apologetic face. 'Sorry. I didn't realise... forgot to set the alarm.'

'Do you still want to swim?'

'Of course.'

'How soon can you be ready? Only last night we said we'd set off at eight, and it's almost nine. We've been waiting ages.'

'Sorry... I'll, er, be as quick as I can.'

'Okay. I'll tell the others ten minutes, yeah?'

'Sure.' Sophie closes the door. She remembers now that they

agreed to have their first swim before breakfast. Normally she would have been up early, costume on, hat and goggles at the ready, flask made, raring to go. But today she feels tired and sluggish, all the stuffing beaten out of her. This trip is supposed to be first and foremost about the swimming, but it has been transformed into something utterly different – at least for her. Now it's a detective mystery, a puzzle, a torture chamber...

She dives into the jumble of underwear and T-shirts in the top drawer of the dressing table and finds her swimsuit. A baggy T-shirt and a thick jumper go on next, then a pair of warm leggings and some socks. Grabbing her dryrobe from the wardrobe, she leaves the room in search of the others.

The house looks quite different in the daylight – shabbier, dirtier, less romantic. Sophie goes into the sitting room with its forlorn sofas and threadbare rugs and looks out of the large window overlooking the garden. Not that you can call it a garden – there are no flower beds or shrubs, just a worn patch of ground edged with brambles. Elise and Keira are already outside, wearing their dryrobes, pacing up and down, looking impatient. Keira spots her and waves.

Grace is in the porch, crouching down, lacing up her boots. Ariel tucks a rolled-up towel under one arm. Sophie joins them, hurriedly doing up the zipper on her robe.

'You okay?' asks Ariel. 'It's not like you to be late.'

'Sorry,' she says for the third time. 'I didn't sleep very well.'

'Tell me about it.' Ariel rubs the small of her back for emphasis. 'That sofa bed kept me awake most of the night.'

'That's a shame. Didn't Keira say she doesn't mind sharing?'

'Yes, but...' Ariel frowns. 'I'd rather be on my own, to be honest.'

They join the others in the garden. Apparently Keira and Elise have been up for hours. Keira has fetched several buckets of water from the stream and Elise has already done a recce of the loch. 'There's a small shallow beach,' she says. 'We should have no trouble getting in. It's only five minutes' walk away, but the path's muddy, so wear your boots.'

'Come on, what are we waiting for?' says Keira. 'I'm dying to get into that water. I don't care how cold it is.'

Ariel laughs. 'You say that now... Just wait! This is Scotland, remember.'

They set off down the path in single file, Elise leading the way. The morning is bright, but the cold is snapping at its edges. Sophie takes up the rear again, watching her step as she picks her way between lichen-covered stones and clumps of rotting leaves. They skirt around a small birch wood. Ribbons of sunlight thread through the branches, which are black and almost bare. For once, nobody is talking, which means Sophie can hear the birds singing. If it weren't for this horrible, impossible situation, she would find it beautiful and peaceful. But there's room for neither beauty nor peace in her world right now.

The swim is truly exhilarating. The cold hurts with an intensity she's never experienced before, but it wakes her at last, sparking connections inside her like thousands of fairy lights. The loch, which was indeed easy to enter via the stony beach, shelves steeply and they are soon out of their depth. Keira and Elise start swimming properly, but the rest of them tread water as fast as their legs will allow, paddling frantic circles with their arms, puffing out rings of breath.

'Oh. My. God,' gasps Ariel. 'Not sure – how long – I can stand this.'

Sophie lowers her goggles, then inhales and sinks. The water pours into her ears, freezing her brain. It trickles icily through her veins. She feels her heart pounding in protest. There's no noise. Her chest tightens and hurts as the oxygen in her lungs expires, forcing her back to the surface. She opens her mouth wide and takes a huge gulp of fresh, zinging air.

Elise is already on the bank, wrapped in her dryrobe. Ariel and Grace are making their way to shore, followed closely by Keira. Sophie is desperate to have a moment in the loch all by herself. She carries on treading water for thirty seconds or so, but her fingers and toes are going numb and she's feeling slightly light-headed. It would be dangerous to stay in any longer. Regretfully she glides towards the shore, scraping her knees on a rock. She stands up and stumbles out.

'That was incredible,' says Keira. 'How long did we last?'

Grace checks her waterproof fitness watch. 'Five and a half minutes.'

'Maybe it would feel warmer if we swam later tomorrow,' says Elise.

'I doubt it.' Ariel rubs herself with a towel while the others dive into their dryrobes to remove their swimsuits.

'Did you enjoy that, Sophie?' asks Elise a short while later, while they are walking back to the house.

'Yes, very much,' she replies.

'You're very quiet. Not your usual bubbly self at all.'

'Really?'

'Come on, we've hardly had a peep out of you since we arrived. Are you still upset about the crash?'

Sophie shakes her head. 'No. Obviously I feel bad about it, but nobody was hurt.'

'I didn't mean you *ought* to be upset about it, I was just wondering. You seem to have a lot on your mind. Is everything okay?'

'Yes, everything's absolutely fine,' she retorts. 'I wish people would stop asking me.'

'Sorry. I was only trying—'

'Well, please don't.'

'Okay.' Elise flinches away, then hangs back to chat to Grace instead.

Sophie strides ahead, silently reprimanding herself. *You've got to do better than this or you'll give yourself away.*

As soon as they get back to the house, Ariel puts a large saucepan of porridge on the stove while the others finish drying themselves off and change into warm clothes. Everybody laments the lack of hot showers. The water in the loch has left them smelling slightly brackish.

Sophie can't get warm. It's as if there's a thin layer of ice just beneath the surface of her skin. She kneels before the log burner, hands outstretched, like a pilgrim at a shrine, begging for help.

'You'll feel better with some hot food inside you,' says Ariel, carrying the vat of porridge into the sitting room.

'Thanks,' Sophie replies. 'To be honest, I don't usually eat porridge.' She dislikes the lumpiness of it, the way it sticks to the back of her throat.

'But we're in Scotland. It's traditional.' Ariel sets the pot down on the table.

'Yes, I know.'

'It'll warm you from the inside out.' She ladles out a bowl. 'Come on, try it.'

'Okay.' Sophie stands up, reluctantly leaving the fire. The others come to the table, and they all eat. Grace has found a jar of honey in the larder and passes it around. Keira sprinkles nuts and raisins, while Elise drowns her bowl in a puddle of milk. Ariel stirs a generous spoonful of brown sugar into hers, and they all pronounce their various versions delicious. But Sophie finds the porridge cloying and heavy; it makes her want to heave.

'Anyone fancy going to the beach today?' asks Keira, who has been reading through the file of notes for visitors. 'It's only about forty-five minutes' walk away, and it's supposed to be really isolated and beautiful. Lots of wildlife and stuff. There's even an abandoned village there.'

'Oh yes, I read about that online,' says Elise. 'One of the old buildings has been done up as a shelter. You can sleep there for free, don't even have to book.'

'I think you'll find it's called a bothy,' Ariel informs them. 'There are lots of them scattered around the Highlands. They're for walkers and campers. Very basic. They make this place seem like a five-star hotel.'

'I'm up for it,' says Grace, helping to clear the table.

'Shall we take our swimming gear?' asks Elise. There's a general shaking of heads. They would love to swim in the sea, but having only just warmed up, they decide to leave it for tomorrow or the day after, depending on the weather.

Sophie helps make up some sandwiches, wrapping them in individual foil packages the way Nan used to when they went on trips to the seaside. They fill their flasks with hot tea and put them in their backpacks. Lively, joshing conversation passes between them as they zip up coats, don woolly hats and lace up walking boots. All the women appear so cheerful and relaxed, yet one of them is her enemy.

Oh, it's all so embarrassing, she thinks, as they tramp through the rough, boggy grass. She's never approved of women who knowingly have affairs with married men; they let the side down. But it's Ryan she should really be directing her anger at; he's the one who has broken his wedding vows. If he were here right now, she'd happily push him into the nearest loch.

They reach the brow of a hill and suddenly there's the coastline, stretching before them. Sophie lets out a gasp of wonder. This is the perfect beach of her imagination. Wild and untouched, beautiful in a slightly desolate way. The bay forms a generous curve of grey-white sand, dotted with tufts of marram grass. Nearer the sea the sand turns to mud. Small rocky islets studded with barnacles rise out of the shallows. Bright green fronds float in rust-coloured pools. Rivulets and runnels of water form dancing criss-cross patterns between the boulders, and everywhere there are clumps of dark, reeking seaweed.

The wind gusts across their faces as they walk closer to the shore. A flock of cackling geese flies overhead and they all look up simultaneously. Without discussion, they separate to explore, each interested in something different – the bracken-stained rockpools, a cosy hollow among the dunes, the chance to make footprints in the sand.

Sophie heads straight for the abandoned village, although it's no more than a few ruined houses nestling together against the assault of time and the cruel coastal weather. The single-storey buildings are built of local stone, pieced together like a giant jigsaw puzzle. They look as if they might tumble down at any moment. Their roofs have long since disappeared, as have their doorways and window frames – rotted to pulp or broken up for firewood, perhaps. She walks among the tiny rooms, imagining families and even animals huddling here during the long winter months. There is a lingering atmosphere of loss and regret.

The bothy is set apart from the other buildings, about a hundred yards further along the bay. It has a new corrugated-tin roof. She walks towards it, eager to see what it's like inside. The door is ajar, so she enters without thinking.

She stops. Somebody is obviously camping here. A fire is glowing in the log burner, emitting just enough light for her to see. A sleeping bag is laid out on a small wooden shelf with a thick jumper rolled up to form a pillow. A rucksack is propped up against the wall, a few items of clothing spilling out. Embers are glowing in the log burner, and the room smells of peat. There is a hefty torch and other items of camping equipment. A waterproof is hanging on a nail. She stares at a saucepan on the small camping stove and an aluminium plate encrusted with what looks like baked beans. Whoever is staying here can't have gone far, she thinks. How trusting of them to leave all their belongings lying around.

Suddenly she feels like an intruder. She retreats, stepping out of the gloomy bothy and back into the stark daylight. She looks about her, but the only people she can see are from her own party. Elise is wandering up and down the shoreline; Grace is investigating the ruins. Ariel has sat down on a rock and appears to be sketching. Keira has disappeared into the dunes.

Then, out of the corner of her eye, she sees a flash of movement. She follows it, turning just in time to see a dark figure, dressed all in black, clambering up some granite rocks on the far side of the beach. There's no mistaking the fact that this person – male or female, it's impossible to tell from this distance – is running away.

They reach the top, then jump down out of sight. A few seconds later, they emerge again, hurtling through the grass and bracken, darting between boulders as if their life depends on their escape. Finally they enter a small birch wood, and she loses sight of their black outline as it merges with the skeletons of trees.

A shiver of fear runs through her. Who was it? Why were they so desperate not to be seen?

She returns to the bothy, this time searching for clues. Picking up the torch, she switches it on and scans the room. There is a pile of papers tucked under the rucksack. Crouching down, she pulls out a map of the local area. This is not in itself suspicious, but when she unfolds it, she sees that the path from the beach to their house has been marked with a line of red ink. She shuffles anxiously through the rest of the papers and finds printouts from the website for Condie's Retreat: photos of the rooms, descriptions of the facilities, instructions for using the equipment, directions to the loch. And there's more. At the bottom of the pile, there's what looks like another printout. It's an article from *The Guardian*. She trains the torchlight over the page and sees a photo of a woman drowning underwater. The headline reads: 'The Dangers of Wild Swimming'. Her heart almost stops.

TWELVE

SOPHIE

Suddenly she can't bear to be in this gloomy, confined space a second longer. She hurriedly puts the printouts back and turns off the torch. Checking to see that everything is where she found it, she escapes the bothy. She stands in the soggy brown grass, buffeted by the wind, the smell of seaweed in her nostrils as she tries to catch her breath.

Her brain is turning somersaults, trying to make sense of what has just happened, trying to work out whether she's right to feel afraid. She could have chanced upon a random stranger who wanted to be alone – in which case she's the one at fault, invading the bothy, rummaging through their belongings. But then she remembers the pages of information about Condie's Retreat, the red line drawn on the map, and that image of somebody drowning... It *has* to be linked.

She shudders. Until a few minutes ago, it has not occurred to her that the threat to her might come from outside the group. She's been concentrating all her energy on the other four women, but now there is a fifth person to consider. Whoever they are – male or female – they are agile enough to scamper up rocks and fit enough to run away at speed. Young, then. Youngish at least. She cannot think who it might be.

Where are they now? They could easily be watching her from the woods, or have crept back to hide behind a rocky outcrop. She imagines them, faceless and dressed in black, jumping into a sandy hollow, peeping through the spiky marram grass.

She needs to get back to the others. There is safety in numbers, at least. She looks across the bay and sees that Elise has joined Ariel on her rock. Grace is still wandering around the ruins. There's no sign of Keira.

She sets off towards them. Now she has to decide whether to tell them what happened. What if this guy – she thinks it probably *was* a man, something about the body shape – turns out to be a burglar, or even a rapist? She should warn everyone to make sure the doors and windows are locked at night and to not go out by themselves. They've all been assuming that they're protected, that Condie's Retreat is some magical place that bad people can't reach. Whereas in fact, if she thinks about it for one second, they are potentially quite vulnerable here. There's no way of contacting the emergency services. If they needed help, God knows how long it would take to arrive. As she tramples the long grass underfoot, it becomes obvious that she should share her discoveries with them.

And most disturbing of all... why did this person have an article about the dangers of wild swimming?

'Because they want to do some wild swimming themselves, I expect,' says Ariel when Sophie relays her findings to the group.

'Yeah, they're probably a beginner,' agrees Elise, 'and they wanted to read up about the dangers involved.'

'I guess...' murmurs Sophie. 'But what about all the info on our place? Don't you think that's creepy?'

Grace kicks divots out of the sand. 'Not necessarily. Maybe they're thinking of staying there at some point and want to check it out. Lots of people do stuff like that. There's no law against it.'

'But why run away like that when they saw me coming? Honestly, they were desperate to escape.'

'Maybe they were scared,' says Ariel, putting away her sketch pad and charcoal sticks. 'You were the one in the bothy, going through their things...'

Sophie feels herself heating up. 'I didn't know someone was staying there. I didn't break in. The door was open.'

'Yeah, but once you saw it was occupied, you should have left.'

'I *did*,' she protests. 'I only went back in when I saw the guy running away from me. I was suspicious.'

'Just now, you said you didn't know whether it was a man or a woman,' says Elise in a slightly accusing tone, as if she thinks Sophie is making it all up.

'I don't know for sure, they were too far away, but I *think* it was a guy. He was dressed completely in black.'

'Hmm... Seems like a lot of fuss about nothing.' She wrenches her backpack off her shoulders. 'Are we going to have lunch now, or what? I'm starving.'

'Me too,' replies Grace. 'Anyone seen Keira?'

'She went to explore the dunes,' says Ariel, taking a foil parcel out of her bag. 'I'm sure she'll come back when she's ready.'

Grace finds a perch on the rock next to Ariel and Elise. Sophie stands apart, observing them as they pour their hot drinks and dive into their sandwiches. She feels churned up inside and has completely lost her appetite. As far as the others are concerned, the matter is closed, dismissed as being of no consequence, but that's because they don't know what's really going on – or to be more accurate, *three* of them don't know and one is doing an impressive acting job.

This situation is impossible, she thinks. *It's sending me mad. They're probably right, and I'm just being paranoid, jumping to conclusions, making everything about me.* She walks off towards the water, trying to compose her thoughts and calm down. The tide is coming in, the thin rivulets widening into streams; she jumps across them, sinking into the soft mud as she lands. The water is so cold she can feel it through the leather of her walking boots. It's hard to imagine how it might feel to swim in it with only a costume on – she probably wouldn't manage more than a couple of minutes. It could be dangerous, she decides. If the person she saw *is* a beginner, they really shouldn't go out there on their own.

The wind is brutal; she can hardly keep her eyes open. A rush of icy water swirls aggressively around her feet and, alarmed, she turns around. How quickly the landscape has changed. Her boot prints have already been washed away and the path she took to the water's edge is no longer available to her. She looks up to see the others waving at her to come back. Keira has turned up and is shouting through cupped hands, not that Sophie can hear what she's saying.

She splashes through the water, jumping across the gullies on to small bumps of sand, picking her way across a group of slimy boulders, trying to keep her balance. Finally she makes it on to dry land, beyond the reach of the sea. She runs up to the others.

'What the hell were you doing?' demands Ariel. Grace and Elise simultaneously roll their eyes.

'Sorry, I didn't realise,' Sophie says breathlessly. 'It came in so quickly.'

Keira gives her a more sympathetic look. 'Are you okay, Sophie? The girls were telling me about some guy...'

'It's nothing,' she mumbles. 'Forget it.'

'Why's he so interested in Condie's Retreat?'

Elise sighs. 'Do we have to go through this again? I'd like to go back now.'

'Yes, it's starting to get cold,' says Ariel, looking up at the lowering clouds. 'Might even rain...'

They walk back in virtual silence, locked in their own thoughts. There is an awkwardness between them that only Ariel tries to smooth over; making occasional comments about the weather, trying to jolly them along with the promise of cake. Keira seems particularly immune to her efforts and trudges along, head down, hands in pockets. Sophie wonders whether her troubled mood has anything to do with the stranger on the beach. She feels bad, like it's all her fault, even though she knows it's not.

The house is cold and gloomy. There are important jobs to do before the light fades – fetching logs from the wood store outside, getting a good fire going, making sure the lamps have enough paraffin for the evening. Ariel makes a pot of tea and produces a home-made lemon drizzle cake, which she cuts into generous slices because 'it won't keep'. Keira takes hers to her bedroom, saying she wants to read for a bit, while the rest of them sit awkwardly in the living room, their plates perched on their knees. The cake is drier than it should be, and the sugar coating makes Sophie's teeth hurt.

It is Elise and Grace's turn to cook tonight, and they go into the kitchen to chop vegetables for a chilli. Bursts of raucous laughter punctuate the otherwise quiet atmosphere, and at one point they belt out a Beyoncé song. The two of them seem to have formed a bond, which doesn't surprise Sophie, as they are similar in age and outlook.

She finds herself alone with Ariel, who gets her sketching materials out and starts assessing her work.

'Hmm... I'm not sure I've captured the essence of the place.

The bleakness, the wild beauty...' She's clearly fishing for compliments.

'Oh, I think you have,' says Sophie. 'There's real movement in those grasses.'

'Do you think so?' Ariel's face lights up. 'Do you paint?'

Sophie shakes her head. 'No, I'm hopeless at art.' She picks up a magazine and starts flicking through it.

Ariel puts down her sketch pad and lowers her voice. 'What do you think is going on with Keira?' she asks. 'She went off by herself for ages this afternoon.'

'Maybe she just needed some time alone.'

'Hmm...' She leans forwards. 'I think it's man problems.'

'Oh. How do you know?'

'She said something a few weeks ago that gave me the impression she was in some kind of illicit relationship.'

Sophie's heart misses a beat. 'Really? What did she say?'

'I can't remember her exact words, something along the lines of being fed up with sneaking around, and wishing things could be out in the open.'

'Like... she was having an affair with a married man – that kind of thing?' Sophie's voice trembles.

'What else could it be?' Ariel folds her arms across her chest, looking very pleased with herself. 'I asked her what she meant, but she said there was no way she could tell me.'

'Why was that?'

'No idea. Anyway, I think it's all gone badly wrong.'

'Oh. What makes you think that? Has she said something else?'

'Not in so many words, but when we were making dinner together last night, she was very jumpy. She took her phone with her to the beach – I think she went off by herself to try and get a signal. When she came back, she was in a very strange state, like she'd just had an argument with somebody.'

'Really?'

'Oh yes.' Ariel nods sagely. 'I'm very sensitive, Sophie. I pick up on other people's moods. I often know what they're feeling before they feel it themselves.'

Just as Ariel completes her sentence, Keira walks in carrying a lighted candle. She's changed into a long, dark dress, and for a second she looks like a ghost from a bygone era. Sophie starts guiltily. What if she was listening outside the door?

'There you are, Keira,' says Ariel smoothly. 'We've been missing you. How does the song go? *What good is sitting alone in your room?*'

'No good at all when it's like being in the bloody Arctic,' Keira says, crossing over to the armchair next to the log burner. 'I was trying to read, but my fingers were so cold I kept dropping my book.' She sits down and drapes her long legs over the side.

Ariel asks her what's she reading, and they have a brief conversation about historical fiction. Sophie quietly watches Keira, the recent conversation running through her head. Is she the one? She is very attractive: slim, even-featured, with clean skin and bright blue eyes. But her hair – which is jet black and possibly dyed – is short, and Ryan has often remarked that he finds long hair more attractive.

Sophie twists a lock of her own hair around her fingers as she contemplates Keira, who has gone back to her novel. Maybe Ryan only said that because he wanted to put her off the scent.

'Right. I'd better lay the table,' says Ariel, as she lights the last of the lamps. She turns the flame up, making her shadow grow large over the wall, then goes into the kitchen to fetch the cutlery.

Keira looks up from her book. 'Well... this is nice, isn't it?' she says, leaning back. Her lips curl into a strange half-smile. 'Just you and me. Alone at last.'

Sophie hesitates. 'Um... what do you mean exactly?'

'Nothing. Just that it's nice to spend some time together. We've been swimming for nearly a year, but I don't really know you at all. I think we could have a lot in common. If we had a chance to get to know each other better, we could be friends. You know, proper friends.'

Sophie looks away. Why does everything she says sound so loaded? Is it her imagination, or is Keira trying to mess with her?

'Keira...' she begins. 'Be honest with me. Are you having...' She breaks off, unable to finish the question.

'Am I having what?' Keira's blue eyes widen.

'Nothing... nothing.'

'No, go on, say it.'

'Really, I didn't mean anything.' Sophie stands up. 'Better go and see if I can help.'

She rushes out of the room and stumbles into the gloomy corridor. Leaning against the wall, she stops to catch her breath. She is not ready to show her hand yet. Soon, but not yet.

THIRTEEN

SOPHIE

Sophie eats her meal in virtual silence, hoping nobody will notice that she's not joining in the conversation, or coming up with witty comments, or enthusing about the food. The chilli is delicious, but she has no appetite. She looks around at her companions' glowing faces. Their voices rise above each other as they compete for attention. Sudden bursts of laughter puncture the air. But she feels separate and isolated, as if sitting on the other side of a thick pane of glass.

Of the three most likely candidates to be her husband's lover – Elise, Grace and Keira – Keira was her third choice. She seemed too sophisticated for Ryan, too – how can she describe it? – self-possessed. Definitely not needy enough. When it comes to relationships, Ryan likes to be the hero, likes to sweep a girl off her feet. And he's a superficial bastard, goes for big tits and long hair. Keira has neither. But that's not to say she's not the one.

She pushes a piece of carrot around in the rich tomato sauce as she battles with her gut instinct. Maybe she simply discounted Keira because she didn't *want* it to be her. Keira is her favourite out of the whole group; she's the woman with whom she has up until now felt the most sympathy. Even though she's not an easy person to get to know, Sophie has always felt that if she *did* get to know her, she would like her a lot.

Keira takes the swimming seriously. She actually swims, for a start, unlike the others, who bob and flap and gasp. Sophie has always believed that Keira *needs* to swim, that it's more than a social activity or a health kick. She gets the water's deeper meaning, just as Sophie gets it. If Keira is the 'other woman', it means that she's been pretending all along, coming to Elizabeth Lake for all these months to laugh and mock and sneer.

Elise tops up Sophie's glass and their eyes connect. Sophie feels like she's asking if everything is okay, so she nods, then looks away. She drinks the wine, which has already gone to her head and replays the hurried phone conversation she had with Ryan in the car park.

He said his lover was dangerous. She has some hold over him, apparently, although he wouldn't explain what it was. He was describing a mad person, and Keira doesn't seem the slightest bit mad. None of them seem mad, though. They all seem perfectly normal and sane, four women on holiday having a great time. Sophie feels she's the demented one, the skull at the banquet, polluting the atmosphere with her suspicions.

Maybe it's all a load of lies and Ryan's gaslighting her. She gasps internally at the thought. That would be so mean; guaranteed to spoil the break she was so looking forward to. It's possible. But why would he do that? Does he hate her that much?

'Such a shame Fern had to drop out,' Grace is saying. Sophie forces herself back into the here and now. 'She discovered this place, booked it, organised it... I feel bad being here without her.'

'Anyone know the reason?' asks Elise. 'I mean, like the *real* reason. She was very vague about it.'

'So? She has a right to privacy,' replies Keira. 'I hate gossiping. It soon turns into bitching, especially if it's all women involved.'

'Men can be just as bitchy,' says Ariel, 'but I agree, we shouldn't speculate about other people's personal lives.'

'I wasn't speculating,' protests Elise. 'I was just wondering that's all. I like Fern. I hope she's all right.'

'We all have secrets,' says Sophie, finally joining in. 'Who knows what's really going on under the surface?' She looks from face to face, searching for a glimmer of a response – a tweak of an eyebrow, a bitten lip – but nobody is giving anything away.

She skulks back into her own world and lets the conversation continue without her. As the wine gurgles in her half-empty stomach, she revisits her theory that Keira is not Ryan's type, whereas she – Sophie – totally is.

She thinks back to how she first met him, twenty years ago. They'd both come to the student health centre. She was suffering from depression, while he had a smoker's cough he couldn't shift. She was eighteen, a fresher studying – ironically – Health and Well-Being in a Social Context. He was in the year above, ploughing his way through Business Administration and Management.

The year hadn't got off to a very good start. She was the first person in her family to go to university and hadn't really known what to expect. These were uncharted waters, and her parents couldn't help her navigate them. They were simply thrilled that she'd passed her A levels, even though her grades weren't good enough to secure the place she'd originally been offered at Exeter. She'd had to go through clearing to find a course, and had ended up – if she was honest – at a third-rate institution she'd never even heard of.

None of her fellow students seemed in the least bit interested in studying and just wanted to go out every night on the piss. Her room in the hall of residence looked out on to a large terrace where students congregated after the pubs shut to carry on drinking and smoke weed. Even midweek, they partied until three or four in the morning, and she couldn't sleep. Sophie wasn't a prude, she liked to go out and have fun, but she couldn't keep up with the punishing pace. Nor could she afford that kind of lifestyle.

She had a weekend job in a DIY superstore, kept her expenses low and yet was still piling on the debt. Her family wasn't able to help out. Everyone else seemed to be having a wonderful time, while she felt lonely and miserable, ashamed of herself for missing her parents and Nan. If she hadn't met Ryan that day in the health centre, she would have probably chucked it all in and gone home.

They were sitting next to each other in the crowded, stuffy waiting room that smelt of sweat and bad breath with notes of marijuana. Three doctors were off sick and there were long delays to be seen. Ryan introduced himself, and before long Sophie was pouring her heart out to him. It was quite unlike her. Until then, she hadn't shared her misgivings with anyone else for fear of appearing uncool.

He said he knew exactly how she felt and that she wasn't alone. Most first years were homesick and pretending to enjoy themselves – he'd been the same. She was just being honest. Like her, he came from a working-class background. He did impressions of strung-out, posh hippy kids, which made her laugh and cheered her up. So much so that when she finally got to see the doctor, she felt like a fraud.

Ryan hung around after their appointments and asked her out on a date. From that moment, they were a couple. He was the magic ingredient that made everything else taste right. She didn't grow to love her time at uni, but he made it bearable. He lived in a shared house in a student area on the outskirts of town, and she spent several nights a week there. But they were not as inseparable as she would have liked them to be. He didn't want to get a place just for the two of them, and he liked drinking with his mates after football. He went home every other weekend and never invited her along to meet his folks, although to be fair, she was usually working and unavailable. She had to fit in with the rest of his life, whereas he *was* her life. When she wasn't with Ryan, she lived in a kind of suspended state, still sitting in that waiting room where they'd met.

The first course has finished, and Ariel is asking everyone to pass her their plate. Sophie stares down at her half-eaten chilli and has a pang of guilt. It was lovely food, cooked under far from ideal conditions, and she's not shown the cooks any respect.

'Sorry,' she says to Elise and Grace. 'It was delicious, but I don't seem to have much appetite. I shouldn't have had that lemon drizzle cake earlier.'

'Ah, so it's *my* fault.' Ariel grins.

'No, not at all. It's just... um... I don't...'

'It doesn't matter,' says Elise. 'I take it you don't want crumble?'

'No thanks.'

She grins. 'All the more for us then!'

Sophie gulps down the rest of her wine. 'I hope you don't mind, but I need to lie down in my room for a bit. Thanks for the meal. Sorry I wasn't up to it.' They look at her curiously as she rises from her seat.

'Take care, Sophie,' says Keira. 'If there's anything we can do, just shout.'

Her words sound hollow to Sophie's suspicious ear. She lights a candle and takes it down the gloomy corridor to her bedroom. Behind her she can hear gales of laughter as the others instantly adjust to her absence. Or maybe somebody has made a joke about her. Who knows?

She puts the candlestick on the little side table and climbs on to her bed. According to her mobile, it's only just gone nine o'clock. Its battery is running low, she needs to charge it. But

Keira is the only one with a solar charger, and the prospect of asking to borrow it tomorrow grates. Everything feels impossibly complicated and unworkable.

The room is very cold and the candlelight too weak to read by. She doesn't know what to do with herself, other than try to get some sleep. However, the chances of that seem minimal right now. She walks over to the window to draw the curtains. As she pulls them across, she sees a small pinhead of light moving slowly through the pitch-black darkness. Her heart skips a beat.

Somebody's out there.

Leaving a gap in the curtains, she runs back to the bedside table and blows out the candle. Then she returns to the window and stares out, her pulse racing as she looks for the light again, but it's gone. Did she imagine it? No, she tells herself, she definitely saw it. Somebody is prowling around with a torch.

Her mind immediately leaps to the guy she saw running away from the bothy on the beach. It has to be him. *Has* to be. She knew something was wrong when she found that map and the information sheets about the house, but the others pooh-poohed it, even told her off for snooping. Now she's been proved right.

She stands there for a few more minutes, still and silent, blood rushing through her ears, eyes trained on the dark nothingness on the other side of the glass. Her brain is on red alert for any unnatural flicker of light. It's like staring into the abyss. Maybe he saw her in the window and turned his torch off, she thinks. But that doesn't mean he's gone. He's still out there, lurking. He could be very close to the house, looking for a way in. Is he a burglar? What does he want with them?

Sophie draws the curtains together tightly, then feels her way back to the bed and relights the candle. Her hand trembles as she carries it out of the bedroom, retracing her steps down the corridor to the sitting room.

Ariel, Elise, Grace and Keira have finished their pudding and are laying out a game of Monopoly. They are busy chatting and don't even notice when she enters.

'Somebody's prowling around outside,' she bursts out.

They turn around simultaneously. 'What?' says Ariel. 'Are you serious?'

'Yes. I think it must be that guy I spotted at the beach.'

Elise puts her hand to her mouth. 'Shit! You mean you actually saw him?'

'No, not exactly – I saw the beam of his torch. He was moving among the trees, like he was looking for a way into the garden. What do we do? We can't call the police, there's no bloody signal.'

Ariel looks doubtful. 'Are you sure it was a person? Maybe it was the reflection of your candle. Or a fox – their eyes glow in the dark.'

'Yes, that's it, must have been a fox,' says Keira.

'No, it wasn't an animal. There was just one light, not two.'

'A one-eyed fox then,' laughs Grace.

Sophie feels her jaw tightening. 'It was coming from a pen torch.'

'Impossible,' says Keira, shaking her head. 'A pen torch wouldn't be any use out there. He'd fall over in seconds, break a leg.'

'He's using a pen torch near the house because he doesn't want to be seen. We need to check that all the doors are locked.'

The four of them exchange glances. 'Honestly, Sophie, I don't think there's anything to worry about,' soothes Elise. 'You've been on edge ever since we got here, ever since you crashed the car, in fact.'

'I *nearly* crashed it, that's all,' Sophie replies sullenly. 'Anyway, this has got nothing to do with that. The guy staying in the bothy is interested in this house. I saw the evidence. And when I approached, he ran away. Now I don't know who he is or why he's snooping around in the dead of night, but it scares the shit out of me.'

'You need to calm down, Soph—' starts Ariel.

'Don't blame me if we're all murdered in our sleep!'

'You're being ridiculous,' Keira mutters.

Sophie feels her hackles rising. 'Okay, fine. You carry on playing Monopoly and I'll make sure we're all safe.'

She rushes over to the patio doors and checks that they're locked. Nobody says anything as she leaves the room, taking her candlestick into the hallway. The front door has a simple Yale lock and no bolts or chain, so there's nothing more she can do to improve the security there. She walks into the kitchen and finds to her horror that the back door has been left unlocked. Her stomach immediately lurches with fear. She turns the key and puts it on the shelf, out of reach, then bolts the door at the top and bottom.

The bedrooms are next. She marches into Ariel's little makeshift room just off the kitchen and checks the windows; does the same in Elise's bedroom, then Grace's, before finally entering Keira's domain. Of course, all the windows are shut but none have locks. There's no double glazing either. Her mouth dries as she imagines a gloved fist breaking the glass.

Casting the light from her candle across the bed, she sees a discarded jumper and jeans, a scrunched-up towel. Keira's mobile sits on the dressing table, still plugged into the solar charger. She is tempted to grab it and search through her texts, but she's frightened of being caught. Besides, the immediate enemy is not within, but without – a one-eyed monster creeping through the blackness.

She goes back to her own room and dives fully clothed under the covers. She will never sleep tonight.

FOURTEEN

SOPHIE

Sophie lies flat on her back, eyes wide open. She is as alert as a soldier on patrol, her senses on a trigger switch. At first the darkness is impenetrable, but gradually her pupils widen and she starts to make out solid blocks of furniture, the heavy drapery of the curtains. Every sound – creaking floorboards, the opening and closing of doors, whispers outside in the corridor – sparks her fear. She can't bear to lie like this a moment longer. Sitting up, she reaches for the box of matches and strikes a light. She puts the flame against the wick of the candle, and it sputters into life.

Now the room is full of ghostly shadows, but at least she'll be able to see any intruder. Before, she longed to sleep, but now she wants to stay awake. *Somebody* has to be on guard...

Her eyelids feel heavy, despite the chemicals surging through her brain. Unbidden images enter her head. She sees Ryan having sex with his lover in some unknown bed. The picture is blurry. They writhe like animals, twisting away from her, offering her only tantalising glimpses of the woman's face. Is that Elise's generous mouth nuzzling into Ryan's neck, or

Grace's painted fingernails scratching down his back? Can she see Keira's shock of dark hair buried in his groin? Even Ariel's voluptuous breasts make an appearance. Sophie tries to get rid of the women, but like the last guests at a party, they hang on, drunk and slightly bolshie, ignoring all her polite hints to leave. She tries more aggressive tactics, swearing at them in her head and thumping them through the pillow.

Finally the spectres seem to tire, and the images become less distinct. The candle sputters and goes out. She falls into a light, spacey almost-sleep, ears still singing, brain still fizzing. But she mustn't drift off, she has to stay on duty...

It's too late. The darkness has crept up on her, and she can feel herself sinking slowly into its folds.

She sleeps heavily, waking next morning with a headache. No prizes for guessing why, she thinks. She drank too much last night, didn't eat enough either.

Heaving herself on to her elbows, she peers into the chilly gloom. Everything looks normal. Ordinary. It's the lack of electricity that gives the place an eerie atmosphere. She never realised until now how dark real darkness is, how much it scares her.

The thought of getting up and greeting the others weighs heavily on her chest. She can't spend the rest of the holiday like this, on a knife-edge, suspecting everyone. She has to challenge the guilty party to come forward. But what if they all deny it, what then? She'll look like an idiot, *and* she'll have offended three perfectly nice people. No, she has to know for certain who it is first and tackle them on their own.

'Morning!' chirrups Elise as Sophie enters the kitchen a short while later. The others are already up and dressed, sitting at the table munching on cereal, yoghurt and fruit.

'Hi.' Sophie hesitates, unsure whether she's welcome. 'Everyone sleep okay?'

'Like a log,' says Grace. 'If the intruder got in and raped me, I didn't feel a thing.'

Ariel charges in straight away. 'Grace! That's a really inappropriate thing to say.'

'I agree,' says Keira.

'For God's sake, it was only a joke.'

'Rape is not a laughing matter. Ever.' Ariel folds her arms.

'I know that. I didn't mean...' Grace sighs irritably. 'I was joking about what happened last night. Sophie tried to creep us all out, remember?'

Now it's Sophie's turn to protest. 'I wasn't trying to creep you out. I genuinely believed someone was out there.'

Grace stands up, scraping her chair back on the slate floor. 'Yeah, yeah, whatever. I thought this holiday was supposed to be fun. What is this, *Nightmare on Elm Street*?' She walks out of the kitchen, leaving a trail of toxicity behind her.

There's a pause, then Ariel says in a low voice, 'I'm sorry, but I can't accept rape jokes. I've worked with vulnerable women – I know what the reality is.'

'You were right to object,' replies Elise. 'She wasn't thinking, just said the first thing that came into her head.' Ariel huffs.

'Look, I'm sorry about last night,' says Sophie, reaching for the packet of wheat biscuits. 'I think I was freaked out by finding that stuff in the bothy. When I saw what looked like a torch beam, I put two and two together and came up with twenty-six.'

'It was a bit strange,' admits Keira. 'Perhaps we should go back to the beach this morning and see if he's still there – maybe have a word...'

Elise looks up from her cereal. 'What – and combine it with a swim?'

'Yeah. Why not? We said yesterday we'd like to try the water.'

'Hmm, I'm not sure,' says Ariel. 'With the wind-chill factor, that sea is going to be incredibly cold, and there's nowhere to warm up properly afterwards. It's such a long walk back to the house, I think it could be quite dangerous.'

'There's a log burner in the bothy,' Sophie says. 'If it's free, we could use it.'

'But what if it's not free? What if there's no wood?'

'Then we don't swim.'

'I'd rather go back to the loch for a quick dip,' says Elise. 'It's only a few minutes' walk away, and it feels safer. I don't mind another trip to the beach, but we were only there yesterday and there are loads of other places to explore.'

'Okay, it was just an idea,' responds Keira, a little testily. 'I was trying to put Sophie's mind at rest—'

'It's fine,' Sophie interrupts. 'Look, nothing happened last night. Let's forget it and move on.'

Ariel looks pleased. 'Good. Let's go to the loch, have a quick swim, come back for hot chocolate and a mid-morning snack, then make a plan for the afternoon.'

'Actually, I won't be joining you,' Sophie finds herself saying. 'I'm going to stay here.'

'You can't do that – you *have* to swim. That's why we're here, that's what it's all about!' Elise puts down her spoon. 'It'll do you good, straighten you out. You're all cramped up and twisty.'

'I'm not,' Sophie replies evenly. 'I just need a bit of time to myself.'

Keira and Ariel make a few more efforts to persuade her to change her mind, but they are in vain. Grace returns and apologises for flouncing off, and Ariel admits she was a bit sharp. The four of them change into their swimsuits, and Keira, Elise and Grace put on their enormous dryrobes. They leave the house looking like a group of heavyweight boxers going off for a fight. Ariel brings up the rear old-style, wearing her anorak and jogging bottoms, a flimsy towel tucked under her arm.

From the patio doors, Sophie watches them until they're completely out of sight. She feels a bit sad about not swimming. Elise was right, it *would* have made her feel better. But this is the only way to have the house to herself. She has decided to search her friends' rooms to look for any evidence linking them to Ryan. Keira is the obvious person to start with.

In the day, her bedroom looks even messier than it did by candlelight. Sophie is surprised. Keira always seems so neat, so organised. She goes straight to her phone, which has been unplugged from the solar charger. The battery is only showing 25 per cent capacity, which means the equipment isn't working very well. Luckily there's no passcode required to get in. Sophie quickly scrolls through Keira's contact list, looking for Ryan's name, but it's not there. She probably lists him as something else, she thinks, just in case. There are entries for 'Plumber', 'Yoga' and 'Ruby', but they all turn out to be genuine. Then she sees the name Fred. For some reason she can't explain, it seems hopeful – in a horrible sort of way. She clicks on the text feed and starts to read.

After a minute or two, she sinks on to the bed, her finger shaking as she scrolls through endless exchanges – some cheeky, some romantic, some very explicit. There are also arrangements for meeting up, apologies for not being able to get away, even a few tetchy remarks about hating having to hide. There was doubt in her mind before, but these messages confirm it. Keira is having a secret affair with somebody whose name is extremely unlikely to be Fred.

She is shocked to find that she's such a poor judge of character. But above all, she feels angry. Incredibly, indescribably angry. It's as strong as it was last New Year's Eve, when she first found out about the affair. She feels like she's going to explode, wants to fling Keira's phone across the room and smash it to smithereens, then destroy the furniture, set fire to the house... But she doesn't do any of that. Her anger coalesces, forming a hard rock in the pit of her stomach. She puts the handset back where she found it and goes back to her own room.

Got to talk to Ryan, she says under her breath. She has to have his confirmation before she confronts Keira. Otherwise she could easily lie and say that Fred is some other guy. There's no choice but to walk all the way back to the car and drive until she reaches civilisation.

She tears a scrap of paper from her notebook and writes a message, explaining that she's gone for a long walk and will be back later in the afternoon, before it gets dark. She puts on her waterproof jacket and laces up her boots. Hat. Gloves. The all-important mobile has almost run out of juice, so she takes her charger too, in case she finds a café, or a library perhaps. And the car key. Mustn't forget that. She rummages in the pockets of her rucksack. Which one did she put it in? She can't remember.

The key is not in her rucksack. She goes through the pockets again, turns the bag upside down and gives it a lively shake. Then she rifles through the underwear she put in the chest of drawers, feeling her way through the socks and pants at first, then throwing everything on to the floor. No key.

She goes into the sitting room and scans the surfaces. She looks under the sofa cushions, inside pots and vases, in the drawers of the sideboard, even though she knows for sure that she didn't put the key in any of those places. She didn't put it *anywhere*. It was in the rucksack.

But now it's gone.

It's not in the kitchen either – not lurking among the food-stuffs or playing with the cutlery. It's not in any of the plastic bags they brought full of shopping, or in the bin. It hasn't fallen out of her pocket on to the floor of the outside loo, or into the log basket. It's not in the porch, playing hide-and-seek with the shoes. She goes through every logical narrative she can think of to explain why the car key, which is on a large plastic fob advertising the hire company, has ended up somewhere strange, somewhere it shouldn't be; which leaves her to draw only one conclusion. Somebody has taken it. But who? And more to the point, why?

It has to be one of the others. Keira is now in the frame for every bad deed, so Sophie goes back to her room and rifles through her stuff. She is feeling desperate now. She needs that key more than anything else in the world. Without it she can't drive the car, can't find a signal, can't talk to Ryan, can't tell Keira what an absolute bitch she is...

The key is somewhere in the house. It has to be. Unless Keira took it with her to the loch. Sophie stops for a second. Yes, of course, that makes sense, dammit. If that's the case, then it's yet more proof that Keira is trying to mess with her.

She hears chatter, the back door opening. Without thinking properly, she rushes into the corridor.

'It was amazing,' says Elise, her skin red raw with cold. 'Freezing but completely amazing. You should have come.'

'Somebody's taken the car key,' says Sophie accusingly.

'What?' Keira looks up from unlacing her boots.

'Nobody's *taken* it,' says Ariel. 'You've mislaid it, that's all.'

'No, I haven't. It was in my rucksack, now it's gone.'

'Have you looked for it?' asks Elise.

'Course I've bloody looked for it. I've searched high and low.'

'Maybe the bogeyman crept in last night and stole it,' says Grace mischievously. Elise shoots her a warning look, and Sophie realises that they've been making fun of her behind her back. She can just picture them treading water in a tight circle, cackling away.

'You don't need it right now,' says Keira. 'I'm sure it'll turn up eventually.'

'Can we please get out of this draughty porch and go to our rooms?' interjects Ariel. 'I'm getting hypothermia here.'

Sophie wants to make them all turn out their pockets, but instead she steps back to let them past.

Forget the car, she thinks. *I'll hitch a lift, walk ten miles if I have to. I've got to talk to Ryan.*

FIFTEEN

THE SWIMMER

I remove my soaking-wet swimsuit and towel myself dry. My fingers are like frozen sausages and I can barely fasten the buttons on my shirt. Pulling on a pair of jeans and some thick socks, I set about rubbing my hair. It's thick and holds moisture easily. What I wouldn't give for a hairdryer... I stand before the mirror, wrapping the towel around my head, squeezing it tight until my forehead hurts.

My reflection grins back at me as I remember how agitated Sophie was just now. She was quite accusatory, I thought. If I lose something, I normally blame myself first, but she came straight out with it. She seems to be cutting herself off from the rest of us. I sniff paranoia.

Last night, after all that fuss about the phantom prowler, she went off to bed in a huff because none of us were taking her seriously. The rest of us stayed up, whispering about her as we played Monopoly. At first everyone was keen to say how much they liked her – including me – and that we were worried about her because she just wasn't herself. A few drinks later and we were all prepared to add that she was being a bit of a pain in the arse. We still liked her, of course. A lot. She was a lovely, generous, warm-hearted person. Without dear Sophie, we wouldn't be here in this fantastic place. We just wished she'd chill out and join the party because... well, she was kind of spoiling it a teeny-tiny bit.

The Monopoly game seemed never-ending, and we were all getting tired and slightly tetchy. I suggested we call it a day, and everyone agreed, making jokes as we went to our rooms about checking for intruders hiding under our beds. I sat up, scheming by candlelight, thinking of ways that I might spook Sophie even more. I contemplated going outside and scraping my fingers down her window, but that felt too much like hard work, and if I was caught, it would have been hard to explain away.

I tried to stay awake. I read until my eyes felt sore and my lids started drooping, then dozed, lurching in and out of dreams. A particularly unpleasant one woke me just after three in the morning – the deadest hour of the night. Easing myself out of bed, I dressed in black, raising the hood of my jacket and wrapping a scarf over my face. Then, taking my little torch, I crept out of my room and made my way down the corridor.

Sophie's door creaked as I opened it. I entered, pushing it behind me so that it rested against the latch, ready for a quick exit. I threw the tiny beam of light over the scene. She was lying on her side facing away from me, submerged in bedding so that all I could make out was the tumble of blonde hair on the pillow. I paused, listening for the sound of her breathing. In and out. In and out. She was deeply asleep, eyelids fluttering rapidly, no doubt.

I felt a bit deflated. There was no point dressing up in my intruder costume if she wasn't at least subliminally aware of me. If I wanted to rouse her, I would have to make quite a noise, which might in turn disturb the others. I thought about shaking her gently, maybe whispering something vile in her ear, but didn't quite have the nerve.

Instead, I cast the torch beam around the room, looking for

her rucksack. She'd tucked it down the side of the chest of drawers. I went over and carefully pulled it free. Putting down the torch, I swiftly rummaged through the side pockets, hoping to find something interesting. My fingers closed around a key fob. Taking it out, I saw that it belonged to the hire car.

I imagined Sophie realising it had disappeared and going into a panic. She'd ask for our help. We'd all be secretly irritated but would join her in the frantic search. Where the hell had it got to? What if it had fallen out of her rucksack on the way here? It could be anywhere, lost for ever. Time would be pressing... what we were going to do without the key? Then I would 'find' it at the last minute and save the day.

Or alternatively, if my plan went badly wrong, I could use the car to escape.

I pocketed the fob and put the rucksack back where I'd found it. Then I crept out of the room, pleased with my night's mischief. Sleep came quickly after that, and I was late waking. The key was still in my jacket. I needed to find a safe hiding place for it, somewhere outside, perhaps, where nobody would think to look. I didn't expect Sophie to notice it had gone missing so quickly. Maybe she was thinking about doing a bunk.

I rub my hair until it's as dry as I can get it and hang my wet towel on the hook behind the door. I have to say, this morning's swim was a-maz-ing. It was so cold the pain was exquisite. And it was a relief not to have Sophie with us, because it meant I could fully enjoy the experience. Whenever I'm with her, I'm on edge, worried that I won't be able to keep up the pretence, that I'll suddenly flip and go for her throat. Deceiving Ryan is much easier, for some reason, which is odd considering how intimate we are. I can zone out with him, imagining I'm with somebody else, or simply not there at all. Sometimes I think about work, or what I need to buy from the supermarket. Sometimes I think about Carly.

I pick my swimsuit off the floor and take it into the garden, squeezing out the water on to the grass. The air smells so sweet. I stand still for a few moments, breathing it in.

Before we left, I fantasised a lot about how I would do it. I pored over photos of rocky mountainsides and dramatic cliff faces. In my head, it was simple: all it would take was a well-timed shove. Sophie would barely notice until she found herself falling, and by the time she landed, it would all be over. But now that I'm here, I can see that it won't be that easy. The landscape is very exposed, and although it's isolated, there are walkers around, not to mention birdwatchers with powerful binoculars. I couldn't be completely confident that nobody had seen me.

No, it has to be a swimming accident, and the loch is the perfect location. This morning, I managed to do a sly recce, swimming away from the group. The water suddenly got even colder. I held my breath and sank a long way down until I touched the bottom, which was very rocky and tangled with weeds. It was brain-numbingly freezing down there. I felt my heart pounding, screaming at me to escape.

I was only in the water for ten minutes, and that was pushing it, so I don't know what the temperature's like around the other side of the loch. There's no easy access, that's for sure, and I reckon the water could be even deeper. The stony beach is the only way to get in safely. Jumping off the bank is never a good idea, and diving is absolutely forbidden. We all know the rules. But an act of carelessness, or recklessness, a slip or a trip... Falling into extremely cold water can send you almost immediately into shock. If you don't know how to respond or if you're injured, it can be fatal.

The biggest challenge will be getting Sophie on her own. We seem to be going around in a clump at the moment, like a flock of sheep. I thought there'd be more splitting off into smaller units. I'd rather not initiate anything; I'll just wait for someone else. Sophie needs to pick me rather than the other way around. Perhaps somebody will suggest pairing off over the next few days, once we've all had enough of the whole group experience. I have to be patient. I've waited nearly twenty years for this, so what harm will a few more days do?

I take out my phone and check for new messages, even though I know there won't be any. It's just habit. I scroll through the dozens of exchanges I've had with Ryan over the past few months, remembering. Funny how sometimes you can search and search for something but only find it once you've stopped looking.

I'd thought about Ryan on and off for years, wondering what had become of him and Sophie, whether they'd stayed together or been torn apart by what happened, whether their love had been so tainted that they'd felt sick every time they kissed. I looked out for him when I went shopping or clubbing. I scanned faces in football crowds, googled his name, searched for him on Facebook, scoured other people's photo galleries for tags. But I couldn't find him. I concluded that either he didn't do social media, or he'd run away to a foreign country, or he was dead. Hopefully the latter.

But somehow I knew he was still alive. I sensed him out there in the ether, going about his life, unencumbered by grief or shame, while my family carried the memory of Carly around on our backs, weighing us down day after day, month after month, year after year. I didn't have a clear idea about what I would do if I bumped into him in the street, but I wanted to know where he was in case one day I decided to do something.

Time passed, but it didn't seem to get any easier. We were dealing with Carly's death in different ways, and none of them had any chance of healing us. Mum had become virtually housebound with agoraphobia and Drew was heavily into drugs. Cousin Billie withdrew into himself. My addiction was sex. I couldn't do the boyfriend–girlfriend thing, couldn't contemplate ever trusting a man enough to marry or have kids.

Yet I needed intimate contact with other human beings, even –
no, especially – if it was loveless and perfunctory. I couldn't
bear to love somebody new for fear that they would leave me, so
I didn't commit and always left first.

I turned to the internet. Normal dating apps were no good
for me. I didn't want to meet fun-loving guys for romantic walks
in the countryside. I wanted stranger danger, anonymous hook-
ups, one-night stands. The apps that catered for married people
wanting discreet encounters suited me down to the ground. If
the guy was already attached, then there was no chance of
things developing, or so I thought.

That's where I found Ryan. It was purely by accident,
although now I think the revenge gods got sick of waiting and
decided to move the drama along a bit. When his picture
flashed up on my phone screen, I swear my heart stopped
beating for a couple of seconds. Not because his good looks and
cheeky smile took my breath away, but because I recognised
him.

The passing years – all nineteen of them – had been good to
Ryan. He still had that freshness about him, the lightly freckled
skin, the clear blue eyes, the sandy hair that fell across his forehead in a preppy kind of way. He'd filled out a bit, but only as
any man would. He looked comfortable with himself – even
cocky.

Why was he using this particular app? I wondered. He had
to be unhappily married, or at least sexually deprived. The
thought gave me some instant comfort. I was desperate to know
whether he'd married Sophie, but of course he didn't disclose
that particular piece of information on his short, provocative
profile.

Did I dare make contact? The idea of having sex with Ryan
made me want to throw up, but there was something deliciously
masochistic about it. I was sure he wouldn't remember me. I'd
changed more than he had over the years, and anyway, he

hadn't taken much notice of me back then. I'd just been the pesky little sister who hung around in the background. Besides, I wasn't using my real name on the app, so it was highly unlikely that he'd make the connection.

I sent him a message, saying how fit he looked and how much I'd like to do outrageous, unspeakable things to him. I also sent him a few provocative selfies, to which he responded very enthusiastically. He wanted to meet me, so I invited him over to my place. I knew it was incredibly risky, but I didn't care. I was going to confront him, maybe even poison his wine or stab him to death in my bed. Oh my God, I had some wild fantasies about how I was going to make him beg for mercy.

But it didn't turn out like that. I found I was attracted to him. The sex was really hot, better than with any of the other guys I'd met. I liked playing games with him, stringing him along, winding him up like a clockwork toy and letting him go. He kept insisting he was just in it for the sex, but I could see that he was falling in love with me.

One evening, when we were lying in bed after a really intense session, he pushed a strand of hair off my face and said, 'It's strange, but you remind me of a girl I once knew. Long ago, when I was a teenager.'

'Really?' I said, my pulse quickening. 'How come?'

'I don't know, can't put my finger on it. You don't look like her, but you've got the same beautiful soft skin.' He bent his head and nuzzled into my neck. 'Mm... and the same smell. I can't explain it.'

'Did you love her?' I asked, trying not to show any emotion, even though it was bubbling up inside me.

'Oh yes, very much,' he replied sadly. 'I didn't realise how much until it was too late. I went off to uni and met this other girl. She kind of took control. Before I knew it, we were living together and... I don't know... it got complicated. I didn't handle it very well.'

'Why? What happened?'

He rolled on to his back, heaving a sigh. His eyes were misty with tears. 'I don't want to talk about it,' he said. 'It's too painful. But I'll never forgive myself as long as I live.'

'And this other girl you met... what happened to her?' I asked.

'Sophie? Oh. I married her... That's why I'm here, I guess. With you.'

After that, my target changed. I didn't need to punish Ryan – he was doing that job perfectly well enough by himself. It was Sophie I wanted to hurt. She thought she'd won the prize, but she'd received faulty goods, damaged beyond repair. Yet a failed marriage wasn't enough. Nor was the fact that I, Carly's kid sister, was having an affair with her husband. I wanted more...

I hear my name being called and shake myself free of my memories. It's lunchtime, and the flock have to eat together. This afternoon we're going for a walk. I turn back to the house and compose myself. Nice smile, soft eyes, cheery voice. A skipping rhyme from school pops into my mind. *All in together girls, never mind the weather girls...*

Out I go.

SIXTEEN

SOPHIE

Sophie sneaked out while the others were in their rooms, drying themselves and getting dressed. Stupidly she forgot to bring the map and now has to try to remember the way back to the road. It's not even forty-eight hours since they arrived, but so much has happened, it feels like weeks. She was in a trance when she made the walk to the house and just followed the group unthinkingly, her head too full to appreciate the scenery or remember any landmarks. Besides, walking in the opposite direction changes the landscape entirely. It all looks completely new to her: the stepping stones over the rushing stream, the steep hill littered with rocks and rough wet grass, the forest of spindly birch trees, the uneven stones and earthy puddles underfoot. It's as if she never passed this way before.

There are a few signposts, thankfully – triangles painted on wooden posts at junctions, indicating a path down to the loch or upwards to the Prince's Cairn, where there is a famous view. She decides to go straight on, although straight is hardly the word. The path twists and turns as it follows the contours of the hillside; one minute she is on a steep, heart-thumping climb, the next she is edging her way down a muddy slope. There is very little to hold on to. If she fell now and twisted her ankle, she would be completely stuck.

She stops by an outcrop of large grey rocks at the top of a hill and takes out her phone. There is a small chance that she might pick up a signal. One bar won't be enough; she needs at least two, ideally more. She doesn't want the call with Ryan to keep breaking up, or to get halfway through the conversation and lose the connection entirely. It would be better to wait until she has decent Wi-Fi and make an internet call. She holds the handset up to the sky, hoping against hope. There's nothing, not even a glimmer of a signal. What's more, her battery is really low. She has the charger with her. If she can just make it to the road in one piece, hitch a lift to the nearest town, find a café, set herself up with a nice cup of coffee and a seat in the corner, plug herself in...

She keeps trudging uphill, the same thoughts rumbling endlessly through her head. Is it Keira? Is Fred her code name for Ryan? Did she take the car key, and if so, why? She didn't give anything away when Sophie questioned her, but then nor did anyone else. If Keira *isn't* having an affair with Ryan and this Fred is some other guy, then reading her messages was a really bad thing to do. Sophie hates the way this situation is turning her into somebody she doesn't recognise, or like. She's never done anything like that before.

Even when Ryan originally confessed, she didn't try to hack into his laptop, or read his texts, although mainly because she couldn't bear to know the gory details. She tried to retain some dignity, although inside she felt ashamed that he'd cheated on her. During those difficult times, when she didn't know who to turn to, she read lots of blogs about infidelity. Other people were feeling exactly the same thing, so it was obviously a common victim response. The couples counsellor questioned her about it several times. *What have you got to be ashamed of? Surely Ryan is the one who messed up.* He agreed that if anyone should feel ashamed, it was him. Except he didn't feel anything of the sort. He was sorry it had happened and admitted that mistakes had been made, but it was all in the passive voice. He wouldn't own the shame, so it was left for her to deal with, like when the kids were sick and she had to mop up their vomit.

Shaming and blaming, that's what the counselling sessions were basically about. Was it all Ryan's fault or had Sophie contributed in some way? By not maintaining her attractiveness, perhaps, or giving too much attention to the kids, or being too tired to have sex. There was this huge bag of marital rubbish and neither of them knew who it properly belonged to, whose turn it was to put it out. Most sessions, they opened up the bag and emptied the rubbish on to the floor, picked it over, tried to remember how the various items had got there in the first place. Occasionally they decided something wasn't rubbish after all and removed it, but mostly they tidied everything away at the end of the session and carried the bag home, as heavy and stinking as before. Sadly, no men in high-vis jackets and a bleeping truck ever came to take it away. It just sat there in the corner of their relationship, waiting to be taken to the next session, where the whole pointless process was repeated until they fly-tipped it somewhere en route between the therapy centre and home.

All that seems a long time ago now, thinks Sophie as she continues with her ascent. The landscape around her is a patchwork quilt, woven in shades of brown. Clouds hanging mistily over the horizon like a gauze curtain. The path follows the line of the massive loch – more like a fjord really – that lies deep in the valley, snaking its way towards the sea. It is an extraordinary view, but today, the epic scale of the scenery barely touches her. She is experiencing everything internally and could be walking anywhere. Right now, the landscape provides nothing more than an obstacle course, preventing her from talking to Ryan.

She needs to hear it from his own mouth, although in one

respect it no longer matters who he has been screwing this past year. Whether it's Keira, Grace, Elise, Ariel (unlikely) or none of them at all, he can't do any more damage than has already been done. The marriage is over, the holiday wrecked, her love of wild swimming ruined for ever. But she would still like to know for sure who the bloody woman is, because she wants to have it out with her, face to face. She wants her to admit the deception and accept the consequences. Two little boys are going to be growing up with separated parents, at least one of whom hates the other. Sophie can't shoulder the burden of shame for three people. Her husband's lover has to be forced to take her share. And so it goes on, churning through her brain. The composing, the rehearsing, the damning lines, the cutting phrases, the irrefutable arguments...

She suddenly has the sensation that she's not alone. Her ears prick and she silences her inner voice. There's the sound of steady plodding footsteps behind her. Hill walkers, she supposes, stopping and turning around. It's a man, on his own, twenty paces or so away. She's surprised that she's only just become aware of him. Where has he come from?

He's wearing dark trousers and a large black waterproof jacket that goes down to his knees. Black boots, black woolly hat. Her stomach sickens as she remembers the figure she saw running away from the bothy; she's sure it was him. Is this a coincidence, or has he been following her all this time?

He raises a hand in a cheery wave, and she finds herself rooted to the spot, as if she's waiting for him to catch up. As he comes towards her, she can look at him more closely. He is in his thirties, she reckons, his features obscured by a large dark beard and bushy eyebrows. There's a small rucksack on his back and he's carrying a long stick, something he might have found on the ground, or snapped from a tree.

'Hi,' he says, reaching her. He's slightly out of breath from hurrying. 'Awesome, isn't it?' He gestures at the scenery.

'Mm,' she agrees. 'Beautiful.'

'I've been walking for three hours and you're the first person I've met. You can't say that for many parts of the UK.'

He takes his rucksack off and finds a bottle of water. They exchange a few more pleasantries while he drinks, although he does most of the talking, asking her if she's on holiday, where she's staying, whether this is her first time in the Highlands. He seems really nice and friendly, but she still feels suspicious. It's the black clothing. And why is he asking all these questions, like he's pumping her for information? She tries not to look in his eyes, keeps her answers deliberately vague and brief.

'You must be staying at Condie's Retreat,' he says, screwing the lid back on the bottle. 'There's nowhere else around here, not for miles. What's it like?'

'Great,' she says.

'It's a large place to hire on your own. Are you part of a group?'

'That's right. Some friends.'

'Are you the swimmers?'

She starts. 'What?'

'I saw some women swimming this morning, in the small loch not far from the house. I don't think you were among them, though. Hard to tell. People look different with no clothes on.' He catches her alarmed expression. 'Not that anyone was naked, I mean, they had swimsuits and hats on. I wasn't spying! I was just out walking and came across them accidentally. As soon as I realised, I went the other way.' His cheeks pinken with embarrassment. 'Sorry if that sounded a bit... I'm not a pervert.'

'What *are* you then?' she asks, testing him.

'A journalist.'

'What sort of journalist?'

'Hmm... I'm mainly interested in ecotourism. I blog – on my own site, as a guest – and do occasional pieces for the nationals.

At the moment, I'm researching a book about the Rough Bounds.'

'Oh. Where's that?'

'Here! We're standing right in the middle of them.' He sweeps his arm in a wide circle. 'From the mountains over there down to the big sea lochs and as far as the coast. The area is incredibly biodiverse but largely inaccessible. There used to be several settlements, but nobody lives here now, not full-time. It's too hard. But ecotourism is edging its way in.'

'Digital detox holidays,' she says.

'Exactly. It brings great benefits to the local economy, of course, but it also threatens the environment.'

'Condie's Retreat has virtually no carbon footprint,' she assures him. 'There's no electricity, a compost loo—'

'I know, it's a cool place. Actually, I was supposed to be staying there this week so I could write a piece, but when the booking agency found out I was a journo, they got jittery and cancelled the booking.'

Yes, she remembers, Fern said there'd been a last-minute cancellation, which was why the house was free.

'I decided to come anyway,' he continues. 'I've been staying in a bothy on the beach, a couple of miles further west. Not exactly five-star accommodation, but it's free.'

His story is making sense. Relief starts to flood through her. 'I know it,' she says. 'It's part of that abandoned village.'

'That's right. This is the last week of the season. After that it's supposed to close, although anyone can break in. There are no locks, it's all done on trust.' He seems to study her face, and she wonders whether he saw her going into the bothy, whether he knows she rummaged through his things, but he's smiling at her and his expression is open and warm. She dismisses the idea.

'So... do you just go on walks every day?' she asks.

'Pretty much.'

'How about at night?'

He makes a scoffing noise. 'Are you kidding? No way. This terrain is dangerous enough as it is. I'd break my neck. I always make sure I'm back at the bothy before it gets dark.'

She remembers the printout, the image of a figure drowning. 'And the wild swimming... are you interested in that too?'

'No thanks, I hate cold water.'

'As a journalist, I mean.'

'Oh. Yeah, I am, actually.'

'Why?'

'Well, it's a thing, isn't it? There's hardly a pond left in the country that hasn't been invaded by menopausal women.' She raises her eyebrows, and he realises he's overstepped the mark.

'That's not why we do it,' she replies sharply.

'No. Sorry, I didn't mean... It's just a joke everyone makes. It seems to attract more women than men, yet it can be very dangerous.' He pulls a sheepish face. 'Why *do* you do it, as a matter of interest?'

'Um... look, it's been nice to chat...' she sidesteps, 'but I've got to press on.'

'Right. Of course. Don't let me keep you. Um... where are you going? Just so that we don't bump into each other again.' He laughs awkwardly.

'Back to the road. I need to make a call.'

'Ah. Best of luck with that. You'll probably have to drive all the way to Mallaig.' He sighs. 'But that's what I love about this place. It's so cut off, so pure, like you're in another time, another world.'

'It's also extremely inconvenient,' she says. 'Bye.'

He waves her off. 'Good to talk, Sophie. Maybe we'll see each other again, eh? If you go to the beach, look me up. I'm here all week.'

She walks away, glad that he doesn't attempt to follow, not even at a distance. She reaches the top of the hill, then immediately starts the descent, following a crooked track marked with rocks and flat stones. Their conversation replays in her head. Was it a chance meeting, or did he deliberately come after her today? Everything he said was in line with the stuff she found in the bothy – the map, the details about Condie's Retreat, even the printout about wild swimming. The only thing he wouldn't admit to was prowling around the house at night, and he'd given a perfectly reasonable explanation as to why he wouldn't do that. She bites her lip. It must have been an animal she saw, or the reflection of candlelight in the glass. Unless he *is* a pervert after all.

Time is getting on. She takes out her mobile again and checks for a signal. Surprise, surprise, there's nothing, and her battery level has gone down to a disastrous 5 per cent. The guy said she'd have to go to Mallaig, and he clearly knows what he's talking about. What was his name again? She sifts through their conversation, but can't find any mention of it. No, they definitely didn't exchange names.

And yet when they said goodbye, he called her Sophie.

SEVENTEEN

SOPHIE

There's a fresh urgency in Sophie's pace as walks on in the direction of the road. She feels scared. What if he's still following her and she's not aware of it? She keeps turning around to check, but he's not there. Her eyes dart around the bleak, rugged landscape. Could he be crouching behind that boulder, or hiding among the birch trees? She imagines him crawling on his stomach through the undergrowth, stalking her like a deer.

Her surroundings feel hostile, conspiring with the enemy against her. Strange that about ten minutes ago they were having quite a nice chat. He certainly did a good job of reassuring her. Now she thinks he must have been watching her that day on the beach and saw her going back into the bothy. She wasn't very careful about putting those papers back where she found them. He knew she'd seen the stuff about Condie's Retreat and decided to deal with the problem head on by 'bumping into her' this morning with the aim of throwing her off the scent. Only he slipped up. Called her by her name when she hadn't given it to him.

All of which means he is targeting her.

He has to be a contact of Ryan's mistress – such a stupid term, like something out of a nineteenth-century novel. But 'lover' is too good for her; it gives her too much status and romanticises the relationship. This mystery guy... is he some kind of hit man, then? She laughs out loud at the possibility, remembering his soft voice and self-deprecating manner, his green credentials. He could have been putting on an act, of course, but that beard was genuine, it must have taken months to grow. The idea is absurd. But then she also remembers the panic in Ryan's voice during that call at the service station, when he begged her not to continue with the trip. He told her she was in danger, but she didn't believe him, not in the sense that she could be physically hurt. But if her rival has hired someone to cause her harm...

I'm taking this way too far, she thinks. *Got to calm down. The toxic atmosphere at the house and the remote landscape are doing my head in.*

Okay... so back on planet earth... what if she *did* tell the journalist her name but immediately forgot? If she could remember *his* name, that might suggest she also gave him hers. She tries a few on for size as she stumbles down a sharp decline, picking her way across moss-slimy stones, skirting around swathes of thick mud. Josh, Rob, Matt, George, Tom, Luke... They are all good fits, but none jogs her memory. Maybe they exchanged names at the beginning of the conversation but she was on autopilot, not really listening or engaging. She's had a lot on her mind these past couple of days; she knows she's been distracted and acting a bit strangely. There is the distinct possibility that she's being paranoid, that he's just a nice, normal guy with a beard who writes blogs about ecotourism.

She reaches the stone bridge over the railway line, thankful to find something she remembers from her outward journey at last, something that's part of the solid, man-made world. Leaning over the brick parapet, she looks down at the tracks.

Trains connecting towns and cities, tarmac, concrete, cars, gas, electricity, petrol, phones, Wi-Fi – all that toxicity she was so keen to get away from, how she longs for it now. She tries to gather herself together. Everything's okay. It's not far to the road, another fifteen minutes' walk at the most. She knows what she has to do. Cadge a lift to Mallaig, find a café, recharge the mobile and make some calls. Ryan first, get that over and done with. After that, she wants to chat to her gorgeous little boys.

Pressing on, she refocuses her thoughts on Ben and Louie. She hopes they're not missing her too much. They get on extremely well with her parents, so they're probably having so much fun they haven't given Mummy a second thought. That's how it should be. But right now, she'd give anything to see their cheeky smiling faces, to listen to their detailed accounts of goals scored against Grandad, or how many muffins Grandma let them eat in one go. When Sophie was a girl, she always stayed with Nan in the school holidays. According to her mother, she was spoilt rotten, but she never saw it that way. The rules were just different at Nan's house.

She retraces the last steps, down a path that runs alongside a fence. As she reaches the road, her shoulders drop. The hire car is still there, thank God – not that she can drive it away, but at least it hasn't been stolen. Her legs are aching; she'd love to sit down and get out of the cold. She goes to the Zafira and checks the doors, on the outside chance she forgot to lock them, but no such luck.

The road is quiet, but there are several cars parked up in the lay-by. It's a popular starting point for walkers heading down to the lochs or up to the cairn. Sophie considers waiting for one of them to come back. Surely, if she told them she'd lost her car key, they'd be happy to help. But all the beauty spots are hours away; it could take a while for anyone to return, and by the time she's reached Mallaig, done what she needs to and found her way back, it might be too late to make the long trek back to the house.

Perhaps there's a signal here. She takes out her phone to check, but the wretched thing has died. She sinks down on the kerb, weary and fed up. It must be lunchtime, because her stomach is gurgling for food. Reaching into her day bag, she takes out a bottle of water and a snack bar. As she chews, she realises that she doesn't want to go back to Condie's Retreat. Not today, not ever. She wants to go home. Or rather, she wants to go to her parents' house, where her boys are. She cannot do battle with Ryan or his mistress – it's horrible and undignified. Let them have each other.

A new plan starts to take shape. First she needs to get to Mallaig. There's bound to be a hotel there, or at least a bed and breakfast. Even a youth hostel would do. She'll call the hire company and ask them to send a replacement key. It could take a day or two, but as soon as it arrives, she'll come back here, collect the car and drive away.

But there are several flaws in this plan. The others think she has simply gone for a walk. When she doesn't return, they'll worry that she's had an accident, and there's no way of letting them know that she's safe. She's got no choice. She has to get back to Condie's Retreat before darkness falls.

She stands up and goes to the edge of the lay-by. Her eyes scan the long, winding road as she waits for a car or a truck to appear. Maybe buses travel this route, she thinks. She can't recall noticing any stops, but it's possible that you just have to flag them down. Her thumb is at the ready. Surely somebody will take pity on her and give her a lift.

A few cars pass. She sticks out her arm and tries to wave them down, but they are travelling at speed and don't seem to notice her. Her surroundings seem bleak and desolate, echoing her mood. Perhaps she'd do better if she stood on the other side of the road, heading back to Fort William. It's further away, but it's a bigger town than Mallaig. However, even fewer vehicles seem to be going in that direction. She tries standing in the road to make herself better seen, even though she risks being run over. A couple of lorries pass, ignoring her completely, and the driver of a minibus gesticulates at her to get out of the way.

If she's not careful, time is going to run out. She feels chilly from standing on the spot, and starts stepping from one foot to the other as she tries to decide what to do. Then, after a few minutes, she hears the sound of people chatting coming towards her. Feeling hopeful, she turns round and goes to meet them at the end of the path.

It's a family, two parents and three kids – a teenage girl and two young boys who immediately remind Sophie of her sons. They are a homogenous group, warmly dressed in identical waterproofs, woolly hats and stout walking boots. Their cheeks are rosy with effort and their eyes are bright.

'Hi,' says Sophie as they emerge at the roadside.

'Hello,' replies the mum, and the dad nods a greeting. The teenage girl looks away, slightly embarrassed, while the boys break free and run towards the family car, which is parked further along the lay-by.

'Um...' Sophie hesitates, unsure of how to start. 'Sorry to bother you... um...'

'Are you okay?' the mum asks.

'No, not really. Actually, I've had a bit of a disaster.'

'Really? What's wrong? Broken down?'

'No. Lost the car key.' She points to the Zafira. 'I'm staying in a holiday rental, you know, way out in the wilderness, middle of nowhere, with some friends. I need to contact the hire company, only there's no signal down there, or even electricity, and now my phone has just died.' She looks at the couple appealingly.

'Oh dear,' says the man. 'Can we help in any way?'

'Oh please. At least, I hope so. I need to get to the nearest town, basically, or anywhere that's got power. I've been trying to hitch a lift, but it's like I'm invisible. I mean, is it against the law in Scotland?'

'Boys! Stay still, this is a main road, not a playground!' he barks at his sons before responding to Sophie. 'No, I don't think it's against the law, but people are wary these days. We're going back to Fort William now. We'd give you a lift, but unfortunately, we're full. Sorry.'

Her heart sinks. 'Oh well, never mind. Thanks anyway.' She turns to go.

'Hold on,' the woman says. 'If you want to make a call, I can you lend you my mobile.' She takes it from a pocket inside her jacket. 'I don't know if there's a signal out here, but it's worth a go.'

'Oh, wow, thank you so much,' says Sophie, her face breaking into a smile. The woman enters her passcode, then passes the handset over. The couple stare at her, waiting for her to make the call. They obviously have no intention of allowing her to walk off with it. Sophie hesitates. She feels embarrassed as she realises that she doesn't have the number of the car hire company with her. Her main aim was to call Ryan, but she can't speak to him in front of these strangers.

'Shit... I didn't bring the number. Is it okay if I call my husband instead? Ask him to sort it out?'

'Yeah, yeah, go ahead.'

'Just don't make it too long a chat, if that's okay,' the man adds. 'The kids are getting cranky – we need to go find some lunch.'

'No, sure, that's fine, no worries, I'll just... er... Excuse me.' She walks away from them and leans against the Zafira. The man goes to their car, while the woman waits, watching her every move.

Luckily she knows Ryan's mobile number off by heart. She

dials it and waits nervously for him to pick up. When it goes to voicemail, she almost feels relieved.

'Ryan, it's me. Listen, this is urgent. I want you to come and get me. You know where I am, I left you all the details. You were right, I should never have come on this trip. I don't know who your... your... who, er... who this *woman* is, but it's driving me insane and wrecking everything. We need to have it out. I just want the truth, okay? I need to know. Just get here as soon as you can. Please? You owe me this.'

She ends the call and turns back to face the woman, who is already holding out her hand for the phone. 'Thanks so much,' she says, giving it back. 'You saved my life.'

'What are you going to do now? Wait for the hire company?'

'No, no. My husband didn't answer, so I had to leave a message. I've got no choice but to go back to the house.'

'How far away is it?'

'About an hour and a half's walk.'

'Okay... Sorry we couldn't squeeze you in. The boys have booster seats, and my husband's a stickler for safety.'

'No, that's fine, I understand. I've got two boys too, about the same ages. Kids are precious, it's not worth the risk.'

'Exactly.' She nods approvingly. 'Anyway, better get on. Best of luck with the keys. Keep looking. They're bound to turn up eventually.'

Sophie thanks her again and they say goodbye. The car makes a U-turn and drives away. She watches until it disappears around the bend, feeling jealous of the happy family. Then, with a heavy heart, she sets off back to the house.

EIGHTEEN

SOPHIE

'Sophie!' cries Elise as she steps through the door. 'Where the hell have you been? We were about to send out a search party.'

'I went for a walk.' She pulls off her hat and gloves. 'I left a note, didn't you see it?'

'Yes, but that was hours ago. It's getting dark.'

Grace enters the hallway from her room. 'There you are! We thought you'd got lost or had an accident.'

'Sorry. I didn't mean to... I just needed some time to myself.'

Elise frowns. 'That's at least the third time you've said that. You sure you're okay? You missed your swim today, that's so unlike you.'

'It wasn't the same without you there,' adds Grace. 'You're like our coach, or our mascot.'

'I'm fine, really I am.' Nevertheless, the two women study her curiously as she fumbles with the zip of her coat.

She takes it off and hangs it on a peg, then removes her muddy boots and walks into the kitchen, where Ariel is chopping vegetables by candlelight. She has a colourful scarf wrapped around her head and is wearing a fisherman's smock and baggy trousers.

'Hi,' says Sophie.

Ariel looks up. 'Hello, stranger. I was wondering whether you'd run away.' She waves her knife. 'Hope you don't mind, but I thought somebody needed to get started.'

'Oh shit, I'm supposed to be cooking tonight, aren't I? I'm so sorry, I completely forgot.'

Ariel smiles. 'It's not a problem.'

'Just let me make a cup of tea, then I'll get stuck in.'

'It's okay, Sophie, I'm quite happy to do it all. I like cooking. There's nothing else to do.'

'Thanks, Ariel.' There's still some water in the kettle, so Sophie ignites the stove and puts it on to boil. She peers into the bread bin. 'Okay if I finish off this crust? I only had a cereal bar and an apple for lunch.'

'Help yourself. There's some honey in the cupboard.'

'Great.'

Ariel continues preparing the vegetables. 'You were out a long time. Where did you go? Somewhere interesting?'

'I went back to the road, actually.'

'Really? All that way? Why?'

'I needed to call my husband.'

She raises her eyebrows. 'Isn't that kind of breaking the rules? This is supposed to be a digital detox, isn't it?'

'Yes, but I was missing my kids. Anyway, by the time I got there, my phone had died.' Sophie smears some honey on the bread. 'Luckily there were some other walkers about. A kind woman let me use her phone, but Ryan didn't pick up. It was a bit of a waste of time, to be honest.'

'Sorry to hear that.'

She swallows her mouthful. 'How about you?'

'Well... we had a lovely walk this afternoon. We were trying to get up to the cairn, but we set off too late and ran out of time. We need to allow the whole day really.'

The kettle whistles. Sophie takes it off the hob and pours

the boiling water over a tea bag. 'Remember I found those papers in that bothy? About this place? Well, I bumped into the guy who's been staying there. He's a journalist, writes about ecotourism. He was supposed to be staying here to do a piece about Condie's Retreat, but the agency cancelled his booking. We had quite a long chat.'

'Oh well, that explains it,' smiles Ariel. 'Mystery solved.'

Sophie sips her tea thoughtfully. 'Hmm... I know everyone thinks I'm paranoid, but... I think he was following me. Deliberately. And er... he already knew my name.'

Ariel creases her forehead. 'What do you mean?'

'He called me Sophie, and I'm pretty certain I didn't tell him.'

'But you had a long chat, so perhaps you mentioned it and forgot.'

'I suppose I *might* have, but... I don't think so.' She traces a circle of wet tea on the wooden table. 'I think he's spying on us. He admitted that he'd watched you swimming this morning, and I've a feeling he was here last night, you know, wandering around in the dark...'

Ariel puts down the chopping knife. 'You think he's a peeping Tom or something?'

'I don't know. It's just odd, isn't it? He seemed like a nice enough guy, quite young, an eco-warrior type. Not your standard pervert.'

'He's probably looking for juicy material for his article,' she says.

'Yes, I'm sure you're right.' Sophie rises from the chair. 'Got to charge my phone. I know I can't use it, but I still like to know the time. Does Keira's solar charger need actual sunlight to work, or does it store power?'

'No idea. Ask her.'

'Okay.'

'And, um... that thing I told you, about Keira, you won't say anything, will you?'

'No.'

'She confided in me, and I shouldn't have told you. It's nobody else's business.'

Sophie checks that no one is in hearing distance, then lowers her voice to a whisper. 'The thing is... and this really is a secret, Ariel, so please don't tell the others... I think the guy she's seeing could, er... possibly be my husband.'

Ariel looks aghast. 'What? Oh my God, Sophie, that's... I mean, how do you know? Are you sure?'

'No, not completely, but it all adds up. Ryan didn't want me to come on this trip. He tried everything, but I wouldn't budge. In the end, he called me at the service station on the way up here and confessed he was having an affair with one of you.'

Ariel blinks in astonishment. 'But he wouldn't say who?'

'No. I've been in absolute turmoil ever since.'

She lets out a low whistle. 'I knew something was wrong, but I would never have guessed, not in a million years.'

'When you told me what Keira had said to you... well, naturally...'

'Of course, it makes sense. But is that all you've got to go on?'

Sophie leans forward, lowering her voice even further. 'I found some dodgy texts on Keira's phone.' Ariel's eyes widen. 'Yes, I know, I shouldn't have been snooping, but I was desperate. She's been messaging somebody she calls Fred.'

'And it was your husband's mobile number?'

'No, I didn't recognise it, but Ryan could easily have bought a pay-as-you-go. That's what people do, isn't it, when they have affairs?'

'I wouldn't know, I've never cheated on anybody.' Ariel pauses, thinking. 'But Keira could just be seeing somebody whose name is Fred. Another woman's husband.'

'Yes... You're right, it's not proof,' Sophie admits. 'It could still be either Elise or Grace.'

'Not me, though.' Ariel gives her a sardonic smile. 'I'm too old, past my best-before date.'

'Sorry, I didn't mean to assume...' Sophie blusters.

'Actually, I'm not that much older than you. You're what, nearly forty? I'm forty-six, that's hardly ancient.'

'No, of course it isn't. Sorry... you're just so not Ryan's type, that's all.'

'Ah. Too much of a hippy?'

'Yes. And anyway, I can't imagine you doing something like that to me.'

'But you *can* imagine the others?' Ariel looks puzzled. 'You surprise me, Sophie. Keira, Elise, Grace – they're all very fond of you. You inspired us to get in the water... you've changed our lives.'

'I wouldn't go that far.'

'You know what? I think Ryan is lying to you. He's jealous. He doesn't like you having a life of your own and he's trying to destroy it. I used to be married to a man like that, I know how they operate. It's called coercive control.'

Sophie looks down. 'I did wonder about that.'

Ariel grasps her hands, squeezing them tightly as she looks her right in the eye. 'Forget Ryan. Talk to the others. They're your friends. Get them together and ask them outright.'

'No, no, I can't. It's too embarrassing. It'll wreck the holiday.'

'Don't you think it's half-wrecked already? Everyone knows you're really pissed off and that something bad is going on. Let's have it out in the open, get it sorted.'

'Maybe...' she says. 'I'll think about it.'

'*Do* it, Sophie. Before it's too late.'

.   .   .

Sophie leaves the kitchen and goes to her room. She sits on the edge of the bed, feeling disorientated. Confiding in Ariel has helped – it's the first time she's told anyone about Ryan's affair, apart from Miriam David, who doesn't count. The weight that she's been carrying feels a little lighter. She feels tempted to go further and talk to the group tonight. But what if Ryan told her the truth? It would be humiliating to share her pain with her enemy. No, she has to be sure of her facts first. Unfounded accusations can easily be denied, and then she'd have to retreat, apologise even. She'd look weak when she needs to look strong – to *be* strong.

She picks up her mobile and leaves the bedroom. She knocks on Keira's door and calls her name. After a few seconds, Keira opens it and stands guard at the entrance.

'Yes? What is it?'

'Um... I was wondering if I could borrow your solar charger,' Sophie says, trying to sound normal.

'It needs sunlight, you'll have to wait until tomorrow.'

'Ah yes, I thought that might be the case. Thanks anyway.' She shifts. 'I'm, er, sorry about this morning... accusing everyone over the missing key. I just got in a panic.'

'I didn't feel accused.'

'Oh, good.'

'I'm having a rest now. See you later.' Keira slowly shuts the door in Sophie's face.

Keira emerges at dinner time and sits next to Sophie at the table. The chatter is lively and full of good-natured humour, but Sophie detects a false undertone. It's as if everyone has been instructed to be on their best behaviour. Maybe Ariel has had a private word with the others, asking them to cut her some slack. She hopes to God she didn't say why. Ariel is a bit of a gossip – she'll have to be more careful in future. She swallows down her third glass of wine, already feeling fuzzy at the edges. The others are drinking heavily too, digging into supplies that are supposed to last them the week.

As the evening progresses, the atmosphere becomes more febrile and unstable. Sophie sways in the dance of the alcohol, leaning into Keira, laughing too loudly at Elise's wisecracks. When Ariel makes a toast to the solidarity of women, Sophie almost lets out a sarcastic cheer. She senses all of them watching her out of the corner of one eye, assessing her state of mind.

'How about another game of Monopoly?' asks Grace later, once they've cleared the table and washed up.

'No, please no,' replies Keira. 'Isn't there anything else?' She goes over to the sideboard and crouches down, digging around among the shelves. 'Scrabble?'

'Boring,' Grace and Elise chorus.

'I'm too pissed,' says Sophie. 'Something easier, please.'

'How about Pop-Up Pirate?'

'I know that one, we've got it at home. It's a kids' game.'

'Yes, I know, I wasn't seriously suggesting it.' Keira rolls her eyes and returns to the others, who are now lolling around on the sofa and armchairs.

The bottle of wine has migrated to the coffee table. Grace tops up everyone's glass. 'If we want to play an *adult* game, I can think of a few,' she says. 'Like Rude Charades... or Would You Rather? We could play Two Truths and a Lie – that's a good one.'

'Do we have to play anything?' asks Ariel. 'Can't we just chat?'

'We've been chatting all day,' says Elise. 'I'm a bit chatted out, to be honest.'

'What about Truth or Dare?' says Keira. 'Everyone knows it, right? We go around in a circle, and when it's your turn, you choose either to answer a question truthfully or do a dare. But there's no wimping out.'

Sophie takes a deep breath. 'Yeah, okay, why not? I'm up for it.'

'Me too,' says Grace. 'Elise?'

She nods. 'Sure.'

'Don't you think we've all drunk too much?' Ariel looks worried. 'We've had a nice evening together, let's not spoil it.'

'Come on, Ariel, it's just a bit of fun,' Elise says. 'If you don't like it, go to bed.'

'Okay, just don't say I didn't warn you.'

Keira does another round with the bottle to drain it, then places it on the rug. 'Elise – do you want to be the first victim?'

'Ha! Why not?'

'We spin to see who gets to ask you a question or give you a dare.'

Elise laughs and pushes her hair over her shoulders. 'Do I have to say first whether I want a truth or a dare, or can I wait to see who I get?'

'You can wait.'

'Okay. Cool. Let's do it.'

They gather round, their faces glowing in the candlelight. Sophie feels her heart racing as the bottle spins past her several times before coming to rest in front of Grace.

'Oh God,' groans Elise. 'I don't trust Grace – her dares will be evil. I think I'd better go for a truth.' She pulls a face of mock terror. 'Eek. This could be so embarrassing!'

Everyone turns to look at Grace, who is grinning all over. 'Um... okay... yup, got one.' She looks straight at Elise. 'Have you ever faked an orgasm, and if so, who with?'

'Course I've faked an orgasm,' Elise cries, 'loads of times. Who hasn't? Honestly, Grace, that's a really tame question.'

'Well, *I* haven't,' remarks Ariel.

'It's not your go,' Grace butts in. 'And Elise hasn't answered the whole question yet. I asked who with.'

Elise shrugs. 'They won't mean anything to you, you don't know them.'

'We want names. Names, names, names!' chants Grace. Keira joins in, giggling. 'Names, names, names!'

'Okay. A guy called Jordan... and another one called...' Elise stops herself. 'No, one name is enough. Jordan was one of my first ever boyfriends. He was very sweet, but he didn't have a clue, so I just made a load of sounds and did some heavy breathing, and he thought everything was fine.'

'You were being kind to him,' says Ariel approvingly.

'Not really. I dumped him two weeks later.' The others laugh. 'Who's next? Are we going clockwise or anticlockwise?'

'Clockwise,' says Grace. 'It's Keira's turn.'

Keira grimaces. 'I hope I don't regret this.' Elise spins the wine bottle. It comes to rest pointing towards Sophie.

Her heart leaps. This is the perfect opportunity to ask Keira outright. *Are you sleeping with my husband?* No, that's too specific. *Have you ever slept with the partner of one of your friends?* She takes a deep breath.

'Have you ever slept—'

'Hang on, I haven't decided what I want yet,' interrupts Keira. She looks at Sophie steadily, taking the measure of her. 'Dare.'

Grace and Elise make an 'ooh' noise, while Ariel looks relieved. Sophie is momentarily flummoxed, the question still sitting in her mouth, desperate to escape.

'Oh, er, right... Um... okay.' She thinks. 'I dare you to go for a swim in the loch.'

'I already did that this morning.'

'I mean now.'

'Now? What, in the dark?'

'Yes. You can take a torch.'

'No, Sophie, that's too much,' says Ariel. 'That's really dangerous.'

'I thought dares were supposed to be dangerous.'

'Not necessarily. Sometimes they can just be gross, like emptying the rubbish bin over your head or smelling some-body's armpit.'

'Okay, she can do that then.'

'No, a dare is a dare,' replies Keira. 'And I play by the rules.'

NINETEEN

SOPHIE

Keira comes out of her bedroom wearing a tracksuit under her dryrobe. 'Ready!' she says. 'Sophie, get your coat on. You're coming with me.'

'No,' Sophie replies. 'This is stupid. It was just a joke – you don't have to do it.'

'Yes, I do. The game was my idea, I said no wimping out and I meant it. You've got to come so you can check I actually get in the water. Put your coat on and bring a couple of torches.' Keira marches into the porch and crouches down to lace up her walking boots.

'You can't do this,' says Ariel, standing over her. 'You're pissed, and it's pitch black out there.'

Keira stands up. 'Come on, Sophie, I'm waiting for you. Anyone else want to come?'

Grace and Elise shake their heads. 'Ariel's right,' says Elise. 'We've all drunk too much to go crashing around—'

'Okay, I'll go on my own then. I'll take some pics of me swimming naked.'

'Keira, stop this now,' says Grace. 'You've made your point, okay?'

'No way.' Keira's eyes are glittering defiantly.

Ariel goes up to Sophie, who is hanging back, feeling guilty. 'You'd better go with her,' she whispers. 'She won't get far in the dark, she'll turn back. Just... you know... look after her.'

'I wasn't thinking, just said the first thing that came into my head.'

'Hmm...' Ariel looks at her disbelievingly. 'Be careful, eh? Don't say anything about... you know. Promise?'

Nodding, Sophie puts on her outdoor clothes. She feels embarrassed, as if she's being punished.

'See you all later.' Keira grabs her arm and almost frog-marches her out of the door.

Outside, it's as dark as dark can be. Their torches make little impact, and Sophie has to train the light on the ground immediately in front of her to find her next step. It's hard enough to make out the edge of the garden and the gate leading to the path. Keira goes ahead, full of bravado and wine, and within seconds has disappeared, as if sucked into a black hole. Sophie can't even make out a beam of light from her torch.

'Not so fast!' she calls, struggling to keep pace. 'I can't see where I'm going, the ground's really uneven...' She sets off down the track. 'I'm sorry, okay? It was a stupid dare – I take it back. Please stop! Keira, talk to me! Turn round – I can't see you.' But there's no response.

The path winds downhill, bordered on one side by a prickly hedgerow and on the other by bare trees, which creak as she passes. She has only been to the loch once and can't remember the way. She can only stumble on half blind. She's scared of tripping over a tree root or a protruding stone, scared of twisting her ankle in a hole. The earth seems to move beneath her, and she slips on a patch of mud. She reaches out in the hope of finding something to hold on to, but all she catches is a handful of darkness. Cursing loudly, she just about manages to save herself from falling. She stops and bends over, catching her breath.

What made her issue such a dangerous dare? she thinks. Was it just a stupid joke, or was a part of her trying to provoke Keira? When she said it, she didn't really think it through. Although the weather is relatively mild, it's still October, and the water will be even more freezing at night.

'Keira!' she calls. 'Wait for me!' She carries on down the slippery slope. 'Hey! Can we just stop now? This is getting stupid.' She stops to listen for a reply, but the air is silent apart from a distant owl, or maybe it's some other night creature, she can't tell. She's a city girl, not made for this.

A twig cracks behind her and she instantly swings around. Did she just see the faint glow of a torch? If so, it's been quickly turned off.

'Keira? Is that you?' Panic rises in her throat. She was sure Keira was in front of her before – did she step to one side to let her go past? 'Where are you? Stop messing about. Say something!' But there's only an edgy silence, as if somebody close by is holding their breath. Sophie sweeps her torch in front of her, but all she can see are the bare tree branches, sticking out like skeleton fingers. She walks towards them, shuddering as they brush against her sleeve. She tries to calm her nerves. Keira went ahead; there's no way Sophie could have passed her without knowing. The noise she heard was probably a fox or a stoat or whatever roams around these woods at night.

She walks on, getting angrier by the second. If Keira won't answer, she might as well turn round and go back to the house. But then the others will be cross with her and they'll worry if Keira doesn't turn up. It'll be all her fault.

The undergrowth is rustling. She imagines small rodents scurrying away, birds roused from sleep. The mud oozes beneath her tread. Another twig cracks behind her. She presses on, walking ever downwards, calling Keira's name.

Suddenly the path opens out and she realises she's reached the loch. There's a new chill in the air, a stingy coldness that pierces her ears. Casting the torchlight around, she finds the edge of the bank, and beyond it a seemingly endless expanse of water – so dark, so flat, so still. She calls Keira's name again, and the sound echoes across the valley.

'Where are you, for God's sake? Just answer me, will you?'

She waves her torch around. Isn't there supposed to be a natural beach here from where you can easily enter the water? All she can see is the edge of a steep bank. She must have taken a wrong turning somewhere along the way and come out in a different place, further around. Maybe that's why Keira's not answering. She must have followed another path and emerged on the other side. She could be preparing to swim – slipping off her dryrobe and her jogging bottoms, hobbling over the stones towards the water.

'Keira!!!' she hollers. 'Please! Don't go in by yourself. I'm coming! Just tell me where you are!'

There's the sound of footsteps behind her, heavy breathing. She turns just in time to see a shape looming out of the darkness. 'Keira?'

The figure grabs her in a kind of rugby tackle, bending low and squeezing her chest, knocking the torch out of her hand. Sophie screams and struggles as she's pushed towards the bank. She tries to break free, tries to keep her feet on the ground, but she's fighting an unstoppable force that's grunting and squeezing and shoving with all their might. She feels the ground slipping beneath her. With one more brutal shove, she's forced right to the edge. *If I'm going in the water, you're coming with me*, she thinks. She grabs hold of some clothing, and they both hit the water with a loud splash.

Sophie touches the bottom, then bounces back up, spluttering, to the surface. The water is indescribably cold, slicing into her brain.

A strange, silent pause follows, and then she feels a hand around her ankle. Before she has a chance to inhale, she's pulled under again. She twists and turns, stabbing with her feet, punching the water with her fists. Her chest tightens, the pain is immense, she's running out of breath. Then suddenly the grip weakens and she is able to kick free. She starts to sink again, but finds the rocky bed and pushes off, slowly rising to the surface.

Her head emerges, eyes wild, mouth open, wet hair falling over her eyes. Her heart is going like the clappers; it's never beaten this fast before. She must be going into cold shock. Fear takes hold of her now. She has to escape before she's attacked again, has to get out of the water before it kills her.

Where is Keira? Still under? No, that's impossible, she must have surfaced. She could be treading water a few feet away and Sophie wouldn't see her. It's so damn dark. But the only splashing and gasping she can hear is her own. Everything is horribly, scarily quiet.

But she can't think about Keira right now, just has to save herself. Emergency mode kicks in. She knows what to do – not to flap her arms or gasp for breath, not to waste valuable oxygen calling for help, not to try to swim. Just lie on her back and float, wait until she can control her breathing. It's counter-intuitive, but if she doesn't follow the rules, she could have a heart attack and drown.

And so, with supreme effort and willpower, she forces the back of her head against the water's surface and lifts her legs. The air trapped between her clothes helps her to stay afloat. She lies there trying not to snatch at breaths but to allow the oxygen to fill her body. The cold is astonishing; she's never experienced anything like it before. Every nerve ending is stinging with pain. But still she lies back and looks upwards. The sky is black; there must be cloud cover tonight, because there are no stars to gaze at, not even a sliver of moonshine to comfort her.

Float. Just float... As if she's in a swimming pool in Spain, relaxing, soaking up the warm Mediterranean sun. Her lovely boys are with her, playing happily in the water. Everyone is safe.

She feels her heart rate gradually slowing to a more normal pace. Good. That's good. Now she can try to swim to the bank. If only she could be sure where it is... The last thing she wants to do is swim into the middle of the loch. That would mean certain death.

She lets her legs drop and turns slowly on to her stomach. Her coat billows around her like an inflatable. Her pupils must have dilated, because she can make out the solid mass of the bank. At least she hopes it's the bank. She starts to doggy-paddle towards it, making gentle movements, keeping her head above water. It only takes a dozen strokes before she manages to grab a fistful of grass. She lunges towards the edge and leans over it for a few seconds, catching her breath. Her upper-body strength is not good, she knows that, and the clothes that were keeping her afloat are now dragging her down. But somehow she has to heave herself out of the water before the loch claims her. Before she's dragged under again.

New strength comes from some unknown place, and she lifts herself upwards and forwards, landing heavily on her chest. From there she wriggles like a worm, pulling with her hands, kicking until at last her feet leave the water. She lies there for a few seconds, her face in the mud, panting. Her extremities have gone numb, she can hardly feel her limbs, but she's alive.

She gradually gets to her hands and knees. She is shivering violently, teeth chattering with cold. Her sodden clothes are sticking to her skin and her boots are full of water. She knows she can't stay here, soaking wet and freezing to death. She has to make a superhuman effort to get back to the house. Call the others. Get help. Somehow. And she has to act fast, before the cold paralyses her and she can't move.

Miraculously, she sees the tiny glow of her torch on the ground. She crawls towards it, her knees scraping over rocks hidden in the grass. As she clasps her numb fingers around the handle, a surge of electricity seems to run up her arm. *Now I have light, I can do this*, she tells herself. Recharged, she slowly she gets to her feet and waves the torch around until she finds the path. She staggers towards it like a monster from the murky depths, dripping slime in her wake.

Sophie doesn't remember what happened next, or how she came to be lying in a crumpled heap halfway up the hillside, but some time later – she has no sense of how long – she's woken by the sound of gentle angelic voices. She blinks open her eyes and sees two blurry faces, the light from their torches creating haloes around their heads.

'Oh my God,' says Elise, touching her coat. 'She's soaking wet.'

Grace nods. 'She must have gone into the water.'

'Sophie, wake up... Are you hurt?'

'Um... no... don't think so... Just tired... cold.'

'Yeah, we're going to take care of you. Where's Keira?'

'Don't... know.'

Grace removes her sodden coat and gives Sophie her jacket. Elise donates her hat, scarf and gloves. They lift her to her feet and, putting an arm around each shoulder, help her back to the house.

Ariel is standing at the front door, holding the paraffin lamp.

'Good God,' she exclaims as they approach. 'Come in, come in.' They take Sophie into the sitting room. 'What happened?'

'We found her on the path,' says Grace. 'I think she was trying to get back to the house. She's been in the water. I'm really worried, she's extremely cold.'

Ariel sets about removing Sophie's wet clothes. 'Where's Keira?'

'Don't know. We thought we'd better rescue Sophie first.'

'Yes, you did the right thing. I knew it was a dumb idea.' She rubs Sophie vigorously with a towel while Elise goes to fetch dry clothes. 'What on earth happened?' she asks. 'Did you fall in?'

Sophie doesn't know how to answer. Images and sensations swirl through her body, but no words come. She remembers being pushed into the water, the tug of a hand around her ankle, kicking out as she tried to free herself, but it could all be a dream.

'We'd better go and look for Keira,' says Grace.

'Yes, God knows what's happened. I hope she's okay.' Ariel sighs. 'Take care.'

Elise and Grace leave. Ariel fetches Sophie's duvet and wraps her up in it. She puts more logs into the burner and fans the flames with the bellows. Then she makes her some tea, although Sophie's fingers are still so numb, she can't take the mug.

Ariel sits on the floor next to her, holding the mug to her lips. 'Tell me what happened,' she says, her voice laced with fear. 'Where's Keira?'

Sophie pauses, then whispers, 'I think she tried to drown me.'

TWENTY

SOPHIE

None of them sleep. After Grace and Elise return from their search – empty-handed – Ariel makes yet more tea, and they drink it in worried silence in front of the log burner.

Sophie is gradually drying from the inside out, but she still feels cold and confused. The alcohol she consumed last night seems to have completely flushed through her system. They are all dead cold sober, although 'dead' is not a word anyone wants to use right now. Nobody has dared to say what they must all be thinking – that Keira is lying at the bottom of the loch and Sophie is somehow to blame.

She told the others what happened – or rather, what she *thinks* happened; it was so dark and she was so drunk that now she can't recall the order of events or the exact details. They are ebbing away from her like the fragments of a dream. All she can remember is the incredible cold and her determination to survive. To see her boys again. Their bright, shining faces kept her afloat and carried her to safety. Everything else is a blur.

It's already been suggested that she simply fell into the water in a drunken stupor, and that if Keira *did* push her, it was just in fun. They've been expecting Keira to turn up, shivering and dripping wet, full of apologies for going too far. But Sophie knows different. She's certain now that Keira is Ryan's lover.

Of course, it was a stupid dare, but Sophie thinks that maybe, on some subterranean level, she deliberately drew Keira out, challenging her to a duel. Keira certainly took the bait. She insisted on going through with it too, and that Sophie come with her. Off they went into the night, Keira storming ahead, refusing to answer Sophie's calls. After that, it got rather murky and vague. Sophie has no memory of seeing Keira in the water, of her coming up for air or of hearing her scream for help. Maybe she went into cold shock and had a heart attack. Maybe Sophie let her drown.

The night paralysed their search, but now the dawn is breaking. The sky is daubed with pink and lavender streaks and the daylight is making everything inside look tawdry and miserable by comparison. Sophie just wants to be back in her own house, making dippy eggs for breakfast, ironing a mountain of school shirts, listening to the joyful sounds of Ben and Louie playing upstairs.

Ariel heaves herself out of her armchair and extinguishes the lamps. 'Okay, it's light enough for us to search again,' she says with a certain authority. 'Maybe Keira managed to get out of the water. God knows what state she'll be in – I shudder to think – but we can't leave her out there a second longer.' She bites her lip. 'It may already be too late.'

Elise immediately stands up and stretches her stiff limbs. 'Don't say that. We've got to be positive.'

'It was bloody cold last night, though,' says Grace. 'Sophie hasn't completely warmed through yet, and she's been in front of that fire for hours.'

'Keira's very fit and she's not stupid – she'll have known what to do,' Elise reminds them.

'The two of you should never have gone out in the first place,' Grace says as she gets to her feet. 'It was utter stupidity.'

Sophie frowns. 'I was trying to stop her.'

'But you gave her the dare.'

'I didn't think she'd go through with it. I kept calling out, begging her to stop, but she marched off ahead, she wouldn't listen.'

'Hold on, that doesn't make sense,' says Ariel. 'You said she came up behind you.'

'I think maybe she hid and let me go past. Or I took a wrong turning and then she came to find me. It was pitch black – I couldn't see a thing.'

'And you're sure she went into the water with you?' Elise's expression is pleading with her to say no.

'Yes… At least I think so. I went under and she tried to grab me by the ankle.'

'Hmm. Perhaps you got caught in some reeds.'

'Well… yes, that's happened to me before, but at the time, it felt like a hand.' Sophie hesitates. 'To be honest, I don't know any more, I was too busy fighting for my life.' She shivers at the memory.

Elise picks up her coat from the back of a dining chair and puts it on. 'We don't have time to analyse this. Are we all going back out there, or what?'

'Yes, we should separate and take different paths,' says Grace. 'How about you, Sophie? Are you feeling up to it?'

'I'm not sure, but, um, yes, I'll come, of course.' She has to show willing, even though going back to the loch is the last thing on earth she wants to do right now.

The others finish getting ready, pulling on boots and hats. Sophie emerges from her cocoon like a reluctant butterfly and makes her way to the porch. Her coat and boots are still soaking wet from last night, so she puts on her dryrobe and a pair of trainers instead.

Ariel opens the door and a blast of chilly morning air whooshes down the corridor. 'Hold on, everyone,' she says.

'Before we separate, I think Sophie needs to explain what's been going on between her and Keira.' She throws Sophie an encouraging look. 'It's only fair.'

Elise stops zipping up her coat. 'What?'

'Um... well...'

'More like going on between her *husband* and Keira,' Ariel says, obviously rather proud of herself for being in the know.

'What do you mean?' asks Grace.

'Well... I'm not absolutely sure, but...' Sophie's cheeks flush pink, 'I think they've been having an affair.'

'No way!' Elise's mouth gapes. 'You're kidding me. Keira and... what's his name again?'

'Ryan.'

'Oh my God! I knew something had gone wrong, but I never dreamt...' Grace turns to Sophie, impressed. 'Wow. So you lured her outside last night and confronted her, is that it?'

'No. Not at all.'

'Did you have a fight?'

'No! She ran at me out of nowhere and pushed me in, I told you.'

The three of them stare at her – she can almost see thought bubbles popping over their heads. They don't believe her. They think she's the one who pushed Keira and got dragged in. It's the logical conclusion.

'I was going to talk to her about it, but I needed to make sure it was definitely her first.'

'What do you mean?' Grace looks at her like she's mad.

'Ryan told me he was having an affair with someone in the group, but he refused to give me their name.' Grace and Elise's eyebrows rise simultaneously. 'Yes, I know, it's incredibly embarrassing.'

They take a few seconds to digest the news and recalibrate their understanding of the night's events. 'Why didn't you say anything?' asks Elise eventually.

'Because I knew three of you were innocent and I didn't want to spoil the trip.'

'Yes, but surely—'

'We can discuss this later,' interrupts Grace sharply. 'I don't really care about innocence and guilt. We just need to find Keira.'

'Sorry, you go ahead,' says Sophie, tying her trainer laces with numb fingers. 'I'll catch you up.'

The others leave. Sophie fetches her phone and takes it into Keira's room. It already feels strange not to be knocking on her door. The place is just as messy as the last time she was in here, but it looks even more forlorn now. Keira's absence is almost palpable. A sick feeling rises in Sophie's stomach as she surveys the discarded clothes on the bed. She goes over to the dressing table, where Keira's phone is still plugged into the solar charger. She's tempted to look at her texts with 'Fred' again, but it feels indecent, like going through a dead person's pockets. Dead – there's that word again. *Please, God, don't let Keira be dead*, she thinks.

Instead she quickly unplugs Keira's phone and plugs in her own. The sun is barely up. Who knows when or even if it will make it into the room, let alone whether it will generate enough power to recharge her battery. But she has to try.

She leaves the house, locking the door and putting the key in the safe. She remembers the message she left on Ryan's voicemail, begging him to come. Either he ignored it or he's on his way to Scotland. She really needs to talk to him as soon as possible. How did people manage before mobiles were invented? she wonders as she walks down the path that seemed as impenetrable as Sleeping Beauty's castle last night, but which today looks ordinary and harmless. The darkness plays evil tricks on the mind, she realises. Maybe she did just fall in...

. . .

Two hours later, they've trodden every path and narrow track in the vicinity of the loch, looked behind every tree and bush, but found no trace of Keira. They've shouted her name a thousand times, but she hasn't responded.

Sophie shows them where she thinks she was pushed into the water, but she's not completely sure it's the right place. Everything looks so different in daylight.

They stand in a row, staring at the expanse of dark green water, not daring to speak their thoughts.

'There's no choice,' says Ariel finally. 'We have to call the police, report her missing, say we think there might have been an accident.'

'We could try and find her ourselves, I guess,' Elise replies, although it's clear from her tone that her heart's not in it. None of them wants to dive in and start groping around for a body. Sophie can't bear the thought of swimming ever again. Just the sight of the water is a trigger. She can sense her heart racing, her stomach clenching with anxiety.

'No, we should leave it to the experts,' says Grace firmly. 'We could be destroying evidence.'

'Evidence?' echoes Sophie. 'I didn't commit a crime. She attacked *me*. I didn't do anything except defend myself.'

'Yeah, so you keep saying. It's just that you're okay and she – well – isn't.'

'Hey, we don't know that, not for sure,' says Elise, putting a restraining arm round Grace. 'She could have hitched a ride to Fort William and be having breakfast in some greasy spoon café by now.'

'You think?'

Ariel raises her voice above them. 'We have to inform the police. I'll walk back to the road and call 999 as soon as I can pick up a signal.'

'I'll go with you. My mobile has still got some juice.' Grace takes it out of her pocket. 'Don't ask me why I bring it every time I go out – just habit.'

'I'm not sure I'm up to that long a walk,' Sophie says. 'Sorry. I think I need to go back to the house and rest.'

'Two's plenty. I'll carry on looking for Keira,' says Elise. 'She may have got lost in the dark and gone further afield than she meant to.'

'God, I hope so,' Ariel mutters. 'Because this is starting to feel really bad.'

They start to ascend the path, Ariel's words echoing through Sophie's head. The growing possibility that Keira drowned last night is too much to stomach. She thinks she might actually vomit at any moment. What if the police don't believe that it was Keira who attacked her and not the other way around? There were no witnesses, she has no defence wounds, there are no CCTV cameras hanging from the trees. And when they find out that she had a motive...

Ariel and Grace say goodbye and branch off in the direction of the distant road. Elise takes Sophie's arm. 'Shall I walk back to the house with you?'

'No, I'm okay.'

'You sure? You look pretty shaken.'

'It was going back to the loch, it freaked me out a bit.'

Elise smiles sympathetically. 'You didn't have to come out to look for her, you know.'

'I didn't want people to think...'

'No, I understand.' She stops to tuck the hair back inside her hat. 'I hope you don't mind me asking, but... was the affair already going on when Keira joined the swimming group?'

'Yes, I think so. Otherwise it's a bit of a coincidence, isn't it?'

Elise curls her lip in disgust. 'I'm surprised at Keira, I thought she was better than that.'

'So did I,' Sophie replies, stopping herself just in time from saying that Keira was once her favourite fellow swimmer.

'Do you know what? I'm going to come back to the house with you. I'm worn out. And now I know what Keira was up to, well, I don't feel quite so inclined to bust a gut trying to find her.'

'I still hope she hasn't drowned,' asserts Sophie. 'I didn't mean to hurt her. I just fought back on instinct.'

'You did the right thing. She's a strong swimmer. I expect she climbed out and ran away, like really embarrassed. But if... you know... if she's, er...' Elise grimaces. 'If the worst comes to the worst, I'm sure the police will understand. Just don't lie about any of it, because they'll find you out.'

'I don't need to lie,' Sophie replies.

They walk the rest of the way without talking. The silence between them grows heavier and heavier as Sophie runs through the calamitous situation in her head. She doesn't want the police to find Keira in the loch, doesn't want to be arrested or convicted of anything. How would she survive in prison, and what would happen to her beautiful boys? Oh, the horrible injustice of it all. How she wishes she'd never met Ryan, never fallen in love, never married him, never forgiven him for the affair. Never started Sophie's Swimmers. She wants to be a child again, whose greatest problem is a broken toy or a scraped knee. If only Nan was here, she'd glue everything back together; she'd pick her up and kiss the pain away.

TWENTY-ONE

SOPHIE

Sophie's chest heaves with sobs as Elise gently rubs her back. 'Hey, it's okay, just let it all out,' she says quietly. They are back indoors, sitting together on the lumpy sofa that is fast becoming Sophie's hidey-hole.

'I'm sorry,' she says, her nose blocked with mucus. 'I just can't take it any more, it's too much.'

'That's hardly surprising. You nearly drowned last night – your body is still recovering. It was a really traumatic experience, I expect you're still in shock.' Elise rolls her tongue over her lips. 'You could do with a stiff drink.'

Sophie shakes her head. 'Not at this time of day. I didn't plan all this,' she continues. 'I was furious, I wanted to confront her, give her a piece of my mind, but I never intended to...' She shudders. '...you know, kill her.'

'Who's talking about killing anyone?' Elise frowns. 'She attacked you, right? You defended yourself.'

'Yes, yes, but given the circumstances... how's it going to look to the police?'

'I don't know, but like I said, you just have to be honest and hope they believe you.'

Sophie sniffs up her tears. Her cheeks are damp, and she tries to dry them with her fingers. 'Don't suppose you have any tissues?' she asks.

'In my room, hold on.' Elise nips out, leaving Sophie alone for a few moments. She has to pull herself together and stop behaving like she's guilty, otherwise the police will arrest her on the spot.

Elise returns with a small travel-sized packet and plants it in Sophie's lap. 'There you go,' she says. Sophie thanks her and takes out a tissue, unfolding it and blowing her nose. 'And no more talking yourself into trouble, okay? Keep it simple. It was a stupid drunken dare that got out of hand, end of.'

'But they're bound to investigate, they'll find out,' Sophie says. 'I don't deserve this. Ryan had the affair, but I could be the one going to prison.'

'That's really not going to happen,' Elise assures her.

'I've tried and tried to be a good person all my life. I've devoted myself to my family – to Ryan and the boys. And this is how he repays me!'

'Yeah, well, this Ryan does sound like a spectacular waste of space.' Elise sits back down, curling her legs underneath her. 'How long have you been together?'

'For ever. We met at uni – I was in my first term, and he was in the year above. We lived together for a long time before I finally managed to drag him up the aisle.'

'And how did he meet Keira?'

Sophie shrugs. 'The usual – online. Some disgusting hook-up app. He told me it was a one-off, a short fling. We had counselling and everything. He was really sorry, said it would never happen again. He was lying through his teeth the whole time. It's been going on for over a year. It's still going on.' Or *was*, she thinks, briefly consigning Keira to the past tense.

'Hmm, not surprised you've reached boiling point,' Elise says. 'And to find out she's been kind of stalking you... that is so not on. To be honest, if I was in your situation, I'd have probably drowned her on the first day.'

'I didn't drown her,' says Sophie stiffly.

'No, I know, I'm just trying to say that I understand how you must be feeling. That kind of betrayal is off the scale.' Elise yawns, stretching her arms above her head. 'It'll be ages before Ariel and Grace get back with the police. I'm going to try and get some sleep. So should you.'

'I don't think I'll be able to, but you go ahead. See you later.' Sophie reaches out. 'And thanks, Elise. For being so supportive.'

'No problem.' She leaves the room, and a few seconds later, Sophie hears the sound of her bedroom door clicking shut.

She lifts her legs on to the sofa and buries herself in the duvet again. It's cold without the log burner on, but she doesn't have the strength – or the know-how – to get a fire going, so she piles on the extra blanket and leans her head against a cushion.

Her thoughts are still in the past, those early days when she was first with Ryan, trying to be the perfect girlfriend. It took months before she felt confident enough to describe herself in that way. Ryan never introduced her as such – never introduced her at all, as far as she can remember. But she glued herself to him like a smiling limpet, hoping other girls would get the message.

At the end of her first year, she had to move out of her student residence, although she'd hardly been living there for months, gradually sneaking more and more stuff into Ryan's shared house, moving in with him by stealth. But there wasn't room for her full-time and she wanted something nicer, more couple-y.

'Let's get a little flat,' she said, 'just the two of us.'

'Nah, I'm happy here with the lads,' Ryan replied. 'Why don't you find somewhere with your mates?'

But the truth was, she hadn't made many friends; she'd been too wrapped up in Ryan. It hadn't occurred to her to team up with other girls, and nobody had asked her either. They'd already manoeuvred themselves into small groups and were busy negotiating with departing third-years to take over their tenancies. Sophie was in danger of being left high and dry. As usual, she'd made assumptions about her relationship with Ryan, and not paid attention to reality.

Then she had a stroke of luck – at least that was how she saw it. At the end of the summer term, Ryan's landlord decided to sell his property and gave them notice. The lads wanted to carry on living together, but they were a large, unwieldy group of six and couldn't find anywhere with enough bedrooms. Things were getting desperate.

Sophie took her chance. She did all the donkey work – scouring the internet, arranging viewings, charming estate agents – and finally found the perfect place. It was a sweet little one-bedroom flat above a mobile phone shop, right in the centre of their stomping ground. She turned Ryan's inherent laziness to her advantage, presenting him with the solution to his accommodation problems just as he woke up to the fact that he was about to be made homeless.

Before they moved in, she scrubbed the flat from top to bottom, dealt with the mould in the bathroom, and hung a pair of hand-me-down curtains, donated by Nan, in the sitting room. She went round the charity shops picking up kitchenware, table mats and candle holders; even an IKEA rug. It was like playing with a doll's house, only everything was scaled up and the people were real.

Ryan didn't do a thing. She almost didn't want him to help, so that she could surprise him and win his praise. Thinking back, she realises it was pathetic trying so hard to please him when all he really wanted to do was hang out with the lads. But she was young. It was her first proper relationship – her one and only proper relationship, as it turned out.

He reluctantly moved into their love nest, and she spent

the next few months trying to persuade him that he'd made the right choice. She cooked meals from her 'eating on a budget' recipe book, did most of the cleaning and never nagged him to do his share, changed the bed and added his clothes to her weekly wash. She even ironed his T-shirts, although he stopped her doing that because he said it made him look like a nerd.

He seemed happy enough. He didn't have to lift a finger and was getting sex whenever he wanted it, which was virtually every night. Sometimes he went out on the lash and stayed over with his old housemates, leaving her alone and bereft, worrying that he was with some girl. But mostly he was there, not studying, just lounging around playing video games, a four-pack of cheap Polish lager at his side.

When she felt it was indisputably official, she wanted to take him home to meet her grandmother. Nan was such a big part of her life, Sophie felt Ryan couldn't really know her until the two of them had met. But he seemed to have no curiosity about her childhood or this wonderful woman she spoke so often about, and always found excuses not to go with her.

Her parents visited once a term, always arriving with a full carload. Sophie had become a depository for all the things they no longer wanted but couldn't bear to throw away: small items of furniture, wine glasses, casseroles, a canteen of cutlery, a juicer, a standard lamp her mother had never really liked, although it had sat in the corner of the dining room for as long as Sophie could remember. There wasn't room for any of it in their minuscule flat, but she couldn't bear to reject these familiar objects, because they reminded her of home.

Ryan always discovered a pressing need to go to the library when they turned up, and Sophie had to beg him to stay around, at least for lunch.

'I can't do this *Meet the Fockers* crap,' he said, searching for the library card he never used.

'But my mum and dad are easy,' she argued. 'All they want to do is get to know you.'

'Why? I'm going out with you, not them.'

'But we're an item.' He winced at her terminology. 'They really like you,' she went on, although her parents had never actually said it. 'They want to welcome you into the family.' She knew by the look on his face that she'd said the wrong thing. Again. 'Not now, I mean, one day in the future, the distant future...'

'They make me feel inadequate,' he said. 'Like I don't love you enough.'

Her reply came instantly, from her gut. 'Maybe you don't,' she said quietly.

'Please, Soph, let's not go there.' He sighed wearily. 'I'm here, aren't I? Playing happy families, like you want.'

'Except you never take me to meet *your* family,' she said.

'We don't get on – I've told you that a million times.'

'Why are you being so mysterious about them? I don't know what they look like, or even their names.'

'You don't need to. We're never going to invite them over for Sunday lunch, okay? They're small-minded, backward-thinking – we don't agree about anything. You wouldn't like them, and they probably wouldn't like you either.'

'Why not?' She looked indignant. 'What's wrong with me?'

'Nothing's wrong with you, it's *them*.' He sighed. 'It doesn't matter, forget it.'

Sophie eases herself out of the past, stiffly and carefully, as she might extract her foot from a tight boot. She's spent too much of her life puzzling over her relationship with Ryan. The sad truth is, it has never been right. There has always been something rotten at the heart of it, a bad smell lingering in her nostrils.

Maybe it's because of what she did all those years ago. Only Nan knew, and bless her heart, she took the secret with her to the grave. Sophie has never told Ryan. She didn't even confess to it during their counselling sessions. She kept it back, afraid that he'd end the marriage on the spot. At the time, she wanted to keep her options open. She was still unsure about what she wanted to do; whether their relationship was fixable, whether she could find it in her heart to forgive him. But a deeper, more important question remains hidden inside her. If she told Ryan what happened that night, would he ever forgive *her*?

TWENTY-TWO

SOPHIE

She studies the quality of the light in the room. What time is it? She has no idea. Not going to bed has brought everything forward, and although she suspects it's only mid-morning, it feels like late afternoon. She throws aside the duvet and gets off the sofa. Her back is stiff from lying awkwardly.

Her thoughts immediately switch to Keira. Will Ariel and Grace come back with a police officer, she wonders, or will they immediately dispatch a diving team? She has visions of people in white paper suits, plastic tape festooning the trees. Then there's Ryan to worry about. What if he's on his way here? What the hell is he going to say when he finds out? Elise advised her to keep her story simple when talking to detectives. Ryan might put his foot in it.

Although she knows it's useless in this godforsaken place, she still wants her phone by her side. Just in case a bar of signal miraculously appears. She leaves the sitting room and walks down the corridor, pausing outside Keira's bedroom to gather the courage to enter. Taking a breath, she squeezes the handle and opens the door.

The room looks different. There are no clothes lying on the

bed, no pile of underwear on the floor. The toiletries have gone, and so has Keira's mobile. Only Sophie's handset remains on the dressing table, unplugged from the solar charger, which has disappeared along with everything else. Including the rucksack.

She stops, her eyes flickering across the bare surfaces, unable to comprehend at first. Has one of the others been in here and taken her stuff? No, surely not. There's only one explanation. Keira must have come back.

A tsunami of relief almost sweeps her off her feet. She runs out of the bedroom and bangs loudly on Elise's door.

'Elise! Are you there?'

The door opens. Elise's bright hair is tousled, and she looks like she's only just woken up. 'What is it?' she asks, blinking her grey-blue eyes.

'Keira is alive!'

'What? Oh my God, that's amazing. Is she all right?'

'Yes, I mean, I think so. She *must* be. I went to look in her room and all her stuff has gone. She must have come back while we were out looking for her.'

'What?' Elise almost pushes her out of the way as she goes to see for herself. Sophie follows and they stand at the entrance to Keira's room, marvelling at its emptiness.

'I'm so relieved,' Sophie says, her heart skipping excitedly.

'Except we don't know for sure it was her.'

'It *has* to be her. There's nobody else it could be.'

'I know, but... The last time you saw her, she was in the water. If she managed to get out, how come we didn't find her earlier? She would have been soaking wet, frozen half to death. Remember the state you were in – you could hardly move.'

'She must have got out and dried off somehow. She's prob-ably been hiding, waiting for us to leave the house.'

'But why sneak back, pack her bag and run away? Looks like she hasn't even left a note.'

'Perhaps she was too ashamed to face us?' suggests Sophie hopefully.

'Hmm...' Elise walks around the room, opening the wardrobe and drawers as if expecting to find Keira hiding there. 'I suppose it could be that.' She sits on the bed, thinking. 'It's still an odd thing to do. *I* would have just climbed into bed and gone to sleep.'

'It doesn't matter. She's alive, that's the main thing. At least it looks that way.'

Elise smiles. 'Yes, I'm sure you're right.'

'I don't want to sound mean, but to be honest, I'm glad she's gone.'

'Me too.'

'It's a pity Ariel and Grace have already gone to call the police. We're going to look a bit stupid.'

'Yeah,' Elise agrees. 'I had a feeling we were jumping the gun, but you know what Ariel's like. She has to be in charge.'

'We can't even ring them to let them know,' Sophie says ruefully, picking up her mobile and seeing that it had only managed to reach 7 per cent before it was unplugged from the charger. Not that she cares so much any more; this good news has trumped everything.

'We should try and catch up with them before they reach the road,' says Elise.

'It shouldn't be too hard. There's only one path, we can't miss them.'

'But what if we bump into Keira?'

'I'm not sure I could cope with that,' Sophie murmurs, simultaneously thinking about Ryan, who could also be on his way. An image of the three of them meeting on the mountain-side and having some dramatic showdown rushes into her head, and she swallows nervously.

Elise pats her arm. 'Okay, I'll go. You should probably rest anyway.'

'Really? You don't mind?'

'I don't actively want to go on a four-hour hike, but there's no choice, is there? The police are going to be mightily pissed off if they arrive and we say "sorry, false alarm". They might even charge us with time-wasting.'

'Yes, you're right... Thanks, Elise, it's so good of you. I feel like it's all my fault. I gave her that dare—'

'No, no, no, don't go there. She's been screwing your husband, she betrayed you. You have nothing to feel guilty about. She's gone, it's over.' Elise stands up. 'Anyway, I'd better get going before the divers turn up.' She walks out of the room, leaving Sophie standing by the window feeling slightly breathless.

Keira may have fled, but the problems in her marriage are bigger than she ever imagined, even during those darkest days when Ryan first confessed to the affair. At first she believed she would never get over it, but after seven arduous months of couples counselling, she had to admit that it no longer hurt quite so much. She could live with the emotional pain, hoping that in time it would fade whilst knowing it would never go away completely. It was like having a chronic illness. She was in that state for a while, aided by the wild swimming and the camaraderie of her new friends, who knew nothing about her troubles – or so she thought. But now she's back to square one.

She hopes Ryan is too cowardly to come and face her. If he does turn up, she'll probably tell him to go away immediately. These next few days suddenly seem precious. Rather than plunge into a deep well of depression, she should gather her strength for what she has to do when she gets home. There are twenty years to unpick and refashion into a new life. Ben and Louie are her priority – she's not sure how she's going to tell them that Mummy and Daddy are splitting up. Then there's the house, and their accumulated belongings. Their friends, their social life. The extended family. Sophie knows she'll be okay; her parents will support her and the boys. It's Ryan who will be left stranded. Will Keira want him once he's no longer forbidden fruit? Sophie realises she neither knows nor cares.

Elise has gone and the house is quieter than ever. Sophie feels herself start to unwind. She walks from room to room, bathing in the solitude. For the first time since they arrived at Condie's Retreat, she's able to appreciate all the place has to offer. She wanders around the house's rough garden, letting her senses feast on the surroundings. The views are spectacular, the air smells sweet, and a gentle breeze is playing on her skin. Shutting her eyes, she holds her face up to the soft autumn sun and takes several deep breaths, in and out, in and out. She is held by the silence. Although now that she's properly listening, she discovers that it's not silent at all. Invisible birds are singing, and she can hear the distant rush of water. This is what she came here for, but until this moment it's been hidden from her. Now she wants to reset the clock and experience the place with a more positive state of mind. She'll take more walks, she'll commune with nature, but nothing will induce her to swim in that loch again.

Ariel, Grace and Elise have been fantastic. Sophie knows she hasn't been pulling her weight with the chores and wants to make it up to them. She fetches logs from the store, sweeps the floor of the compost loo, then goes to the stream and refills the water can. Maybe she'll cook tonight, although she has no idea what's on the menu, or what remains of their supplies. They might have to do another shop, which would be a nuisance. Then she remembers that the bloody car key is still missing. She should have asked one of the others to call the hire company and arrange for a spare to be sent.

She flicks through a couple of magazines and reads a chapter of her book. To her shame, she finishes a packet of digestive biscuits, washing them down with several cups of strong tea. After five hours, the blissful solitude is starting to pall. She starts to worry that something's wrong. Did Elise manage to catch up with Ariel and Grace? What if she missed them? She starts to fret again, feeling guilty for not going with her. She is struck by the speed at which her mood changes, from happy to desperate, combative to defeated. She even starts to wonder whether she's right about Keira being Ryan's lover, although just a few hours ago, she was totally convinced.

It's starting to feel really cold in the house. She tries to pass the time by setting a fire in the log burner, screwing up pieces of newspaper and making a Jenga-style arrangement of kindling as she's seen Ariel do so expertly. But when she places a larger log on the top, the edifice collapses. Cursing, she removes the wood and starts again.

'Hi!' a voice calls out. 'We're back!'

'Thank God,' says Sophie under her breath. She gets to her feet, shouting a greeting as she walks into the hallway to meet them. Ariel, Grace and Elise are all there, jostling in the porch as they fling off coats, hats, scarves, gloves and boots.

'I never thought we'd make it,' says Ariel breathlessly. 'I'm completely knackered.'

Sophie watches them anxiously. 'What happened? Everything okay?'

'Yes, in the end.' Grace looks up from untying a knot in her left boot lace. 'Unfortunately, we'd already called the police. We were waiting for them in the lay-by when Elise turned up. They took bloody ages to come, and then we had to send them away again.'

'We had to do a lot of grovelling,' adds Ariel, 'but they were actually quite relieved not to have to search the loch.'

Grace hangs up her jacket. 'Let's face it, we all were. I was really scared.'

'Did you... um... see Keira at all?' Sophie asks. They shake their heads.

'I hope to God we're right and she's not lying at the bottom of the loch,' says Ariel.

'Stop it,' says Grace. 'She *has* to be alive. Who else could have cleared out her room?'

'I know. But she should have left a note. It's not on, making us worry like this. I mean, how is she going to get home?'

'I expect she's fine. There's nothing we can do about it anyway.' Sophie looks at them appealingly. 'Shall I make some tea?'

'Tea? It must be wine o'clock, surely? Look, the sun is going down... well, sort of. Give it another hour or two.' Elise grins. 'Come on, girls, it's been a very long day. Let's crack open a bottle and snuggle down in front of the fire.'

Sophie insists on cooking and dismisses all offers of help. She puts a sheet of ready-made pastry into a pie dish and fills it with a medley of leftover vegetables. Their supplies are indeed running a bit low, despite Ariel's careful planning, but Sophie decides not to raise the subject. Nobody has any interest in walking back to the road yet again, and there's still this annoying missing key issue. There's nothing she can do about it tonight, so she concentrates instead on making leaves out of the spare pastry and brushing them with beaten egg. The activity soothes her. She finds herself wanting to please her friends as she once wanted to please Ryan – cooking his favourite food, making sure there were always beers in the fridge, that he had a clean, ironed shirt for work. Well, she won't be doing any more of *that* when she gets home, she thinks.

The atmosphere over dinner is subdued, with everyone making an effort to be pleasant. Sophie's hotch-potch pie goes down well, and she's finally able to join in the conversation properly. They flit from subject to subject, avoiding the controversial. Only Ariel wants to speculate about exactly what happened to Keira.

'Maybe she didn't actually fall into the water,' she muses, waving her glass of wine around. 'She never would have survived the night outside if she was wet. Hypothermia would have set in for sure.'

'I guess we'll never know,' says Grace, sounding bored.

'I'm just trying to establish the facts.' Ariel turns to Sophie. 'I know at the time you were sure she went in with you, but do you think you could have been mistaken?'

Grace rolls her eyes. 'Give the girl a break.'

'I'd rather not go through it again. It's kind of traumatising,' Sophie replies.

'I think we all need a break from it, to be honest,' agrees Elise.

Admonished, Ariel gathers up the dirty plates. Elise changes the subject to tomorrow's swim, sensitively suggesting that they go to the beach instead of the loch.

'Yes please,' says Sophie immediately. 'I'd love that.'

'It'll be super-super-freezing,' warns Grace, 'but I'm up for it. You know me and cold water.'

'I'd also like to check out the bothy again, see if that guy's still staying there.'

'Ooh! Already moving on, eh? I like it.'

'Don't be silly, Grace. I just want to ask him how he knew my name.'

'Duh, because you told him.'

'Yes, except I don't think I did. And there was definitely somebody out there with a torch the other night.'

'Please can you not go all paranoid on us again, Sophie?' says Ariel, her tone exasperated. 'We've had enough of ghosties and ghoulies and things that go bump in the night.'

'I just want to ask him, that's all.'

'Wants to ask him *out*, more like,' laughs Grace.

Ariel puts her hand on Sophie's arm. 'Look, we understand why you were so on edge before, but that's all over. Keira's gone, it's just the four of us now. You're safe.'

Sophie nods. 'I know, you're right. I'm being silly. Forget it.'

TWENTY-THREE

SOPHIE

It's a cold morning. They hurriedly strip off, dryrobes first, then various sweatshirts, woolly jumpers, T-shirts and vests, until they are standing in nothing but their swimsuits. Sophie is the last to get undressed. She puts a large stone on top of her pile of clothes and pulls on an orange swimming cap. The others are waiting for her, shivering in the chilly breeze. The weather is dry, and the sun is poking intermittently between the clouds, but it's still bitterly cold.

'Sorry,' she says, tucking a few strands of hair beneath the cap. 'Ready now.'

'Race you!' shouts Elise. 'Last one in the sea cooks tonight!'

Laughing, they scamper towards the incoming tide, weaving a path between rock pools and clumps of slippery seaweed. Sophie's skin tingles with goosebumps, thousands of fine hairs standing on end, her psychic efforts concentrated on imminent submersion in freezing-cold water. Ariel is the first in, striding out until it's deep enough, then launching herself forward with a defiant splash. Grace and Elise enter more cautiously, gingerly holding their arms aloft – ankles to knees to thighs to hips to waist. They release the customary squeals as they finally give in and dip their shoulders under.

Sophie remains at the edge. She was so looking forward to this, but now that she's here, she's not so sure she can do it. A wave runs over her feet, the cold water instantly triggering a memory. Her heart starts to race as it did that night. Suddenly she's in the loch, in the darkness, caught by the ankle, being dragged down... She jumps back.

The others are waving at her to join them, but she turns on her heel and hurtles back up the beach. All her excitement has turned to fear. She's desperate to put distance between herself and the cold water. As she reaches base, she pulls off her cap and grabs her clothes, re-dressing with frantic haste. Then she sits down on a rock and starts to cry, wiping her face with the sleeve of the dryrobe, which was meant to be soaking up seawater rather than tears.

The others are still frolicking in the waves, but they won't be able to stand the cold much longer. Sophie opens her day bag and takes out her flask. She unscrews the cup and removes the stopper, her hand shaking as she pours the tea. She cradles the thin plastic cup and looks around, hoping the scenery might calm her.

The ruined houses are to her right, clustered together against the elements that ravaged them decades ago. About a hundred metres beyond them is the bothy. There's no sign of any smoke coming out of the chimney. Maybe the journalist guy has moved on. She sips the scalding tea and feels her heart rate slowing.

The others are coming out of the water now, skipping towards her, skin red and blotchy with cold, swimsuits dripping, faces wet and joyful.

'What happened, Sophie?' asks Elise. She grabs her dryrobe and throws it over her head, disappearing for a few seconds.

'I don't know,' Sophie mumbles.

'You missed something really special,' says Grace, shivering visibly.

Ariel pulls out her towel and rubs her face dry. 'It was so refreshing. Why didn't you go in?'

'I just couldn't do it.' Sophie shrugs. 'As soon as I touched the water, it brought it all back.'

'What, like PTSD?' asks Elise. Sophie nods in uncertain reply.

Grace looks sceptical. 'But it's completely different to swimming in the loch, and it's daytime – sunny.'

'If you'd dived straight under without thinking, you would have been fine,' Ariel adds.

'Maybe. I'm not ready yet.' Sophie shakes the last drips of tea on to the sand, then screws the cup back on the flask. 'I'm going to pop over to the bothy while you're getting dressed.'

'Going to meet lover boy, eh?' grins Grace.

'No! I just want to see if he's still staying there, that's all. I won't be long.'

She leaves them to get dressed and have their hot drinks, walking back up the beach where the sand is drier and finding a path across the dunes. Grace's jibe about her fancying the guy irritates her like an insect bite. Nor was the younger woman very sympathetic about her inability to get into the water. I can't help it, she thinks. You didn't experience it – you don't know how frightening it was.

When she reaches the bothy, she walks around the outside looking for signs of life, but finds none. Even so, she knocks on the door, just in case.

'Hello?' she calls. 'Anyone there?' There's no reply, so she pushes it open and enters.

The guy's stuff is still here – the sleeping bag laid out on the shelf, the rolled-up jumper, the rucksack leaning against the wall. But the log burner is stone cold. It seems like he left some hours ago, probably on another trek. She feels a flash of disappointment that she won't see him today. Not because she fancies him, as Grace implied, but because she wanted to ask him how he knew her name.

She stares at his possessions as if trying to conjure him forth, thinking back to their conversation on the path. Being a journalist, he asked a lot of questions, and he was very interested in the wild swimming. She told him that she'd started the group on Facebook. Did she mention what it was called? She hadn't meant to name it after herself, but she had to give the page a title, and Sophie's Swimmers was all she could think of. They don't use the name much, only when they're teasing her. But if she'd told the guy, he would obviously have assumed that she was the Sophie in the title. She feels a wave of relief lapping over her.

Not wanting to be caught snooping, she leaves the bothy and shuts the door. Her eyes dart between the sand dunes and the cliffs further to her right, but there's no sign of him. She walks back to the others, who are now fully dressed and finishing off the last of their hot drinks and morning snacks.

'Well?' asks Elise. 'Was he at home?'

'No. His stuff is still there, but the fire had gone out.'

Ariel squeezes out her costume, dripping water on to the sand. 'Shall we go now, or do you want to explore a bit more?'

'I'd like to go back to the house,' says Elise. 'But we don't have to stick together the whole time. If anyone wants to hang around on the beach, or walk further...'

'I'm up for going back,' says Grace. 'Swimming always gives me an appetite. By the time we get there, I'll be so ready for lunch.'

Nobody seems to have much desire to stay, so they start the uphill walk to Condie's Retreat, chatting in various pair combinations or going in silent single file when the path dictates. Sophie senses that the others are taking it in turns to be lumbered with her. Her conversations with Grace, then Elise, then Ariel, then Elise again are forced. Once their inspiration, now she's the leper of the group. The name Sophie's Swimmers suddenly seems horribly inappropriate. Maybe she should go home today, she thinks. They will have a better time without her.

When they reach the last sharp incline, she makes an excuse about needing the loo to rush ahead. She's panting for breath as she reaches the house. Punching in the four-digit code to open the key safe, she unlocks the door, leaving it on the latch for the others. As she bends to remove her boots, she hears noises coming from the sitting room. She stops, listening.

'Hello?' she calls out nervously. 'Who's that?' There's no reply. She stands up and walks to the door, slowing pushing it open and peering round the frame.

Keira is on her hands and knees, arranging logs in the burner.

'Keira!' Sophie cries. 'What... what... You're back!'

She starts in surprise and twists round to face her. 'So I am,' she says. 'Hi.'

Sophie holds on to the door frame, unwilling or unable to go any closer. 'We... er... thought you'd gone home.'

'Yeah, sorry... Um... things have been a bit... um...'

'Where have you been?'

'Sheltering in a shepherd's hut. It was really grim – I'm frozen to the bone. That first night, I was so drunk I got completely lost and couldn't find my way back. I thought I was going to die of cold. In the morning, I managed to get back here to pick up my things.'

'Yes, we saw. That's why we assumed...'

'I *was* going to go home, but then I thought... how the hell, you know, with no transport. I badly needed some time to myself, to think, straighten out. So I went on this massive long walk and found this little hut. Last night was hellish, I couldn't take it. And I felt bad because I didn't leave a note and I knew you'd all be worried, and then I thought, this is ridiculous, just go back, Keira, finish the trip.' She lets out a small self-conscious laugh. 'Sorry.'

Sophie draws a breath. 'For what exactly?'

'You know, disappearing.'

'Ri-ight...'

'It was a really stupid thing to do, going off in the night. I mean, it was your dare, but I shouldn't have accepted it.'

The others have just arrived. Sophie turns around and goes back into the hallway to meet them.

'She's back!' she hisses. 'Keira's back!' Astonishment sweeps across their faces. 'She's behaving like nothing happened. I don't know what to do.'

'Leave it to me,' says Ariel, walking past her and into the room.

'Where has she been?' whispers Grace.

'In a shepherd's hut or something.'

'Come on,' says Elise, kicking off her boots. They follow Ariel into the sitting room. Keira is still kneeling on the floor by the log burner, trying to light the fire.

'I'm sorry,' she's saying. 'I didn't mean to make you worry.'

'We looked everywhere for you,' Ariel replies. 'We thought something terrible had happened.'

Mission accomplished, Keira gets to her feet, rubbing her dirty hands on her thighs. 'I'm really sorry. I shouldn't have run off like that and I should have left a note when I came back to collect my stuff. My bad.'

'You pushed Sophie into the water,' says Elise slowly. 'You nearly drowned her.'

Keira frowns. 'What? No, I didn't.'

'Yes, you did,' Sophie says, finding her voice. 'Don't deny it. You went into the water with me and then you tried to pull me under.'

'I did no such thing!' Keira protests. 'What the hell are you talking about?'

'Sophie nearly got hypothermia,' adds Grace. 'If we hadn't found her, she probably would have died.'

'Well, that had nothing to do with me. I didn't see her. I went down to the gravelly bit and waited, but she never showed. That's the truth! You know how pissed we all were. Eventually I started walking back, but I accidentally strayed on to a different path and got lost. I was walking around in circles for ages and my torch died. I was really scared.' She pauses, taking in the others' disbelieving expressions. 'Honestly! That's the truth.'

'So you're telling us you didn't go in the water?' asks Ariel.

'No. No way! I'm not stupid.'

'I was pushed,' repeats Sophie. 'I didn't make it up.'

'Okay, maybe you were, but not by me,' Keira snaps. 'I'd never do anything like that. I mean, why would I?'

'Because you want to get rid of me.' Sophie feels the edge of her voice hardening. 'I know what's been going on, Keira. I know about your affair.'

Keira's eyes open wide. 'What affair?'

'Oh, come on. You and Ryan.'

'Me and *who*?' She looks at Sophie blankly. 'Sorry, but I haven't a clue what you're talking about. Ryan – is that your husband?'

Sophie sighs impatiently. 'You're an amazing actress, we all get that, but now's the time to own up.'

'I don't have to listen to this,' says Keira, hands on hips. 'This is utter crap. I've never even met your bloody husband – I wouldn't recognise him if I fell over him in the street.'

The others stand there silent, mouths half-open. Sophie takes a step forward. She is feeling so angry she thinks she might actually strike Keira.

'You told Ariel you were having an affair with a married man.'

'I did not.' Keira shakes her head in disbelief.

'Well, you implied it,' Ariel blusters. 'You said you'd had enough of sneaking around, so I assumed you meant—'

'Jesus, what is wrong with you people?' Keira fumes. 'I said no such thing.'

Ariel goes to protest again, then thinks better of it. Keira looks like she wants to leave the room, but Sophie stands in her way, arms folded, jaw set tightly.

'Okay, then, who's Fred?' she asks, playing her trump card.

'None of your business.' Keira scowls. 'Have you been looking at my phone? My God, you sneaky little bitch.'

'Fred's your code name for Ryan, isn't it?'

Keira laughs. 'No, you fool. You've got it all wrong – completely wrong.'

'But Ryan told me...' Sophie cuts herself off. Ryan *didn't* tell her that he was having an affair with Keira, just somebody in the group. She looks at the other three, still standing there in a line like rubberneckers at a crime scene. An icy chill runs through her. If it's not Keira, who is it?

'He was lying. Honestly, Sophie, we are not having an affair, you must believe me.' Keira reaches out for her, but she backs away. 'I knew you were being a bit off with me, but I couldn't work out why. I understand now. The dare... that was because you wanted to have it out with me, yes?'

'No. You were the one who insisted I went with you, not the other way around,' Sophie replies sullenly. 'You came up behind me and pushed me.'

'How many more times, I wasn't anywhere near you! You're making stuff up.'

'I don't think there's much point continuing this conversation,' says Ariel after a pause. 'Obviously Sophie's going through some personal difficulties at the moment and it's making her... you know... imagine things.'

'I was pushed,' says Sophie again.

'Not by me.' Keira's eyes flare.

'Then who?'

'How the fuck should I know? Out of my way, please. I haven't slept for two nights, I need to lie down.'

TWENTY-FOUR

THE SWIMMER

Well, well, well... Sophie knows her husband is having an affair with one of her swimming buddies, which means Ryan must have told her, even though I warned him against it, tut-tut. Interestingly, he didn't tell her which of us it was, which shows that he's just as capable of torturing Sophie as I am. Even more so.

I have a feeling he dropped the bombshell when we stopped at the service station on the way up. She had a phone conversation with him, and after that, she wasn't the same woman.

If I'd been in her place, I would have got everyone back in the car and challenged us there and then, refused to start the engine until somebody owned up. *Come on, which of you bitches is shagging my man?* Or something along those lines. But Sophie didn't do that. She chose to keep the info to herself and carry on as if nothing had happened. That must have taken some guts. She has crept up a notch in my estimation. Perhaps she wanted to take revenge by devising her own 'tragic accident'. I have to say, it puts the dangerous drunken dare in a whole new light. Maybe she planned all along to have a midnight showdown at the loch. Maybe I'm more in danger from her than she is from me.

I go to my purse and take out the photo of Carly that I keep tucked behind my credit cards. It's one of those booth shots; the two of us shoved together on the little revolving stool, mouths open, tongues out, looking like a couple of clowns. Had we had smartphones back then, we would have taken hundreds of selfies, but this is the last picture I have of the two of us together.

'Hey, big sis,' I whisper. 'Guess what? I only went and wrecked their marriage! Aren't you proud of me?' I stroke her tiny face and give it a kiss.

Okay, so Ryan wasn't actually married to Carly, but it was on the cards, especially as far as she was concerned. She'd been planning the wedding since she was fifteen. She was going to wear one of those strapless ballgown dresses with a long wispy train that looked like a net curtain. She knew what 'accent colour' she wanted – for her bouquet, the bridesmaids' outfits, the groom's tie and the table decorations. Peach. I wasn't too keen, but she insisted it would go well with her skin tone. She knew stuff like that because she was training in hair and beauty.

As her only sister, I thought I should be chief bridesmaid, but she told me I was too young and that the job would be shared between her three best friends. They were going to marry in church because it would make a better backdrop for the photos, and the reception would be at a nice hotel, not in the upstairs room of our local pub. Carly put more effort into planning her wedding than she did into revising for her GCSEs. She didn't know any quotes for her English Lit. exam, but she could already recite her vows off by heart. She was a simple girl, really. Old-fashioned. She loved Ryan and he loved her, that was all she needed to know. Under pressure from her, they got engaged on her seventeenth birthday, just before he went off to university. She never took that cheap diamond ring off, not even when she went to bed.

Ryan's mum, Jill, was desperate to buy her wedding hat – a peach one, no doubt. She loved Carly almost as much as we did; she was the daughter she'd always wanted. But Ryan was holding back the female tide. He said he and Carly should wait until he'd graduated and had settled into a good job. He couldn't save a penny while he was a student. Weddings were ridiculously expensive – 'all that fuss just for one day'. When the economic argument didn't work, he announced that marriage wasn't necessary. They didn't need a piece of paper to prove how they felt about each other, and neither of them was religious, so what was the point?

Carly was disappointed, but she had no choice. Ryan was always in charge of that relationship, and she didn't seem to mind. She trusted him completely. It never occurred to her for one second that he might be involved with someone else, even though there were clues. He hardly ever came home to see her during term time and refused to let her visit him at his 'mouse-infested student shithole'. I don't think she even had the address.

I'd love to know how and when Sophie found out about her. My guess is that she confronted Ryan straight away and made him choose between them. How did she react when she heard that Carly had died? Was she overcome with guilt, or did she crack open a bottle of champagne? Maybe one day I'll force her to tell me.

It's getting chilly in here. I put my phone down and pull the duvet across my legs. I'm going to have to be very careful from now on. At the moment, Sophie's too confused to know who to trust, but she may yet work it out in her stupid little brain.

There must be no slip-ups, no botch jobs. I may even have to abort my mission altogether and wait for another opportunity, although it will be hard to find a better one in the future. No more digital detoxes in the middle of nowhere, I imagine. I'm finding it quite satisfying that her passion for wild water has been tainted for ever. I wouldn't be surprised if Sophie's Swimmers falls apart now. Shame in a way, because I do love it so.

It's Thursday today... how time flies when you're having fun. I'm up early, fetching water from the stream. I'm carrying the two buckets back to the house, salivating at the thought of a nice cup of tea and a slice of stale toast, when I glimpse a figure threading their way through the trees. I pause. Is that Sophie's mystery man? No, I don't think so, his clothes are too townie. Could it be...? No, surely not. Oh shit, it *is*. It's bloody Ryan. What's he doing here?

He stops and takes a piece of paper out of his pocket, which he consults with a furrowed brow. I'm not surprised he's feeling lost. According to the map, you're already there, but you can't see the house because it's hidden in the valley. I pick up my pace as I try to reach him before he moves on. The water slops over the edge of the buckets and on to my feet.

'Ryan!' I hiss, as soon as I'm close enough for him to hear me. He looks around, as if a spirit has called him from the trees. 'Over here!'

'You!' he cries, as if surprised that I'm still alive.

'Yes, me.' I put the buckets down. 'What the hell are you doing here?'

'Sophie called me,' he says. 'She asked me to come.'

'But there's no signal here.'

'She borrowed somebody's phone or something, I don't know. She left a message.'

'Oh, right – that was Monday, wasn't it? You took your time.'

'I couldn't get off work. I came as soon as I could, I drove all night. She sounded in a bad way. What's been going on?'

I give him my best supercilious smile. 'Oh, we've been having a wonderful time, thank you. Eating cake, getting pissed,

playing silly games, trying to drown each other in the loch... it's
been fabulous.'

'Very funny.'

'Really, I'm not joking.'

He frowns, neither understanding nor believing me. 'Does
she know?'

'What? That I'm the one?' He nods sheepishly. 'Hmm... not
sure. It's been touch and go. At the moment, she's in turmoil,
doesn't know what to think. Everyone is under suspicion,
Monsieur Poirot.' I laugh, trying to maintain the upper hand,
but in truth, Ryan's arrival has rattled me. It changes everything.

'You've had your evil fun, but now it's over,' he says. 'I'm
going to tell Sophie everything.'

He makes to leave, but I grab his sleeve. 'No,' I say sharply.
'I won't let you do it.'

'It's my life, my marriage. You can't stop me.'

'Can't I?' I shoot him a thunderous look. He's not going to
spoil it for me, not now, not when I'm so close.

'I'm not leaving her with you,' he says. 'You're mad. This
has gone far enough.'

I raise my hand. 'Oh no, it's not gone anywhere near far
enough yet. I'm in control of this, Ryan, not you. I dictate terms.
I promise that if you tell her who I am, I will completely wreck
your miserable little life.'

'It's already wrecked. I told her ages ago that I'd had an
affair.'

'You did *what*?!' I am genuinely shocked.

'I told her it was just a fling and I'd ended it. We had
months of therapy – it was torture. She forgave me.' He looks
down at his suede boots, which are muddy and ruined. Serves
him right. 'I'm a shit, I know it.'

'Yeah,' I agree, cross with myself for not realising he'd been
lying to me too. 'So why did you tell her it was still going on?'

'Because you joined the bloody swimming group, that's

why! She founded it because I'd cheated on her and she was depressed.' He kicks a stone. 'It's time to be honest, cut the crap and tell her the truth. We'll split up, for sure. My kids will hate me, I'll lose my home, everything.' He looks up. 'So you see, there's nothing you can threaten me with.'

'Don't be so sure, Ryan,' I snap. It takes all my strength not to remind him that Carly never got to walk down the aisle, never got the chance to have kids. 'If you think you're safe from me, you're very, very wrong. I could destroy your life just like that.' I click my fingers in his face.

He flinches. 'Really? Like how?'

Yes... like how? I pause dramatically, trying to make it look like I'm about to whip some devious plan from my sleeve. Then the obvious solution occurs to me.

'I'll go to the cops and tell them you forced me to have violent sex. That you stalked me and wouldn't leave me alone. That you threatened to kill me if I told anyone.'

'They wouldn't believe you,' he scoffs. 'We met on a hook-up site, for God's sake. If anyone's been doing the stalking, it's you.'

'But you see, Ryan, the thing is, I've got footage to prove you raped me.'

He gasps. 'You what? But that's... that's completely untrue!'

'I made secret recordings of some of our little sex games,' I lie, wishing now that I *had* put a hidden camera in my bedroom.

He reddens. 'That's what they were – games! Between consenting adults. And *you* were the one who wanted to be tied up and stuff. I was just doing what you asked me to do.'

'I know that, and you know that, but it's not how it looks on camera. Our performances are astonishingly good – me the victim, you the perpetrator. You could be looking at a long prison sentence.' I let out a sarcastic sigh. 'Oh dear... poor little Ben and Louie, growing up with a sex offender for a dad—'

'Stop it! Stop it! You leave my kids out of it!'

'I just think you should know what's at stake here.'

'I don't get it. Why are you doing this? Do you hate all men, or is it me in particular?'

'Oh, Ryan, I'm not going to tell you that. You're going to have to work it out.' I stare at him, challenging him to recognise me. 'Funny... you have no idea who I really am, do you? Not a bloody clue.'

'What the fuck do you mean?' He grabs me by the shoulders and shakes me. 'Who are you? Tell me! What's going on?'

'Take your hands off me, or I'll scream, and then it'll all be over for you.'

He releases his hold, arms falling limply to his sides. 'I don't understand,' he murmurs.

'You don't need to.' I narrow my gaze at him, imagining a target in the centre of his forehead. 'Like I said, *I'm* in charge, not you. You're going to tell Sophie that you made it up, okay? You're going to swear that you've never even met any of us, let alone had sex with one of us. You'll beg for her forgiveness, which she probably won't give you. And then you're going to turn around, go back to the car and drive off into the sunset. Without Sophie.'

'She won't believe me.'

'Oh, I'm sure you'll manage to convince her somehow. You're so good at lying. But if you tell her the truth, be prepared for what's going to happen next.' I let my words hang menacingly in the air. 'Go on. Off you go. You just have to follow the path round – there's only one house, you can't miss it. I'll be along in a few minutes for the fake surprise. And don't you dare so much as look me in the eye.'

He chews his lip for a few moments, weighing up the options, perhaps. 'I hate you,' he says finally.

'Not as much as I hate you,' I reply acidly. 'Now piss off, before anyone sees us.'

I watch as he makes his way along the path, losing sight of

him when he turns the corner. My heart is pounding, palms sweating. I so nearly told him the truth just then. The words were queuing up in my mouth, desperate to be let out. *It's me, you idiot! Carly's kid sister! Why doesn't it even occur to you that all this is because of her?* I kick one of the buckets in frustration and it topples over, the water soaking into the earth. I pick it up and storm back to the stream.

TWENTY-FIVE

SOPHIE

'Ryan!' Sophie cries when she opens the front door. She stares at him for a few seconds, shocked.

'I got your message,' he says. 'Sorry I'm late.'

'I'd given up. I thought—'

'I tried to come straight away, but they wouldn't give me the time off. I drove up overnight, called in sick this morning. Can't stay. Have to be back for tomorrow's shift.'

'Oh. Do you want to come in?'

'Not really. I just want to talk to you... On our own. In private.'

'All right. Go round the side and wait for me in the garden.' She gestures at her dressing gown. 'I need to get some clothes on.'

She shuts the door and quickly goes into her room, throwing off her pyjamas and dressing in jeans and a jumper. Ryan's *here*... She'd almost forgotten she called him.

It's early, just after 7 a.m. She's been awake for a couple of hours, but it seems like the others haven't stirred yet. Probably just as well, she thinks as she pulls on a pair of thick Fair Isle patterned socks. There's been enough washing of her dirty linen in public. She grabs her coat and enters the back garden via the patio doors.

He is standing at the bottom of the ragged, overgrown lawn, hands in pockets, head down, nervously stepping from foot to foot. A sickening sensation fills her stomach as she walks towards him. It feels like an important moment in their relationship, perhaps *the* most important one. He has responded to her command, driven through the night, walked for nearly two hours to get here. Surely he must be ready to come clean.

She arrives at his side. They stand there staring into the trees, neither knowing how to start. She is close enough to touch him, but it feels like they're a thousand miles apart, like he's a stranger.

'I lied,' he says eventually.

'That's hardly news,' she quips. There's another pause. 'Which particular lie are you referring to?'

'About having an affair with one of the girls in your group.' *Women*, she corrects silently. 'I'm sorry, it was spiteful. I was just feeling jealous. These days you seem to care more about them than you do about me. I'm not saying I don't deserve it, but... Anyway, that's why I did it. I was trying to hurt you, I guess. I wanted us to go away together, just the two of us, to heal things.' A pained expression crosses his face. 'It felt like you'd given up on me. I was angry, so I made it up. To spoil your trip.'

Sophie looks down at the ground. The grass is wet with dew; it looks like tears. 'I don't believe you,' she says quietly.

'Well, it's true. I don't know any of these women. I've never even met them, let alone... you know. The affair ended months ago, just as I told you.'

'You reacted very strangely when you saw that photo,' she reminds him. 'You ran out of the house like it was an emergency.'

'No, I didn't, you're exaggerating.'

'You didn't come back for hours. Where did you go?'

'I told you before, I was driving around. The photo brought it home to me, that's all. I was jealous. I know I didn't have a right to be, but I was.'

'That's bullshit. You don't care that much about me, Ryan, you never have. I've always been the dominant one in our relationship. We went through all this with Miriam. You said yourself you'd sleepwalked into—'

'I don't want to go through all that again. I love you, Sophie, you're my wife. Honest to God, I've not been having an affair with one of your friends. Like I said, I've never even met them before. The reason I didn't name names was because I couldn't bloody remember any!'

'You're lying.'

'I'm not,' he insists. 'Not about this, anyway.'

Sophie paces up and down, creating a muddy track in the grass. 'Okay, so let's get this straight. You *did* have an affair—'

'It was a hook-up,' he cuts in, 'nothing more.'

'Oh sorry, I forgot, *hook-ups* are fine,' she snaps sarcastically.

He takes one hand out of his pocket and wipes away a tear. Or maybe it's the cold that's making his eyes stream, she thinks bitterly. She doesn't know what to think. He seems rattled, like he's under pressure.

She takes a deep breath. 'I'm going to ask you a question, and I want you to look straight at me and tell me the truth... okay?' He nods. 'The woman you had the hook-up with. What was her name?'

'I don't know. I expect it was a false name – people tend to do that on these sites.'

'Do they? Well, you're the expert.' She glares at him. 'And what name did you use?'

'Um... does it matter?'

'It wasn't Fred by any chance, was it?'

'No.' He laughs nervously. 'Why did you say that?' She doesn't answer. 'I used my own name, if you must know.'

'Not afraid of being caught, then.'

'Look, this is old territory, Sophie. I came here because you left me a message saying you needed help. I could tell that you were suffering, and I thought I should come and... you know... explain.'

'It just seems rather convenient to me that—'

He grabs her hands urgently. 'Sophie, please, you have to believe me. I made it up. I don't know any of these women. Just forget I ever said it!'

'It's Keira, isn't it?'

'No. It's not any of them. I promise.'

She pulls away from him. 'You were right to be scared. She pushed me into the loch. She tried to drown me, Ryan! She's denying it, but I know what happened. She's been behaving really strangely, *and* I found a load of dirty texts on her phone, sent to someone called Fred.'

'That's not me.'

'After she nearly killed me, she disappeared for a night, and when she came back, it was like, "Oh, sorry, I just needed some time alone". Yeah, right. Did she walk back to the road and call you? Did she tell you to get your arse over here and smooth things over?'

'No. Absolutely not. *Definitely* not.' It's the first thing he's said that actually sounds genuine. 'I don't even know which one Keira is,' he adds. 'I don't know any of them.'

'Let me introduce you, then. I'm sure you'd like to apologise for wrecking their holiday.'

'No, don't make me do that. I need to go now.' He starts to make his way back up the garden.

She follows him. 'Don't be a coward. If you're genuinely sorry, face the music for once.'

'I've got to get going.'

'But I thought you were here to take me home.'

'No... I don't think... It wouldn't work... You should stay

here with your friends... finish the trip.' He rounds the side of the house and reaches the path, stopping to reorientate himself. 'It's this way, right?'

She grabs his sleeve. 'What's wrong?'

'Let me go,' he says sharply, then softens. 'Please, Sophie. I have to go. I've said what I came to say and now it's best that we, um... that you... have some time to think it over. Maybe, when you get back—'

'Ryan! For once in your life, just tell me the truth. I'm begging you.'

He swallows hard. 'I'm *not* having an affair with any of your friends,' he says slowly.

'Really? Honestly?'

'Yes. Honestly. I swear.'

Her mind is reeling. 'Oh. My. God. How could you be so cruel? You put me through all that just because you were jealous?'

'Yes. Basically.'

Could he be telling the truth? She remembers New Year's Eve, how he accused her of flirting with the guy at the party. That was how it all started. They rowed, and then he confessed...

'I'm so sorry, Sophie, so sorry,' he says, talking over her thoughts. 'Look after yourself... please, take care,' he adds, his voice breaking. 'I love you.'

She releases him without reply, and he turns away. She watches him go, feeling like it could be the last time she ever sees him. He doesn't even look back before he turns the corner.

Sophie crouches down, emotionally spent. Of all the terrible conversations they've had over the last year, that one ranks among the worst. Now what? Does she walk back into the house and carry on like nothing's happened? She can't face the others right now, particularly Keira. She almost believed her when she came back from her mysterious night in the forest, tired and cold, full of apologies for having made them worry. Now Sophie thinks she probably hitched a ride to Mallaig and stayed in a hotel. How else did she manage to dry her clothes? Ryan was vehement in that particular denial, but it could have just as easily have been a lie like all the others. All she knows is that he wasn't himself, although she's not sure who the real Ryan is any more.

She opts for the path that leads down to the loch. After a few minutes, she reaches the fork and takes the left track, the one she mistakenly took the other night in the dark. The ground is damp, even though it hasn't been raining. Her boots slide on the loose stones and she has to lean backwards to keep her balance. Grabbing hold of a branch to steady herself, she pauses for a moment. Why is she doing this? The loch is the last place she wants to go, and yet something is pushing her forward; a vague intimation that maybe, once she's standing close to the edge of the water, she'll remember something significant.

She carries on down the track. It's so quiet she can hear her heart thumping in her chest. Her memories pursue her, closing in with every step. Her blood chills, and suddenly she's back in the loch, flailing in the freezing water, chin bobbing just above the surface, snatching breaths out of the darkness. Now something is wrapping itself around her ankle, and she gasps as it pulls her down and under...

She stops and bends over to steady her breathing. It's no good, she can't put herself through this. After a few moments, she straightens up and turns around. She has to go back to the house. Talk to the others.

Ariel spots her from the window and meets her at the front door. 'Sophie, are you all right? I was starting to worry.'

'About what?' she blinks.

'That guy you were talking to in the garden...'

'Ryan.'

'That was *Ryan*? Your husband?'

'Yes.'

'Oh. I thought it was the journalist. I wasn't spying, but it looked like a serious conversation, I didn't want to interrupt. Why is your husband here? Where is he? Is he staying over?'

'No, he's gone.'

'Already? How come?'

'It's complicated,' Sophie replies. 'I need to talk to everyone together. Are the others up?'

'Yes, we were about to go for a swim. I was hoping you might feel up to joining us this time.'

'I need to talk to them first.' She almost pushes past Ariel to enter the house. Throwing off her coat and boots, she walks into the sitting room. Grace and Elise are already in their dryrobes, looking like a couple of greyhounds eager to get out of the traps. Keira is clearly not in so much of a hurry, lounging on the sofa drinking a cup of coffee and eating a cereal snack bar.

'Morning,' she says through her mouthful. 'Who was that guy you were talking to?'

'We're all dying to know,' Elise adds. 'Ariel said—'

'It was Ryan.' Ariel answers for her.

'Ryan?' Grace and Elise echo simultaneously.

Sophie looks from one woman to another. Who is faking? Maybe none of them, maybe all of them. 'I know this is really awkward and embarrassing,' she starts, 'but we need to talk. Together. As a group. I need to know.'

'Need to know what?' asks Keira, sipping her drink.

'You know what she's talking about,' says Ariel, perching on the end of the sofa. 'Go on, Sophie, fire away.'

'Ryan told me he'd made the whole thing up. He swears that he isn't having an affair with any of you, that he was jealous and was just trying to spoil the trip.'

'I knew it!' Ariel cries. 'I absolutely knew it! He's been gaslighting you, Sophie. It's classic.'

'Well, maybe... I don't know what to think and I need to be sure. So I'm afraid I'm going to have ask each one of you individually...' She pauses. 'Look, I don't actually care that much any more, because I'm done with him, it's over. But I do need to know once and for all.' There's no response. 'You've already humiliated me, so please at least have the guts to admit it.' Nobody flinches or makes to speak. Sophie looks at them all in turn, searching for the slightest hint, but the four of them remain inscrutable.

'Keira?' she asks finally.

'You accused me before and I said no,' she replies grumpily. 'I really resent this. It's like we're at school and somebody's broken a window and not owned up.'

'It's a bit more serious than breaking a window.'

'You know what I mean.'

'Okay, I accept your answer.' Sophie turns to the next candidate. 'Elise?'

'No, Sophie, I'm not having an affair with your husband,' she replies simply.

'Nor me,' adds Grace. 'I wouldn't do a thing like that. You're my friend.'

Elise nods. 'Same here, I hope that goes without saying.'

Sophie turns at last to Ariel. 'You're going to say it's not you either, aren't you?'

Ariel smiles. 'Yes, I am... but you already knew that.'

'Do you think it could be Fern?' asks Grace. 'Maybe that's why she pulled out. She lost her nerve or something.'

'No, it can't be her,' says Sophie. 'Ryan already knew she wasn't coming on the trip.'

'Looks like you're going to have to believe him,' Keira says after a pause. '*And* us.'

Sophie feels tears pricking behind her ears. 'I knew this would happen. Now I feel like a complete dick.'

'No, you had to ask,' says Elise. 'We understand.'

'I knew he was trying to turn you against us,' Ariel announces, sounding rather pleased with herself. 'It's what they do. I've seen it countless times in my work. As soon as you make friends or form any kind of social group, they break it up. He wants to destroy your support network and make you feel isolated.' She stands up and goes over to Sophie. 'Well, we're not going to let him!'

'I'm sorry, this is the last thing I wanted to do. I feel so bad...' Sophie begins, but Ariel shushes her with an embrace.

'We're on your side. All of us. Aren't we, girls?' She beckons them forward. 'Come on. Group hug. We all love Sophie, right?'

Grace and Elise immediately come over, while Keira puts her tea down and slowly gets off the sofa. Ariel opens her arms and gathers them in, and they smile into the circle, like the members of a football team. Sophie stands in the middle, barely able to breathe.

TWENTY-SIX

SOPHIE

It's the evening now. Darkness has put its generous arms around the house, and everything looks cosy in the flickering light of the paraffin lamps. The log burner is blazing away, and the five women are gathered around it, glasses of wine in hand, blankets spread across their knees. Alcohol supplies are running low, so they've rationed themselves to two glasses each and as a result are only gently drunk. The atmosphere is convivial – there will be no lairy games tonight.

On the dining table, their dirty plates wait patiently for somebody to take them into the draughty kitchen and begin the bothersome task of washing up. Strictly speaking, it's Ariel and Elise's turn to clear, but nobody seems interested in reminding them. It would break the circle, loosen the bond that has been tightening between them all day.

Sophie is surprised at how different she feels tonight. Not exactly happy; it's too early in the process for that. Something nearer to relief, perhaps. The last eighteen months have been tough. The battle with Ryan left her with emotional injuries that wouldn't heal. She treated them as she would any chronic condition: trying to ignore them, taking remedies that didn't work, feeling hopeful then desperate, determined then defeated. She became so used to the pain that she was barely aware of it any more. But now that it has gone, she feels the absence of it. A weight has been lifted from her shoulders. Her posture is different; there's no knot of tension at the back of her neck. She feels lighter and elongated. But no miracle has taken place. This has only happened because twelve hours ago, she finally took control of her life. It turned out to be surprisingly easy. All she had to do was end the relationship with Ryan. End it and *mean* it.

When he first confessed to having the affair, she wanted to make some dramatic gesture like chucking him out in the middle of the night or stuffing his clothes into bin liners and taking them to the charity shop. She felt physically violent towards him, which she'd never felt about any other human being before. The anger scared her, but she couldn't keep that level of emotional intensity going indefinitely. Ryan's remorse wore her down. He was so appalled by his behaviour, and so genuinely sorry, that she suppressed her instincts and gave him another chance, agreeing to counselling because that was what civilised people did. Now she sees that she only tried to save the marriage for the sake of the boys, not because *she* wanted it. She still feels bad about how Ben and Louie will cope with the divorce, but she can't go on putting other people first and ignoring her own needs. Ultimately children need happy parents, regardless of whether they're together or apart.

Elise passes around a box of chocolates and Sophie takes one, allowing it to sweeten her thoughts. She still has so much spinning through her brain, she hasn't been able to join fully in the conversation, but tonight – for the first time this holiday – it hasn't stopped her feeling part of the group. The others have been kind and attentive towards her all day, treating her as if she has the flu or some kind of physical injury. She's been included, but nothing has been expected of her, which she really appreciates.

'So... why are we here?' asks Ariel after a reflective pause.

Elise pulls a face. 'Ooh, that sounds a bit philosophical,' she says, exchanging a wink with Grace.

'I mean, why are we attracted to wild swimming? What does it do for us?'

'Freezes our tits off!' Grace laughs and the others join in. 'I don't know. I just enjoy it, that's all. It's free, it's good for your mental health, you meet amazing women...' She raises her glass in a general salute. 'What's not to like?'

'You just said it,' responds Keira. 'The cold water.'

'But that's precisely why we do it,' Sophie says, joining in at last.

'Absolutely,' Elise agrees. 'I hate it and love it at the same time.'

'We're all addicts,' says Ariel, helping herself to another chocolate. 'Every Tuesday morning I wake up dreading it, and yet I'm also really excited because I know I'm about to get my hit and the rest of the day I'll be buzzing. I've got to the point where I *need* it, like a drug. My work is really stressful, and sometimes it's hard to disentangle myself from other people's problems. The cold water is cleansing. Purifying, even.'

Elise snorts. 'Not getting all spiritual on us, are you, Ariel?'

'I don't know... maybe... Yes, why not? There's nothing wrong with spirituality.'

There's a pause. Sophie senses that the others are considering whether to continue with the subject or move swiftly on to something else. They've never spoken with each other in this way before. It's slightly alarming. Like Truth or Dare but without the dare option.

'I started swimming because I felt I had to *do* something,' she says. 'Just for me. Nobody else. Not for the kids, definitely not for Ryan. I was trying to connect with myself and what I truly felt.'

'And did you?' asks Elise. 'Connect?'

Sophie hesitates before answering. It's a good question. If she'd been asked it a few months ago, she would have replied in the affirmative, without hesitation, but now she realises that she's only been treading water – literally and metaphorically. 'I thought I was taking action, but actually I was avoiding it,' she replies at last. 'It wasn't until I was dragged under that I started to fight back.'

'That's so interesting,' says Ariel, chewing on her toffee.

'I'd like to say something about that,' Keira begins as four pairs of eyes turn to look at her. 'It's important.'

'Do we really need to go back over stuff?' says Elise.

'Yeah, I think we should just move on,' agrees Grace. 'Put all that shit behind us.'

'I *didn't* push Sophie into the water,' Keira persists. 'I was on the other side of the loch. I didn't see or hear anything.'

Sophie tenses. 'Are you saying I made it up?'

'No, not at all. But you were very drunk. Well, we *all* were, but you were in a strange mood, like you didn't trust any of us, especially not me. You'd been looking daggers at me all evening. To be honest, I think you became disorientated, fell in and then got caught up in some weeds.'

Sophie's forehead creases into a frown. 'It felt very real at the time.'

'I'm not and never have been having an affair with your husband,' says Keira.

'Sophie knows that,' intervenes Ariel. 'Ryan admitted he made it up.'

'Yeah, but I'm not sure she believed him.' Keira studies Sophie's face. 'Well? Did you?'

'Um, I... It's hard... he's lied so much... I *did* believe him this time, but only because I believe the rest of you more, if that makes sense.'

'I'm not sure this is helping anyone,' interrupts Grace.

Elise takes the last chocolate. 'Yeah, I agree.'

'But I need to get this off my chest,' continues Keira. 'Because Sophie suspected me and she went through my stuff, including my mobile, and I'm still feeling quite pissed off about it.'

Sophie's stomach clenches. 'I'm sorry. I know I shouldn't have done that, but I was going out of my mind. And...' She pauses, not knowing whether to carry on. '...the thing is, Keira, I *did* find those texts.'

'My *private* texts.'

'Yes, I know. But it looked like you were having some kind of... er... illicit relationship with somebody...'

'Which was none of your business.'

'Except if it's with my husband, it becomes my business too.'

'But it's not, so you had no right—'

'Hey, girls, please let's not go there,' interrupts Ariel. 'We've been having such a lovely evening, and everyone's been so open and positive. Let's not spoil it.'

Keira draws in a breath. 'As it happens, I *have* been having an affair – if that's what you want to call it – with somebody who's already in a long-term relationship.' There is a collective catching of breath, and Elise and Grace exchange the swiftest of glances. 'You can judge me if you like. I'm not particularly proud of it, but... it happened. It got way too serious and I didn't want all that responsibility, so I ended it just before we came away. That's why I've been a bit distracted.'

Waves of guilt wash over Sophie. 'Oh,' she says. 'I'm really sorry.'

'Yes, so you keep saying,' Keira snaps. 'Look, I don't want to be mean, but this trip is not all about you. You're not the only one here with issues.'

'Of course I'm not – I'm aware of that. I never meant—'

'We all brought emotional baggage along,' Elise says. 'I know *I* did.' She laughs self-consciously. 'Obviously nothing as heavy as yours, but... What I'm trying to say is, I know you've been having a rough time too, Keira, but you've got to understand – Sophie has been to hell and back. Her marriage basically ended this morning. That's huge.'

Sophie turns to Keira. 'Why didn't you explain?'

'Because it's private. I'm not into all that sharing stuff... it's just not me.' Keira fiddles with the edge of her jumper, picking away at a loose strand of wool. 'I'm sorry. I should have pulled out of the trip. I thought it would do me good to get away, do lots of swimming, spend some time thinking, et cetera, et cetera. And I didn't want to let the rest of you down.'

There is a long, awkward silence. 'Anyone else with anything to confess?' quips Grace. 'Come on, girls, admit it. We've all acted against our fellow sisters at some point in our lives.' She looks from one to another of them. 'How about you, Sophie? Have you ever been with a married guy?'

'No, absolutely not.'

'Or someone who already had a girlfriend?'

'No!'

'Really?' presses Elise. 'Hasn't there ever been a bit of an overlap? We've all had overlaps, surely!' The others laugh knowingly.

'I don't like things to be messy,' Sophie says.

'Wow... that's impressive.'

'Not really. Ryan was my first serious boyfriend. I haven't had much experience.'

'I had an affair with a married man once,' admits Grace. 'I didn't know to begin with, and I *did* end it, but not as soon as I should have done. I fooled myself for a few months before realising he was never going to leave his wife.'

'I had a brief thing with a guy who was engaged,' says Elise.

'The bizarre bit was that his fiancée knew about it and she was doing the same. It felt exciting at the time, but then they got married and it was over. God knows whether they're still together. Doubt it.'

'Well, like Sophie, I've only been a victim of adultery,' Ariel says, pouring herself another glass of wine. 'And I can tell you, it's a really horrible thing to go through. Utterly humiliating. I was physically and emotionally abused. It wasn't my fault, but I blamed myself and it made me very depressed. Women who have affairs with married men are traitors to womankind.'

'Hey! If we start judging each other, this is going to end in tears,' says Elise. 'Look, we've all done things we regret, and we've all been shat on from a great height. That's life. It's complicated. Now, enough confessions. Can we just play a game or something? Cards, maybe?'

'Good idea,' says Grace.

'There's a pack in the sideboard,' Keira adds, 'but it's incomplete.'

Sophie unfolds her legs. 'I brought some, they're in my room.' She stands up, pleased to have an excuse for a time-out. Picking up a candlestick, she leaves, making her way down the cold, dark corridor to her bedroom. She puts the candlestick down on the chest of drawers and picks up her rucksack, rummaging through its pockets. Her fingers touch a packet of tissues, a pen torch, a comb, a lipstick, a small notebook and a couple of biros. No playing cards. She tries another pocket, and touches something hard and metal.

'I don't believe it!' she says aloud, pulling the object out and holding it under the light. It's the key to the hire car. How did she miss it before? She's sure she emptied all the rucksack pockets, but here it is, exactly where she thought she'd put it in the first place. She laughs at her own idiocy, relieved to be in harmony with the universe again.

Forgetting the pack of cards, she rushes back to the sitting room, candlestick in one hand, key in the other. She holds it up triumphantly. 'I've found it!' she cries.

'Found what?' asks Ariel.

'The car key – look!'

Keira smiles. 'Phew! Where was it?'

'In my rucksack.' There is a collective groan. 'I'm sorry, everyone. I obviously didn't look properly. I wasn't in a fit state...'

'The important thing is that you've found it,' says Ariel.

Elise claps her hands. 'Yay! Now we can go and buy more booze and chocolates!' She picks up the empty box and rattles it.

'Did you find the cards, Sophie?' asks Keira.

'Oops – forgot!' She goes back to her room. Everything's going to be okay. She's with friends, and providing they stick together, they'll be safe. If she managed not to see the car key when it was right under her nose, she could easily have imagined being pushed into the water. The holiday is nearly over, but for Sophie it's only just begun.

TWENTY-SEVEN

SOPHIE

Sophie lies on her back, starfish-shaped, stretching towards each corner of the bed. Everyone has retired for the night after several games of blackjack and whist. They are back on good terms with each other, and she feels almost calm.

This is how it will be from now on, sleeping alone night after night, undisturbed by Ryan's snores and snuffles and coughs. None of his daily detritus to deal with – dirty underwear on the floor, crumpled tissues under the pillow, stray hairs on the sheets. No toilet seat to close several times a day. No more petty arguments about the temperature setting on the heating thermostat, whose turn it is to put the bins out, or whether it would be a good idea to get a dog. She'll be free to make every decision by herself.

But she'll be alone – that's the price. No more family holidays. No more putting the world to rights over a cup of tea in bed. No more seeing the funny side of something and breaking into uncontrollable giggles. No more cosy cuddles in the morning or passionate sex at night. She will miss all that, although to be honest, she can't remember the last time they made love. They've been running on empty for a long time now. The tanks are dry, and they've finally come to a stop.

At least she will still have Ben and Louie. They'll live mainly with her, in the family home. Ryan will want to spend time with them, and that's fine. He's a good dad. It's just being a husband he's shit at. They'll come to an amicable arrangement. She won't weaponise her children as some parents do.

She blinks into the darkness. Soon it'll be time to leave this strange place and return to real life. It's highly likely that Ryan will still be at home, hoping perhaps for a reconciliation. If he refuses to leave, she's not sure what she can do. When everything blew up last year, she made him sleep on the sofa bed in the spare room, but after a few days he crept back in, complaining that the mattress was giving him backache. But she won't share a bed with him any more. Not even for one night.

She could go to her parents' place perhaps, while Ryan sorts out his accommodation. They would welcome her for sure. But although she adores them, she could never live with them permanently again. When they retired, they moved down from Sheffield to be closer. Sometimes it feels too close. They still treat her like a teenager, even though she's nearly forty and has developed her own domestic routines and family traditions, her own behaviour handbook for the kids. It would be confusing for everyone not knowing who was in charge of whom. She would rather be in her own place, on her own terms. And Ben and Louie need as little disruption to their lives as possible.

No, Ryan has to be the one to leave. But where will he go? she wonders. Not to *his* parents, that much is certain. He never visits them or invites them over, not even at Christmas. They've never accepted Sophie as part of the family, and the boys are closer to the neighbours than they are to their paternal grandparents.

All that can be sorted out. In the meantime, she owes it to the others to salvage something positive from this ill-fated trip.

They are determined that she'll swim with them tomorrow morning.

'It's like when you fall off a horse, you have to get straight back on or you'll never ride again,' Grace said before they went to bed. 'Not that I've ever been on a horse,' she added, which made them all laugh.

'It's true,' agreed Elise. 'You can't give up wild swimming, not when you've already lost so much.'

'Okay, I'll try,' Sophie said, mainly to stop everyone going on about it. She wants to swim, but she's not sure she's ready. She keeps having flashbacks to the other night, and although the rational part of her accepts that she could have imagined being pushed into the water, a more instinctive, emotional part of her still doesn't believe it. At the time, she was sure that Keira attacked her, shoving and pushing her towards the edge of the bank. She remembers gripping her jacket as they both toppled in. But maybe she was just pissed and disorientated by the darkness; slipped and fell, became caught up in the weeds...

No, she must put all that out of her head.

She puts her swimming costume on as soon as she gets out of bed. She does this on the coldest mornings, when she doesn't feel in the mood. It stops her chickening out later on. There's nothing more defeatist than removing a dry swimsuit. She layers up with jogging bottoms, two T-shirts and a thick jumper, then leaves the bedroom in search of the others.

Grace is already up, make-up on as usual, including the famous painted eyebrows, which make her look permanently startled. She's sitting at the kitchen table pressing lumps of solid butter on to a heel of bread. 'Morning,' she says.

'Hi. Sleep okay?'

'Like a baby.'

Sophie reaches for the box of cereal and empties a few dusty crumbs into a bowl. 'Oh dear.'

'Everything's running out,' says Grace glumly. 'I think we should go to the nearest town and have fish and chips for lunch.'

Sophie picks up one of the apples from the bowl. They're going a little wrinkly, but they're the only fruit they have left. 'I know there's only one day to go but we do need some other stuff. Bread, milk, bananas...'

'Wine. Gin.'

'Yes, all the essentials.' She grins.

'Seriously, we deserve a treat,' says Grace. 'Next time we're going on a pamper weekend at a spa, okay?'

'If there *is* a next time.'

'Why shouldn't there be? We're friends for life now, aren't we?' She gives Sophie a mischievous wink. Sophie is still trying to interpret it when Ariel breezes into the kitchen.

'Morning, girls,' she says. 'It's a beautiful sunny day. I hope you're both up for an early dip in the loch.'

'Count me in,' says Grace, raising a hand.

'Sophie?'

'I've already got my swimsuit on.'

Ariel hacks away at the last remaining bit of loaf. 'That's brilliant news. Feel the fear and do it anyway, eh?'

'Something like that.'

'Right...' She gestures at Grace to pass her the marmalade. 'We just need to get the lazybones out of bed, then we can all go down to the loch together.'

'It's only just gone eight,' Grace says.

'I know, but if we're going up to the Prince's Cairn today, we need to make an early start.'

'Grace and I were just saying we probably need to prioritise a trip to Mallaig or Fort William. For supplies.'

'And fish and chips,' Grace adds.

'Really? Can't we manage?' Ariel frowns. 'There's no meat

left, but I'm sure there are enough vegetables. I could easily whip up a curry.' Grace pulls an agonised face behind Ariel's back, and Sophie tries not to giggle.

'Let's see what the others think,' she says. 'I'll give them a shout.'

It's another hour before all five of them are ready for the swim. As the week has gone on, everyone has slowed down, finally shaking off the relentless pace of city life and adjusting to having so much time to fill. They arrived in brand-new outdoor gear and coordinated leisurewear. Now they are all wearing mismatched clothes and have given up brushing mud off their coats. Sophie quite likes the scruffiness, although she can't wait to have a hot shower when she gets home. *When she gets home...* She suddenly feels desperate to be there, to see Ben and Louie. But she can't deal with that right now. She needs to join in with the others, gather her strength, prepare herself for the challenge ahead. Try and have a good time, for God's sake.

Keira leads the way down the path from the house. It's narrow, so they walk in single file. Grace, then Sophie, then Elise, their orange swim hats making them look like a giant caterpillar. Ariel brings up the rear, flasks of coffee and the last chunk of lemon drizzle cake in her rucksack should anyone need a quick sugar fix afterwards.

Sophie's heart starts to beat faster as they near the loch. The path widens out to the small beach from where it's easy to wade in. She looks around, her gaze drawn to the other side of the loch, where all the drama happened. There's a muddy track that skirts the bank, indicating that it would probably be possible to reach that part from here on foot. She'd like to go and check the ground to see if there are any signs of a struggle. Just to put her mind completely at rest.

The others are already stripping off, laying their clothes on the ground and securing them with stones. The dryrobes always go on top, so they can be grabbed quickly as soon as the women emerge from the water.

'Come on, Sophie, you can do it,' says Keira. 'The important thing is not to hesitate.'

'Yes, I know.' She takes off her boots, socks and jogging bottoms before putting on her swimming shoes. The dryrobe is reluctantly discarded next, and then her top clothing. The sun has disappeared behind a bank of clouds and a sharp breeze is blowing across the surface of the water. She shivers, wrapping her arms across her chest as she hobbles over the pebbles, following the others. Elise and Grace are holding hands to steady each other. They cry out simultaneously as they hit the icy water, and Grace swears loudly.

Ariel is already in. She does a few desultory breaststrokes, then bobs up and down on the spot, grinning from ear to ear. Keira isn't far behind, running in and flinging herself immediately into the water. She swims a few strokes, then dives under.

'Oh my God, it's colder than ever!' she cries as she pops up a few metres away, her face dripping wet.

'Great. Thanks for telling me!' shouts Sophie from the beach. The water is licking the toes of her thin swimming shoes; she can already feel how icy it is. She wants to swim, and yet...

Elise comes back for her, holding out her hand. 'Come on, Sophie,' she says kindly. 'You'll be fine once you're in.'

Sophie nods and takes a step forward, the water pooling around her ankles. Her skin is pimpled with goosebumps and her extremities are starting to hurt. She needs to submerge herself and let her body acclimatise. She needs to swim.

'I c-can't,' she stutters.

'Yes, you can.' She lets Elise drag her in, deeper and deeper, the icy water hitting her calves, then her knees, thighs, hips. 'Shoulders under,' Elise commands, and they dip beneath the surface together. Sophie feels the cold fastening around her neck like a collar.

'Well done!' says Grace, swimming like an elegant old lady, chin up, face dry. 'I knew you could do it!'

'Yes, thanks. It feels... good.'

Ariel and Keira join them, and they gather in a floating circle, treading water.

'You okay, Sophie? You keep looking over there.' Keira points towards the other side of the loch.

'Do I?'

'Yes! Is that where you fell in?'

'Yeah... think so...'

'Ignore it,' says Grace. 'Look the other way.'

'I'm just thinking,' Sophie continues. 'I'd like to know if there are reeds underwater. I got all tangled up, you see. At the time it felt like somebody was dragging me under, but...' She catches Keira's expression. 'I'm not saying that's what happened. It's what it *felt* like.'

'Okay, then let's investigate,' replies Keira, her tone slightly off. 'Put your mind at rest.'

'I didn't mean—'

'We could all go,' says Elise. 'It'll only take a few minutes to swim there and back.'

Grace looks at Sophie. 'You sure about this?'

'Yeah... I think so.'

'Race you!' shouts Elise, breaking into a crawl.

Keira is the strongest swimmer and soon overtakes her, unafraid to put her face in the water, arms curving gracefully over her head. Ariel and Sophie follow with breaststroke, while Grace calmly doggy-paddles her way across.

The water is even colder in this part of the loch, suggesting it must be deeper here. Sophie feels her heart racing as it deals with the plummeting temperature. She tries to stop herself gasping, telling herself to calm down. But it's not just the cold that's scaring her.

'I think it was around about here,' she says. 'See that stretch of bank? That's where I climbed out, I think. You can see where the grass has been flattened.'

'You sure?' Keira asks. 'There are no reeds or anything, and the water's really deep.'

'I think we're too far out. If you fell in, you would have been much closer to the edge,' suggests Elise.

'Good point,' says Keira. 'I bet there are a load of reeds underwater by the bank.' She starts swimming towards it.

'This cold is too much for me. I'm going back to base,' says Grace.

Elise nods. 'Me too. How about you guys?'

Ariel turns to Sophie. 'You don't have to do this. Keira's just trying to prove a point, that's all.'

'I know. I didn't mean to accuse her all over again.'

'Come on, Sophie!' Keira shouts.

'Don't get too cold.' Ariel smiles at her before swimming after Grace and Elise.

Sophie takes a deep breath to steady her nerves, then joins Keira. The water is still surprisingly deep, even though they are only a few yards from the bank. It's also surprisingly clear of vegetation.

'There's nothing here I could have got snagged up in,' she says. 'Sorry... this must be the wrong place. It was dark, difficult to tell... I think we should go back now before we get too cold.'

'I'm going to see what it's like at the bottom,' Keira announces. She adjusts her goggles, then dives under.

Sophie sighs. This was supposed to be a healing swim, but all it's done is make her feel worse. And she doesn't want to get into another row with Keira.

Suddenly Keira bursts to the surface, spluttering and gasping. 'Oh God! Oh God!' she says.

'What? What is it? Tell me!' The whites of Keira's eyes are large, her mouth is open, gulping in water. 'Are you okay? What's wrong?' Sophie presses. 'Are you hurt?'

Keira splutters as she speaks. 'No... There's... there's a body down there! A fucking body!'

'What? Are you sure?'

'I saw it lying on the bottom. I touched it!'

'But... but...'

'We've got to call the police.'

'Who is it? What do they look like? What are they wearing?'

'I don't know! What does it matter? They're dead! We've got to get help. Tell the others. Swim, Sophie, swim as fast as you can!'

TWENTY-EIGHT

SOPHIE

They stand on the bank shivering, as much from shock as the cold. Sophie zips her dryrobe up to the neck and plunges her hands into its deep pockets.

'I *knew* somebody pushed me in,' she says through chattering teeth. 'I kept... trying to believe, but in my heart I knew. I... I should have... reported it to the police.'

'We did,' Ariel reminds her.

'I know, but we sent them away.'

Elise pours the water out of her shoes. 'We thought it was Keira, remember?'

'Oh, so it's my fault, is it?' Keira snaps.

'No, but you have to admit, you confused things. If you hadn't gone walkabout without telling anyone—'

'I needed some time to myself.'

'You didn't come back that night – what else were we supposed to think?'

'The worst, clearly. Sophie gets it into her head that I'm having an affair with her husband, so obviously it stands to reason that I must want to kill her.' Keira squeezes out her wet costume angrily. 'You lot are unbelievable.'

'Stop it. This isn't helping,' rebukes Ariel, hurriedly getting dressed. 'There's a dead body down there.'

'I know, I found it! Have you any idea how traumatising that is? But nobody seems to care about how I feel.'

'That's not true...'

'Everyone's been against me this whole trip,' Keira huffs. 'You've no idea what I've been going through these past few days.'

'Keira had nothing to do with it,' interrupts Sophie. 'It's my fault.'

Grace shakes her head. 'No way.'

'I pulled that person into the water with me.'

'You were defending yourself, simple as.'

'I let them drown.'

'They were trying to drown *you*.'

'Yes, but who is "they"? Who is it down there?' Sophie cries out. 'I don't understand.'

'Girls, we can't stand here debating,' interjects Ariel. 'We need to get back to the house or we're going to get hypothermia. Once we've warmed up, we can make a plan.'

They finish putting on their socks and boots in silence, then troop back up the steep path to Condie's Retreat. On the way, Sophie tries to remember more details about that terrible night, as if she's being questioned by a detective. How tall was her attacker? What were they wearing? Did they speak? Why did she pull them into the water? Did they cry out for help? Why didn't she try to save them? Why didn't she report it to the police straight away?

As soon as they arrive back, everyone rushes off to their room to dry off properly and change into fresh clothes. Then they gather in the lounge. The mood is sombre, and Keira still seems to be stewing with indignation. Sophie feels sorry for her. It must have been a terrible shock, and it's true, she's not receiving much sympathy.

Ariel makes a pot of tea and brings it in on a tray. Nobody says much, other than a dull please or thank you, but Sophie is sure that each of them has a hundred questions churning through her head.

'Okay, so what do we now?' asks Grace finally.

'Call the police, of course,' replies Ariel.

'Except there's no bloody signal.'

'Obviously. We'll have to walk back to the road until we get one.' Ariel sips her tea. 'Personally, I think Sophie should go. She's the main witness. And she's the driver. She might have to travel to the police station in Fort William, you know, to make a statement. At least one of us should go with her. For support. We should set off as soon as possible.'

'Yeah, that makes sense, but it's not exactly an emergency, is it?' says Elise. 'Whoever it is lying down there is... well, dead. No disrespect, but don't we need to talk it through first? Make sure we've got all our facts correct.'

Keira nods. 'Absolutely. I think Sophie should start by telling us exactly what happened that night.'

'I've already told you,' Sophie replies. 'I'm not lying.'

'You were out there too, Keira,' says Elise. 'To be honest, I'm surprised you didn't hear anything.'

'Well, I didn't, okay?'

'The big question is, who is it?' says Grace.

'Come on, it's got to be the guy from the bothy,' Elise answers. 'Has to be. He accosted Sophie on her walk, he admitted he'd been spying on us at the loch, which proves he knew the place...'

'And Sophie, you found those documents about Condie's Retreat,' adds Ariel.

She nods. 'Yes, including that leaflet about the dangers of wild swimming. And when we went to the beach the day after, all his stuff was still in the bothy, but the log burner was stone cold.'

'Yup. Plus you thought you saw somebody with a torch out in the garden one night,' says Elise. 'I know we didn't believe you, but... that was probably him.'

'He's a pervert and he got what he deserved,' announces Grace. 'Good riddance, I say.'

'We don't know for sure that it's him,' says Sophie. 'Not until... you know...' She shudders. Images of divers and white tents and plastic tape spring instantly to mind.

'The police will want to know whether it was a random attack or whether he was targeting you specifically,' says Keira. 'Have you any idea who he might be?'

'He said he was an eco-journalist, that's all.'

'But he used your name and you said you couldn't remember giving it to him,' she presses.

'Yeah, but afterwards I remembered telling him about Sophie's Swimmers... At least, I *think* I did. I've lost track now...' Sophie tails off.

'Well, the police are probably going to question you under caution, so you'd better make sure you've got your story straight,' says Keira. 'There were no other witnesses. Only two people know what really happened, and one of them is dead.'

'For God's sake, Keira, there's no need to scare the shit out of her,' Elise says. She turns to Sophie. 'You've done nothing wrong, okay? All you have to do is tell the truth.'

'Yes...' Sophie murmurs, although right now the truth feels like a slippery thing she can barely keep hold of. It's all part of the nightmare that started when Ryan called her at the service station. Could there be some connection? Could Ryan have paid the bothy guy to kill her? The idea is utterly preposterous, but right at this moment, anything seems possible. Should she mention it to the police? It could be important, but she doesn't want to put them on the wrong track, doesn't want to falsely accuse Ryan and make things worse...

'What did he look like?' asks Grace, interrupting her thoughts.

'Just a regular guy. Quite tall. In his thirties, I think. He had a beard.'

'When you met him, did he give you his name or mention which magazine he worked for?'

'No... I think he said he was a blogger or something.'

'Did he have a Scottish accent?'

Sophie shakes her head. 'No. Definitely not. He just spoke normally.'

'What's normal? Midlands, like us? London? Welsh? Irish?'

'I don't remember... Nothing distinctive.'

Elise puts down her mug of tea. 'Maybe a couple of us should go to the beach and see if his stuff is still in the bothy. The police will want to seal it off, I guess. We could stand guard until they arrive.'

'Is that necessary?' asks Ariel. 'Nobody's about and the police will get there soon enough. We don't even know for sure if it *is* the guy. He could be alive and just have gone out for a walk. We can't go rummaging in his things.'

'Fair enough,' accepts Elise. 'I wanted to do something positive, I suppose. We're just speculating here.'

'Let the police investigate,' says Ariel, rather self-importantly. 'One of us should go with Sophie and the others should stay here so we can show the divers where the body is.'

'In that case, *I* should stay,' says Keira.

'I'll stay too, if that's okay,' says Grace. 'I twisted my ankle yesterday and would rather not do that long walk.'

'I'm happy to go with Sophie,' says Ariel. 'You okay with that?'

'Yes, fine. Thanks. Whoever. I'd just rather not be on my own, that's all.'

'Then I'll stay here too,' says Elise. 'We could start clearing up, getting ready to leave. I mean, we're not going to want to stay, are we? Not now. We'll give our statements to the police and then we'll be off, yes?' Everyone nods in agreement.

'And I thought this trip couldn't get any worse.' Grace laughs grimly.

Sophie and Ariel set off on the long walk back to the road. Having said she wanted somebody to come with her, now Sophie wishes she was on her own. She doesn't want to call the police and set something in motion that she can't control. What she'd really like to do is drive off in the hire car and never come back.

Every hundred metres or so, Ariel stops and takes out her phone to see if she can get a signal. As they're going to make an emergency call, any network will do. Sophie watches as she raises her arm and waves the handset in the air as if trying to command the attention of some god in the heavens.

'No. Nothing doing,' she declares.

They carry on, hardly saying a word. Sophie feels more anxious with every step, as if she is trudging towards some miserable fate. This shouldn't be happening to her, it's not fair. If only she hadn't agreed to swim in the loch today. She *knew* she hadn't got tangled in weeds and that somebody had grabbed her by the ankle and tried to pull her down. Damn Keira for trying to prove her innocence. They would have left Condie's Retreat tomorrow morning and nobody would ever have known that there was a body in the water. Sophie could have lived the rest of her life in blissful ignorance.

True, somebody probably would have reported the guy missing eventually. The police would have found his stuff in the bothy and searched the surrounding area, but with hundreds of small lochs dotted around, they were unlikely ever to have found him. More likely they'd have concluded that he'd gone swimming in the sea and drowned. End of story.

She knows it's wrong, but a large part of her wants to turn back and persuade the others to keep quiet, to pretend none of it happened. What if nobody believes it was self-defence? Could she be charged for not trying to save her attacker's life? Not that she could have rescued him. It was hard enough saving herself.

They have reached the birch wood. More leaves have fallen in the past couple of days, and the ground looks as if it's covered with golden coins. If only she'd turned back at the service station, none of this would have happened. If only, if only... She's going to be repeating that phrase for the rest of her life.

'You okay, Sophie?' asks Ariel, breaking the silence.

'Yeah... I'm just worried about how the police are going to react,' she replies. 'It's going to look really suspicious.'

'It'll look more suspicious *not* telling them. We called them before, remember, saying we thought Keira had drowned. If somebody else finds the body weeks or months later, well, it'll be on record, they'll know it was us.'

'It's not likely, though, is it? That he'll be found. He's not going to be washed up. And he's not in a part of the loch where people would normally swim.'

Ariel stops in her tracks. 'Sophie! What are you getting at? We can't *not* report it. That would be a criminal offence in itself.'

'I suppose so. It's just that... I've been through so much. I'm not sure I can...' She feels tears pricking behind her eyes. 'It doesn't make any sense. Why *me*? That's what I want to know.'

'It was probably a random attack, but the police will investigate, they'll find out.'

'What if they think I killed him?'

'They won't.'

'But what if they do?!'

'We *have* to report it,' Ariel says sharply. 'I can't believe we're even discussing this.' She takes out her phone and waves it around again. 'Unless there's something you haven't told me...'

'Of course there isn't. I'm just saying... sometimes—'

'Forensics find stuff, so there's no point in keeping things secret.'

Sophie sighs. 'I've nothing to hide. I'm just worried, that's all. Wouldn't you be?'

'Ha! I've got a signal,' Ariel says. 'It's only one bar, but it's worth trying.' She turns to Sophie. 'Look, I understand how awful this is for you, but it'll be okay. You have nothing to fear.'

Sophie gulps as her friend dials 999.

TWENTY-NINE

THE SWIMMER

Funny how sometimes you get what you want without trying; how it can come from a completely different source than expected.

There's a drowned man lying at the bottom of the loch, and soon the entire area will be swarming with police officers with Scottish accents. I suppose I should feel sorry for the guy, but it sounds like he attacked Sophie, so he probably got what he deserved. There's going to have to be a full investigation. I don't suppose she'll be charged with murder, but manslaughter, perhaps? What *is* the legal position here, I wonder? There were no witnesses, so it's Sophie's word against that of a dead man. She's already admitted that she pulled him into the water with her and didn't try to save him. Does that count as self-defence? She's got to be guilty of *something*. I expect she'll wriggle out of it eventually, knowing her, but she's going to have to face some rigorous interviewing, maybe even a trial. I'd like to see her in the dock. I want her to suffer. We'll be there in the visitors' gallery, of course – Sophie's Swimmers, loyal to the end.

But now I'm in my bedroom, waiting for the drama to start. The window is misty with condensation; beads of water have gathered on the windowsill and there's a faint smell of mould. I draw a heart with my fingertip and write Carly's name in the centre. We were always drawing on glass when we were kids – in the car when we were in a traffic jam, or in the lounge when it was raining and we were stuck indoors. Now it's my way of connecting with her, imagining that I'm writing in her ghostly breath.

'Wouldn't it be great,' I whisper, my lips almost kissing the glass, 'if Sophie were charged with causing death by drowning.'

Very fitting, she replies in my head. *I hope she goes to prison for a very long time.*

'Me too.' I kiss her name, then rub everything off with the side of my sleeve.

I can almost see her sitting on my bed – barefoot, the hem of her jeans rolled up. Her toes are separated with bits of screwed-up toilet paper and she's painting her nails with red glittery varnish. She always liked a bit of sparkle, did Carly. When I was little, I used to beg her to paint my nails too, but Mum told her she wasn't allowed. Sometimes she did my toenails secretly, but only in the winter, when I could hide them under socks.

That bottle of nail varnish still sits on the dressing table in her bedroom back home. I don't think anyone's tried to open it, but it must have dried up by now, surely. Her fingers and toes were painted with it when they fished her out of the canal. Mum wanted to identify her that way, didn't want to have to look at her face. She told them she'd know her daughter's hands anywhere, but the police said that wasn't enough for a formal identification. They *made* her look, and I don't think she ever recovered.

I never saw Carly's body. I was too young, and anyway, I didn't want to. She'd been in the water for two days – God knows what that does to the skin. We weren't there when they pulled her out. We were gathered at home, anxiously waiting for news, hoping against hope that she was still alive but knowing in our gut that she wasn't.

Now the canal basin is bursting with cool bars and fancy restaurants, but back then parts of it were still rough and undeveloped. The towpaths were badly lit and the canals were full of rubbish. The police tried to piece together Carly's last movements, but the few old pubs along that stretch had no CCTV, and nobody came forward to say they'd seen her.

Carly had a Saturday job at Topshop. After work, she usually popped home to have some tea and get changed, then she'd go out for the evening with friends – or with Ryan on the rare occasions he came back for the weekend. But on that Saturday, she didn't turn up. Mum texted her asking where she was and if she was okay, but she didn't get a reply, which was odd because Carly and Mum were always texting – *Thinking of you... Love you lots!... Let me know when you're on the bus*. It was a bit oppressive, I thought.

Mum was in a stew all evening, ears on stalks listening for the sound of the front door opening or a comforting message pinging on to her mobile. She rang Carly countless times, but it went straight to voicemail – she wasn't allowed to take calls at work and clearly hadn't switched it back on.

'I've a funny feeling something's wrong,' she told me, several times. 'Did Carly mention anything?'

'No, she never tells me jack shit,' I replied, which was true.

Mum picked up her phone again, willing it to play its tinny ringtone. 'It's not like her not to get in touch. She's always so good.'

'Perhaps she left her phone at the shop.'

'Hmm...' Mum wasn't buying it. 'Is Ryan home this weekend?'

'Dunno... maybe. How should I know?'

'I expect that's what happened. He probably surprised her after work and whisked her off for a pizza.' She rolled her eyes.

'I hate the way she drops everything as soon as that boy turns up, without a thought for anyone else. I'd made shepherd's pie as well.'

'I know. We ate it earlier, remember? I live here too, Mum.'

But she didn't react to my pointed remark. 'I left hers in the oven, but it'll be stone cold and all congealed by now,' she said instead, rising from the sofa. 'I'll put it in the fridge, then she can stick it in the microwave when she gets in,' adding in an irritated tone she would later regret, 'whenever *that* is, the little madam.'

She was acting cross, but I could tell she was really worried, because she forgot to tell me to go to bed. I was still watching telly at eleven o'clock when she started ringing round. She was one of those mums who insisted on having all your friends' numbers. She rang Ryan first, but he didn't pick up. Then she tried Carly's friends. Most of them didn't pick up either, but those who did said they hadn't seen or heard from Carly. She even tried Ryan's mum, Jill, who said she was pissed off with her son because he hadn't been in touch for weeks.

At midnight, Mum rang the police, but they said we had to wait twenty-four hours before reporting Carly as a missing person, so there was nothing we could do. Drew came home and sat up with Mum. I was yawning my head off and feeling quite bored, so I went up to my room and fell asleep.

As soon as the twenty-four hours were up, the police started searching. It didn't take long. Carly's red shoes were found on the towpath, along with her matching handbag. Her purse and mobile had gone, but her name badge from Topshop was still inside. Divers were sent down, and they found her body at the bottom of the canal just a few yards away. Then they fished out her mobile. It looked like she'd been mugged and pushed into the water. But the detective in charge said it was also possible that she had dropped her bag and somebody had stolen its contents at a later stage. She might have fallen in accidentally, or even – dare he say it? – jumped. Apparently people often took their shoes off before committing suicide.

Mum wouldn't accept that Carly had killed herself. She insisted that she'd been a happy young woman, training to be a beautician, engaged to be married. For once, to say that she had everything to live for was not a cliché.

Waiting for the results of the autopsy was agony. Mum was terrified that Carly had been raped before she was killed. The pathologist found high levels of alcohol in the body, but no evidence of assault. We were relieved, but still puzzled. What had Carly been doing at the canal basin in the first place?

Ryan came home straight away and made a great show of his grief. There was huge competition between him and Mum to be chief mourner at the funeral, but afterwards he went back to university and didn't keep in touch. It was months later when we heard about his double life. According to a mutual friend who'd bumped into Ryan in Gloucester, he'd been seeing a girl called Sophie for nearly two years. They even lived together.

Drew and Billie went to confront him, and there was an ugly scene. He claimed Carly hadn't known about Sophie, but the lads didn't believe him. They threatened to kill him unless he confessed, but Mum said she didn't want to lose any more of her family because of that bastard, so he was let off with a bruised ego and a black eye. His parents moved away shortly afterwards. They were ashamed, and allegedly never forgave their son.

Drew, Billie and I have sat in Carly's bedroom for hours talking about what really happened that night, pondering every possible scenario, going round in circles, never reaching a conclusion. We have different theories about how she died – accident, suicide, even murder – but the one thing we agree on is that Ryan was to blame. Somehow. Unfortunately, we don't have a shred of evidence to prove it.

But I'm going to get justice for Carly and succeed where my

brother and cousin failed. I pick up her photo again and hold it up to my lips.

'What do you reckon, sis? Is it game over for Sophie, or am I still going to have to kill her?'

Wait and see, she says. *Just wait and see.*

THIRTY

SOPHIE

'This is where we hit the water,' says Sophie, showing DS McKenzie a patch of flattened grass. 'I think so, anyway. The body's somewhere over there.' She gestures. 'That's right, isn't it?' She turns to Keira.

'Hard to tell from the bank,' she replies, 'but yes, more or less.'

'Well, it gives us a starting point.' The detective looks at his spindly young constable. 'Get some photos,' he orders before taking out a small black notebook and pen.

Sophie was surprised by how casually the police took the news that there was a dead body lying at the bottom of the loch. Either it was a common occurrence, or they didn't believe it, she thought. The group had expected an emergency response, with helicopters flying overhead and officers sealing off the area. But these two are all that were sent – a scruffy sergeant in corduroys and wellington boots who looks on the brink of retirement and a fresh-faced constable who could easily pass for fourteen.

'So...' says McKenzie, 'when did this happen?'

'When was I attacked or when did we find the body?'

'The attack first.'

'Monday night, at around ten or eleven.'

He raises his bushy eyebrows. 'What were you doing down here at that time of night?'

'We were... er...' Sophie exchanges a glance with Keira. Ever since the policemen arrived, she's been feeling increasingly nervous about how she's going to describe all this without sounding suspicious. 'It's hard to explain.'

'Out on the skite, were you?'

'Sorry?'

'Drinking.' She nods. 'I'm listening,' McKenzie says, pen poised.

'We were playing a game. Truth or Dare – you know it? I'd dared Keira to go for a swim.'

'In this loch, in the dark?' Sophie blushes. 'That was some dare.'

'It was a joke – I didn't think she would actually do it. She left the house and I went after her – I was trying to stop her, only I got lost and ended up here.'

'Where a random attacker just happened to be waiting.'

'Basically, yes.'

'Out here, in the dead of night, middle of nowhere? This isn't Glasgow city centre, you know.' He winks at his constable, who laughs weakly. 'Why didn't you report it immediately?'

'We did. Sort of. But we thought it was Keira because she'd gone missing, only then she turned up so we, er... withdrew... cancelled, whatever. It'll be on record, you can check.'

'Aye, we will.' He makes a note. 'Let's backtrack a wee bit. Why did you think it was your friend here that tried to drown you? You're here on holiday together, is that right?'

Sophie looks at the ground. 'We'd had a bit of a falling-out. So when I got pushed, I immediately assumed... I didn't see their face, you see, they didn't speak. It was pitch black and they rushed at me from behind.'

'I *did* keep telling everyone it wasn't me,' says Keira hotly. 'I had nothing to do with it. I was on the other side of the loch, I didn't even hear anything.'

'So, no witnesses...' He makes another note.

'Sophie was extremely drunk,' she adds.

'We were *all* drunk, Keira, you included.'

'Yeah, but you were completely wasted. And you were spoiling for a fight.'

'That's not true!' Sophie retorts.

'It totally is.'

'Okay... okay!' DS McKenzie raises a hand. 'We need to get some facts straight here, girls. I've got a team of divers on their way – that's not cheap, as I'm sure you understand. If this is all some stupid argument between you, it needs to stop right this minute, or I'll be charging you both with wasting police time.'

'There's definitely a body down there,' says Keira, folding her arms firmly.

'You saw it too?' he says, turning to Sophie.

'Er... no, not exactly. We were all swimming together, but only Keira was diving. When she told us, we panicked and got out of the water straight away.'

'The thing is, I know these lochs. Once you're out of your depth, you can't see a damn thing. There are stones, boulders, other obstructions... plants and weeds and stuff. You can't tell what's what. The imagination can play terrible tricks.'

'I didn't imagine it. The body is lying face down, fully clothed,' Keira says. 'I saw it and I touched it.'

'You were looking for it?'

'No. I wanted to see what is was like down there.'

'Why?'

'Because I thought Sophie had probably got caught up in some reeds. I wanted to prove that it wasn't me – that she'd imagined the whole thing. I wasn't expecting to actually find a dead body, okay? I'm not bullshitting. He's down there and you need to fish him out.'

'What I actually need right now is a nice cup of tea,' the detective says, rubbing the base of his spine. 'That was a long hike. Shall we go back to the house and carry on in comfort? I need to take statements from yourself and the other lassies in your group.' Sophie and Keira nod. He points a finger at the constable. 'You stay here and wait for the team, Gregor. Don't let anyone in the water or on the bank. This whole area's a potential crime scene, so don't go tramping about.'

'Okay,' the young man replies, shifting uneasily from one foot to the other.

Sophie and Keira lead DS McKenzie back to Condie's Retreat, where the others are waiting anxiously for an update. Ariel goes off to make hot drinks and the detective sets himself up in the sitting room. He calls for Sophie first. She shuffles in guiltily, feeling as if she's been hauled up in front of the head teacher.

'Okay, take me back to the beginning and tell me everything you remember about that night. When you were attacked.'

'Yes, I'll try... But before I do that, can I tell you something?'

He nods. 'Aye, go ahead.'

'I have a feeling I might know who my attacker was.'

'You do?' He leans forward.

She tells him about the guy in the bothy, the map with the route to Condie's Retreat marked in red, the information sheet about the dangers of wild swimming, how he accosted her on the path. He nods as he scribbles notes on his pad.

'I also think he was prowling around the house a couple of nights before – I only saw a torch beam flickering, but I think it must have been him.'

'Sounds likely. When you met him out walking, what did he say?'

'Just normal stuff about the scenery. And he admitted he'd been watching my friends swimming in the loch.'

'Did he? Ah, now we're getting somewhere. Why didn't you mention this at the start?'

'Sorry... I, er... I wasn't sure...'

'He was staying at the bothy, you said? I'll send someone down to the beach to check it out.'

DS McKenzie laboriously writes out Sophie's statement, and after a few amendments, she signs it. Then Keira goes in. Grace and Ariel remain in the kitchen, seated at the table waiting for their turn.

'This is going to take all day,' Sophie says, joining them.

'I don't know why he wants statements from us three,' Grace replies. 'We had nothing to do with any of it.'

Ariel gives her a patronising look. 'He'll want to corroborate, check the timeline, that kind of thing. Our evidence is just as important as Sophie and Keira's.'

'Not really.'

Elise comes in through the back door carrying a canister of water. 'The divers are here,' she says. 'It shouldn't take them long to bring him up.' Sophie shuffles along so that she can sit down. 'So what's happening?'

Sophie lowers her voice. 'Keira's in there now. I don't think McKenzie believes there's a body.'

'Well, none of us went to check, did we?' says Elise.

Ariel groans. 'Oh God, that would be so embarrassing.'

'But when I told him about the bothy guy, he cheered up a bit,' Sophie continues. 'I think he was worried about wasting money on a search.'

'This is all so horrible,' whispers Grace into her mug of tea. 'I can't bear it. It's been the worst holiday ever. I just want to go home.'

'Me too,' says Elise, and Ariel agrees.

Sophie doesn't respond. Going home might signal the end of this trauma, but for her it means the beginning of another one. Since Keira found the body and she went on that long walk to call the police, Ryan has been relegated to the back of her mind, but now he's pushing himself forward again. Where will he go once she's chucked him out of the house? How will they tell the boys? Problems loom before her like a high brick wall she has no hope of climbing over. And there's the recent shock, of course, the realisation that another human being tried to cause her harm – even kill her.

'Well, I think we might as well pack up,' says Ariel. 'There's no point hanging around. We should be allowed to go once everyone's given their statements.'

'The sooner we get out of this place the better,' agrees Elise.

They go to their rooms to start the process. It's already after two in the afternoon, but nobody has even thought about lunch. Ordinary activities like eating seem inappropriate when something so extraordinary has happened.

Sophie opens her wardrobe and stares at the few items of clothing hanging there. It will literally take about ten minutes to pack – there's no urgency, and right now she doesn't have the strength. Sitting on the bed, she picks up her phone and uses valuable battery power looking at pictures of her children, quickly scrolling past any that include Ryan. The boys are the only thing keeping her sane. She needs to be with them, to hold them in her arms. What if the police don't let her leave Scotland? She's alive and unhurt while the person she claims attacked her is dead. There are no other witnesses to back up her story, not even Keira (which Sophie doesn't believe; she must have heard something). It doesn't look good. Panic starts to rise, and she feels light-headed. She can't stay here by herself. She *won't*.

There's a knock on her bedroom door. 'Yes?' she calls out.

'It's DS McKenzie, may I talk to you?'

'Er... coming.' She climbs off the bed and opens the door. 'Yes?'

'Our divers have located the body,' he says. 'They're fetching it out of the water now.'

'Oh... right. That was quick.' Suddenly her knees give way and she has to hold on to the door frame.

'Obviously this is going to trigger a full investigation.'

'Yes... I see.' She takes a breath. 'Will I be able to leave? It's just that everyone wants to get away and I'm the only driver.'

'Oh no, not yet, I'm afraid. I need to go back to the station and update my boss. It doesn't help that there's no damn phone signal out here.' He sighs. 'Like living in the bloody Dark Ages... Anyway, sit tight, don't go anywhere.'

'Okay.'

He walks back down the hallway and leaves by the front door. As soon as she hears it shutting behind him, Sophie breaks down, crumpling to the floor in tears.

'Hey – you okay?' says Elise, coming out of her bedroom.

'No! Of course I'm not fucking okay. I've killed someone!'

'No, you haven't. They attacked you. At worst, it was self-defence.'

'I can't prove it.'

'Look, he was a stranger, a pervert. Once they identify him, they'll know. There'll be clues, he might even be on the sex offenders register.'

'I've got to see him,' Sophie says, getting to her feet. 'I've got to know if it's the bothy guy.'

'Mm... they probably won't let you.'

'I'll make them.'

'Sophie...'

But she pushes past Elise and runs into the porch, pulling on her boots without lacing them and running down the path towards the loch. Her heart pounds loudly in her chest as she stumbles over stones and splashes through muddy puddles. She has to see his face... she has to *know*.

She takes the same narrow path she took that night,

branching off from the main route, and within a couple of minutes she reaches the loch. She stops and takes cover behind some trees. Three people in wetsuits are standing on the bank, talking to the young constable. Their backs are turned to her and they have no idea that she's there.

The body is lying on the ground several metres behind them. It's been temporarily covered with a large piece of black plastic, the soles of a pair of dark boots visible at one end. She only just manages to stop herself gasping out loud. A few days ago, this lifeless lump was a living, breathing human being. If she hadn't fought back, if she hadn't managed to escape, it would have been *her* body lying here...

She has to see his face, and this is her only chance. Very soon the whole scene will be roped off – a tent erected over the body, the area swarming with forensic investigators, uniforms guarding the perimeter.

She creeps forward, boot laces dragging through the mud, trying her hardest not to breathe or make her clothes rustle. She knows she has to do this in one quick movement; that if she hesitates, they'll hear her and it'll be too late.

She reaches the body and crouches down. With trembling fingers, she pulls back the plastic sheet to reveal a bruised, puffy face, swollen with water. She screams.

THIRTY-ONE

SOPHIE

Sophie runs from one bedroom to another, banging on doors, shouting names.

'Elise... Keira... Ariel... Grace! Everyone to the sitting room now!' Her tone sounds so urgent that they emerge immediately.

Ariel speaks first. 'What is it? Have they found him?'

'Yes... I mean no... It's awful, so awful...'

'Are you okay, Sophie?' asks Elise. 'You look like you've seen a ghost. What on earth has happened?'

'I need to talk to you together,' she replies, trembling. 'Please.' She gestures at them to follow her to the sitting room.

They troop in one after another, exchanging worried glances. Sophie hovers on the rug, not knowing whether to stand or sit, or how to begin. She's still reeling from the shock and can barely comprehend what she's just seen.

'They've got him out of the water, right?' says Elise. 'The bothy guy.'

Sophie shakes her head. 'Yes, but it's not him.'

Grace frowns. 'Really? You mean there's some other pervert out there?'

'No! Don't say that. It's not... not what you think... Please, you need to listen.'

'We *are* listening,' says Ariel, 'but you're not telling. Come on, what's the news?'

'Everyone needs to sit down first.'

Elise, Grace and Ariel take the sofa, while Keira perches on its arm. Grace takes hold of Elise's hand and they all look at Sophie expectantly.

'Okay,' says Ariel, taking an ostentatiously deep breath. 'Give it to us.'

'It's... um... Sorry, I don't know how to say this.' Sophie swallows. 'But the body they just pulled out is... I'm afraid it's... it's Fern.'

There is a collective gasp.

'Fern?' echoes Keira. *'Fern?'*

'Yes. I'm sorry.'

'I think I'm going to be sick.' Grace puts her hand to her mouth and rushes out of the room.

'How can it be Fern?' says Elise after a few seconds of silence. 'That's... impossible. She didn't come with us, she's back at home, there must be some mistake.'

'Believe me, I *saw* the body and I know it was her,' insists Sophie. 'I thought it was going to be the journalist guy. I never expected it to be Fern, not in a million years. It was a total shock. But... I'm sorry... there's no doubt.'

She shudders. The horrific image will be for ever seared on her brain. Fern's body bloated and discoloured, her once beautiful skin looking like soggy brown paper that would disintegrate at the slightest touch. Her nose and mouth still in place, but only just. Her hair, always so precisely cut and highlighted, matted with mud and plastered against the sides of her head. Sophie wouldn't have recognised her for sure had it not been for the scarf knotted around her neck. She'd admired it once and been told that a dear friend had knitted it for her. It was a gorgeous scarf – the wool soft, the heathery colours picking out the blue of Fern's eyes.

'It makes no sense,' says Ariel.

Sophie clasps her fingers together. 'I'm sorry... I'm sorry... I didn't know how to tell you... I still can't believe it myself, but it's true.'

Ariel screws her face up sceptically. 'I think we should all take a look. Just to be sure.'

'No way,' says Grace, coming back into the room.

'But it might not be her. The body's been in the water a couple of days, Sophie could be mistaken...'

'I'm not. It's her,' Sophie repeats. 'Anyway, you don't want to see her... not that they'd let you. They've probably taken her away by now.'

Suddenly Keira jumps up and runs to the wall, banging her fist on the plaster. 'Nooooo! Nooooo!' she screams. 'Not Fern! It can't be, can't be!'

'Keira!' calls Ariel. 'You're going to make a hole in the wall!'

'She came for me!' Keira cries. 'She wanted *me*! Oh God... this is all my fault. All my fault!' She bursts into loud, angry sobs, sinking to the floor and curling herself into a ball.

The others gape at her, then look at each other.

'What do you mean, she came for you?' asks Ariel.

'It was all my fault. I wrecked her life, she lost everything because of me and now she's dead! I might as well have drowned her myself.'

Nobody knows what to say. The atmosphere is electric. Sophie senses the thoughts sparking through their brains. Ariel gets up and crouches down next to Keira. 'I know this is a terrible shock for you, for all of us,' she says, gently stroking her back. 'But you mustn't lose control, you have to stay calm. Tell us what you mean. Please. Nobody's going to judge you, we're your friends.'

Gradually Keira uncurls, lifting her head. 'We were having

a thing... me and Fern.' She pauses, waiting for their reactions. 'Nobody knew?' They all shake their heads slowly.

'I could tell you were close, but I had no idea that you were... you know... together,' says Grace.

'Nor me,' says Elise.

Sophie doesn't say anything. She's too busy trying not to look too shocked. Like the others, she had no idea the affair was going on. But then she didn't know much about the private life of anyone in the group. They came to swim, that's all. That was part of the attraction.

'To be honest, I didn't even know you were a lesbian,' says Elise. 'Not that it matters.'

'I'm bi, actually,' replies Keira. 'But it was all very new for Fern – scary.'

'Well, it would have been,' says Ariel. 'A married woman with kids...'

'I didn't seduce her or anything. Neither of us meant it to happen. It was just a friendship at first, but then...' Keira bites her lip.

'Did you meet at swimming?' asks Elise.

'Yes.'

'You kept it very quiet.'

'I'm a private person, and obviously with Fern being married, it had to be a secret.' Keira sniffs back her tears.

'So... what happened?' asks Ariel.

'We'd been seeing each other for several months. It was kind of intense, more than I wanted, really. You know what Fern's like – *was* like,' she corrects, her voice cracking. 'She was very committed. I was fond of her, but I hated all the sneaking around, lying to you guys, deceiving her family...'

'So those texts,' says Sophie, thinking aloud. 'They were to Fern, weren't they? Fred was your cover name for her.'

'Yes, it was our joke.' Keira heaves a huge sigh. 'Oh God... I can't believe she's dead.'

'None of us can,' says Grace. 'Do you need a drink? I think there's some whisky in the cupboard.'

'Not a good idea,' chips in Ariel. 'The police will want to interview her, she needs a clear head.'

'Fuck the police. The girl's in shock.' Grace walks over to the sideboard and takes out a bottle of single malt. She removes the stopper and pours a large measure into a cut-glass tumbler. 'Here, get this down you.'

Keira sips at the whisky, wincing as it burns her throat. 'Thanks, Grace,' she murmurs. 'Needed that.'

Ariel looks slightly miffed. 'I still don't get why Fern was here, or why she attacked Sophie.'

'It was me she was looking for,' says Keira. 'She was angry, said she wanted to kill me.'

'How did it go so wrong?'

Keira swallows. 'Fern thought what we had was real and for ever, but I knew I was simply a catalyst. She hadn't been happy in her marriage for years – our affair just brought it to the surface. She came up with the idea of this trip so that we could be together for a whole week. She was so excited. I wasn't sure, I thought it would be difficult, that you were bound to work it out. She said she didn't care, she wanted us to come out as a couple. She wanted to leave her husband and move in with me. I panicked. It was all getting way too serious. I didn't want Fern living with me. I didn't want to be involved in her divorce, dealing with the fallout, being some kind of stepmum to her kids... I realised I'd made a huge mistake.'

'So you ended it,' says Sophie. Keira nods. 'And that's why Fern pulled out of the trip.'

'Yeah. Trouble was, she'd already told Peter – that's her husband – that she was leaving him for me. He reacted very badly. I think the fact that she'd been seeing another woman made it worse somehow. He felt kind of emasculated. And her kids went mental, they were really horrible towards her. She turned up at my flat in a terrible state, blaming me for everything, then started attacking me, throwing things around. I nearly had to call the police. She stormed out at about two a.m. and I didn't hear from her again. That was the night before we came away. I was very shaken up. And I was worried about her, wondering where she'd gone, what she was doing. I was desperate to find a signal I could call her, but it was impossible. Honestly, I had no idea she'd followed me here.'

'But it's not surprising,' says Grace. 'She knew exactly where to find you.'

'Perhaps she was staying in one of those shepherd's huts,' suggests Ariel. 'There are quite a few dotted about.'

'That's so not Fern's style,' says Elise. 'She was probably in some nice hotel in the next town, or an Airbnb.'

'No, I think Ariel's right,' Keira replies, taking another swig of whisky. 'She must have been camping nearby, spying on us, waiting for a chance to get me on my own.'

Grace pulls a face. 'But how come we never saw her?'

'She was careful. This place is a wilderness, there are heaps of places to hide.'

'Do you think it was deliberate, pushing Sophie in, or do you think Fern meant to attack *you*?' asks Ariel.

'How should I know? She liked Sophie, she liked all of you. *I* was the one who'd ruined her life.'

'You didn't ruin it – you're not to blame,' insists Grace.

'True,' says Elise. 'Fern was a grown-up, she knew what she was doing.'

Sophie stays silent, not wanting to judge. She feels so strange, like a balloon that's been released from somebody's hand. Keira was the target, not her. And although Sophie is shocked and horrified that Fern is dead, part of her feels relieved, which in turn makes her feel guilty. Because it's no longer about her. The real drama was going on under her nose, but she couldn't see it. Nobody could, not even Keira.

The conversation has returned to the night of the attack. Elise is pressing Keira for more details. 'You were out there too, only a hundred metres or so away. I know it was dark, but I don't understand how you didn't hear anything,' she says.

'I already told you. I'd stormed off into the forest, I didn't know where I was going. I had no idea Fern was around and I wasn't listening out for strange noises. This is just as much a shock to me as it is to you.'

'Okay, okay, I was just asking.'

'It's important to go through it now. The police will want to know everything,' says Ariel. 'You need to get the story straight in your mind.'

'It's not a story, it's the truth,' replies Keira.

'Yes, but if the police suspect you, they'll try to catch you out. If you're inconsistent or contradict yourself, they'll pounce on it straight away.' Ariel turns to Sophie. 'You too – you're in a vulnerable position. You were the last person to see her alive.'

'Only because Fern tried to drown her,' butts in Grace.

'Yes, but we only have Sophie's word for that. And Fern was a friend, not just some random stranger. That fact changes everything. I'm afraid it puts the suspicion right back on you, Sophie.'

'You can't say that, Ariel!' protests Grace. 'It's not fair.'

'Let's leave it to the detectives, shall we?' says Elise. 'They'll sort it out.'

Ariel huffs. 'You think? Don't be so sure. I know what it's like not to be believed. You think you're there as a witness, and before you know it, you're being charged with something you haven't done. Keira and Sophie need to be careful.' She pauses, looking from one to the other. 'We *all* do. We need to check our facts and make sure we're all saying the same thing. Because if any of you are lying, I promise you, you're about to be found out.'

THIRTY-TWO

SOPHIE

For a few seconds after she wakes, she thinks she's back home, in her own bed. Then she realises that the window and door are in the wrong place and that she doesn't recognise the furniture. Suddenly she remembers where she is – that she and Ryan have split up and Fern is dead. Reality sweeps over her like a giant wave.

Cold water. That's what she needs right now. She wants to feel her heart pounding, her nerve endings tingling. She needs to feel alive.

The room is still in semi-darkness. It must be very early, she thinks, checking the time on her phone. It's 6.30. She sits up and swings her legs around to the side of the bed. The floorboards are icy. Getting to her feet, she pads over to the wardrobe, where her swimsuit is hanging on the door handle. She fingers the fabric curiously. How come it isn't dry yet? Then she works out that less than twenty-four hours has passed since they went swimming and found the body. Their lives have changed so much in that short time that it feels like days. Weeks. Years.

Gingerly she steps into the damp swimsuit and drags it up

her legs; pulls the straps over her shoulders and tucks in her breasts. She's already shivering, and quickly adds layers of clothing – T-shirt, thin jumper, thicker jumper, jogging bottoms. It's cold in the room but could be colder outside. The temperature of the water will be extreme, but that's what she craves.

She can't and won't swim in the loch. It's been sealed off by forensics, but in any case she'd never go near the place again anyway. Only in her nightmares, where she visits it a lot. No, she's going to swim in the sea instead. It'll take her about three quarters of an hour to walk to the beach, downhill virtually all the way there and a stiff climb on the way back. She knows it's dangerous to swim alone, but she can't bear to be around the others at the moment – the atmosphere is too tense. She won't go out of her depth; just submerge herself for a few minutes, jump up and down, splash about, then run back up the beach to safety.

Popping her towel, swimming shoes and cap into a bag, she puts on her dryrobe and quietly leaves the house. Everyone else is still fast asleep. She'll probably be back before anyone discovers she's gone, so she doesn't bother to leave a note.

She begins the descent on the stony path, picking her way between muddy puddles and moss-covered rocks. Her body feels heavy, as if her thoughts are physically weighing her down. She slept better than expected last night – probably because she was too emotionally exhausted to put up a fight – and hasn't fully woken yet. The air is sharp and the leaves are tipped with silvery dew. Giant cobwebs hang between the branches, glistening in the morning sun. Above her, the sky is bright blue, as solid and unchanging as a Pantone colour. Picture-postcard perfect. She wishes she could appreciate it properly, but her head is too crowded with other, uglier images to let any new ones in.

Fern's face, swollen and ravaged. The woollen scarf wrapped around her neck like a noose.

Yesterday afternoon, they took her body away on a stretcher. Two guys had to carry it all the way to the road because they couldn't get a vehicle on to the site. Sophie and the others were told to stay indoors, but they didn't want to watch anyway. They kept to the house for the rest of the day, mostly walled up in their own rooms. Nobody felt like eating, so nobody cooked. Ariel even stopped making endless pots of tea.

The investigation has taken a new direction. No doubt Fern's husband will have journeyed up to Scotland last night to identify her. Sophie wonders whether he'll visit the loch. She'd like to offer him some support but guesses he won't want it – not from her. He might think she killed Fern. The police may even agree with him. Yet another reason why she has to swim in the sea this morning, in case she's arrested and locked up. Confined spaces make her feel anxious at the best of times, and if she's going to be falsely accused... It doesn't bear thinking about. She walks on, trying to focus on the breathtaking views of the coastline that stretch before her.

After they took the body away, DS McKenzie returned with the senior investigating officer, who immediately wanted everyone to go through their witness statements again – 'in the light of recent developments'. While the events of that awful night remain the same, the context has changed utterly. Fern wasn't some random stranger; she was part of the swimming group. More importantly, she was Keira's lover.

At one point yesterday, Sophie overheard the SIO refer to Fern as 'the victim', which really worried her. If she's the victim, what does that make *me*? she thought. The detectives are trying to sniff out a motive, and McKenzie has definitely changed his attitude towards her.

So far she hasn't mentioned her own marital problems – they're irrelevant to this case and even sound a bit petty compared to what's happened. More importantly, she doesn't want to confuse the issue. But maybe that's a mistake.

This is their last day at Condie's Retreat. They're supposed to leave by the ten o'clock deadline, but who knows whether the police will allow them to go home. Maybe she'll have to return to Scotland for further questioning. There's bound to be an inquest – she'll have to give evidence. Unless she's charged with something... but what? Failing to rescue the person who tried to drown her?

Gradually the landscape opens out. Earth meets sand and she trudges through the dunes, tufted with spiky marram grass. The air tastes salty and a breeze is whipping off the sea. Unfortunately, the tide is out, making it more difficult and riskier to swim. If the currents are too strong, she'll just go for a paddle, she thinks, stopping by some rocks to change into her swimming shoes. Strands of hair are flapping across her face, slipping into her mouth. She spits them out, then puts her cap on, tucking in the stray bits.

These rocks are the last spot where she can safely leave her things. Beyond this point the sand is like mud, drenched with water, soft underfoot. The temperature has plummeted. She doesn't want to get undressed and expose her skin to the elements. Her desire to walk all the way down to the tideline is waning. But it's always like this, especially by the sea and when there's a cold wind blowing like today. It's an obstacle you have to get over. She knows from experience that afterwards, when she comes out of the water, she'll feel invigorated and wonder why she hesitated for one second. But right now, it's too much pain for not enough gain.

She sits down on a rock, annoyed with herself. This is silly. An hour ago, she was desperate to swim. She's walked all this way; it would be stupid to turn back now. She gazes around at the handful of ruined houses that line the upper part of the beach, hoping for some inspiration. People lived here for generations, eking out an existence from the sea and their meagre livestock. It must have been a very small community. How did they cope with the isolation? Did they all get on together, or did they fall out? They must have been so strong to survive here.

Her gaze extends to the bothy beyond the ruins. To her surprise, she can see smoke coming out of the flue in the corrugated roof. Somebody is clearly staying there – maybe it's the journalist guy. She immediately stands up and, holding her walking boots by their laces, starts walking towards the hut.

The door is half open, but she knocks all the same. 'Hi,' she says, pushing it gently. 'Anyone there? Can I come in?'

'Hang on!' After a few seconds, he comes to the door. It's him, the guy she met on the path, the guy who until yesterday she feared was at the bottom of the loch. He smiles, recognising her immediately.

'Hello, Sophie,' he says.

'Oh. You remembered my name.'

'Sophie's Swimmers – it's got a good ring about it.'

'I'm sorry, I don't remember yours,' she replies.

'Don't think I gave it to you... It's Andy.'

'Hi.'

He steps out, looking beyond her. 'On your own?'

'Yeah... I came for a swim, but the tide's out and it's really freezing.'

'Isn't that the whole point?'

'Yes, sort of.' She pulls off the orange cap and her hair springs forth, standing on end with static. 'I saw the smoke – thought I'd better come over straight away.'

'Right... Why?'

'Haven't you heard?'

'Um...'

'About what happened... at the loch.'

'Which loch? There are dozens.'

'The one near Condie's Retreat, where we've been swimming.' He looks at her blankly. 'Sorry, I assumed the police came down yesterday, looking for you.'

'No. Why?'

'Somebody drowned.'

'Drowned?' His face instantly puckers. 'Fuck! Who?'

'Her name's Fern. She was part of our group.'

'Fern,' he repeats. 'God, that's terrible...'

'We didn't know she was here until they found her body. She was supposed to be with us, but she dropped out at the last minute. We think she might have been camping out in one of the shepherd's huts.'

'Actually, I might have seen her. Is she, er... a bit overweight, with short brown hair? Mid forties?'

'Yes, that sounds like her.'

'I spotted her when I was out walking a few days ago. She was on her own, quite smartly dressed, not like your normal scruffy rambler. She looked a bit lost. I thought I'd go and say hello, but as soon as she saw me, she ran off. I thought it was a bit weird. Most solo walkers like bumping into other people.'

'That's interesting. The police will probably want to talk to you about that.'

'The police? Why?' He frowns.

'It's evidence.'

'I never saw her in the water. She was just hanging around.'

'Sorry, I didn't mean to imply...' She pauses to reset. 'Her death wasn't a swimming accident. Well, it *was* – an accident, that is – but only as a result of her trying to...' Her voice fades.

'Trying to what?'

'It's really hard to explain.' Tears well in her eyes.

'Hey, are you okay?'

'Not really.' Now that she's allowed one tear to fall, others are quickly following.

'Please don't cry. Come in and warm up. I've just made a brew.'

'Thanks... Sorry about this.'

'No need to apologise.' Andy beckons her into the gloom of the bothy. 'It's not very comfy, but at least it's out of the wind.' He takes the kettle off the stove. 'You're lucky. There's just enough water for another cup. No milk, I'm afraid. Can you drink it black?'

'Yes, if it's not too strong... Thanks.'

She sits on his sleeping bag, which has been folded up to form a floor cushion. While he makes her tea, she finds a tissue in her pocket and blows her nose. She looks about curiously, although she's been here before, of course – twice, in fact. 'You've got it quite cosy,' she says.

He hands her a mug, white enamel with a chipped navy-blue rim. 'This is my last day. The bothy is supposed to close for the winter. Don't know if anyone will actually come to chuck me out, but I've had enough anyway. Need to get back to work.'

'I thought this *was* work.'

'Yeah, yeah, it is. I need to get back and write it up. No electric or Wi-Fi here.'

'No, of course not.'

He sits down next to her on the stone floor. 'So, what happened to your friend? How come she drowned?'

Sophie takes a sip of her tea – it's bitter and bites the back of her throat – then tells him the story, at least as far as she understands it. He listens carefully, every so often emitting low grunts of sympathy or small gasps of surprise.

'That must have been terrifying,' he says. 'But how are you going to prove she attacked *you* and not the other way around?'

'I don't know.'

'After you fell in, you didn't hear her splashing about, or calling out for help?'

'No.' She looks into her tea. 'But anyway, I was trying to get away from her, to save myself. My guess is she went into cold shock and had a cardiac arrest, but the autopsy will work it out.'

'Hmm... so she attacked you, but you're okay and she's dead,' he says after a few moments' thought. 'Do the police believe you?'

'I don't know. They *should* do. If I deliberately killed her, why did I lead my friends to the spot and let them find her body? It doesn't make sense.'

'Maybe you were all in it together.'

She rolls her eyes. 'In which case, why did we call the police? Why didn't we just go home? Nobody would ever have found her.'

'Double bluff?' he suggests. 'Murderers often turn up at the scene of the crime, get involved in the search party, that kind of thing. I'm not saying that's what you're doing, just that it happens. The police are wise to it.'

'I'm not a murderer, Andy.'

'No, obviously not. I didn't mean...' He stops, embarrassed. 'Sorry. That was a dumb thing to say. I was looking at the story from all angles – you know, like a journo.'

'Yeah, I get it.' She hands back the mug and sighs.

'You need to be careful. You're in a tricky position, it could all go horribly wrong.'

'I know, and I'm worried sick about it.' She stands up. 'That's why I overreacted. Sorry... I shouldn't have barged in, shouldn't be telling you all this.'

'You needed someone to listen and here I was. Happy to help.'

'Thanks for trying.'

There's a long pause, then Andy gets to his feet too. 'Hey, why don't we go for a walk? It's a beautiful day, stupid to be stuck inside. I can show you some really cool places nearby. Views to die for. You can't leave the Rough Bounds without seeing them.'

She purses her lips. 'I'd like to, but I should go back. The police will probably turn up again.'

'It's very early. They won't arrive for hours. Come on, this is your last chance.'

'But I didn't tell anyone where I was going.'

'A short walk, that's all.'

'It's tempting, but I really came to swim.'

'Okay, we can do that too. After our walk.'

'*We?*' she echoes.

He nods. 'Yeah, I'll come for a dip with you.'

'You sure? Do you know how cold the water is out there? If you're not used to it...'

'I'll be fine.' He smiles at her eagerly. 'Let me go with you, Sophie. It's dangerous to swim alone.'

THIRTY-THREE

THE SWIMMER

I should be pleased that Sophie's in trouble, but to my surprise, I'm feeling deflated, like a balloon at the end of a party, shrivelling up as the air slowly hisses out of me. My sense of purpose has gone and I've no energy left. Just the thought of getting dressed this morning feels like too much effort. I've had enough of this place. All my clothes need washing, and I haven't had a proper shower for days. I want to go home and be myself – if I can ever find her again. I haven't been me for a while. I'm exhausted with all this pretending, and annoyingly, it's not over yet.

From the clatter of sounds beyond my room, everyone's in the kitchen, eating porridge and stale bagels (there's nothing else left) and wondering why I haven't yet got out of bed. I'll join them in a few minutes – to stop them gossiping about me if nothing else.

It'll be okay. We'll drink tea and say for the thousandth time what a lovely woman Fern was and that we still can't believe she's dead. Sophie will bleat on about how it wasn't her fault and how worried she is that the police don't believe her. I'll dole out a warm dollop of sympathy and assure her that it's all going to be fine, although I'm hoping it won't be.

What really happened that night at the loch? I'd so love to know. Did Fern attack Sophie thinking she was Keira, or did Sophie attack Fern? She's portraying herself as an innocent bystander, a victim of mistaken identity, but maybe she was part of a love triangle. Maybe Keira dumped Fern for Sophie. I doubt it somehow. Sophie's as straight and boring as they come.

But Keira and Fern were definitely an item. Who knew, eh? Not me, for starters, and I'm usually good at spotting secret connections between people. They certainly kept it very quiet; never arrived together for our weekly swims, or hung around afterwards trying to be left alone with each other. Keira never laughed too loudly at Fern's jokes, or vice versa. They never complimented each other or exchanged knowing glances or found excuses to touch. And yet their relationship was so serious that Fern left her husband. Or at least she *thought* it was serious until Keira gave her the big heave-ho. She's really upset now, is Keira. Weighed down with guilt. But who wouldn't be? It's a bad situation. I'm not saying she's to blame, but people need to be more careful with those who love them. Especially if they don't love them back.

It's all very tragic, but it has nothing to do with me. I've got my own drama to attend to, and it's not going according to script. Our jolly digital detox was supposed to end with *my* climactic moment. I'd written a big reveal – Sophie and me balanced precariously on a mountaintop in a strong gale. 'It was me all along!' I was going to say, shouting above the wind. 'I'm the one who's been screwing your husband. I ruined your marriage – I destroyed your happiness. And shall I tell you why?' Cue loud cackles of laughter. She was going to nod, shocked and bewildered, and I was going to tell her that I'd come to avenge the death of my sister. Then I was going to push her over the edge. It would have been certain death, easily explained away as an accident. No other witnesses, no CCTV cameras. Oh, I had it all worked out.

But that scenario has been torn up, and now there's going to be a different ending for Sophie. Sudden death has been replaced by a long prison sentence (with a bit of luck). I should be delighted because I'm not implicated in any crime, but the truth is, I wanted to be the one to do the deed. I wanted to see the look of terror on her face as her foot slipped and she fell backwards into the abyss. I wanted to go home and tell Drew and Billie that I'd finally achieved justice for Carly. How proud they'd be of me. And I wanted Ryan to feel guilty for the rest of his life.

Somebody's knocking and calling my name. Actually, it's not my name. I borrowed it from Carly, just as I used to borrow her crop tops – without asking. She used to get really annoyed with me because I always pulled them out of shape, and I'd argue that she never wore them anyway so what did it matter? She never used her second name either, so I'm working on the same principle.

'Yes?' I reply, shuffling over to the door and opening it just wide enough to poke my head through.

'Ah, you're up,' says Ariel. She's fully dressed and wearing one of her stupid turbans.

'What is it?'

'Sophie's disappeared,' she announces.

'Really?' I reply, trying to sound like I give a shit. 'When?'

'We don't know exactly. Very early, we think. Did you hear anything?'

'No. I've only just woken up.'

'Nobody knows where she's gone.'

'For a walk, I expect.'

'Well, she shouldn't have. The police told us not to leave the house in case they need to talk to us again,' Ariel reminds me importantly. 'I've a horrible feeling she's done a bunk.'

The possibility makes my heart skip, but I adopt an expression of doubt. 'Surely she wouldn't do that. That would be really stupid. It would make her look guilty.'

'Exactly!' Ariel says. 'Oh dear, I don't know what to think now. Maybe she *is* guilty after all. Grace is beside herself, and poor Keira is catatonic with grief.'

'Let me get dressed. I'll be right out.'

'Thanks, Elise. You're so good at calming things down.'

I smile modestly and shut the door.

Carly Elise Woods. It has such a pretty ring to it. Apparently Mum named her after Carly Simon, the singer. I don't know where 'Elise' came from; maybe that was Dad's choice. By the time it came to naming me, they'd run out of steam and I was given boring old Lauren. There were three of us in my class at primary school, for God's sake, and as Lauren W, I always came last. I was jealous of Carly in many ways – her name was just one of them.

After she died, I wanted something of hers as a keepsake, but I wasn't allowed to have her bedroom, or her clothes, or that special place in Mum's heart. So I took 'Elise' out on permanent loan, tucked it away where nobody would find it. For years I didn't dare use it in public. It felt sacrilegious. I was worried that Mum or Drew or someone else in the family would find out. But when I started using hook-up sites, I wanted a false identity – not so much for security, but to give me confidence. 'Elise – what a sexy name,' the guys would say, letting it slide off their tongue, and I'd purr with satisfaction. Even Ryan said it once. Either he'd forgotten it was Carly's middle name or he chose not to mention it.

The messed-up, self-disrespecting Elise who has sex with strangers is altogether different to the one who goes wild swimming. That one is kind and compassionate, always says encouraging things, never puts other people down – she's more like the original owner of the name, in fact. Carly Elise Woods was a nice girl, everyone liked her. In death, she became even nicer and more liked, but the truth is, her reputation grew from a very high base. If Mum was a Catholic, she'd have applied for her to be beatified. Probably would have succeeded too.

That's the Elise I channel when I'm with my fellow swimmers, especially with Sophie. In this way I've been able to explore a whole new side of myself. Sometimes the line between Lauren and Elise blurs and they cross over into each other's territory. At work, for example, I've caught myself feeling sympathetic towards people I used to look down on and sticking up for colleagues I despise. Lauren is softening. It makes me wonder whether I'm not as bitter and twisted and angry and mean as I think I am – or as I think I should be, perhaps. I carry a lot of pain around for Carly. I was hoping to hurl it off the mountain along with Sophie, let it crash to the bottom and break into a million pieces. I was going to walk away light and free.

I finish getting dressed and leave the bedroom, my Elise mask hooked invisibly over my ears. Following the sound of voices, I go into the kitchen and find Grace and Ariel sitting at the table. Grace's eyes are rimmed red with crying – she's not wearing any make-up and looks about twelve years old. Ariel is leaning across, holding her hands, bludgeoning her with platitudes.

'We've got to be strong,' she's saying. 'Life is ten per cent what happens to you and ninety per cent how you react to it.'

'I know, I *know*,' Grace mutters, as if Ariel has just uttered an undeniable truth.

'Where's Keira?' I ask.

Ariel looks up. 'She's in the garden – trying to meditate, bless her.'

'Really?' I suppress a sigh of irritation. 'Any more tea?' I lift the lid of the pot. There's a drain of stewed liquid left, which I pour into a mug.

'I still can't believe it,' says Grace.

'Can't believe what?'

'That Sophie would drown Fern.'

'It was self-defence, wasn't it?'

'That's what she said, but now she's run away...'

'It doesn't look good,' Ariel butts in, passing me the carton of milk.

'How do we know she's run away?' I ask. 'Has she taken her stuff?'

'No, just her day bag. We checked,' says Grace.

'What about her dryrobe?'

'Um... not sure.'

I march out of the kitchen and into Sophie's bedroom. Drawing back the curtains, I look around. The bed is unmade, a pair of crumpled pyjamas lying across the sheet. I look behind the door and in the wardrobe. No dryrobe.

'She's gone for a swim,' I declare, returning to the kitchen.

'A swim?' repeats Grace. 'What – at a time like this?'

Ariel looks doubtful. 'She can't have gone to the loch. It's out of bounds.'

'Then she must have gone to the beach.'

'It's a long way to go. And she wouldn't swim by herself, it's not safe.'

'Well, it's the only explanation I can think of,' I reply, almost snapping.

'I do hope she's not going to do anything stupid,' Ariel murmurs after a pause.

Grace looks alarmed. 'Don't say that.'

'I know what you mean, though,' I say. 'Sophie's in a very tight spot. I'm sure she's completely innocent, but ultimately, the police will go by the forensic evidence. If the autopsy reveals—'

'Don't say that word!' Grace covers her face with her hands. 'It's all too horrible. I can't take it – I want to go home.'

Ariel lowers her voice as she turns to me. 'Maybe Sophie is scared of what they might find.'

'That's what I'm wondering.'

'She could be panicking.'

'Tell you what, I'll go and look for her.'

Ariel's face floods with relief. 'Would you? I'd come with, but I ought to stay here to look after Keira and Grace.'

'Of course. And the police are supposed to be coming back, remember – we can't all disappear.'

'I'll explain that you're looking for Sophie.'

'Okay.'

'Thank you, Elise, that's so good of you. Persuade her to come back and face the music. Tell her honesty is always the best policy.'

Another bloody platitude, I think, but I just nod in agreement.

I put my jacket and boots on, then leave the house. My heart surges with hope as I quicken my step. Just as I thought I wasn't going to be able to complete my mission, the perfect opportunity has dropped in front of me. It's time for the final showdown.

THIRTY-FOUR

SOPHIE

'This way,' Andy says. 'There's a secret place I want to show you.' They take a rough path through moor grass, then clamber up a small rock face to a clump of trees. He pushes through some branches and suddenly they're in the middle of a woody glade. The wind immediately drops, and the air becomes still. The atmosphere is magical. She holds her breath for fear of breaking the spell.

'These are ancient,' he tells her. 'The trees have been allowed to grow and fall as they wish. The birches are different to the ones you get further south – rougher, stronger, taller... Look at the way the oak has twisted into that crevice. It looks like a giant bonsai, don't you think?'

'Mm, I see what you mean... beautiful,' Sophie murmurs. 'I had no idea this place was here, so close to the sea. It's like another universe.'

They stand at the foot of a small waterfall, watching a stream tumble through a narrow ravine. Feathery ferns are tucked into every available niche, hanging from the crooks of branches like extravagant armpit hair. Sophie gazes in awe at the stones and boulders of various shapes and sizes piled randomly on top of each other, drenched with shimmering green moss.

'What's the bird I can hear singing?' she asks.

He listens for a moment. 'A robin.'

'Oh.' She feels disappointed. 'We get those in the garden at home.'

'They're everywhere. The robin is one of the few birds that sings virtually all year round, although its song seems to change according to the seasons. It sounds bright and hopeful in spring, more melancholy in the autumn.' He points the bird out, poised on a low branch a few metres away.

'I do love robins,' she says. 'They always make me think of Christmas.' She pauses, suddenly engulfed with thoughts not of Christmases past, but of the future. Will she have to share Ben and Louie – one year with her, the next with Ryan? How will she bear to be apart from her boys? It will make every other Christmas seem pointless.

The robin sings again. 'He sounds lonely,' she says.

'You're wrong, he's not lonely at all. The males and females split up at the end of the summer and find a place to see out the winter months by themselves. They're very territorial. He's actually telling you to piss off.'

She laughs. 'They choose to be alone?'

'Yes. Nothing wrong with that.'

'I suppose not.' She studies his face. 'I'm guessing *you* like to be alone.'

'Sometimes. Not always.' He turns away and starts walking again. 'The other birds you see and hear a lot are redwings and fieldfares. They overwinter here, living off berries, particularly from rowan trees.'

She follows, picking her way across the vivid carpet of moss. 'How come you know so much?'

He shrugs. 'I've always liked being in nature,' he says. 'It helps calm me down.'

'Why? What do you need to calm down *from*?' He shoots her a strange look. 'Sorry, I shouldn't have said that – I didn't mean to intrude.'

'Everyone stresses out, don't they? That's just life.'

'I guess.'

He looks up at the sky. 'Time's getting on. If you still want to swim…'

'Yes, I do. Are you sure you want to join me?'

'Of course. I didn't bring any trunks, so I'll have to go in in my boxers, if that's okay with you.'

She laughs. 'I promise not to look.'

He leads her out of the dell, and within a few minutes they are back in the rough, windswept landscape not far from where they started. Sophie follows the track he makes through the straggly grass. The terrain is boggy in places, littered with holes and hidden rocks. He shows her an area where he's spotted deer grazing, but there's no sign of them today.

As they enter the dunes. Sophie peers through the marram grass to look at the vast expanse of flat sand, dotted with feeding birds.

'Hmm… maybe this isn't such a good idea,' she says.

'Why, what's the problem?' Andy asks, already undressing.

'It's low tide. Could still be on the way out. You should never swim on an outgoing tide – it's dangerous.'

'I was watching it earlier and it's definitely on its way back in now.'

'You sure?' She tuts. 'I should have checked the timetable.'

'Honestly, the tide has turned.' He takes off his jumper and T-shirt, revealing a pale, hairy chest.

'It's a long walk to the water. Feels even longer when you come out freezing wet.'

'Then we'll run!'

She smiles. 'All right, but don't say I didn't warn you.'

Andy strips down to his stripy boxer shorts, which are made

of thin cotton and are slightly baggy at the waist. Sophie unzips her dryrobe, then peels off her clothes. He's watching her out of the corner of his eye. It feels faintly sexual, as if they're about to go to bed.

'Don't suppose you've got any swimming shoes?' she asks, aware that her swimsuit is revealing a lot of cleavage.

'No, sorry.' He jumps up and down, hugging himself against the cold.

'Okay, well just watch where you're treading. There might be weever fish.'

She puts on her shoes, tightening the string to make them as watertight as possible, then pulls on her orange cap. At least one of them will be visible, she thinks. Not that she intends to do any proper swimming. It's impossible to know what the currents are like out there. Wading in up to her knees will be enough to give her the cold-water fix she needs.

'Right. Race you there!' shouts Andy, and they run across the flat sand, scaring away a small flock of curlews. Sophie feels her breasts bouncing uncomfortably on her chest as her shorter legs struggle to keep up. The wind is icy, and she's soon covered in goosebumps, the hairs on her arms sticking up. She has to close her mouth to stop her teeth from hurting.

Andy reaches the water's edge, then stops and turns, smiling as he waits for her. 'I won!' he cries triumphantly.

She slows down, suddenly feeling awkward. What on earth is she doing? This is wildly inappropriate. She's in the middle of a tragedy. One of her friends is dead, there's a police investigation going on, she's just split up with her husband and she's about to frolic in the waves with a man she hardly knows.

'Come on!' He holds out his hand, and she notices that his fingernails are dirty.

'Sorry. This is wrong. I shouldn't be doing this.'

'It's safe. The tide is definitely coming in, look.' He points to a patch of wet sand.

'It's not that. I ought to be getting back.'

'Look, we're here now... Hey, come on, Sophie. Just have a dip with me.'

She acquiesces with a reluctant sigh. He grabs her by the fingers and leads her into the water. They start to wade out, pushing against the tide, which is indeed sweeping in at a fast rate. Soon the sea is swirling around her bare thighs. The coldness is shocking to the point of painful. She needs to get her shoulders under, have a quick swim, then run back out.

But Andy won't let go of her hand. He seems scared, and yet he's the one pressing on, dragging her forward.

'Hey, this is far enough,' she says, but he ignores her. The water has reached his boxers now; the fabric is plastered against his thin frame. His upper body is visibly trembling with cold. 'Let me go, please.'

'No.' He grips her more tightly.

'Are you okay? You *can* swim, can't you?'

He doesn't reply, but ploughs on, going deeper and deeper. She stumbles on a rock and starts to fall, but he yanks her up roughly. 'Andy, this is dangerous. I can feel the current.'

He stops abruptly, then turns to face her, releasing her hand and grabbing her by the shoulders instead.

'What are you doing?' she says, thinking for a brief moment that he's about to try and kiss her. 'Andy, please.' Then she sees the look in his eyes – hard and full of hatred. 'What is it? Why are you looking at me like that?'

'This is where it ends, Sophie,' he says, his lips starting to turn blue.

'What?'

'It ends right here, right now. In the water. Just like it did for Carly.'

She stares at him, dumbfounded. *What* did he just say? Did she hear right? It's so noisy out here, with the wind blowing and the waves crashing and the gulls screaming overhead.

'I'm s-sorry, I d-don't understand,' she stutters.

'Don't bullshit me.'

'Please, let me go.'

His fingers dig into her shivering flesh while the waves heave around them, almost knocking them off balance.

'Hey, Andy, let's go back, yeah? Before we get too cold.'

'That's how Carly died,' he says. 'In freezing, stinking water.'

'Who's Charlie?'

'You fucking know. Don't lie!'

'I'm not lying,' she answers, trying to keep her voice steady. 'I don't know who you're talking about.'

'Carly. My sister. Your husband's fiancée!'

'My husband's *what*?!'

'She killed herself because of you.'

'This is crazy. Please, Andy, let me go or we're both going to freeze to death here.'

'I don't care. I don't want to live any more.'

'Well, I do!' She lifts a leg and knees him in the stomach as hard as she can. He tries to hold on to her as he falls backward, but she manages to push him away. As he hits the water, a large wave breaks over them both and he disappears for a few seconds. She staggers back, winded.

'Get up!' she shouts. 'Get up! Now! Nobody's drowning — do you hear me?'

He rises out of the water, his hand reaching for her, trying to pull her down. She takes it and tries to pull him up instead, but he won't budge. They engage in a brief tug-of-war before she lets him go, falling back into the water herself.

'Fuck you!' she shouts. 'You can drown if you want!'

Scrambling to her feet, she starts to move away, pushing through the water, letting the tide propel her forward to the shore. She doesn't look back. Once she reaches dry land, she breaks into a run.

The distance back to the dunes seems further, even though now there's less beach to cover. Her shoes slap heavily on the wet sand. She skirts around an outcrop of slimy rocks, jumping over swathes of brown seaweed.

A woman is standing by the rocks, next to their piles of clothes. She can tell who it is by the pinky-red hair flapping about her face.

'Elise! Elise!' she shouts, hurtling towards her. She stops, bending over to catch her breath. 'Thank God, thank God...'

'What are you doing, Sophie?' Elise replies coldly. 'We've been looking for you bloody everywhere.'

'The guy from the bothy,' she pants. 'He's in the water. He tried... he tried to...' She cannot find the words.

'Tried to what?'

'I don't know... We were wading out for a swim, and he just turned on me, started saying all these mad things.' Sophie looks back towards the sea. It's hard to see through the waves, but there's no sign of him. 'Now he won't come out of the water. Elise, you've got to help me. I can't have another drowning on my hands, I can't!'

'Jesus Christ, Sophie, what's wrong with you?'

'I don't know! One minute we were friends, then he...' She shrugs her shoulders, bewildered. 'Please, we've got to save him.'

'Okay. It may be too late, but...' Elise unzips her jacket and quickly removes her outer clothes until she's standing in her bra and pants. Sophie shivers before her, water dripping off her costume on to the sand. Her extremities are already feeling numb and the thought of going back in terrifies her, but she has to try.

They run together towards the shoreline. Elise is younger and fitter than Sophie and is soon charging ahead. Sophie lollops after her, already out of breath. A stitch bites into her stomach and she feels her chest tightening, but she makes herself accelerate and catch up.

'There he is!' she cries as they splash through the water. 'Can you see him? Look, his head, it keeps bobbing up.' He is turned away from them, so they can't see his face.

'Fucking idiot,' Elise curses. 'What's he playing at?'

'Andy!' calls Sophie. 'Andy! Just stay calm, we're coming to get you!'

He doesn't turn round. His head carries on bobbing for a few more seconds before it's engulfed by a wave, which then rushes at them, knocking them off their feet.

They splutter to the surface. Elise starts to swim out against the tide and Sophie follows. Her legs and arms feel weak, and the undertow is dragging her to one side. Where is he? She can't see him any more. Has he sunk? The cold water is taking over, slowing her down, blurring her vision.

Then he pops up a few yards away from them. He's facing them now – eyes startled, mouth agape.

'Lauren!' he gasps.

'Oh fuck,' Elise says, almost going under herself. 'Drew! For fuck's sake. Drew!'

Sophie stares from one to the other as another wave crashes over her. 'Wha... what? I don't get it... Why did he call you Lauren?'

'Oh, Drew, what the fuck were you doing? Hold on, babe, I'm coming!' Elise starts swimming towards him.

'Who is he? How come—'

'He's my brother... Drew, it's okay, I'm here. Look at me, try to stay calm.'

'Your *brother*?'

Elise turns round, spitting out her words. 'Yes, my brother, Andrew! Now shut up and listen! He can't swim. You've got to help me, bitch. If he drowns, so do you!'

THIRTY-FIVE

SOPHIE

They half carry, half drag Drew back to the bothy and sit him down on the sleeping bag. Elise empties his rucksack to find shirts and jumpers. She dresses him like a child, pushing them over his head, poking his arms into the sleeves.

Sophie fetches logs and kindling from outside and tries to light the wood burner. She searches for newspaper to scrunch, but there doesn't seem to be any left. There's no choice but to use the information sheets she found that first time she explored the hut. She rips up the pages one by one, briefly scanning the photocopied article about the dangers of wild swimming. It seems so ironic now. She takes the picture of the drowning figure and screws it into a ball before stuffing it into the burner and lighting it with a match.

'Shall I make some tea?' she asks, gesturing towards the camping stove.

Elise is rubbing Drew's back, trying to keep him awake. She looks up at Sophie, her expression hard and contemptuous. 'No, I'll do it.'

'Is he going to be okay?'

'Think so. We got him out just in time.'

Sophie stands up and walks towards the door of the bothy. She hesitates and turns back, blinking at the gloom. In her heart she knows she doesn't need to ask this question, but if she doesn't, it will gnaw away at her for ever.

'It's you, isn't it?' she says. 'You've been having an affair with Ryan.'

Elise casts an anxious glance towards Drew, who seems to be drifting off. 'I don't want to talk about it now.'

'What's he doing here? Why did he attack me?'

'Revenge,' Elise replies. 'He didn't trust me to do a proper job.' A flash of bitterness crosses her face. 'That's big brothers for you.'

Sophie looks at her, bewildered. 'I don't understand... Revenge against who? Ryan?'

'Hadn't you better go? The detectives will be there by now, wanting to question you about Fern's murder.'

'I didn't kill—'

'Yeah, so you keep saying. Difficult to prove, though. I think you're in trouble. Personally I hope they lock you away for a very long time.'

Sophie turns and leaves. She climbs the long hill back to the house, tears streaming down her face the whole way.

'Her name's not Elise, it's Lauren,' she explains later. 'She's been screwing Ryan.' Ariel, Grace and Keira are sitting at the kitchen table, their tea going cold as they listen with open mouths to her edited account of what happened at the beach.

'So he was lying about... well, lying,' says Grace. For the first time this week, she hasn't painted on eyebrows, and she looks fresh-faced, like a child. 'You know, I had a feeling that was the case, but I didn't want to cause trouble.'

'Me too,' admits Keira. 'I thought it was either you or Elise.'

'Oh thanks!'

'Only because there were no clues. She's an incredible actress, you have to hand it to her.'

'Yes... she had me totally fooled.' Sophie doesn't add that Elise was at the very bottom of her list of suspects. She'd always been so kind and thoughtful, offering a shoulder to cry on – the peacemaker of the group. Of course, that was the giveaway.

'And the bothy guy is her brother,' marvels Keira. 'And she didn't know he was here?'

'No. She seemed genuinely surprised when she saw him.'

'But what were they up to? What was the plan?'

'I don't know.'

'They must have some kind of hold over Ryan,' says Ariel. 'Have you any idea what it could be?'

Sophie shakes her head. She *does* have an idea, of course she does, but she's not going to go into details with them. The whole thing is humiliating enough as it is and she needs to keep her counsel.

'Perhaps they've been blackmailing him,' suggests Grace. 'Maybe he's committed some crime, like fraud or drugs or porn.'

'For God's sake, let's not go there!' Ariel reprimands. 'We've already got one police investigation going on, there's no need to make it worse.'

'I need to talk to Ryan,' says Sophie. 'He owes me the truth.'

'Yes, but men like that don't always pay their debts.'

Keira turns to her. 'Are you going to report the bothy guy? What's his name?'

'Andrew.' Sophie bites her lip. 'No, it'll only complicate things.'

'You're right to leave it,' says Grace. 'You've got enough on your plate.'

As if on cue, there's a loud knock on the front door. 'Shit,' says Sophie. 'That must be the police.' She pushes back her chair and goes to answer, pausing briefly in the hallway to look in the mirror. Her face is blotchy with crying. She smooths her cheeks and tries to brighten her eyes.

'Hello,' she says, opening the door. DS McKenzie is standing there with his young constable.

'Morning. Mind if we come in?'

'Yes, I mean no. Please.' She takes a step back to let them enter.

'Hi, fancy a cup of tea?' offers Ariel, coming into the hallway.

'I won't say no. A drib of milk and two sugars please,' McKenzie replies, walking into the sitting room with his boots on. Unsure, Sophie follows.

'Um... so is there any... any news?' she asks.

'Not yet. It's early days. We're waiting on forensics, toxicology.' He sits down on the sofa, while his constable takes the upright chair by the window. Sophie stands there helpless, not knowing whether to stay or go.

'Why are you here? Only I went through my statement again yesterday. There's nothing more to add. I know I can't prove it, but I didn't *do* anything – she pushed *me*.'

'Okay, calm yourself down, Sophie. I'm not here to arrest you. This is just an update. You're supposed to be leaving today, is that right?'

'Yes.' She nods.

'Well, the booking after you has been cancelled. The owners are upset, but we can't have visitors traipsing about while we're still investigating.'

Ariel brings in two mugs of tea and puts them on the table. 'That's the last of the milk,' she says. 'Sorry. We were supposed to stock up on supplies, but...'

'As far as we're concerned, you can go home,' McKenzie continues, reaching for his mug.

Sophie gasps. 'Really?'

'We've got all your details. If we need to talk to any of you again, we know where to find you. You'll be called as witnesses at the inquest, but there's no point you hanging around for that.'

'Oh, right,' responds Ariel. 'Thanks, that's good to know.' She turns to Sophie. 'What do you want to do? You're the driver, so it's up to you.'

'I just want to get out of here as soon as possible.'

'Okay. I'll tell the others.' Ariel bustles out of the room, glad to have some important information to impart.

'You seem agitated, Sophie,' says McKenzie after a pause.

'Do I? I'm still very upset about Fern, I suppose. It's been such a shock.'

'Are you sure there's nothing else you want to tell us?'

'No, I can't think of anything.' Sophie looks away. 'I've said all there is to say,' she adds firmly.

McKenzie and his sidekick take their leave, wishing them a safe journey home and advising Sophie to take care on the roads. As soon as she shuts the door behind them, she breaks down in floods of tears. Of relief, not joy. McKenzie seems to have accepted her account, at least for now. There's a chance that forensics will dredge up some new evidence – she'll deal with that if and when it happens. She just wants to concentrate on getting away from this wretched place and driving home safely. She closes her eyes as she imagines holding out her arms as Ben and Louie rush toward her, pulling them into her embrace.

'Right. Let's get out of here,' she says.

They go off to their rooms to finish packing. According to the instructions, they're supposed to leave the house clean and tidy, but none of them cares any more. They just want out.

Sophie is putting the last items into her rucksack when Ariel knocks, then immediately pokes her head around the bedroom door.

'Elise still hasn't come back,' she says.

'Good,' Sophie replies sharply, pulling the drawstring tight.

'It's just that... I've been wondering, don't you think somebody should tell her what's happening? If she comes back and finds we've gone...' She trails off uncomfortably.

'She'll be stuck. So what? She deserves it. Anyway, she's with her brother.'

'But all her stuff is here. Maybe one of us should go to the beach and tell her that—'

'She's been deceiving all of us, not just me.'

'I know that.' Ariel looks down at her feet. 'But the rest of us haven't had a chance to talk to her. This feels like running away.'

Sophie huffs. 'You can stay until tomorrow if you want, you can *all* stay, I don't care. I'm leaving now, so if you want a lift—'

'Okay, okay, calm down. Let's be grown up about this. Elise deserves—'

'She doesn't deserve a thing. She's not one of us, she's evil! She's never been interested in swimming, she joined our group to get at me, no other reason. God knows what she planned to do to me this trip – I'm lucky to be alive.' She picks up her rucksack and dumps it on the bed. 'Please tell the others I'm leaving in ten minutes.'

Ariel nods and scurries out. Sophie fills up with fury as she stomps about, throwing the last bits and bobs into her day bag. She picks up the car keys, wondering fleetingly whether Elise stole them to torment her then sneaked them back later on. Not that she's going to hang around to ask her. She checks under the bed, does a final sweep of the wardrobe and drawers, then heaves her rucksack on to her back.

The atmosphere in the car on the journey home is very subdued. Ariel, who is clearly still feeling disgruntled, sits at the very back this time, while Grace takes the front passenger seat. There is no singing, no banter, not even much conversation other than to discuss where to take their next break. Sophie retunes the radio to a station that plays classical music and tries to let its soothing tones ease her troubled mind. She feels exhausted, but doesn't want to stop driving. Her fingers clutch the steering wheel as she stares ahead, mile upon mile of anonymous motorway stretching before her in the darkness.

It's ten o'clock by the time they leave the M6. There's still a lot of traffic on the roads, and she has to concentrate really hard to make sure she gets in the right lane. It's too late to pick the boys up now, she decides reluctantly. They'll be fast asleep. Besides, her parents aren't expecting her until tomorrow. She'll go home tonight and collect them in the morning, maybe stay for lunch.

Home. She's not sure what that word means any more. Will Ryan be there, huddled in his man cave, playing video games? Or will he be out on the piss with the lads? She hopes he isn't drinking tonight. They need to talk, and she wants him to be sober.

'Don't miss the turn-off!' calls Keira.

Sophie swerves the car to the left. 'Sorry!' she calls, following the signs for the city centre.

She offers to take each of them home, but they all agree that she's done more than enough driving for one day; if she can drop them off at the station, they can catch a train, bus or taxi.

She finds a parking space, then opens the back door of the Zafira, and they take out their rucksacks and bags.

'Thanks,' says Keira. 'That driving was heroic.'

'I'm just glad we made it back safely.'

Grace gives Sophie a hug. 'Take care, hon. Keep in touch. I'll text you, okay?'

'Okay.'

'Sorry to ask,' she adds, 'but what about Tuesday? Are we swimming or what?'

They look at each other questioningly. Nobody wants to be the first to answer.

'Um... not sure I can face the water any more,' says Sophie. 'But there's nothing to stop the rest of you meeting up. Let's see how it goes, eh?'

'Okay. Bye, everyone, see you soon!'

Grace heads off in the direction of the taxi rank and Keira rushes to catch a train. Ariel remains stubbornly by the car. She looks as if she's about to make a speech that she's been composing all the way back.

'This is drop-off only,' says Sophie. 'I don't want to get a ticket.'

'No, of course not.' Ariel smiles weakly as she hoists her rucksack on to her shoulders. Sophie wonders whether she's going to apologise for being in a bad mood the whole way back. 'Right. This is it,' she says. 'I expect I'll see you at Fern's funeral, if not before.'

'Oh. I hadn't thought about that. Not sure the family will want us there.'

'We're her friends, aren't we?'

'Yes, but I don't think... in the circumstances...'

'Well, we can decide later. Look after yourself, Sophie,' Ariel says kindly. 'You've been through a lot, and it's not over yet.'

'No,' she replies. 'It's not.'

'Good luck sorting things out with Ryan. If you need someone to talk to...'

'I really must get home.'

'Of course, sorry.'

Sophie gets back in the car and pulls out of the station concourse. It's only a fifteen-minute drive to the house, a route she knows extremely well. As she approaches the final set of roundabouts, she feels her mouth dry with nerves.

The lights are on in the living room, suggesting that Ryan's at home. She parks on the road and takes out her rucksack and bag. The car bleeps and flashes to lock. She walks up the front path and lets herself in with her key. Her heart starts to pound.

Ryan lumbers into the hallway. He's unshaven, already in his pyjamas – or rather, a pair of stripy bottoms and an old T-shirt. 'Sophie! Why are you so late? I was starting to worry...' He catches her expression. 'Hey, what's wrong?'

'There was an accident,' she says. 'Somebody died.'

'*Died?*' Panic flits across his face. 'Who?'

'Don't worry, it wasn't your mistress. It was Fern.'

'Oh... How did it happen?'

'She drowned.'

He puffs out. 'Oh God... That's awful, I'm really sorry.'

'It's an absolute tragedy. A terrible waste of a life. I'll tell you about it later.' She eases off her jacket and throws it over the banister. 'Make me a coffee, please – strong and black.'

'Yeah, of course.' He starts to go, then turns. 'I just want to say, I don't have a mistress—'

She holds up her hand. 'Stop right there, Ryan. I *know*... Elise confessed.'

'Really?' He looks at her disbelievingly. 'But she made me say... she *threatened* to go to...' He stops himself.

'I don't want to talk about Elise right now.' She takes a deep breath and lets the past come flooding back. 'I want to talk about her sister.'

He frowns. 'Her *sister?*'

'That's right. Her sister. I want to talk about Carly.'

THIRTY-SIX

SOPHIE

'Carly?' he echoes. 'You mean Carly *Woods*?' He shifts uncomfortably, unable to look at her directly.

Sophie shrugs. 'I don't know. I'm talking about the Carly you were engaged to.'

He starts to waffle. 'Yes, yes, that's her. That was ages ago, when we were teenagers. But, um, her sister wasn't Elise. She was called... er... what was it? Can't remember... She was a lot younger than Carly, a right pain in the arse. We ignored her most of the time.'

'Does the name Lauren ring any bells?'

'Yes, that's it, Lauren, although everyone called her kiddo, which she hated.'

'Right.'

'So how come... I thought you said Elise was...'

'Elise is Lauren.'

His eyes widen. 'What? No, no way.'

'It's true. Elise is a false name.'

He sits down, shaking his head several times as he tries to process the news. 'She's Lauren? Carly's little sister? But... I don't understand.'

'It wasn't a coincidence, Ryan. I think she targeted you deliberately.'

'But this is insane. I... I had no idea. I didn't recognise her. I mean, why would I? The last time I saw her, she was about twelve.' He takes a deep breath in and expels it on a sigh. 'You're sure about this? That's just like... unbelievable.'

Sophie studies him, noting his reactions – the way his hands are trembling, the constant jigging of his right knee. He seems genuinely shocked, as if he didn't have a clue. She wonders what calculations he's making in his brain right now. Whether he's going to start telling the truth, or keep lying to her as he's done for the last twenty years.

'Carly died, apparently,' she says. 'She drowned or something?'

'Yeah, yeah, that's right. She fell into a canal. She was on her own, at night. It was a terrible tragedy – she was only eighteen.' He pauses. 'Did Elise tell you that?'

'More or less. She blames you, Ryan. That's why she tracked you down. She wants revenge. You destroyed her family, now she's out to destroy yours.'

'I had nothing to do with Carly's death,' he mumbles. 'Nothing at all.'

'She doesn't agree. Nor does her brother.'

His head snaps up. 'Drew? What's he got to do with it?'

'He was there too, hiding out in some shelter, waiting to attack me. He tried to drown me, although the stupid idiot couldn't swim, so I ended up saving his life instead.' Her eyes narrow. 'This is what I've been put through, Ryan, and it's all your fault! If you hadn't had the affair, if you hadn't lied to me...' She crouches down and shakes him by the shoulders. 'Don't you realise I could have died! Ben and Louie nearly lost their mum.'

'I'm sorry, so sorry... I didn't know, didn't have a clue. As soon as I realised Elise was one of your swimmers, I went to see her, told her to back off. She wouldn't listen. I thought she was just being... you know... a bunny boiler. That was bad enough, but honestly, I had no idea she was Carly's sister. This is insane.'

Sophie sits back on the rug, feeling wretched with exhaustion. 'Tell me about Carly,' she says. 'What happened?'

He looks down. 'I don't think I can face talking about it right now. It's too much to take in. You've only just got back, it's late...'

'I need to know. Please. It's important.'

'Okay...' He stretches his neck and looks up at the ceiling, fingers clasped together. 'We met at school. I was only fourteen, she was in the year below. She was pretty. Very sweet, kind, loyal. Devoted to me. I loved her, as far as I knew what love was at that age. We got on well. She was always round my house, and my mum and dad adored her, treated her like a daughter. Everyone said we were made for each other. As soon as she turned sixteen, she wanted to get engaged. I wasn't bothered either way, but she wanted a ring on her finger and I kind of went along with it.' He sighs. 'She was a lovely girl. She didn't deserve someone like me.'

Sophie leans back, trying to picture Ryan as a spotty fourteen-year-old, Carly clinging to his arm, looking up at him with adoring eyes. 'So when did you break it off?'

He chews his lip for a moment. 'I didn't. I wanted to, but I didn't know how. It was so difficult. Once I started at uni, I realised I wasn't ready to settle down. Carly was lovely, but she wasn't...' He breaks off with a sigh. 'I know it sounds awful, but she wasn't enough for me any more. I needed someone with more... I don't know... someone with more intelligence, more ambition. And then I met you.'

'Why did you never tell me about her?'

'I was a coward. Scared of losing you, I guess. I started avoiding going home. I wouldn't let Carly visit me, stopped phoning her every day. She must have known something was wrong, but she never asked. She trusted me. Or maybe she just didn't want to believe it. And I didn't want to hurt her. I was leading this double life, and it was a mess. I didn't know what to do about it.'

Sophie closes her eyes for a few seconds, breathing it all in.

'It's a terrible thing to say, but when Carly died, it kind of solved my problem. I was in a really bad place. I was devastated because I still loved her, you know, and I felt so guilty for the way I'd treated her.' His eyes glisten with tears. 'The only good thing was she never found out about you.'

Sophie pauses. 'Are you sure about that?'

'Absolutely. Nobody from back home knew. I was super-careful to cover my tracks. I even had a separate mobile for Carly.'

'Gosh. You went that far...'

He blushes. 'I know, I'm a shit. But I had nothing to do with her death, I promise you on our sons' lives.'

'Don't say that.'

'But it's true, I swear.' He reaches out to her, trying to grab her hands, but she flinches away.

'So how come she died? What was it, an accident or something?'

'Nobody knows. The police never got to the bottom of it. It's always been a mystery. The coroner's verdict was death by misadventure.'

'It must have been very hard on the family. Not knowing what happened.'

'Yes, it was. Hard on my family too. Everyone was very confused, couldn't make sense of it. Why was she even down at the canal basin that night? On her own. Pissed. That just wasn't Carly... Then a couple of months later, Drew found out I'd been cheating on her, that I was living with you in Gloucester. All hell broke loose.'

'What do you mean?'

'Suddenly it was all my fault. Carly's mum decided she'd committed suicide because I'd called off the engagement, but that's not true. I should have called it off, but I didn't have the guts.'

Sophie pauses, considering. 'She didn't leave a note or anything?'

'No! She had no reason to kill herself – she was happy.'

'Yeah, but only because she didn't know about me.'

'Then her cousin Billie started going round telling everyone I'd murdered her and thrown her body in the canal. He even went to the police. They interviewed me, but there was no evidence, and anyway, I had an alibi for that night. I was in Gloucester, drinking with the lads. Billie always hated me – we were in the same class at school, and he was jealous because I was a better footie player than him *and* I was smart.'

'Did your parents blame you too?' she asks.

'Of course.'

'That's why we hardly ever see them. Why they hate me.'

'Probably... Who knows? We've never really talked about it.'

'Oh, Ryan, what a mess.'

He fixes her with an imploring gaze, his eyes brimming with tears. 'Honestly, I'm innocent, you have to believe me. I would never have hurt Carly – that's why I didn't call it off, because I knew how upset she'd be.'

'You should have told me. You had so many chances over the years – when we first met, before we moved in together, before the wedding. Why didn't you confess when she died?'

'I thought you'd finish with me. I didn't want to lose you too.'

'Maybe we could have worked through it.'

'It was too risky.'

'So instead you decided to keep it a secret. You've been making a fool of me all these years.'

'No, *I'm* the fool, not you. You've been amazing. Forgiving me for the affair, standing by me... I love you, Sophie. I had no idea that Elise was Carly's sister, you've got to believe me. She must be mentally ill, like her brother. He's been in and out of psychiatric hospitals.'

There's a long, heavy pause. Her limbs are turning to mush; she's not sure she'll be able to stand, let alone climb the stairs.

'I'm going to bed,' she says finally. 'By myself.'

'Okay, I understand. I'm so sorry. If only I could explain...'

She waves his words away. 'Not now.'

'We'll talk again in the morning, yeah? Properly. We'll have it out. The truth, the whole truth and nothing but the truth.'

The whole truth? She's not sure about that.

'I'm going to collect the boys first thing,' she replies briskly. 'I've missed them so much. I want to spend the weekend doing ordinary stuff, having fun. Just the three of us. Obviously.'

'Oh. You want me to go, then?'

'Yes. I don't want them to have any clue about what's going on. I'll stay for lunch with Mum and Dad and come home in the afternoon. That should give you a chance to pack a bag and find somewhere else to stay.'

He raises his arms in a gesture of hopelessness. 'Like where?'

'I don't know. That's your problem, not mine. Ben and Louie need to be at home, surrounded by their own things. They're back at school next week. I want everything to be as normal as possible.'

He frowns. 'Coming home and their dad not being there isn't very normal.'

'No, but it's something they're going to have to get used to.'

He starts back in surprise. 'What's that supposed to mean?'

'Oh, come on, do I have to spell it out? It's over. You and me. Our marriage. It's as dead as dead can be. It was a miracle it lasted as long as it did.'

He grabs her arm. 'No, Sophie, it doesn't have to be like that. We can start again. Go back to Miriam David.'

'No way. I've been humiliated enough, thank you.'

'But I want to tell you everything. I want you to understand. I've felt so guilty all these years – about Carly's death, about lying to you. I hated myself. That's why I started using hook-up sites, it was a kind of self-harming. Punishing myself for all the bad things I've done.'

'Oh, Miriam would love that!' she sneers. 'Poor you, so full of self-loathing, no wonder you went around having sex with strangers – you just couldn't help yourself. Sorry, but I'm not buying the psychobabble. You're a spineless, cheating coward. You don't hate yourself, Ryan, you *love* yourself! You think the world revolves around you and you're entitled to do whatever—'

'That's not true!' he protests. 'I've been haunted by Carly's death for years. It's eaten away at me. I need to get it all off my chest.'

'I'm sure if you explain to Elise and her brother, they'll forgive you,' she retorts sarcastically. 'I'm going to bed.'

She leaves the room, almost tripping over her rucksack as she walks towards the stairs.

THIRTY-SEVEN

SOPHIE

It's the day of Fern's funeral. Sophie puts on a knee-length black skirt and, after meeting some resistance, manages to zip it up at the back. The weight she's gained these last few weeks is starting to show. She's not swum once since she came back from Scotland, and she's been doing too much comfort eating: chocolate biscuits at work; a glass of wine with peanuts once the boys have gone to bed.

Taking a patterned shirt out of the wardrobe, she holds it up to the mirror, wondering whether its colours are subdued enough for the solemn occasion. She doesn't want to wear all black, but neither does she want to offend. Her presence today is controversial. Not that anyone in Fern's family believes she is to blame in any way. They have accepted that she was in the wrong place at the wrong time, and that there was nothing she could have done to save Fern. The police are of the same view, and last week Sophie was told that their investigation had concluded. She's in the clear. Free to carry on living her life. She expected to feel relieved, but when the news came, she felt numb and deeply sad. Fern's death was a waste, just as Carly's was a waste. They both died long before their time.

She puts on the shirt and buttons it up, then finishes off her make-up. There are grey patches beneath her eyes that no amount of concealer can hide. She's had too many sleepless nights recently. The bed feels cavernous without Ryan lying next to her. She hates to admit it, but she misses the warmth of him, even misses his snoring. But that doesn't mean she wants him back.

He's staying at a cheap hotel near the airport where he works. At first they told Ben and Louie that Daddy was living away because he had an important job to do. At only eight years old, Louie swallowed the lie, but Ben quickly worked it out. Other kids in his class have separated parents or are being brought up by a single mum. It's relatively normal these days. Even so, he was upset when he realised Ryan might not be coming back. He asked Sophie why Daddy didn't want to live with them any more. She tried to reassure him that it was nothing to do with him and Louie, it was the grown-ups who were having problems. Ben said he understood, but he still cried himself to sleep that night. Sophie's heart broke when she heard his muffled sobs through the bedroom wall. But she can't make it right for him. It's not possible.

Ryan is still taking the boys to gymnastics on Wednesday evenings, and he collects them from the after-school club when his shifts allow. Tomorrow he's taking them to their first football match. Sophie fears they're slipping into a dangerous pattern, where she's the boring parent who makes them do their home-work and eat healthy food, and Ryan does all the fun stuff. She'll have to talk to him about that, but at the moment, she's avoiding serious chats. She lets him come into the house when he drops the boys off, but he only stays for a few minutes. She refuses to spend time alone with him or to talk about the past. As for the future... well, at some point she's going to have to go to a solicitor. File for divorce. How on earth will she afford it on her part-time salary?

She can't think about that right now.

She brushes her thick, wavy hair and puts it into a short ponytail, hoping it will make her look suitably demure and more controlled than she's feeling inside. The bedside clock tells her it's time to go. She's meeting Ariel and Grace at a coffee shop around the corner from the crematorium.

Keira won't be there. Apparently Fern's husband sent her a letter saying he forgave her, but her children have refused to allow her to attend. As for Elise... nobody has seen or heard of her since they left her behind in Scotland. Surely she won't dare show her face today.

The chapel is full to bursting. Sophie, Ariel and Grace accidentally find themselves sitting towards the front, next to what appear to be some older family members. Everyone is grim-faced, holding back the emotion, keeping conversation to a minimum. The normal things people say at funerals are not appropriate – Fern didn't have a good innings, and her passing wasn't a merciful relief from suffering. Nobody is talking about her lesbian affair or the lurid circumstances of her death, but everyone must be thinking about them. Later on, when everyone's had a few drinks inside them, there'll be gossiping in corners, sly references, maybe even direct questions. It's all very public, embarrassing for Peter and the children.

Sophie steals a glance towards the family. Fern's son is wearing a dark suit, sitting with his face buried in the order of service. Her daughter, who looks about fifteen, is dressed entirely in pink, her mother's favourite colour. The flowers on the coffin are pink too, trimmed with glittery ribbons and foil hearts. Fern liked her bling.

'How are you doing?' whispers Ariel. She's wearing a black cloche hat pulled over her ears, and a purple coat.

'Not too bad,' Sophie lies.

Ariel is studying the order of service, frowning at the choice
of music and the sentimental poems. Apparently Fern was an
ABBA fan, and so her body will be committed to the sounds of
'Dancing Queen'.

'Honestly!' she tuts. 'Couldn't they have chosen something
more tasteful?'

'At least it's not "Money, Money, Money",' says Grace.
'That was more Fern's style.' Sophie suppresses a giggle.

The service begins. Everyone stands to sing the opening
hymn, trying to remember the tune and mostly failing. Rather
than rising to a crescendo, the singing peters out embarrassingly
until there are just a couple of old ladies warbling away. The
vicar says the stuff that vicars usually say, and then introduces
Fern's husband, who's going to 'say a few words'.

'This should be interesting,' whispers Grace, and Sophie
pinches her arm, warning her to be quiet.

Peter tells everyone what a wonderful wife and mother
Fern was. There's no bitterness in his voice, only pride. Sophie
is jealous of his magnanimity. He admits he took her for granted
and never stopped to wonder if she was as happy in their
marriage as he was. He says he missed the signs – not because
they were hidden, but because he wasn't looking properly.

'I don't know what I'm going to do without her. If I could
turn back time... Sorry...' He clears his throat. The piece of
paper he's holding is fluttering like a bird. 'The worst thing is all
the questions that go round your head, day and night. Why did
Fern go to Scotland? What was her plan? When she fell into
the water, did she try to save herself or did she let herself
drown? Who was she thinking about in her final moments? Me?
Our children? Her lover?' There is an audible gasp from the
congregation. The vicar looks anxiously at the front row, and a
woman, possibly Fern's sister, starts to get out of her seat, but
Peter gestures at her to sit down.

'I know this is not the way people usually talk at funerals, but I can't keep pretending. My wife fell in love with another woman, so much so that she was prepared to leave me and her family. That woman, who's not here today, rejected her. Fern felt like a fool. She asked me to forgive her, and I was so hurt and angry, I rejected her too. *That's* what killed her. The feeling that nobody loved her.' He pauses to swallow his emotion, and when he speaks again, his voice sounds all shaken up, as if he's being thrown around the room. 'But that wasn't true. We all loved her, still do. Look at all the people here today. I just hope that if Fern's looking down on us now, she'll realise how much...' He breaks down. 'I'm sorry. I'm sorry. Play some ABBA, please. That's what she wants to hear, not me blathering on.'

'Oh. My. God,' says Ariel, clutching Sophie's arm as they leave the chapel some time later. 'I've been to a lot of funerals, but never one like that. It was like something out of *EastEnders*. Bit vulgar for my taste.'

'I thought he was incredibly brave,' says Grace. 'So honest. I'm sure his kids were squirming, but... hats off to the guy. He really bared his soul.'

Most of the other mourners have gone to look at the flowers, of which there are a great many, but Sophie and her friends decide to make a quick exit and not go to the local pub, where there are drinks and a buffet laid on. They don't want people to realise that they are the swimmers who were part of that fatal trip. Sophie felt incredibly uncomfortable while Peter was speaking, scared that he was going to point her out and ask her to describe Fern's final moments.

'It's the not knowing that's the killer,' says Ariel as they walk towards the cemetery gates. The skies are leaden, and there's a penetrating dampness in the air.

Grace frowns with those thick painted eyebrows of hers. 'What do you mean?'

'When you don't know exactly what happened, or why, it eats away at you. For years and years. I've seen it a lot in my work. Teenagers walk out and their parents never hear from them again. They don't know whether they're dead or alive, whether they were murdered or simply ran away. People die, and nobody knows if it was an accident or suicide. The only person who knows the truth is dead, but it doesn't stop their loved ones asking the same old questions. They get stuck in a groove, unable to move forward. It's very sad. Destroys entire families.'

'Sounds grim,' agrees Grace.

They walk to the bus stop. Ariel and Grace are going in one direction, Sophie the other.

'Our bus is due, so we'd better say goodbye,' says Ariel. She gives Sophie a hug. 'We'd love to see you at the lake again, you know. It's not the same without you. We can't keep calling ourselves Sophie's Swimmers if you never turn up.'

'I'll think about it, okay?'

'You do that.'

Sophie embraces Grace, and their bus rounds the corner. She watches them climb aboard and waves goodbye. Then she crosses the road to the stop opposite and waits, her thoughts a muddle of Fern and Carly. Two drownings, both connected to her in strange ways. Two deaths that have changed other people's lives. It's like what happens when you throw a stone into a lake. The kinetic energy of the stone ripples through the water, gradually dissipating until it's undetectable and the water appears still again. But it's an illusion. The energy can never be destroyed; it's always held there in the water, emanating in endless invisible circles, unable to rest.

Ariel is right, of course. Not knowing why or how your loved one died can kill those left behind.

She takes out her phone and dials Elise's number.

THIRTY-EIGHT

SOPHIE

Sophie walks up the front path of Mrs Woods' small, neat house, her stomach a twisted knot of nerves. It's Saturday afternoon; Ryan has taken the boys to the football match. He has no idea that she's doing this.

She hesitates before ringing the doorbell. Elise took some persuading to organise the meeting. 'I need the whole family to be there,' Sophie said. 'Your mum, your brother, anyone else involved.'

The door opens while the bell is still playing its melody. 'Hi, Elise. Thanks for—'

She cuts in immediately. 'Don't call me that. I'm Lauren here. That's really important.' She lowers her voice to a whisper. 'Elise was Carly's middle name. If Mum finds out...'

'No, no, I understand.'

'And you and Drew have never met before, okay? Mum knows nothing about Scotland, or about me and Ryan. If you spill the beans, I swear—'

'It's okay, I understand.' They agreed terms in advance through a series of texts.

'Just be careful, that's all. I'm taking a big risk here.' Elise sighs. 'I must be mad.'

Sophie steps inside and is led into the lounge. Carly's mother is seated on a leather sofa. She's a large woman with generous breasts, wearing a saggy jumper over loose Lycra trousers. Her face has a worn-out look.

Drew is wedged next to her, holding her arm. The last time Sophie saw him, he was lying in the bothy, on the verge of hypothermia. He can't bear to meet her gaze; keeps his eyes fixed on his lap, his fingers picking nervously at a rip in his jeans. Another man – about forty years old, thin, balding, roughly shaven – is sitting in an armchair by the television. He is leaning back with his legs wide open, but Sophie isn't fooled. He looks the most nervous of them all.

'This is my mum... my brother, Andrew, and this is our cousin Billie,' says Elise, squeezing in on the other side of her mother. 'Sit down, Sophie.'

'Thanks,' she replies croakily. Her mouth is dry; she could really do with a glass of water. She takes the other armchair. It's low and squashy and she feels as if she could sink into the cushions and disappear. The thought of disappearing is quite appealing right now. It has taken all her courage to come here today.

'It's very good of you to agree to see me,' she begins. 'I gather... er... Lauren has explained. I'm Sophie. I'm married to—'

'Yes, we know who you are,' says Mrs Woods sharply. 'I don't want you in my house, if I'm honest, but Lauren says you've got something important to tell us about Carly.'

'Yes, I have. Look, I understand how difficult this must be for you...'

'If you've come to gloat—'

'No, not at all, absolutely not. I want to help.'

'You can't bring her back to life,' says Billie tersely.

Drew huffs. 'Nobody can, mate.'

'I know that.'

'Then why say it?'

Elise raises her hand. 'Hey, let's listen to what Sophie's got to say, shall we?'

'The truth, that's all I'm interested in,' Mrs Woods says.

Sophie nods. 'That's exactly why I'm here. To tell you the truth.'

She has practised this speech so many times over the past few days, she should know it off by heart. But now that she's here, confronted by the family, she's not sure where to start. She looks around the room. The furniture is cheap and old-fashioned. The carpets are threadbare, stained with dirt by the patio doors. There are photos of Carly on every surface, taken at various stages in her life, from baby to little girl to teenager. Her eyes rest on a portrait in a silver frame, and she lets out a small gasp. Yes, that's Carly. Exactly as she remembers her.

'Go on then,' says Billie, 'let's have it.'

She looks at them in turn – mother, sister, brother, cousin. 'Ryan never told me about Carly,' she begins. 'But I found out...'

She discovered the secret phone under some football gear in his sports bag. She wasn't snooping, she was putting on a wash and needed some more coloureds to make it worthwhile – like her mother always did. Ryan had gone into college for a tutorial. The flat was a mess, so she'd decided to spend the morning playing housewife.

It was one of those cheap pay-as-you-go phones you can buy in supermarkets. She had never seen it before and was curious, so she turned it on. After a few attempts, she guessed the passcode and found there was only one entry in the contact list: for someone called Carly.

Her heart started to race. She went into his texts and started reading. There were dozens, maybe even hundreds of them. Carly sent a lot more messages to Ryan than he did to her. Her texts were either soppy and romantic – *Love you lots... Miss you loads... Can't wait to see you* – or needy and complaining – *What's wrong?... Why don't you call me?... When are you coming home?* Then there were the practical arrangements for meeting up, most of them featuring Topshop. *Meet me outside after work... I finish at six. Don't be late this time.*

She read every single text, and by the time she'd finished, she understood the whole story. Ryan had a girlfriend back home, and they'd been together for a long time, certainly since before he started uni. It was a one-sided love affair – Carly was clingy and desperate, while Ryan was cool and distant. It was clear to Sophie that the relationship was on the rocks, but this girl didn't seem to be aware of it.

She was surprised by her calm reaction to this revelation. Instead of being angry with Ryan, she felt sorry for him. And for Carly. There were lots of pictures of her on the secret phone, but none of them gave Sophie much cause for alarm. She was sweet but ordinary-looking.

No, she didn't feel angry. Nor was she particularly shocked. It was very common for people to arrive at university with a girl-friend or boyfriend back home. Sophie had turned up baggage-free, but she'd been in the minority. Lots of those relationships didn't make it beyond the first term. Some limped on, but by the start of the second year, most had gone the way of all flesh – petering out during the summer vacation or finishing graciously by mutual consent. Some ended very messily, usually when there were other people involved.

Ryan was too nice, she thought. He clearly wanted to finish with Carly but was afraid of hurting her feelings. Oddly, it didn't occur to Sophie that he'd been lying to her for the last eighteen months, or that he probably had sex with this girl every time he went home. She felt pleased with herself because she was obviously the preferred choice. Ryan lived with her in their cosy love nest. They were a proper couple in a grown-up relationship, whereas he and this girl had only been going out. She was just a kid who, judging by her texts, had very little to talk about other than clothes and make-up.

She put the mobile back where she'd found it and got on with the housework. She felt different inside. Adult and worldly. Sophisticated. As she hoovered and dusted and hung up the washing, she thought about how she was going to tackle the subject with Ryan. She was disappointed in him for not telling her about Carly, but there was no need to make a big fuss about it. What was the point of acting all jealous when she was the winner? Besides, she'd have to admit that she'd been going through his stuff, and he might not believe she'd only been looking for dirty washing. She decided not to mention it. But the situation couldn't continue. She had to step in – sort it out once and for all.

She worked out a plan. First she told Ryan she was going to visit Nan for the weekend, which was true, although not entirely. He didn't question her. He had a football match on Saturday and fully intended to get pissed out of his skull afterwards, so was quite happy that she wouldn't be around.

Haventry had two branches of Topshop, so she rang them both, asking to speak to Carly. The second shop said she was busy and not allowed to take personal calls. Armed with the address, Sophie caught a train on Saturday afternoon, arriving just before five. She went straight to the store.

Carly was pushing a clothes rail around the floor, putting items back in their rightful places, adjusting the hangers, doing up the buttons. Sophie peeped through a forest of summer dresses, observing her as she might a wild animal. Carly was wearing a red tiered skirt, a white top and a matching hairband, which kept her long mousy-brown hair off her face. She looked young and innocent, apart from a pair of pointy red shoes on her feet. Sophie wondered how she managed standing on the shop floor all day in those thin heels.

Leaving the shop, she went to a café opposite, where she ordered a milkshake and sat in the window waiting for her quarry to finish her shift. As the time ticked by, she felt increasingly nervous, but she kept telling herself that she was doing the right thing. The poor girl needed to know the truth.

The *Closed* sign went up dead on the dot of six o'clock, and the sales assistants trooped out shortly afterwards. Carly was one of the last to leave. Sophie jumped up from her seat and ran out of the café. She followed her down the street for several metres before catching up and tapping her lightly on the shoulder.

'Hey, Carly?'

She spun round. 'Yeah? Who are you?'

'The name's Sophie. We haven't met before.'

'So how come you know my name?'

'I'm, um... not sure how to put this... I'm Ryan's girlfriend.'

Carly frowned. 'Sorry?'

'Shit. He hasn't told you about me, has he?'

Her face creased. 'You talking about *my* Ryan?'

'Yup, that's the one.'

'You mean Ryan my *fiancé*?' She raised her left hand, turning it round to reveal a small diamond solitaire on her third finger. It looked fake, like something you'd find in a goody bag, but it was still an engagement ring. For a moment, Sophie felt floored. She hadn't bargained for this.

'We should talk,' she said. 'Shall we get a drink?'

They went to a wine bar at the other end of the shopping mall and sat in the corner, away from the other drinkers. Sophie bought two packets of crisps and a bottle of Chardonnay, three glasses of which Carly downed immediately, barely pausing to breathe.

'I'm sorry it's such a shock,' Sophie kept saying. 'I know how you must feel. Ryan and I have been an item since the Christmas before last, and I've only just found out about you.'

'Bastard,' Carly muttered, waving the empty bottle. 'We need another of these.'

'Okay, but go easy. Have some crisps at least.' But Carly didn't want to eat. She wanted to get drunk – as fast and as hideously as possible. Sophie ordered another bottle and watched her rival set out on the road to oblivion.

'Did he send you to dump me?' Carly asked half an hour later. She was slumped across the table, trailing the sleeve of her blazer in some spilt wine.

'No. He doesn't know I'm here – he'd be absolutely furious with me if he realised we were talking to each other. Ganging up on him.' Sophie laughed weakly. 'Girl power.'

'Huh!' Carly paused to fill her glass again. 'I kind of knew. Not about you. But I knew it was dying. When we were at school, we were never apart. But since he went to uni...' She sighed. 'He hardly ever phones. I have to beg him to come home weekends.' Her words were starting to blend into each other. 'Every time I mention the wedding, he changes the subject.'

'It must have been horrible for both of you, knowing it was over but not wanting to face up to it.'

'Don't feel sorry for him – the lying, cheating bastard.'

'He just didn't want to hurt you, Carly.'

'Nah... He couldn't give a shit about me.' She drained her glass.

'Are you okay? How are you going to get home?' Sophie was starting to worry. Carly had drunk the best part of two bottles of wine and hadn't eaten a single crisp. She was looking pale, and her eyes were pink and watery. 'Can you call your dad and ask him to pick you up?'

'My dad? Ha!' she scoffed. 'He's another bastard. Went off with some tart years ago.'

'Oh, sorry.' Sophie helped her to her feet and took her

outside. As soon as they hit fresh air, she started to keel over and had to be propped up.

'Is there a taxi rank nearby?' asked Sophie, but Carly was too out of it to answer. She looked around her. They were in a retail area, but all the shoppers had gone home hours ago and the shops had their shutters down. There were no other bars or restaurants, and the streets were eerily quiet for a Saturday night.

'Let's walk,' she said. 'You need to sober up a bit, or you won't be allowed in a taxi.'

Carly was slumped against the wall like a rag doll. Sophie put one arm around her shoulders and the other across her waist, then tried puppeteering her along, step by floppy step. Not knowing which way to go, she chose a side street that sloped down to what looked like some kind of walkway.

The puppet was groaning and swearing incoherently. Sophie glanced at her watch. She had a train to catch tonight – the last one left in thirty-six minutes, and she couldn't miss it. Nan was expecting her. If she didn't turn up, there'd be trouble.

They reached a narrow towpath running along a canal. It was unlit, and the water looked still and inky. Carly stumbled over the cobbles in her silly red heels and Sophie had to keep setting her back on her feet.

'Where are you taking me? What are we doing here?' she chuntered. 'Too dark... Ouch! Don't like this. Gotta get out of here.'

'I'm sorry, I didn't realise,' Sophie said. 'Give me your phone, Carly. Let me call someone.'

'Gonna call Ryan.'

'No, don't do that. He's in Gloucester anyway. You need someone to come and get you, take you home.' She slipped Carly's handbag off her shoulder and snapped it open.

'Gerroff! I'll do it!' Carly snatched the bag and rummaged

around until she found her mobile. She stabbed randomly at the keypad. It gave a few protesting bleeps, then died.

'Fucking thing!' she cried, hurling it into the water. It landed with a small, ominous splash.

'Here – use mine,' Sophie said, passing it over. 'Just don't throw it in the canal, okay?'

Carly staggered off to make the call. Sophie couldn't tell who she was speaking to – she hoped to God it wasn't Ryan. She checked her watch again. If she didn't set off for the station soon, the train would leave without her. There was no way she was going to hang around this godforsaken place all night.

'Everything okay, Carly? Is somebody coming?'

'Yeah, yeah...'

'Do they know where to find you?'

'Yeah! Sorted.'

Sophie prised her mobile from Carly's fingers. 'Look, I have to go now.'

'Good!'

She hesitated. 'I'm so sorry, Carly. About Ryan.'

'Yerwelcometim,' she slurred.

'Don't go anywhere, promise me? Stay here until someone comes.' She turned on her heel and ran.

THIRTY-NINE

LAUREN

We sit there open-mouthed while Sophie rattles on, making herself out to be the heroine while she tears us apart with her confession. As if telling us that Carly spent her last hours distraught and rejected is going to bring us closure! We already knew deep down that she must have found out about Sophie. We just didn't know how. And I don't believe Sophie left her there either. I think she killed her.

I shoot daggers in Sophie's direction. I could go into the kitchen right now and pick up a knife. Stab her to death. Who cares if I spend the rest of my life in prison? It'd be well worth it. I start to rise from the sofa, but Mum seems to know where my mind's going and pulls me back down.

'It's okay,' she whispers. 'Stay calm.'

'You left her by the canal? In that state?' Drew asks. He's trying to sound calm and authoritative, like he's a barrister, but he's twisting his fingers together the way he does when he's about to have a panic attack. I know what he's thinking, because I'm thinking it too. Why didn't the two of us drown the bitch when we had the chance?

The accused bites her lip. 'Yes, I had to leave her. I did what I could, but I had to catch a train.'

Mum looks at her in disgust. 'Why didn't you come forward as soon as you heard she was missing?'

'I didn't know, that's why. Honest to God. I went to visit my nan for the weekend, then I went back to uni.'

'But Ryan must have said *something*!' Mum clutches her heaving chest. 'You must have known!'

Sophie shakes her head. 'He'd already gone back to Haventry. He left me a note saying he had some family stuff to deal with. I assumed Carly had demanded he come home. I was expecting him to have a go at me for telling her about us, but... he never mentioned it.'

'Proves how much *he* cared,' mutters Billie. 'He was never good enough for her. She deserved better.' He grits his teeth. 'Slimy bastard... If I ever see him again, I'll punch his—'

'Shut up, Billie,' Mum barks. She turns back to Sophie. 'Didn't you think that was strange? That he never said anything?'

She shrugs. 'Um... I don't know. I was a bit confused, yes, but... you believe what you want to believe, I guess. When Ryan came back, he was very quiet, not his normal self. I knew something was up, but I didn't think Carly was... you know. I checked his mobile and there were no more messages from her. I tried ringing her number, but it was unobtainable. I decided she must have changed it, to cut herself off from him.'

'It never occurred to you when you left her on her own, drunk and upset... you never once thought that she might have come to harm?'

'No.' Sophie's eyes are blinking rapidly. 'I didn't know she'd died that night until Andr—'

'This is all lies,' I cut in quicky. 'She pushed her in.' I release myself from Mum's grasp and stand up. 'That's the truth, isn't it, Sophie? You got Carly shit-faced, then deliberately led her down to the canal and—'

'No! I don't know what happened after I left her. As far as I knew, someone was coming to help her. I thought she was safe.'

'Sit down, Lauren,' Mum says. 'We're going to be civilised about this.' I huff, and plonk myself on a dining chair. My fingers are itching to close around Sophie's throat; I want to strangle the truth out of her. 'And stop tapping the table!' Mum adds.

'Who did Carly call?' asks Drew after a pause.

Sophie bows her head. 'I'm sorry, I don't know. But it had to be somebody close, because she knew their number off by heart.'

'Ryan,' says Billie. 'It's obvious. He'd be the first person she'd call. He came down, they had a fight, and he pushed her in. I always said it was him.'

'Ryan was in Gloucester that night,' Mum says. 'He had an alibi, remember?'

'Maybe his mates lied for him.'

Drew is still knitting with his fingers. 'Do you still have the number?' he asks Sophie.

'No, of course not. It was twenty years ago, I've had loads of mobiles since then. Anyway, why would I have needed to keep it?'

He sighs irritably. 'Because it was evidence.'

'Yes, but I didn't know she was dead, did I? Ryan never told me.'

'This is all total bullshit,' I say. 'She's just trying to shift the blame on to some fantasy person. Carly didn't call anyone that night. If she'd rung one of you, you'd have come to pick her up and she'd still be alive today.'

'Maybe she just pretended to call someone,' says Sophie, backtracking now. 'Or maybe they didn't turn up... I don't know. She said it was sorted, that help was on its way.'

There's a long pause. The air is thick with silent accusation. Mum looks from Drew to Billie, then lands her gaze on me. 'Well?' she says.

I bang my fist on the table. 'Don't look at me! I was twelve years old, remember? I was at home with you, watching telly.'

'Yeah, Mum,' says Drew. 'And I came back about midnight. We sat up together, waiting for her to come home.'

We turn to look at Billie, who's gone very quiet. He looks down at his shoes.

'What about you, Billie?' asks Mum. 'You and Carly were close. She thought the world of you. After Ryan, you were probably the first person she'd call if she was in trouble.'

He covers his face with his hands and starts to sob. Drew and Mum exchange glances. My heart has leapt into my throat, and I can hardly breathe. It's as if time has stopped, or we're in a movie and the screen has frozen. My mind's turning somersaults and I'm thinking, what does this mean? Why is he crying? Is it because of what Mum said about Carly thinking the world of him, or is it simply emotion pouring out? Could it even be...

'What is it, Billie, love?' Mum presses gently. 'Is there something you need to tell us?'

'I loved her,' he says from behind his fingers. 'Loved her way more than he ever did.'

'Yes, I know. You loved her like a sister.' Mum heaves herself off the sofa and goes over to him, her knees cracking as she kneels down. 'Did she call you that night, Billie? Did she ask you to come and pick her up?' He nods. 'You went down to the basin, right? On your scooter?' He mumbles something. 'Take your hands away, love, we can't understand what you're saying.' She gently peels off his fingers, revealing his stricken, tear-stained face.

'You've got to tell us, man,' says Drew. 'Did you find her? Was she dead?'

Billie sniffs up his tears. 'She was sitting on the towpath, all crumpled and groaning, like she wanted to throw up but couldn't. I asked her what had happened, but her speech was slurred and I couldn't understand what she was saying. The only word I heard was "Ryan". She said she hated him. I asked her why, but she just burst into tears.'

'Then what happened, Billie?' Mum asks.

'I pulled her up. She'd taken her shoes off. There was broken glass on the ground, and I was trying to get her to put them back on, but she said she couldn't walk in them, they hurt her toes or something. She started swearing about Ryan, saying he was a bastard, and it was over, finished. She tried to take her engagement ring off, but it wouldn't come.'

I'm picturing it as he speaks. I can see the tears pouring down her face, her mascara smudged, her nostrils thick with mucus. She always looked so ugly when she cried. I can hear her shrill voice wailing into the darkness, cursing Ryan, saying how she was going to kill him. It's as if I'm standing there watching the scene play out.

'Jesus Christ, man, why didn't you tell us before?' mutters Drew. 'You should have told the cops...'

'Then what happened, Billie?' Mum says. 'She's upset. You've got her to her feet and you're trying to help her...'

'I'm sorry,' he says, suddenly raising his voice 'I didn't mean to... I *loved* her, you see. Not like a brother. I loved her for real. I know we were cousins and you're not supposed to... but I loved her so much.'

'What did you do?' Mum's tone sharpens. 'Come on, Billie, tell the truth now. We need to know.'

He takes a deep breath. 'I told her I was glad it was over with Ryan. I said she was beautiful and kind and lovely, and he didn't deserve her. She fell into my arms, sobbing into my jacket, thanking me for coming to rescue her. I was stroking her hair, telling her it was going to be okay.' He stops abruptly, as if a stone has lodged itself in his throat.

'And? What else did you say?'

He exhales. 'I said I loved her, and she said she loved me too. I kind of got the wrong idea and I tried to kiss her and she... er... she pushed me off. She was shocked, I think... and angry. She was swaying about, waving her arms. The look in her eyes... it was like she *hated* me. I tried to explain, but she started screaming at me to go away. She was about to keel over, so I went to catch her, but she... I don't know... She kind of turned away, and the next thing I know, she's fallen into the canal. It was dark, so fucking dark, I couldn't see her. She must have gone straight under. I called out for her, but... she'd disappeared.'

Mum is stunned. She kneels before Billie like a statue, mouth open, jaw slack, eyes glazed over.

Drew stands up. 'Did you try to save her?' Billie shakes his head. 'You can swim, can't you? Why didn't you dive in?'

'It was pitch black... there was nothing I could do...'

'So you stood there and watched her drown, is that what happened?'

'No! I ran along the towpath calling for help, but there was nobody about, the place was deserted. I tried to find a lifebelt, but there wasn't one. It was too late anyway, she'd gone under. She'd dropped to the bottom like a stone.' He breaks down completely in uncontrolled sobs.

Mum unfreezes and embraces him. 'It's okay, love,' she says. 'It's okay.' They hold each other tightly, rocking from side to side.

Drew clasps the sides of his head. 'It's not okay,' he says. 'It's not fucking okay.'

I reach out to him. 'Drew...'

'I can't deal with this. I need some fresh air.' He marches past me and flings open the doors to the patio. A blast of cold air rushes in. It's as if Carly's spirit is swirling around the room.

'I think I should go,' says a disembodied voice, and my heart jolts. I twist my head to see Sophie perched nervously on the edge of the old armchair. I'd forgotten she was here.

'Yeah, you should,' I say gruffly.

She stands up. Her cheeks are bright pink and she's a little breathless from all her storytelling. She hovers, not knowing whether to say goodbye to Mum, who's still holding Billie. They are locked together, sobbing, lost in their pain.

'I hope you're happy now,' I snarl. 'There's no going back from this, you realise that. The family's fucked. I mean, we were struggling before, but Jesus, now there's no hope. So thanks, Sophie, for sharing your "truth" with us. I bet you feel so much better for getting it all off your chest.'

I see something switch in her face. She straightens up, looks me in the eye. 'You're the ones who wouldn't leave it alone,' she says, her voice gathering strength. '*You* tracked Ryan down, *you* went after me. You wanted revenge! You'd have killed me if you'd had the chance, your brother tried to drown me and all this time, it was *him*!' She points a quivering finger at Billie. 'I mean, you're all insane.'

'Shut up!' I screech. 'Shut up and get out!'

Sophie fires a parting shot at the room. 'You asked for the truth, and I gave it to you. Now deal with it.' She scrapes up what's left of her dignity and leaves.

I'm fuming. There's so much anger inside me I think I'm going to self-combust. I'm furious with Sophie, of course I am, but she doesn't know the damage she's caused. Doesn't understand the half of it.

I know exactly how this is going to turn out. When the hugging and the wailing stops and Mum refuses to leave the house and Drew starts using again and Billie has a nervous breakdown, *I'm* going to get the blame. It'll be my fault for digging up the past – not that it has ever been buried. It's been rotting in Carly's bedroom, stinking the place out.

It'll be my fault for letting Sophie blow the family to pieces. My fault that Ryan was a two-timing bastard, that Carly found out, that Sophie got her pissed, that Billie forced himself on her when she was at her most vulnerable. All. My. Fault. I might as well have pushed her into the water myself.

EPILOGUE

SOPHIE

Sophie pulls into the car park and switches off the engine, pausing for a moment to compose herself.

It's the first time she's been to Elizabeth Lake in five months. She looks around, surprised to see so many cars parked up, given how early in the day it is. The Shack is still there, although it's not open yet. They used to do a wicked hot chocolate, she remembers. Maybe she'll have one later.

Taking her backpack out of the car and putting on her dryrobe, she sets off down the slope towards the lake. Everything looks so neat and safe. The bushes have been cut back and new rope rails have been erected on either side of the path. It's a far cry from the Rough Bounds of Scotland.

She halts, closes her eyes and resets. She promised herself she wouldn't think about that today.

She walks on, her stomach rippling with some of the old excitement as she anticipates the shock of cold water on her skin. It's been so long. She remembers how important the swimming used to be to her, how it kept her sane through those dark days – how she even thought it might save her marriage. She laughs grimly to herself. That hope is long gone. After limping on for eighteen months, it's stopped breathing, marked 'Do Not Resuscitate'.

Ryan knows everything now. She told him as soon as she got back from Carly's mum's house. They sat the boys down in front of a movie and went to the bedroom to talk. At first he couldn't believe that she'd kept it from him for so long – then she reminded him that he'd done the same to her. They were as bad as each other with their secrets and lies, and it sickened them both.

She thinks back to that night, sitting on the last train to Sheffield, feeling partly triumphant, partly ashamed. Her rival had been annihilated – not literally, but certainly metaphorically. She was worried about leaving her in that drunken state, but reminded herself there'd been no choice. Nan was expecting her, and she wasn't somebody you messed around. Hopefully Carly was curled up on the back seat of a taxi by now. She'd wake up with one hell of a hangover, that was for sure. Poor kid.

Nan told her off for arriving so late. 'I was starting to panic,' she said. Then she saw the look in Sophie's eyes and asked what was wrong. Before she knew it, Sophie was telling her the whole story. That's what Nan was like – you couldn't pull the wool over her eyes. She had a gift for extracting the truth from people.

'You shouldn't have let her get so drunk,' she said, her hands around a mug of hot, sweet tea. 'It was cruel.'

'I couldn't stop her. She was out of control.'

'You should have waited until her friend turned up.' Nan let out a long, disappointed sigh. 'I'm surprised at you, Sophie. I thought you were a nice girl.'

'I *am* a nice girl! I was doing her a favour.'

'Some favour.'

'She needed to know what was going on.'

Nan folded her arms. 'If you want my advice, I wouldn't

bother with a man like that.'

'No, no, you don't understand. Carly was a loose end. Ryan doesn't love her. He loves *me*!'

She raised her eyebrows. 'If you say so.'

'Honestly! We're for ever.'

'Hmm... I'd watch out for that one. Once a cheat, always a cheat.'

Sophie comes back to the present. If only she'd taken Nan's advice...

Several women are already in the water. She counts nine brightly coloured hats bobbing about – that's more than ever turned up when she ran the group. Of course, it's May now and the weather's a lot warmer. The numbers will rise over the summer and then plummet when autumn sets in.

She stands on the bank, waving. Somebody waves back and then swims towards her. As she approaches, Sophie sees that it's Ariel, still wearing the same purple swimsuit.

'Hi there!' She walks out of the water, her bare feet stumbling over the gravel. 'What a surprise! Lovely to see you!' She gives Sophie a dripping-wet hug. 'How are you?'

'Old, tired and single, but apart from that...' Sophie forces a smile. 'How are *you*?'

'Same as ever... Have you come to swim?'

'Yes. It's been a while and I'm really out of shape, but I realised how much I missed it.'

'Brilliant. I'm so glad, Sophie. We've missed you.' Ariel picks up her towel and dries her face, then drapes it over her shoulders. 'The water's so refreshing.'

'Is Grace here? I can't tell, everyone looks the same with their goggles on.'

'No, she's got a cold, so she didn't come today.'

Sophie starts to undress. 'What about Keira? Does she ever turn up?'

'No. She got a new job, moved to London. It's just me and

Grace from the original group. The rest are all newcomers. Lovely women, actually. I'll introduce you.'

'Thanks.' She looks back at the water. The swimmers are in a circle, chatting and laughing.

'If you want me to go back in with you, you'll have to hurry up.'

'Sorry.' She takes her swimming shoes out of her bag and sits down to put them on.

'How are you, Sophie?' Ariel says. 'As in, how are you *really*?'

She considers the question for a few seconds. 'Hard to tell. It's been tough... I've had to face a few harsh facts about myself. Ryan and I have split up, but I've still got my boys and that's all that really matters.' She smiles thoughtfully. 'Yes, I think I'm going to be all right.'

'What doesn't break you...'

'Yes, you're right.' Good old Ariel, always there with the platitudes. But for once, it rings true. She *does* feel stronger.

'Shall we swim, then?'

'Yes. Let's swim.' She takes Ariel's hand, and they head into the water.

A LETTER FROM JESS

Thank you so much for reading *My Husband's Lover*. If this is your first Jess Ryder book, you might want to try my other psychological thrillers – *Lie to Me*, *The Good Sister*, *The Ex-Wife*, *The Dream House*, *The Girl You Gave Away*, *The Night Away* and *The Second Marriage*. You can keep up to date by signing up at the link below. Your email address will never be shared, and you can unsubscribe at any time.

www.bookouture.com/jess-ryder

I am often asked where I get my ideas from. Well, the springboard for this novel turned out to be right outside my door. I used to live on the south coast, overlooking the English Channel. One day I was gazing out of my office window – looking for inspiration, perhaps – when I saw a group of women walking across the beach towards the sea. It was a chilly autumn day. The sky was grey and the sea looked very uninviting. I knew the water would be perishingly cold. I started to imagine who these women were and why they wanted to put themselves through what seemed to me to be a kind of physical torture. Before long, I was reading books on the subject and discovered that some of my friends were passionate about open-water swimming. Everyone seemed to agree that it was great for your mental and physical well-being, and that the cold water even had a healing quality. I pulled together my cast of characters and began to develop a plot. The Scottish setting came about because I needed to trap the swimmers together, preferably somewhere that was remote and off the grid. Such places are hard to find these days, so I have used some artistic licence, mixing up real locations with completely imagined ones. There is no such place as Condie's Retreat, although some elements of the landscape may be recognisable to those of you who know the west coast of Scotland.

I hope you enjoyed reading *My Husband's Lover*. If you'd like to write a brief constructive review and post it online in the appropriate places, I'm sure other readers would find it useful.

With best wishes and thanks for your support,

Jess Ryder

jessryder.co.uk

facebook.com/JessRyderAuthor
twitter.com/jessryderauthor

ACKNOWLEDGEMENTS

I would like to thank the following people who have helped me in the writing of this novel.

Brenda Page, my researcher, who is incredibly resourceful and never gives up, even when I ask her for information that's very difficult to find. I'm also grateful to her for picking up on typos and errors in the early drafts.

My literary agent, Rowan Lawton at the Soho Agency, who is a great champion of my work and is always there to offer guidance and support. She also handles the foreign translations of my books, enabling me to reach out to readers across Europe, which I love.

Christine Glover, my media agent at Casarotto Ramsay & Associates. This year has been very exciting, as my Bookouture novel *The Ex-Wife* has been made into a TV drama. It has been a long-held ambition to see one of my psychological thrillers on screen, and Christine made it happen!

My editor, Lydia Vassar-Smith. We work together well, from brainstorming initial ideas through to the final draft. Lydia is a very positive person who is always focused on finding solutions to any problem, no matter how big or small. A great quality to have in an editor.

Everyone on the Bookouture team. They work incredibly hard for their authors, and I really appreciate it.

And finally, my amazing family – my parents, my grown-up children, their lovely partners, my gorgeous grandchildren, and of course, my fantastic husband, David.

9 781803 145204